LOVE IN DUE TIME

GREEN VALLEY LIBRARY BOOK #1

L.B. DUNBAR

WWW.SMARTYPANTSROMANCE.COM

COPYRIGHT

DEDICATION

For the love of libraries and the right to read books of our choosing.

CHAPTER ONE

DEWEY DECIMAL CLASSIFICATION: 040
UNASSIGNED

[Naomi]

I'm going to be forty.

Someday.

Soon-ish.

And I'm thinking these things as I stand in the baking aisle of the Piggly Wiggly late at night, while the world is out partying, and I'm grocery shopping. Alone. At ten-fifteen.

Sigh.

Okay, maybe not the world. Just Green Valley, Tennessee. It's Friday night and most of Green Valley is attending the weekly jam session, a night of musical talent and good things to eat, at the community center. I don't attend for several reasons.

I used to go, though.

When I was a teen, I was a wild child. *Naomi, God put a spirit in you, girl*, my mother would say.

It wasn't a god, though, at least not one I readily believed in. The spirit wasn't something placed in me, but something I was born with —something I tried to contain. Daughter of a preacher and a woman

1

who thought she wanted to be a nun, my home was ultraconservative growing up.

Don't drink. Don't smoke. Don't dance.

As soon as I was told not to do those things as a teen, it's exactly what I wanted to do. Then I turned twenty-one. Recollection of that night pulls my heart in opposing directions, like a tug-of-war within my chest.

I reach for a box of brownie mix to chase away the memories. Chocolaty squares of heaven solve everything. Truthfully, I could make these from scratch. I have a great recipe and guilt gnaws at me as I consider the boxed mix. I volunteered to bring a dessert to a luncheon hosted at the library. I could always order something premade from Donner Bakery or grab something from the pre-pack-aged goods section here at the grocer, but where's the fun in that? Adding water, oil, and an egg to the dry mix will make me feel as if I've accomplished something.

Julianne MacIntyre can probably sniff out a box-made dessert, and my holistic approach to life prefers I remain all natural. My beliefs are different from the norm. I'm a Wiccan. I celebrate nature, purity, and most importantly, the spirit of women. Mother Nature is my guide. She's the Goddess Supreme, or rather the Triple Goddess is my ruler. Local rumor is I'm a witch, but my story is nothing fantastical. I'm a librarian at the Green Valley Public Library.

I look left and right, make certain no one notices me, and add the brownie mix to my handheld basket. *Sometimes, you just need to break the rules.* Tonight, I need quick and easy, I console my conscience as I head for the checkout lane. Ten items or less. I always want to take a red pen to the sign. It's ten items or fewer. At this time of night, I don't see how many items a person carries would matter. I'm the only one in here except for Sara Stokes.

"How's it going, Ms. Winters?" Sara Stokes has the misfortune of once being married to Deveron Stokes, the dry cleaner. He was not a good man and his ex-wife suffered the repercussions of reproducing with him. He was a child support dodger to the nth degree, thus her job working the night shift at the Piggly Wiggly. As a woman roughly my age, it was strange she called me Ms. Winters, but then again, all the mommas were used to formally addressing me in front of their children.

"Just fine, Sara, and yourself?" I'm only half listening to her response as I place my plastic basket on the conveyor, preparing to set my items on the belt when I feel a presence next to me. Someone tall, solid, burly. The scent alone signals he's all spicy male, and without thought, my head turns. Then my breathing halts.

Nathan Ryder.

Standing six plus, double my size, and with a chest covered by a leather jacket, he peers down at me with silver-colored eyes I'll never forget. He nods in greeting but I don't respond. My tongue swells three times larger. *My tongue.* The same one that tangled with his and licked his—*oh my.* My gaze drifts down to the very spot I shouldn't be remembering, a place on him I shouldn't be imagining.

My hand comes to the collar of my linen peasant blouse, and I tug.

Is it warm in here? Why is the heat on in September? Am I experiencing hot flashes already?

Still drawn to him, my eyes climb up his mountain height and fall again on the unusual spark in his eyes. His hair—more chrome than ink—matches the metallic stitching in the black leather of his jacket. His hair isn't as long as I remember, being cropped close to his head, almost military in style.

"Ms. Winters?" Sara says, interrupting my perusal of this hunk of man and calling attention to the fact that my basket sits on the belt, but I haven't unloaded the items, keeping the handle looped over my arm, and fighting the tug of the conveyor. I look ridiculous.

Shaky fingers come to my long white and gray streaked hair, and nervously comb back the strands. My appearance adds to the witch rumors—wild curls of premature gray, clothing made of natural fabrics, and black lace-up boots. A finger catches in my hoop earring and I struggle for a second with myself. A sharp tug and the silver circle releases, flinging from my sensitive earlobe and flicking Nathan in the chest.

Ow. My eyes sting with the release but I notice he catches the jewelry as it ricochets off the hard plains of his pecs under the soft-gray Henley he wears. He holds my earring out in between thick fingers I instantly recall tweaking my nipples once. Maybe twice.

With noticeably trembling fingers, I reach for the hoop.

"Sorry about that," I mutter, as if I did it on purpose. Right? Who would purposefully stick her fingers in her own nest of hair, get said finger hooked on her dime-store earring, and flip it at a burly man dressed like he's in a motorcycle club?

I'm a hot mess.

Did I mention how warm it is in the Piggly Wiggly?

I lower my eyes, willing myself to look away from him when I notice he holds only one item.

Is that a box of condoms?

Sweet Goddess, grant me strength.

My eyes flick to his zipper region again, and then I turn away. My cheeks flood with heat, undoubtedly matching the maroon swirls in my ankle-length skirt. I'm fifty shades of red and then some.

"You only have the one item?" I question, no longer able to look in his direction as he taps the box on the metal edge of the counter. I tug my basket upward and step back. "Why don't you go ahead of me?"

There isn't enough space between the checkout counter and the rack of candy behind me for the two of us, yet he shifts his large body to face mine and steps forward, pinning my back to the bars of chocolate and bags of trail mix behind me.

His eyes catch mine for a moment, widening in surprise before narrowing in question. He doesn't appear to recognize me and why would he? It's been a long time. He gives his head a shake, more like a twitch, and straightens. A mischievous curve appears at the corner of his lips and leaning toward me just the slightest bit, he says, "You sure you don't want to go first?" And just like that I'm propelled back in time to a night I've told myself to forget, and yet, never have. The deep timbre of his voice melts over me like drizzled caramel, suggestively hinting at something I know he doesn't mean. A pulse beats at the cookie crunch in my center while I stare back at him, swollen tongue and all.

"Thanks, sweetheart," he adds when I don't respond. His rough tone drips like nougat and fills my mind with candy-coated metaphors. My head shakes to dismiss his gratitude and he slides forward. And I mean slides, allowing his body to glide across mine in a leisurely drag. His firm upper body narrowly misses my face, but his lower area does not escape my belly, which does its own roundoff back handsprings as the awkwardness of something other than a candy bar—yet strong and yummy—swipes over me. The pressure lasts no more than a few seconds, but I'm like a champagne fountain come to life without a single glass to collect the bubbly drink.

What has come over me?

A thick hand comes to my upper arm as Nathan twists away from me and warmth seeps through my body. Then my blouse continues moving with him. My mouth pops open to say something, warn him, as my shirt opens wider at the neck, exposing my nude bra as my blouse follows the twist of his body.

I'm stuck on him.

"Um …" I hold up a finger, and he turns to glance down at me. I freeze. All thought escapes me as his eyes dip lower and heat rises up my neck. I lick my lips. Another second and I'm certain I'll be frothing at the mouth despite my embarrassment. I'd like to say I understand my reaction when he looks at me like he is—silver eyes glistening. But I don't. I'm a thirty-nine-year-old sexually-repressed librarian who practices self-love in hopes of reviving her inner goddess.

I'm still waiting for divine inspiration to spring forth.

With that thought, the fabric springs free of his protruding belt buckle and his hand releases my arm.

Thank you, Mother Earth.

I risk a quick glance up at him to see if he noticed our attached clothing, but it appears as if he missed everything. Instead, he looks like a god with his broody-edged jaw layered in white with a smattering of lion-brown in the mix, not to mention his hulking body. While Wiccan practices remind me life is about balance, it also teaches me I don't need a man on the other side of my seesaw. At least, the way I celebrate my religion.

I blink. I blink again. Then I reach for my shirt, tugging the hem forward to notice a small hole caused by our caught clothing. How appropriate considering the hole he left inside me. And just like the time before, he doesn't even notice what he's done to me. He doesn't look back at me, like he didn't look back then.

Rough fingers with short nails like they'd been bitten come to his belt buckle and absentmindedly press at the metal confine. He straightens it against his waist, leaving his callused digit on the tip a bit longer than necessary. Then he smooths his hand down the front of his zipper.

My mouth falls open. *Swollen tongue.* Then it snaps shut.

Nathan chuckles softly to himself and glances up at Sara who is slack-jawed and wide-eyed, watching us with interest. I don't imagine the night shift offers much entertainment, and right now, the sexual tension vibrating off me is higher than a Passionflix rating of five heats.

"It's your turn," I say, nodding toward the clerk, and he turns his body, giving me his back as he steps forward. Harley Davidson, I read across his broad back and take in the symbol underneath. Is he a member of a motorcycle club? Not versed in the who's who of area bikers, I know enough of the Iron Wraiths, the local MC presided over by the incarcerated Razor Dennings, to make me shiver.

Nathan's box of condoms swipes over the scanner and Sara lowers the package for a bag.

"Oh, I won't need a bag. Keep the environment safe and all that." His eyes drift to the carrier over my shoulder, the one I use to collect my groceries. Environmentally friendly, women in Africa make these bags as a way to raise money for an education which could lift them from oppression. My heart leaps in my chest. He cares about the environment. "Not to mention, I'll be opening the package soon enough."

Or not.

He turns to Sara and winks. Fingers come to her pinkened cheeks while her other hand reaches for the twenty he offers for his purchase.

Quickly understanding his meaning, I begin removing items from my basket, setting them on the belt with more force than necessary. *Why would I care that he's going to use a condom soon?*

Brownie mix. Rice cakes. Tampons.

I look over at the magazine rack to my left and reach for a novel from the ten bestsellers at the top of the display. I don't even read the title. I simply grab the book with the cover of a bare-chested man ripping the bodice of a woman in a floor-length gown and drop it down on the belt with the remainder of my things.

"Looks like an interesting night," Nathan says, eying my stuff as he holds out his hand for his change. Sara seems to be taking her sweet time doling out the bills and pressing coins in his palm.

Did she just stroke his fingertips?

My brain mutters a litany of profanity, but my mouth tweaks up in a false smile.

"Well, we can't all be as interesting as you." My brows tip up as my eyes flip to the box in his hand.

What the ... Nice retort. Am I in high school?

Nathan leans toward me, his head lowered, and his voice deepens. "Plan on it being very interesting. Want to join me?" He smirks—*literally*—with a rough chuckle. A raised brow matches mine and that damn corner of his lip creeps upward again. *Is that a dimple?* Sara's eyes flick between him and me, her mouth clamping in a grimace as her head tips just the littlest of bits, almost encouraging me to follow him.

"No thanks," I mumble, sweat trickling down the center of my back, coating my spine. You're lying, my brain taps my forehead.

Deny. Deny. *Deny.*

His eyes focus on my breasts for a moment. *Maybe I'm imagining it?* Then he tips his chin upward like he's a movie star and I'm lingering paparazzi. "Okay then, Naomi."

It takes a moment to register he said my name. I've seen Nathan a few times in the last year, but he hasn't acknowledged me. I assumed he forgot me, like he must have forgotten my phone number. I, however, have never forgotten him. My chest clenches—a sensation like my ribs are caving inward—and I want the tile floor to open and swallow me whole.

Sara watches me as she scans each of my items slowly, her expression stoic but I sense the question churning inside her. *Him? You?* Her eyes shift once again to Nathan's retreating back as he exits the store and then to me. I remain focused, following the swipe of each item before they are placed in my environmentally friendly bag. My toes wiggle in my leather boots and my fingers twitch, tapping a crisp twenty on the raised counter waiting to pay as I refuse to watch Nathan's departure. My entire body flickers with a flame I haven't felt in a long time.

I will not live my life in the past.

Sara reaches for the impulse purchase, scans the back, and then holds the book up to face me, as if waiting for an explanation.

Tonight is not going to be an evening of stellar, stimulating, quality literature like we host at the library. No, tonight will be a late night of unadulterated smut and self-soothing pleasure.

"You tell anyone, and I'll never let you check out the *9 ½ Weeks* DVD from the library again."

Sara slams the book into my bag and winks.

Interesting evening indeed.

CHAPTER TWO

DEWEY DECIMAL CLASSIFICATION: 612.6
REPRODUCTION, DEVELOPMENT,
MATURATION

[Naomi]

It's almost October and in a few days, we will decorate for Halloween, a Green Valley Public Library favorite. Fall used to be a dreaded time for me. Summer was life when I was a teen. As I grow older, I appreciate the crispness of the changing seasons, the preparation for shorter days, and the necessity of a revolving life cycle. Like the season, I'm in the autumn of my life, desperate for a change, but not knowing what such a change should be.

This time of year is also a crossroad for me. The locals celebrate through the annual Halloween party at the community center, but I refuse to attend organized functions at the former school, especially on the night of such a commercial holiday. The lore of vampires, werewolves, and witches isn't really my thing, being that I'm rumored to be one.

Samhain is my holiday. It marks the beginning of a new year—celebrating harvest and happiness. The night is bittersweet with both a reflection of my accomplishments throughout the past three hundred and sixty-five days and a remembrance of long-gone ancestors.

Seeing Nathan Ryder has been a painful reminder of a night which brought both celebration and devastation to my life. Since running into him at the Piggly Wiggly, I've been thinking of him too often over the last few days. It's been a struggle to face my history when all I've done for eighteen years is repress the memories. Yet seeing Nathan stirs up old yearnings; yearnings that I haven't allowed myself to explore with anyone else.

I'm a follower of the social media sexpert Vilma Louise who has helped me work through my desires, turning urges inward to please myself, not seek pleasure from others. *You do not need another person to complete you.* As a social media sensation advocating women's individual sexual awareness, Vilma's motto is *your self is the center of your personal universe.* Diane Donner-Sylvester, a former library patron, introduced me to Vilma's videos, encouraging me to develop my inner sexuality and the wonders of my own womanhood. Diane had similar issues after years without sex with her husband. She thought I was too uptight and might need a little sex education to loosen me up. She wasn't wrong, but I hadn't found a man to experiment with. I didn't want to be with just anybody.

You are your own circle of sensuality. The mantra repeats in my head as I round the check-out counter at the library for the children's section. I pass Sabrina Logan as I near the reading rug and my thoughts of Nathan and sex dissipate.

Sabrina replaced Bethany Winston six years ago when she—*eternally rest in peace, my sister booklover*—passed. Sabrina could never replace Bethany in my heart, though, which is still full from the goodness Bethany offered me. I was twenty-one when I came to the library. As the mother of seven children, Bethany took me under her proverbial wing, a fairy godmother of sorts, and the rest is my history. When Sabrina started, she had been the same age as me when I became a librarian. I want to be her friend like Bethany was for me.

At first, I misunderstood Sabrina's awkward silence, considering her standoffish, almost aloof, but eventually, I realized she was just painfully shy. The characteristic was foreign to me. Shy was not a word many would have used to describe me at twenty-one. At thirty-nine, my persona is a different story.

With the addition of Sabrina came her now nine-year-old nephew Harry who beams up at me from his spot on a comfy purple beanbag big enough for two people. We have three others in various sizes scattered through the section. Blue. Orange. Green. *They look like planets,* he said to me when we first met. He wouldn't look at me then and I thought his timidness equal to his aunt. Eventually, I realized his lack of eye contact was something he couldn't control without some practice. Harry has autism.

Spending time with children is one of my favorite things about the library. Harry and I have a routine. He tells me about the planets, or we skim through a Harry Potter picture book together, which is what we are doing when Sabrina enters the children's area.

"I ..." Her lips clamp shut. "He ..."

My brows pinch. Not one to stutter, it's evident she doesn't know how to explain what she needs.

"There's a man." The words stumble out, awkward and incomplete. I tilt my head trying to see through the stacks in the general direction where she points.

"Excuse me, Harry," I say to him, struggling to remove myself from the beanbag. One can never gracefully stand from a lumpy sack of beans. When I stand, I crane my neck and Sabrina and I both gawk over the shorter shelves in the children's department at the sliver of a large man.

"What does he want?"

Sabrina's face heats a deep shade of red as her eyes lower to her feet. *Oh my.* What could that mean? I nod as if I understand, smooth my hands down my skirt—today I'm wearing a full denim skirt with a long sleeve, black T-shirt—and walk toward the waiting patron.

Turning down the aisle, I have a better visual of him. Brownish jacket, sturdy and stiff, and typical of men who work outdoors. Construction boots both scuffed and covered in dirt. Jeans which hug the curve of his ... *two firm planets.* I blink and force my eyes away, but the attraction is too strong and my focus returns. This man knows how to wear denim. With that unsettling thought in mind, he turns, and I'm met with sterling laser beams.

"Naomi?" He says in a voice rough and smoky, as if he just woke from a nap. *I'd sleep with him. Oh wait, I already did.*

The thought catches me off guard and I audibly gasp. Nathan's head tips to the side at my reaction and I try to calm my racing heart by smoothing over the denim at my hips one more time. It's a nervous habit. My hand lifts for my chest instead, cupping the black tourmaline crystal hanging from my neck. The anxiety-ridding stone in my palm soothes me.

"Nathan." My voice squeaks like a mouse under the scrutiny of a lion. His size reminds me of one, the color of his coat matching the skin of the jungle king. My eyes flit to his hair like they did the night at the Piggly Wiggly. Almost all silver, his chin holds a patch still mixed with light brown. He has black dots on each ear, like flat earrings. His sudden movement draws my attention to his arms, which stretch behind his back holding something hidden behind the broad mass.

My eyes squint as if I can see through him.

"May I help you?"

His eyes roam down my body and up again. I blush although there's nothing exposed on me. My standard lace-up black boots cover my ankles to the edge of my skirt and my T-shirt comes to my neck. I slide the crystal on the leather strap—another anxious motion—as he scrutinizes my appearance.

"A book, perhaps." I interrupt whatever he's thinking, and he ducks his head to peer through the shelves. He won't find the other librarian, Julianne MacIntyre, here today. She has the day off. He's already frightened poor Sabrina. I'm his only hope.

His eyes flit to the shelf at his right and then back to me. I step forward for a closer examination.

Health. Female health. Young female health.

My eyes leap to his for an explanation.

"I need a book about ..." He pauses, leaning toward me. His breath holds a hint of cinnamon. "You know, your cycle."

I stare at him a moment, unclear of his meaning but also dazed by the intensity of his silver eyes. In the dull light of the library, they gleam with an outer rim of granite.

"My cycle?" *Bicycle?* A tricycle. The cyclical rotation of the seasons.

He clears his throat before he speaks. "Men*struation.*"

My fingers come to my lips as if he's muttered a dirty word. For some reason, a part of me thrums. He closes his eyes a second and exhales. His thick knuckles rub under his chin and the scruff makes a scratchy sound, causing tingles to erupt over my skin.

"My daughter is eleven and I think she's going through the change."

"The change …" I mumble.

"I thought a book to explain everything might help. I don't want her getting random *sh* … stuff … off the internet."

I gape at him as if he's speaking a foreign language, although I fully understand his meaning. I'm female. Of course, I know what he's talking about.

"She doesn't have a mother," he clarifies.

The statement stops my heart and forces me to blink in sympathy.

"I mean, Margie … her mother … she doesn't live here. With us. With Dandelion." His rambling becomes rather sweet. He's flustered sharing this information.

"Dandelion? That's an interesting name," I offer, lightening my voice to ease his discomfort.

His expression relaxes, his face filling with a growing smile. He's proud of his little girl. "It's a nickname."

"*The Dandelion Seed* is one of my favorite children's books," I say but he stares at me like I'm the one suddenly speaking a different language. I wait for more explanation about the nickname, but Nathan's eyes flick to the bookshelf.

"So the … um … change. Her mother didn't explain it." It's rude to ask, and I stop myself before I start fishing for answers to questions that I have no right to ask like: *is he married?* Nathan's large shoulders fall, and the curve of his lips drop a little.

"Let's just say I'm both parents."

I smile softly as if I understand and Nathan's eyes lower to the floor. I take a deep breath, ignoring the pinch in my chest, and go into superpower mode. I'm a librarian. I can help him find answers.

"Okay, we have several books about the young body and … the changes … it goes through. Eleven seems a little late to discuss these things, though." I glance up at him, not wanting to judge his parenting, but a young girl should know these things a little earlier in life.

My fingers troll the spines of books like a pianist expertly skimming the keys of a piano.

"I think this is one of the better books for a young woman." I hold out the book with an illustration of a light pink bloom on the cover. "*I Have a Vagina* is an excellent read."

Nathan sputter-coughs, choking on his gum. He bangs at his chest with a fist, and for a moment, I'm worried I'll have to administer the Heimlich. *I'd rather administer mouth-to-mouth.*

Nathan rereads the title for himself and his eyes fly upward to mine, then quickly divert. Stay in super librarian mode, I warn myself.

"It includes visuals with age-appropriate vocabulary and an explanation of how to use tamp—I mean, feminine hygiene products."

Nathan's eyes roll upward as his head tips back. His cheeks pinken. *Is he embarrassed?* If he thinks this is awkward for him, what about me? He's the one who has experience with the fact I do have a vagina. Experience doing wonderful things to my vagina. Which happens to pulse more rapidly than the life-sustaining organ in my chest at the moment.

This cannot be good. I don't want my vagina to beat to the rhythm of Nathan. I don't want any body part to hammer at the thought of him. Too late, though. My heart races as my mind fills with memories.

Are you sure about this?

I've never wanted anything more.

I was so naïve.

"There's a companion book as well." I swallow as I offer Nathan the second book in the collection. At some point, I've stepped closer to him and I smell him. Sandalwood and musk. Manly and sharp. And something else. Sawdust. Is he a construction worker? My eyes drift down his broad body.

Only the length of the book separates us. A distance I want to shorten.

"*I Have a Penis,*" he reads. Instantly, I'm inflamed by his statement. I am a sacrifice to my goddess and I gladly give of myself, if he'll be the horny god to take me. Horned God, I mean. God with a horn on him. A horn for plundering and ...

"Yes, I do," he adds, his voice low as his twinkling, teasing eyes find mine.

Deep exhale.

Here's the thing, I'm aware of the appendage on Nathan like he's familiar with the special spot on me. Unfortunately, the experience was a long time ago, and I'm quite certain he's forgotten all about my womanly parts especially if he has a daughter.

His eyes widen as he reads the title again and then the corner of his lip curls. I don't see it at first, but I know it's under the fuzz on his cheeks. A dimple lurks beneath the silver and *Sweet Goddess* if it isn't the sexiest thing I've seen in years.

"Naomi?" His questioning tone forces me to realize I'm practically pressed into his chest. Taking a step back, my necklace catches on the zipper of his jacket. The leather tugs at the back of my neck.

Not again. "I'm stuck on you."

His breath hitches before he speaks. "Is this becoming our thing?" His brows rise, and he chuckles, a rich mixture of rumbles. Then he shakes his head as I struggle to pull myself free, drawing back and jiggling the crystal-zipper combination. Nathan's hand wraps behind my neck, pausing my jostling. A thick finger swipes up my nape, curling under the leather string, and I shiver at the intimate touch.

"Let's just take this off," he whispers with smoke and ash in his voice, as he lifts my hair with his other hand and removes the strap over my head. More shivers slither down my spine, and in another moment, I'm going to be a puddle on the floor. He's said these words once before to me.

Yes, take it off. Take it all off.

My face heats. It's suddenly very hot in the library.

I think I'm having another hot flash like the one in the Piggly Wiggly.

Is there a pattern to hot flashes I should be aware of? Hot man. Hot flash. Maybe I should check out a book about things at the other end of the … you know … change cycle.

After he slips the leather from my neck, he unhooks it from his zipper. Dangling it from two thick digits, he holds it up.

"This is cool."

"Thank you," I mumble, reaching out my hand for my pendant but he curls his fingers into the leather strap and lifts the accessory over my head. Lowering it to my shoulders, he swipes my hair upward, cupping the massive curls in one hand. His curved fingers stroke down the string, narrowly missing my breast as he straightens the elongated crystal to hang between them. I should consider it forward. Women press charges for this kind of behavior, but all I want to do is press against him. My nipples respond instantly, standing erect and visible through my thin shirt.

"Thank *you* for the books, Naomi."

The way he says my name sends another river of shivers washing over my skin, and I decide to risk a question plaguing me. "So you remember me?"

His finger taps on something solid just over my heart and I look down to see my name tag.

Naomi.

"This is your name, right?"

Without answering his question, it's clear he's answered mine. Nathan Ryder has no recollection of me. Even though he teased me at the Piggly Wiggly and called me by name, he doesn't remember me. I must have been wearing my name tag that night, too. My nose prickles and my eyes burn. The hurt of my twenty-one-year-old self returns to my almost forty-year-old heart.

"Will this be all you need?" Suddenly, I want Nathan out of the library, away from me, and out of my memories. I don't need a reminder of the things we did, the pleasure lingering in my fantasies coupled with the pain of my actions.

I don't want to think about his backside firm and snug in his jeans.

I don't want to notice the dimple peeking through his silver scruff.

I don't want to see his eyes sparkling at me with a questioning look.

It's been eighteen years and all that time Nathan Ryder hasn't remembered me, so why should it sting that he doesn't recognize me now? I don't need his recognition, but strangely, I want it. I want the acknowledgment of this man who changed the course of my life, and yet, I won't give into him. I've already done that. I've learned my lesson. Nathan Ryder plus me equals catastrophe.

CHAPTER THREE

DEWEY DECIMAL CLASSIFICATION: 302
SOCIAL INTERACTION

[Nathan]

Naomi.

So you remember me?

Could I ever forget her?

Her name tag tells me her name, but is it really her? Naomi isn't common, and I've never met anyone else named the same. Can it really be that after all this time, she's still here? What are the chances I've seen her twice in one week when I haven't seen her once since I returned to Green Valley?

When I saw her a few nights ago in the Piggly Wiggly, I dismissed the sneaky suspicion of familiarity curling inside me when her eyes met mine. The longing in them. The history. I didn't want to believe it could be her even when I called her by name. But I couldn't shake the hint of something suppressed passing through my memory. I didn't want to allow myself to believe it was really her. It'd been such a long time.

Still.

I'm stuck on you.

The words whisper like a door in a dark room slowly opening to allow light. There was a girl with curly raven hair and eyes the color of chrome, deep pockets of granite gray, peering up at me. The crinkles in the corners of this woman's eyes throw me off. Still, when she looks at me, there's something I can't ignore. An undeniable sense she knows me, and I know her.

This woman with silver and white streaked hair, dressed in clothes covering every inch of her, seems nothing like the girl I once met. The girl who danced and whooped and begged me. But there's something unforgettable about her hair—the weight of it—as I wound it upward and righted her necklace. The out-of-control curl hints at tresses once a different shade—midnight and wild—spilling over a motel pillow.

I'm stuck on you.

My memory pulls up the Fugitive—a bar off a treacherous mountain road. A typical night of rambunctious bikers and reckless drinking. An unusual girl celebrating on the dark side. It would be hard to recall one in twenty of the women I'd slept with over nearly the same number of years, but Naomi always stood out. That one girl your mind refuses to forget.

I watch her turn away from me and suddenly there's too much here reminding me of all I want to forget but never could quite let go.

Perhaps it was the timing. At least I've told myself that over the years, but that's not the whole truth. That night changed everything for me, and a shiver ripples down my spine with the memory.

So you remember me?

I never forgot her, but I don't want to admit to the sharp ping of hope and the deep jolt of pain at seeing her again in Green Valley. She hasn't exactly acknowledged me, either. Sure she said my name, but it isn't the deep recognition of what we shared. Then again, how do you bring up something like that night?

Hey, Naomi, remember when we ...

I exhale.

People change, Nathan, my brain reminds me.

She isn't the same person from eighteen years ago and neither am I.

This woman is old ... *er*. Her hair. Her eyes. In miles of denim draped around indistinguishable legs, she is not the Naomi of my memory. But even in her altered state, she's pretty and I blink, a little startled by the realization.

Strangely, I wonder what she's wearing under her matronly outfit.

I have a vagina. The statement almost brought me to my knees, and I swallowed my gum. I'm a little doubtful the girl I knew is inside this woman.

Still.

I remember her. Under me, she was once curves and skin and life. Vibrant. Electric. Blooming.

I'm stuck on you.

Her sweet, quiet voice rings in my ears like the seduction of a siren at sea. Ironic even more so as I've never stuck to anything in my life. I thought I was on my way one night. The club. The girl. Then everything fell apart.

One thing is for sure about this *new* Naomi, she looks like she wants to lick me, and I feel strangely compelled to let her. Her eyes linger as if she's fighting the impulse to take a walk on the wild side of my body. It's a nice sensation—her so obviously checking me out. The stirrings inside my chest haven't been like this for a long time.

But just as I thought our conversation was heading somewhere, she seems ready to dismiss me.

My eyes wander to Naomi's backside as I follow her to the lobby. What's under all that denim, I think once again until we stop at the check-out counter, which she uses as a barrier between us. Suddenly, my phone peals. A loud fire alarm ringtone echoes through the quiet of the library lobby.

"End of lunch," I say, fumbling for the damn thing in my pocket and struggling to shut it off. She points to a sign printed in black ink on white copy paper slipped into a display stand.

Let freedom ring, but not your cell phone. Turn it off and your brain on.

Naomi taps a pencil on the edge of the plastic, as if sternly emphasizing my lack of rule following.

"It's a reminder I only have ten minutes before my lunch break ends," I explain. I work construction for Monroe & Sons. Bill Monroe is my boss, and while he isn't a stickler, I don't want to piss him off by being late. The trip to the library was a last-minute decision after fighting with my older daughter Dahlia last night.

"I need you to explain some things to your little sister," I asked my seventeen-year-old.

"Just buy her a book like Gramm did for me."

I didn't have time for a bookstore run in Knoxville, so the library was the next best thing.

Naomi nods, acknowledging my explanation but obviously no longer wishing to engage in conversation. She twists the corner of her lips with her teeth, and I notice the deep maroon color. It's bloodred, and tempting, a hint of who she might be underneath the yards of denim and black cotton. There's one final way to find out if she's the girl of my memory.

"So, Nae—" I use the name she asked me to call her that evening. *Call me Nae,* a sweet voice whispers breathlessly through my head.

"I don't go by that name anymore." The sudden flare in her ashen-charcoal eyes stops me short. Her brows furrow forming a deep dimple between them. The sharpness in her tone solidifies my query.

It's her.

"These are due back in three weeks," she adds louder, avoiding further eye contact. Sliding the books to me across the counter, I reach for her wrist, pressing her hand flat over the short stack.

"Hey." Without realizing it, my thumb strokes the tender skin on the underside of her wrist. "Was it the penis thing?" My brows wiggle, teasing her, flirting with her. "You know, I'm not offended to admit I have one."

"Just stop," she warns. Her eyes are buckets of coal looking to set me on fire.

"If I recall, you didn't say that before." My voice drops deeper. I don't know why I'm taunting her, but my heart races with the thought she might have forgotten me.

Walk away, Nathan. This chick is not your speed—slow and dowdy. She's not *your* Naomi. Not anymore.

"As you don't recall who I am, I don't suppose it matters what you think I did or did not do before."

Shocked by the snap of her tongue, my grip on her wrist tightens and my thumb strokes harder, rubbing deeper at the pulse of her vein.

You're the girl I can't forget, and I don't want you to have forgotten me.

"Of course, I remember you. I saw you at the Piggly Wiggly last week." It's not what I intend to say, but I'm struggling to come to terms with all I want to tell her. Her mouth pops open and she blinks. The sudden expression brings another flash of memory. A girl shocked by the things I said I wanted to do to her and then a slow smile giving me permission. A grin written for sin. A mouth that made a man linger as I did that night.

"I don't even know who I am most days, how can I expect you to remember me." Her lids lower and she turns her face away from me. Her quiet self-reflection, muttered under her breath, is eerily familiar.

Who am I? I wonder most days.

"Three weeks," she reminds me, tapping a finger on the books. Then she tugs her arm to release herself from my grip. I don't know why, but I don't want to let her go.

I'm stuck on you.

Once outside, I try to shake the weird vibe radiating over my skin. I'm going to be late from lunch and I don't miss the irony of Naomi as my cause.

One more kiss. It's the reason I was late, once upon a time.

I'm still puzzled by the woman inside the library as I sling a leg over my bike—a 2012 CVO Softail Convertible Harley—and set the books inside my side satchel. On days like today, I love my motorcycle just a little bit more. A brisk ride through fresh air and over quiet roads will reset me. Clear of Naomi's presence and those leering lick-me eyes, I relinquish thoughts of her.

I don't need the local librarian.

I have Charlese.

With conviction, I decide to pay her a visit on Friday night and rid my mind of one mysterious library worker. The idea rumbles through me as the sound of my metallic baby roars to life. After my two daughters, Dahlia and Dandelion, this machine is my life. The vibrating hum is music to my ears, although she's running loud today, as I peel onto the road leading to my current build. *Maybe I need the engine checked.* Maybe I enjoy the noise, drowning out the sounds in my head. Ones I wish to forget from a particular night eighteen years ago. I will myself not to think of *then*, telling myself I'm just wound up from seeing Naomi again.

Then I glance over at my side view mirror and notice two bikes flanking my rear.

Shit.

More reminders I wish to forget.

The Iron Wraiths. Specifically, Catfish and his sidekick, Drill, are behind me. It's rare to see the two separated, however, the first time I saw Catfish after returning to Green Valley he was with Dirty Dave. I'm surprised the old buzzard Dave was still alive. Actually, I was surprised to find Catfish still living. All the shit the Iron Wraiths have done makes my skin crawl, even though I know that most likely not every member has participated in the various rumors I've heard.

You owe me. His voice rings through my head—deep, determined, and dangerous. It's the new tone of my old acquaintance, Curtis Hickson, aka Catfish. I can no longer give him a friendly label. I deserted him, and he will spare nothing to remind me of it. When I returned to Green Valley, I did my best to avoid him. I flew under the radar for months until I went to the damn racetrack with my older brother Todd, and his best friend, Big Poppy. Catfish was as surprised to see me as I was to see him. Sixteen years banished from my home. Had that night been a mistake? Undoubtedly, the Iron Wraiths would have been the biggest mistake of my life.

"You were never to come back here again," Catfish growled.

"I have family here. Kids. A home. A job."

"So, you're living the straight and narrow life, and you think all can be forgiven?"

"Have I done you wrong in the years I've been gone?"

My response had stumped Catfish. He knew I was right. I hadn't shared a club secret in all the time that had passed. I didn't know anything new about them other than what the general public heard. Incarcerations. Disappearances. Suspicious activities. I wasn't anymore a threat to the Wraiths than anyone else.

Still.

I did know a few incriminating details, and I'm sure Catfish remembers one particular night involving me. Our secrets keep us locked together, circling each other, but I want to stay on the periphery, not at the center.

I turn into the drive leading to the construction site and release a breath. I don't look over my shoulder as I cut my engine and hear their bikes continue down the mountain road.

If Catfish wanted to run me off the road, he could have done it.

You owe me.

If he wanted to shoot me in the back, he would have done it.

You owe me.

But Catfish hasn't done any of those things. Yet. He has other plans. He wants me to patch in again. Been there. Done that. And not a chance of Jon Snow resurrecting Eddard Stark will I return to the Wraiths. They could run me off the road or shoot me in the back, and even then, I wouldn't consider being one of them. I paid my time. I did my banishment. I just want to live in peace.

I enter the job site, grateful Bill Monroe isn't present, and head for the third floor of the monstrosity we are building. Among the stud-framed walls, peacefulness triggers a certain someone with lick-me eyes and deep maroon lips. I shiver at the possibility of her anywhere near my history, even when she's a slivered part of said past. She's too good for me. I knew it back then. I know it now.

I don't have to fully recall what she wore, or what we did, or what we said. I remember the *feeling* of her as if it was yesterday. *I'm stuck on you.* There's something about her—something *different*—unique even. But Naomi looks complicated, and I don't do complicated, I think as I find my toolbox on the third level, strip off my jacket, and strap on my toolbelt.

I've had enough complication in my life. Been burned twice by complicated women already. What I need is Charlese—simple, sensual, specified. The routine of her keeps me away from random barflies and one-night stands—both of which have been trouble for me in the past—so I stick to a regular girl now. My girl Friday.

I'm stuck on you. I shake my head and double-check the plan for the bathroom I'll be framing out, but my mind wanders.

Charlese isn't someone I'd bring home to Ma and the girls, but I like her just fine. When I want the physical interaction of another body, Charlese is willing. We don't need to talk. We don't share feelings.

Get in. Get it on. Get out.

It works.

It works *well enough*, my heart thumps.

It's a mutually beneficial arrangement as Charlese has no interest in a serious relationship. We keep things between us carefree and low-key. Easy. However, my heart hammers within my chest, my memories swirling like a buzz saw. A wild beauty acting recklessly in the wrong bar. Teasing me. Wanting me. Giving in to me.

The woman in the library merges with the girl in my mind's eye. Long curly hair of gray and silver blur over the raven color in my memory. Eyes the hue of smoldering charcoal brighten a little to sterling silver. A twist of red lips whisper of sweet kisses turned eager and electric.

I'm stuck on you.

The remaining condoms in my satchel come to mind, and I'm suddenly thinking of using a few with someone other than Charlese. Eccentric clothes, silver waves, and bloodred lips are not a combination I thought would attract me—but I find myself bewitched nonetheless.

CHAPTER FOUR

DEWEY DECIMAL CLASSIFICATION: 306.85
SINGLE PARENTHOOD

[Nathan]

"I got you some books today, Dandelion," I tell Clementine when I arrive home after a long day on the site. I've placed the books in a paper bag, so she doesn't immediately read the title. "Ask Dahlia if you have any questions."

Clementine looks up at me with her big blue eyes behind thick dark-rimmed glasses. She has buttery yellow, out-of-control curls which frame her face just like when she was a baby, reminding me of a dandelion—hence, the nickname. Lately, I've teased her the name fits because she's growing like a weed.

"You went to the library?" she inquires, a squeal of excitement in her voice as she pulls the books from the bag. Clem loves books. Me, I struggled with reading.

Please don't read the title aloud, I think. *Please. Pretty please.*

Thankfully, Clementine reads the titles to herself and sets the books on the kitchen table where she has been doing her homework. I never have to ask her to do her work. Dahlia, on the other hand ...

"Thanks, Dad," Clementine says amused and disinterested at the same time.

I reach under my chin and scratch. "If you have questions, ask Dahlia," I repeat. Clementine blinks up at me and gives me a placating smile. She's so easygoing. God, I love this child.

I'm also grateful she isn't a twenty-four seven reminder of her mother, like Dahlia is of hers. Yeah, that's right, two girls, two different mothers. Karma is laughing at me.

"Sure, Dad." She returns her attention to her homework. A pot boils on the stove to signal someone has started dinner. Ma typically takes care of anything related to the kitchen. Dahlia's on laundry. I have the yard and repairs. We're a team, but sometimes I feel like we should be more, like we're missing a piece to our unit.

"So, Dandelion …" I begin not even certain why I'm asking or hesitating. "Do you know a Miss Naomi at the library?"

"Isn't she the witch?" Dahlia asks walking into the kitchen. Her dull blonde hair is streaked with lighter tones. She's thin compared to the solidness of Clem, and her clothes accentuate the subtle curves of her body. She's every bit her mother, and I shiver with the thought. Then I think, when did my baby girl grow into a young woman?

"Why would you say such a thing?" I question Dahlia, bracing myself for seventeen-year-old sarcasm and a million uses of the word 'like' in the explanation.

"It's what all the kids call her, like, with that wild hair and her, like, dowdy clothes. Some kids say she cast, like, a spell on them when they go to the library and, like, talk too loudly. Others say she walks into the woods, probably to, like, conjure up some spell or something. Kill a kitten and, like, use the blood for a potion." Dahlia wiggles her brows at me.

"Dahlia," I warn, my eyes shifting to Clem who is sensitive to all living creatures, not to mention, the obvious exaggeration of such a description.

"Anyway, the boys talk about her." She shrugs.

My brows pinch. "What do you mean? Who talks about her?"

Dahlia shrugs again as she turns her back to me and reaches for the overhead cabinet. "Something about capture the witch, but, like, how would I know. I'm not from here." Her jab stings. She wasn't happy about the decision to move to Green Valley but being here was the right thing to do—for all of us.

"She's not a witch," Clementine defends, her head popping up from her books. "Miss Naomi is the best. She loves Harry Potter and all things fantasy, and when she does read-alouds, she uses all the voices."

I'm wondering why I've never questioned Clem before about the librarian when Dahlia interrupts.

"Because she's a witch. She can, like, speak in tongues. *Wha-ha-ha.*" She throws her own voice in a spooky cackle, lifting her hands and wiggling her fingers to emphasize her point.

"She does not," Clem whines, and then her voice shifts to dreamy. "She's amazing."

I'd chuckle at the interchange between my girls, but I'm intrigued by their differing perspectives.

"Why's she amazing, Dandelion?"

It occurs to me that in the nearly two years since moving back to the Valley, I haven't encountered Naomi. Then again, with her changed appearance, I don't think I'd recognize her without inspection.

And I want to inspect her further.

"She's nice to me," Clem mumbles under her breath, shrugging her shoulder and returning me to the conversation at hand. Her head lowers. Clem has had trouble making friends at school, and I worry most days that she's lonely. Moving here was an adjustment for her—leaving behind good friends and her mother whom she only sees twice a year now. For Dahlia, the change was a necessity. She was getting in with the wrong crowd, hinting at repeating my history. Dahlia hasn't seen her mother since she was one and Becca decided she no longer wanted to be a parent.

"She's a witch," Dahlia repeats, drawing out the words in a haunting tone.

"Just stop," Clem says, and I'm drawn back to the library earlier in the day.

Just stop.

"Do you see Miss Naomi often when you go to get books?" My mother is the one who takes Clem to the library. I try to be an involved father but there are some areas I'm lacking—the library is one of them. Books haven't ever been my thing. However, I want my girls to be intelligent and independent, not like the women I seem to hook up with. Dahlia's mother had no ambition other than to be a club rat, and Margie—Clem's mom—she wanted more as long as it involved crisp paper in a certain shade of green with Benjamin Franklin's image in the center.

"Gramm and I see her every time," Dandelion answers me. "She's my favorite. Mrs. MacIntyre is too strict, and Miss Logan doesn't really speak. Naomi is the best. She gets me."

The comment softens me, but I still correct her. "Miss Naomi." My girls will have manners, too.

"She's a witch," Dahlia mumbles as she pours dry pasta into the pot.

"Dahlia," my mother shrieks as she enters the small kitchen space. My ma lives with us. "You shouldn't say such a thing." Emma Rae Ryder is a force despite her four eleven stature and heavy accent.

"I didn't say bitch, Gramm. I said witch." *So much for manners.* My mother's brows rise, and she swipes a hand at my daughter.

"Good girls don't talk with trash mouths." I don't need to see Dahlia's face to know she is rolling her eyes at her grandmother. Ma loves the girls and I can't thank her enough for taking on children again, but some days ...

"Nathan, when you going to bring home good girl? Stop hooking up with the riff-raff."

Hooking up? Riff-raff? I shake my head, knowing I'll be meeting up with Charlese the next night. She isn't riff-raff, and we aren't hooking up, but my chest tightens with thoughts of what exactly we are doing. My conscience gives me a little poke when I remember our last meeting, after my stop at the Piggly Wiggly. We weren't as good as we had been, and I pause to consider what that means. An image of someone else under me flits into my head, and I wonder for the briefest moment if the lackluster night was because a certain someone was tapping at my subconscious. I shake my head.

Those thoughts are only my mother's words messing with me.

When you going to bring home good girl? My heart repeats. If only I knew one. *But you did ...*

Ignoring Ma, I step out of the kitchen to clean up for dinner.

CHAPTER FIVE

DEWEY DECIMAL CLASSIFICATION: 304
FACTORS AFFECTING SOCIAL BEHAVIORS

[Naomi]

"Expelly your anus," a male voice mocks from behind me as I slip the bills to Amir, the night manager of this establishment, according to the sign next to the register. The Stop-and-Pump is just outside of Green Valley and has the cheapest gas prices. My eyes meet Amir's, black and wide, and I expect him to say something to the teens behind me making derogatory comments and roughhousing in his store. I don't realize the suggestion is directed at me until the second one speaks.

"Broom, broom, broom, I'd love to take a ride on you." My body ripples in disgust at the thought. They can't be more than sixteen, seventeen at the most. I momentarily close my eyes and take a deep breath. My heart races, but I will myself not to overreact.

It will never happen again.

Amir's eyes widen when I open mine to speak up, to tell those boys they can't talk to me like that, but I notice Amir staring over my shoulder. A scuffle happens behind me, and I risk a glance. My entire body shifts completely when I see Nathan, draped in leather and looking fierce, holding one boy by the scruff of his neck.

"Your daddy know you're talking like that?" he asks, hissing at the boy's ear.

"My pop don't care how I talk," he snaps. The lanky male is almost as tall as Nathan but three times thinner. He's a child in a near-man's body, and there's something familiar about him with his spiky hair and smirky grin.

"Let's just give Dwight a call and see if that's true?" Nathan gives the kid a little shake and pulls his cell phone from his back pocket. He dramatically holds it out before the teenage boy, his thumb hovering over the home button. I can't say I recognize the boys although I'm acquainted with many children in Green Valley. If a child doesn't frequent the library, though, I'm not likely to know them as is the case with these two teenagers. However, this dark-haired one ... I can't put my finger on it.

"I can't get in no trouble," the first boy warns his friend as he slowly backs toward the door. His ripped jeans show he's just as gangly as the boy under Nathan's grip. Long, blond bangs cover his eyes.

"Seems trouble is exactly what you wanted. Now apologize." Nathan jiggles the teen he's holding by the neck.

"I'm sorry," he mutters, wincing a little.

"Say it like the man you should have been," Nathan demands.

"I'm sorry," he says louder, his voice cracking like the boy he is.

"It's okay," I offer, waving a hand, attempting to defuse the tension, but sharp silver eyes meet mine.

"It is not okay." Nathan's smoky voice remains gruff as he releases the boy with an easy shove. "Get out of here. And don't think I won't be telling your daddy about this." The teen tips his chin at Nathan with one final look of defiance and then they both shuffle out the door. With Nathan watching them, I turn back to Amir.

It will never happen again.

My fingers shake as I reach for the change he offers. Turning for the door, my entire body trembles.

"Thank you," I murmur, my voice shaky, as I try to pass Nathan, but he grips my forearm and stops me. He's dressed similar to the night I first saw him—black jeans and a leather vest. A white T-shirt accentuates his broad shoulders, solid waist, and low-slung pants. He wears a few silver rings on his fingers and a bandana around his forehead. He looks sinister and sexy, and totally forbidden.

He spins to stand at my side, and his hand slips to my wrist. Gently leading me, he walks us out the door. As we take a few steps into the lot, my skin tingles under his thick fingers, a puzzling reaction to his tender touch. The sensation reminds me of his hand over mine on the stack of books he checked out, and I try to tug free of his hold, but he doesn't release me.

"I'm okay," I lie. In my head, I know I'm fine, but the message escapes my body. The boy's voice has triggered a memory—but my recollection fogs in Nathan's presence.

It will never happen again.

"You're shaking like a leaf, sweetheart." He stops us and looks around the lot. Then his eyes narrow at my car, the only other vehicle at the station.

"A convertible," he snorts. "Not very practical." I own a lime green VW Bug with a soft top. It isn't practical for the mountains, frivolous even, but it was second-hand, and Cletus Winston gave me a deal when my Corolla died.

"Neither is a motorcycle," I retort, which is ridiculous as many locals in the area own bikes. "At least, my ride came with a flower." A little vase suctioned to the dash holds a single Gerbera daisy in deep red. Nathan's face turns to mine and his eyes fall to the corner of my lips which I'm chewing. Slowly, his mouth curves and the stern edge of his expression softens.

"A little sass, huh? You're making a joke." His eyes twinkle, shifting from cold dawn to midnight.

"It's the best medicine." I strive to believe what I say. A little laughter and my nerves will settle, but for the moment, I'm still trembling. I can't decide if it's the boys' mockery, Nathan's surprise appearance, or the fact he just played a hero. Adrenaline rushes through my veins, and I reach for the black tourmaline hanging at my chest.

"Let me give you a ride home." My gaze shoots to his bike—monstrous, metal, and mean.

"I don't ride," I tell him. It's true. I'll never put my body on a bike again.

Give me a ride I'll never forget, I'd flirted with him. That was then.

"What are you doing here?" I glance around the Stop-and-Pump which sits at a crossroads. Head south and the next stop is Cedar Gap, my hometown and a place I never intend to pass through again. His hesitation tells me he has plans for the night. He's headed out—out of Green Valley—to any number of biker bars nearby. The Iron Wraiths own the main ones but heading south and over the mountain is the Fugitive, a place I visited once. Where I met a man. *Who I gave my ...*

Another thought occurs.

"Needed another pit stop, perhaps," I snark, remembering the large box of condoms from the Piggly Wiggly.

Sweet Goddess, does he already need more?

"I'm here for gas," he states, tweaking up an eyebrow and looking around us as if it should be obvious. "Now, about that ride—"

"I'm all set." I tilt my head toward my car.

"How about a drink then?"

"I don't drink." It's true, too. I gave it up, along with dancing and cavorting, as my parents called it.

I gave it all up.

This is all your fault, Naomi. God is punishing you for your behavior. Punishing us.

"Not even coffee?" he asks, not missing a beat like that's what he intended in the first place. Actually, I drink tea, and I'd love a good cup of chamomile. "Daisy's Nut House," he suggests. "I could follow you."

Daisy's place is famous for doughnuts and a bit more, and it's also located in the opposite direction. Sugary treats and I have a love-hate relationship. I love them—they hate me—but a sweet tooth was something I couldn't part with no matter how hard I tried to suppress everything else, and a doughnut does sound good. *I must be allowed one guilty pleasure in my life.*

"I'm sure you have other plans this evening," I note, looking him up and down in his dark clothes. He tugs at my wrist, reminding me of his hold on me, and I stumble toward him, my feet tangling. My chest collides with his, and I scoff at the awkwardness. My hand flattens against soft cotton and hard pecs to break my fall. He's firm—*very firm* —and his free hand slips into the hair on the side of my head, holding my face close to his.

Will he kiss me? It's the craziest thought I've ever had.

"No plans," he says, his voice turning ashy like it did in the library the other day. His eyes capture mine and the only word I can find to respond is, "Okay."

<hr />

The loud rumble of his engine cuts off after he pulls up next to me at Daisy's Nut House. For the millionth time, I tell myself this is the craziest thing I've ever done—next to thinking he'd kiss me—only I know it isn't true. Ironically, the last crazy thing I did was also with this man.

I puzzle for a moment over the thought of being kissed. Do I want him to kiss me? Why do I want him to kiss me? I know exactly how long it's been since I've been kissed, and maybe the length of time is the reason. Maybe it's just been so darn long since it last happened. Or maybe the truth lies deeper. It's him. It's Nathan. Nathan Ryder. The last man I kissed, and I want a repeat.

He hops off his bike and startles me by opening my door as I struggle with my skirt. My choice in clothing is a bit unconventional, for my age, for the era, but I take comfort in it. I feel safe within it— baggy tops and fuller skirts. While I stand out, it also sets me apart from others. It keeps me separate from those who don't understand me. *If the suit makes the man*, as the saying goes, then my long skirts are my armor.

To my surprise, Nathan offers me a hand to help me from my car and he doesn't let go as we walk to the entrance. Daisy's Nut House is owned by Daisy Payton, daughter of one of the most prominent families in the area. She's regal like an African queen with big black eyes and bright red lips. Upon seeing us, she smiles like warm honey. The Nut House had a shoot-out this last summer, but the place is all cleaned up now. Hearing what an officer of the law did was downright frightening. It's one reason I don't call the sheriff's department every time kids taunt me. *Who would believe me anyway?* Unfortunately, racial prejudice is still a thing and religious misperceptions run a close second. Because of my practices, some people consider me different enough not to bother to understand that my beliefs don't harm others. Quite the opposite, actually. I'm often misjudged. Sadly, I'm used to it.

"How are you this evening, Ms. Winters?" Daisy addresses me as I step up to the counter. She was Bethany Winston's best friend and I've shared many nights of giggles with both of them. My heart aches a little at the loss of those moments since Bethany's passing.

"I'm well. How are the girls? How is Adolpho?" Daisy has two gorgeous, intelligent daughters, and a genius son who's handsome in his own right, and they all regularly frequented the library until that one time Julianne kicked Simone out for watching porn on the computers.

"Simone's staying busy with Roscoe Winston in D.C. Oh, to be young and in love, right? And Poe is in California, finishing up his fellowship in planetary astrophysics. That boy always did reach for the stars."

I chuckle with her and don't miss how she avoids information on Daniella. This summer was a trial for her oldest daughter.

After placing my order for chamomile tea, I reach into my oversized patchwork bag for my wallet.

A few tampons.

A half-eaten protein bar wrapped in a napkin.

My favorite homemade lip balm. I had wondered where that went.

A hand comes to my lower back, and I still. Nathan reaches around me before I can find my way through the bottomless mess and places a bill on the counter. Hyper-focused on his warm palm just above my backside, I hardly hear his order.

"I'll take a coffee. Black, please." His voice still sounds rough, and I turn to him.

"Thank you for the tea."

"I'll bring you your drinks. Have a seat," Daisy interjects, giving me a knowing look, although I don't know what she thinks she knows. Nathan winks at her and leads me to an empty booth in the corner. We pass Deputy Sheriff Jackson James and the new, replacement deputy, Wyatt Monroe. There's a stereotype about finding law enforcement in a doughnut shop, but looking at these men, it's evident doughnuts have no effect on their physiques.

"Good evening, Naomi," Jackson addresses me as we pass. I tip my head and grin, not trusting my voice with Nathan's hand still on my lower back and Jackson glaring at the connection.

I fold into the final booth and Nathan sits across from me.

"Thank you again for stepping in tonight. That wasn't really necessary." While I would have gone into librarian mode, effectively using my stern voice of reprimand to put those boys in their place, I am grateful for Nathan's intercession. They weren't exactly young school children.

"There's no reason for Dwight's son to be speaking to you like that. I'd like to think his daddy would be appalled by his behavior, but unfortunately, knowing his father as I do, I don't think so. Either way, it was disrespectful and unacceptable."

I dismiss him with a wave, lowering my eyes to the tabletop. "It happens." It's painful to admit the truth. People talk behind my back all the time. The ignorant. The unfamiliar. They're uncertain what to think of me. It's a conservative Christian community, and I'm an outlier. I'm a little embarrassed of my acceptance at being an anomaly.

Nathan's quiet for a moment and when I finally peer up at him, he's squinting as if he's searching for something on my face.

"How often?"

"How often what?"

"How often does it happen?"

My head turns for the window. The night is dark. The air is crisp. *'Tis the season.*

"It's that time of year," I mutter. Surely, he's heard the rumors, even if he's been gone for eighteen years. *Eighteen years.* Some nights, I think I might have dreamed him up, but then painful memories return. With the recollection, I wish the night had been a dream, instead of the nightmare it turned out to be. But when I glance back at Nathan, and take in his piercing silver eyes, the curve of his lip, and the hint of a dimple, my heart skips a beat, and I curse my thoughts. Nathan might have been a foolish decision, but I don't wish him away. Instead, I marvel at the fact I'm sitting here with him.

"Fall?" he questions, interrupting my wandering thoughts.

"Pumpkins, pumpkins everywhere. Witches in the air …" My voice falters on the Halloween rhyme. I wave my hands in a spooky manner, but the mocking motions are weak. His eyes narrow further. Assuming I'm a witch isn't the worst people have thought of me. A long time ago, I accepted the fact that people are going to believe what they will. I'd learned that lesson the hard way, starting with my parents. *Jezebel.*

"I don't understand." But something in his tone tells me he's heard a thing or two. He continues to watch me like he doesn't know what to think, and then his head tilts and his brow twitches in question. "But it isn't true? The witch thing."

"Are you asking me or telling me?" Does he believe the rumors? Would it matter to him what I practice? What I believe? Then I remind myself, Nathan Ryder doesn't know me, any more than I know him, and his opinion shouldn't matter. Strangely, it does.

"I'm stating a fact. It doesn't matter to me." He leans forward, his clenched hands sliding over the tabletop, stretching forward as if he intends to reach for me. My hands remain under the table, twisting the material of my skirt, sweaty palms gripping at the all-natural fabric.

What would his touch feel like after all these years? Would he be gentle or rough? Would he be smooth or scratchy with that scruff? Would he kiss me like he did, like I was the only girl he ever wanted to kiss?

"If you're looking to dip your wand into my cauldron, you'll be sadly disappointed," I blurt, immediately regretting the words as they leave my mouth.

He sputters as his eyes blink. "My *what* in your *where?*"

"Your wand," I state slowly, twirling my finger as I point at him. "Into my cauldron," I say, aiming my thumb back at myself. Nathan stares at me like I have two heads.

I'm acting like I have two heads. One for not thinking straight. And the other for sounding like a fool.

I lower my hand to my lap, clutching at my skirt and curling my fingers into fists.

"Witches humor," I mutter, pausing a beat. "Never mind."

Could the tile floor please open and swallow me whole?

Thankfully, our warm drinks arrive, distracting us for a mere second.

"Enjoy," Daisy says, smiling at Nathan before giving me another pleased look I can't interpret.

"I really should have paid. It's the least I could do as you played the hero." I attempt to recover my failing social skills with graciousness.

"I'm definitely no hero," he snorts, and there's something cryptic in his tone. His eyes harden, and he focuses on the steaming mug before him. We're silent for another second, each keeping to our thoughts. Sitting across from Nathan feels a little surreal, and my mind is a jumble, like a scrambled jigsaw puzzle.

What am I doing here with him?

I don't go out much. I don't have many friends. I work at the library. I come to the Nut House on Wednesdays with my sister. Otherwise, I'm a homebody and I don't know how to converse with an extremely attractive man unless he wants to talk about books. Thankfully, Nathan breaks the silence.

"How old are you?" His question surprises me.

"I'm thirty-nine. Why?" I want to remind him I was twenty-one when we met and it's been eighteen years, so do the math, but I don't. I watch as his eyes travel over my hair, untamed and static-y in the dry heat of the doughnut shop. I answer him before he speaks. "It's the hair. I went prematurely gray."

"It's the clothes," he adamantly states as if it isn't hurtful to put down my attire. "And the attitude. It's like a shield around you. You're different now." He pauses, roaming over my face, which I'm certain expresses my shock. "What happened to you?"

My mouth falls open and then slowly closes. "I'm the same as I've always been."

"Really? I don't believe it." In many ways, he's right, but I won't justify myself to him. To the man who didn't call when he said he would. To the man who disappeared, never to be seen again.

My arms cross and I glare at him across the table. He isn't the same either, but then I note his broader body and the twinkle in his wise eyes. His silvery hair giving away the years. He's exactly the same in some respects. Hot. Smoldering. Tempting. And the way he's looking at me ...

Deny. *Deny.*

It's suddenly warm again. *Is this another hot flash?* Maybe it's the tea, but I haven't drunk any yet.

Then I remember that he borrowed books for a daughter. Is he married?

I sit up. "I don't think we should be here." I shift right to look over my shoulder and then left to peer out the dark window again.

"Why not?"

"What if your wife sees us?"

"That would be tricky, seeing as I don't have one."

I blink at him. "But you have a daughter."

"Two actually. But no wives. No exes either, just to clear that up." He watches me. "What about you? Got a husband I need to worry about? How about a boyfriend?" It's almost as if his questions tease me.

"No," I choke. I'm not sure I understand his meaning. *No exes.* Has he never been married?

"Is there a problem then? That I have the girls?"

"No," I reply a little too eagerly, my voice lilting. "Why would it be a problem?"

Leaning on his elbows again, Nathan draws closer to me. "Because I'm finding I'd like to see you again."

My face heats and I'm literally fanning myself.

It's hot in here, right? Maybe it's the doughnut machines causing all the heat.

"Oh." It's astonishing I consider myself an intellectual with my lack of vernacular recall around this man.

"That's all you have to say?" He chuckles, leaning back and reaching for his coffee. He lifts the mug, slips his lips over the rim and sips. I don't know if I've ever been so interested in the process of someone drinking. But I'm interested, *so interested.* I watch the roll of his throat as he swallows, and my tongue licks behind my teeth. I want to nibble his neck. Observing his lips curl over the edge of the mug for a second sip, I remember those lips sucking at my skin. Tugging at a nipple. Giving me kisses. I shiver.

He gazes at me over the rim of his mug, and I realize I've taken too long to answer him.

"Yes." Again, stellar verbal skills.

"Yes, to seeing me again, or yes, to all you have to say?"

"Aren't we seeing each other now?" I don't know why I respond with another question or with such snark. I'm nervous. It feels like a date when it shouldn't feel like a date because it isn't a date. It's just two people drinking hot beverages in the same place, at the same time, at the same table. My face heats further. *Because it's bloody hot in here.*

I don't wait for him to answer and ask another question boring a hole in me. "Where have you been?" *These eighteen years* lingers unspoken. I have so many questions, but I'm afraid of the answers.

"Go out with me and I'll tell you everything," he says, a hint of a lie in those words. He holds a secret, and I sense it when his eyes avoid mine. Instead, he focuses on my tea.

Aren't we out right now? I think but don't say. This isn't a date.

"What's in that? It smells like grass." His nose wrinkles in a way that's too cute for an edgy man as he tips his chin toward my tea.

43

"Chamomile. Soothes the nerves. It will also help me sleep tonight."

"Do you not sleep?" His eyes shoot up to look at me.

"Sometimes." I am not about to explain how my lack of sleep lately stems from seeing him, which has brought back a ton of guilt, a wave of nightmares, and unexplained desire. *Why am I drawn to him?* It's only been me for all these years, so I can't explain why I'm reacting so strongly to Nathan. However, Nathan makes for good fantasy, as my inner goddess is a little underwhelmed with my self-soothing practices lately. The fantasy doesn't compare to the reality in my memory, and I get caught up in the recall of *his* fingers on me. *In me.* Doing things to me.

He leans forward again. The corner of his lips curl and the hint of a dimple teases me. "I know some other remedies to help you sleep at night." His low, seductive timbre washes over my skin, and I hear my inner goddess yelp, *Yes, please.* She wants to indulge.

Deny. Deny. My subconscious weakly warns, losing enthusiasm.

A singular headlight beams across the restaurant front, startling us both, and a motorcycle parks in the lot. A man hastily hops from the bike and storms for the door.

"Shit," Nathan mutters. The door hinges open with too much force and slams back in place behind the customer. A lean, lanky man in his mid-thirties stands just inside the entrance. I can make out his outline from the reflection in the window behind Nathan. I also note the absence of the deputy sheriffs, Jackson and Wyatt.

"You touch my kid?" he growls at Nathan, strutting toward our table. A stiff finger points in our direction.

"Now, Dwight, calm down," Nathan commands, shuffling out of the booth and holding up both hands to the irate father. The name raises the hairs on the back of my neck, and I realize I wasn't paying attention when Nathan mentioned it at the gas station.

"You don't put your hands on my son, Nathan." If a bull could be personified, this man would be it. His nostrils flare. His cheeks flame red. Smoke might whistle out each ear any second.

"He was disrespectful and rude. Insulting of his elders." *Ouch.*

"What did he do?" Dwight snaps without losing steam.

"He called her a witch, mocking her literally behind her back." Nathan's hand sweeps toward me and Dwight turns. His breath hitches. He recognizes me. And I recognize him.

"You," he murmurs so low I'm hoping Nathan doesn't hear him. The shock on Nathan's face tells me he didn't miss it.

"What does that mean?" The sharpness of Nathan's tone forces Dwight to turn back to him. Dwight's shoulders lower as he shakes his head.

"My son's just calling it like it is." The image of his son in the Stop-and-Pump comes to mind and the familiarity falls into place. The spiky dark hair. The lanky build. The defiant smirk on his face. His child is the spitting image of him at that age.

I'm working the corner of my lip, nearly chewing off the delicate skin. *I need to get out of here.* But Nathan steps closer to Dwight, closing off my exit from the booth and squaring off with him.

"And what the hell does that mean?"

"If the broom fits—"

Scooting to the end of the seat, I interrupt the remainder of Dwight's comments. I slip out of the booth and stand. I don't need this kind of attention, and with Nathan inching ever closer to Dwight, I'm worried they'll fight right here in the Nut House. I don't want any trouble for Daisy.

Dwight takes a huge step to the side, widening the space between us, as if my nearness might singe him, only that's not how he behaved when he was seventeen—not him nor his friends. The trembling returns, and this time it has a reason.

Nathan steps to my side, his arm sliding around my back and a hand lands on my hip. Dwight's eyes open wide, wheels of surprise.

"What's this?" he hisses as his lids lower to slits.

"I'm watching you," Nathan warns in response.

"You making a statement?" Dwight counters.

"And if I am?" There's a threat in Nathan's tone, and I don't understand what I'm witnessing. The two men eye one another for a long minute before Nathan gently prods me to turn, ushering me forward to the door, with his arm securely around my waist. Once outside, we stand beside my car, as we wait for Dwight to exit. Nathan's in bull mode as well, breathing heavily as he holds me in place—a hand at my hip, the other on the roof of my convertible caging me in.

"What was all that about?" he demands, his temper rising, but not directed at me as he watches Dwight order a doughnut, exit the diner, and stalk to his bike. He takes two quick bites of his sugary treat before he peels out of the parking lot.

"Let's just say the apple doesn't fall far from the tree."

Nathan's eyes search my face, the irises nearly eclipsing all the aluminum color in them. Two hands cup my face, fingers delving back into my hair. He leans forward and my mouth waters. I roll my lips inward and then back. I haven't been kissed in eighteen years. I won't know what to do if he kisses me.

It's like what they say about riding a bike, I tell myself. Only I always wonder who "they" are, and I haven't ridden a bike in a long while either.

It's silly to think he'd kiss me. I mean, why would Nathan Ryder kiss me after all these years?

My heart races. My thighs separate as his knee gently nudges between them. A pulse at my core thunders to life like someone opened a gate at the racetrack—sprinting and galloping forward hoping for a finish line.

Sweet Goddess.

His fingers dip deeper, fisting into the tresses by my ear, and then …

"Ow." One of his rings is stuck in my hair. He pulls forward, and the strands yank in response "Oh."

"It seems I'm stuck on you."

Our eyes meet, and we both chuckle. I'd shake my head, but I can't move. Wild curls tangle in the metal accessory. He frees one hand to work at removing the twist of the other. When it doesn't work, he slips his finger from the offending ring instead and then unravels my locks from the band.

"We seem to have a history of jewelry malfunction," I tease. His eyes leap to mine. The playful gleam of light silver returning. His fingers cup the edge of my chin and he steps forward, closing any space between us.

"I think we have other history, and there was no malfunction in that." Then, he kisses me.

CHAPTER SIX

DEWEY DECIMAL CLASSIFICATION: 160
LOGIC

[Nathan]

My mouth crashes into hers, desperate for a taste. There's just something about her and the way she looks at me. I want to remember her, remind myself of her flavor, how she feels under me, what it feels like to connect.

Lick me, those eyes say.

But she isn't licking me.

In fact, her lips aren't moving at all. No response comes from the initial connection of mouth to mouth, nor the softening sucks I offer after the hard contact. She remains frozen as if I've startled her, as if she's never been kissed.

Maybe she doesn't want to be kissed by you, idiot. Shit.

I pull back abruptly and stare down at her. Her eyes remain pinched shut, her lips rolling inward again.

"I was bad at that, wasn't I?" she says, and I fight the urge to bust out in laughter.

Instead, I huff. "It normally goes a little better," I mutter, scratching under my chin with my knuckles. I've really messed this up—misinterpreted her signals—and I take a step back to give her some distance. I'll take her resistance as a big negative to seeing each other again.

Her eyes widen at the inches I put between us. Then, her shoulders sink. Her head lowers and her fingers fiddle with the crystal near her breasts. Her body language says she's a little disappointed, but I'm feeling a lot rejected. I'm so fucking confused.

"I'm sorry. I just—"

"It's okay," I say, cutting her off. She doesn't need to explain herself, and I don't think I want to hear her reasons anyway. "I'll just follow you home to make sure you're safe, if that's okay. I don't trust Dwight."

Dwight Henderson works with me. He talks big but basically, he's an asshole. He used to be some bigshot Green Valley football star back in his day, but when he got his girlfriend pregnant, he lost his scholarship. Seems Notre Dame didn't want to take a boy who got a girl *in the family way* out of wedlock. At seventeen, he had a kid—Junior, the name finally comes back to me. Dwight's a thorn in my side on a good day. A full-blown pricker bush on a bad one. He's lazy, inconsistent, and a bit dangerous, and I've heard rumors he's trying to patch in with the Iron Wraiths. Seeing his reaction to Naomi has me wondering if something happened between them.

And I realize I don't want to follow her home. I want to understand what just occurred here.

"That won't be necessary," she says, keeping her head lowered, her eyes avoiding mine. She dismissively waves away my suggestion and then tucks her hair behind her ear. Her eyes shift up to my lips and then drift to the side.

What's going on here? I don't want to press her, question why she didn't kiss me back, but I'd like an answer. Then again, her body language tells me not to ask. I exhale heavily in frustration.

"Okay, well, I guess I'll just see ya around then." I don't want to walk away. I don't like how this is going down. I want her to say something. Explain her reaction. Explain what happened.

What did I do wrong?

"Yep," she sharply replies. Her face lifts and a mask makes her expression unreadable. Was she even remotely affected by our lips connecting? "Next time you need a vagina …" Her eyes pop up to mine, horror filling them. Mine might actually mirror the surprise in hers.

"I mean a *book* about vaginas." She coughs, covering her mouth with a fist. "I mean—"

"I think I know what you mean," I say, sparing her by holding up a hand. I also know it means she won't be wanting my penis.

Reaching around her for the door handle, she steps to the side and I get a whiff of her scent—herbal and sharp and addicting. I open the door and wait for her to settle into the seat. Instead, she steps forward. Both hands raise, and my breath hitches with anticipation.

"Nathan, I …" She pauses before swallowing back whatever she wanted to say and lowers her hands without touching me.

I nod, pursing my lips. "I misread the situation. I apologize."

"No, Nathan, that's not it …" Her voice trails off again. *It's not you, Nathan. It's me.* I've heard it before and decide to let her off the hook again.

"I get it. It's okay." There are a number of reasons why she shouldn't be with me anyway. Although I'm certain she doesn't know anything about what happened to me after I left her. Guilt. Exile. Loneliness.

It was a long time ago and I've paid my penance.

"Nathan, you're not letting me explain." Her tone turns sharp, frustrated. Her hands fall to the open car door and I stare at her. Her eyes are so unusual, sparkling brightly despite the dim light. She looks exotic and I want to unveil her. I got lost in those eyes one night. One night which changed everything for me.

"Explain," I tease, lacking humor. I brace myself for excuses.

"I don't know how to explain myself. I just … I don't kiss strangers." She swallows and something tells me it isn't the truth. Not that she *does* kiss strangers, but she isn't telling me her real reason for not kissing me back.

I want to point out we aren't exactly strangers. We have carnal knowledge of each other, but then again, that was a long time ago. Instead, I decide to let her go. I don't need her excuses.

"Don't worry about it. Be careful driving home." It's a hint to get in the car and end my misery. While she hesitates another second, she finally acquiesces and lowers for the seat.

I close her door and step back as she starts up the engine. Waiting until she pulls to the highway, I hop on my bike and fire it up with one aggravated kick.

I'm an idiot. I moved in too quick. What was I doing here anyway? Charlese is waiting for me and now I'm over an hour late, but I find myself following the taillights of her little bug of a car. I don't care what Naomi said about seeing her safely home. I trail her as best I can without drawing suspicion, because I don't trust Dwight. Plus, I need the time to clear my head, and then I do the most unexpected thing. I go home on a Friday night without visiting Charlese.

CHAPTER SEVEN

DEWEY DECIMAL CLASSIFICATION:
306.8754 SISTERS

[Naomi]

I didn't kiss him.

Why didn't I kiss him?

This question plagues me, preventing me from sleep as I lay in my bed, staring up at the dark ceiling.

I froze up.

Although that isn't really true as every part of me tingled like when you turn the gas on the stove and hear the *tick-tick-tick* before the flame ignites. I was seconds away from bursting forth—all orange and blue and bright—crackling to life when he pulled back. It all happened so fast.

His lips crashed onto mine. Then they softened. Then he stopped.

And I'm a fool.

I don't kiss strangers.

Really? Really, Naomi, that's your excuse? He was a stranger when I met him and gave myself to him. Obviously, I'm not fast on my feet for thoughts, but the truth is my greater fear is opening myself up to him.

Admitting how I felt surprises even me. I wanted his mouth on mine. I wanted his hands to dig into my hair and tug. His fingers to roam over my skin and massage. His lips to skim down my body and please me. I didn't realize how much I've craved the intimacy of another until the recent touches from Nathan. Fingers around my wrist. A palm on my lower back. Hands deep in my wild locks.

But I hesitated because I couldn't reconcile suddenly seeing Nathan and the reminder of my brother.

Because on the night I met Nathan, my brother died.

Because of me.

This is all your fault, Naomi. God has punished us for your sin.

Guilt lives deep inside me, festering like another flame, one made of brimstone, ready to scar me if I admit I want the man I was with *that* night. The sexy, persuasive stranger, who danced with me, spoke sweetly to me, and kissed me like I was the only woman he ever wanted to kiss.

The same man who left me without a reason. The man who didn't return as he promised. So I called my brother.

It's been a long time since his death, and I often miss him. My family blamed me when it happened, and I came to terms with their reproach. I've accepted it by denying myself. I don't drink. I don't smoke. I don't dance, date, cavort.

But now.

With Nathan.

Denial is becoming a struggle. I wanted to kiss him back, but I didn't because Nathan plus Naomi equals catastrophe. A man died the last time I was with Nathan and I refuse to place myself in a similar situation again.

Am I being realistic or just ridiculous?

I need to talk to someone, and Bethany Winston had been one of the best people to talk to about these sorts of quandaries. I can almost hear her voice telling me not to ignore the *signs* in life, those gut feelings hinting at decisions. *The universe works in mysterious ways, my friend.*

Is Nathan a step forward or back? Is seeing him again a positive or negative sign?

Vilma's Videos would tell me I don't need a man. Self-love. Inner stability. Personal awareness. But somehow, I feel like I do. I need Nathan Ryder. This isn't some submissive quirk or alpha-male obsession. I've read those fanciful romances. This draw to Nathan is something on another level.

The universe talking.

My inner goddess calling.

Would the heavens collapse if I kissed Nathan Ryder again?

The morning after the failed kiss, these questions continue to fill my head as I drive the curving switchbacks to my sister's farm deep in the valley. Although she's six years older than me, my sister—Beverly Townsen—is one of the only people I consider discussing my confusion with, which is a huge risk. I love my sister, but we don't always get along. She can be ornery and unpredictable, and unreasonable on a bad day.

I try to visit her once a week. She's homebound, more by choice than circumstances. Ten years ago, she was in a horrible accident, and thank the Sweet Goddess, she survived, but her spirit died. The doctors said her legs could work again—over time. Instead, she's devoted her time to sulking and whining about her misfortunes.

Prior to the accident, her husband was a bit of a philanderer, eventually leaving her with their then seventeen-year-old daughter and a struggling farm. Beverly remains bitter about her no-good ex-husband and sour about her daughter's line of work, although she's the reason her daughter works where she does—the Pink Pony. After the accident, Hannah stepped up to care for her mother, giving up her own youth to work two jobs, one of which is stripping. I keep my opinions to myself toward Beverly and my niece's choice of profession, because the few times I have opened my mouth, Beverly assaults me with her bitterness.

"If your Goddess is so good to women, why isn't she helping me?"

I remind Beverly help comes to those who help themselves first.

She isn't helpless, just without hope. At a young age, she threw herself at Howard Townsen, who provided her a way out of our small town, Cedar Gap, which is an armpit in the woods south of Green Valley. Too young, she found herself pregnant and strapped to a farm, like a hired hand instead of a beloved wife.

Howard spread his plentiful seed elsewhere and when Beverly found out, she lost herself. Drinking. Stalking. It's how the accident occurred. She went looking for her wayward husband and the woman rumored to be his latest conquest—a woman from the Pink Pony of all places. My heart-scorned sister went a little berserk. A few too many drinks. A red light she didn't obey. A motorcycle in the crossroad.

The doctors told her she'd always have a limp and that's when Beverly shut down. As a person who uses a wheelchair, she could use arm braces or a walker even, and stand on her own two feet again, but she stopped trying.

"What's the point of continuing with all this if I'm always going to be a cripple?"

I tell her cripple is a crippling word. She's differently abled, which doesn't mean things are impossible.

When I arrive, I notice a silver pickup parked near the old barn. Two-by-fours fill the bed of the truck. Hammering resonates from inside the decrepit building. Beverly hasn't shown interest in her property in years, so I'm curious as I enter her two-story house. I don't find her in her typical spot. She likes to sit at the front window and watch the road, which always seems a bit depressing to me. I have no idea why she'd want Howard to return. Today, she sits in her bedroom. It's the former dining room, so she doesn't need to tackle the stairs. From this vantage point, she has a clear view to the side yard and the drive leading to the barn.

Silently, I walk up behind her as she sits in a rocking chair, and even though the wooden floor squeaks, she doesn't flinch.

"Whatcha doing, Bev?" The seat is almost fitting as my sister looks like a spinster with her graying hair severely pulled back to the nape of her neck. Frameless glasses perch on the edge of her nose. Her shirt is a tiny floral print which looks like something our mother would have worn and plum-colored slacks cover her legs. Slacks. Not dress pants. Not jeans. But old-fashioned looking polyester pants. *Where did she get those things?*

"Shh, I'm listening."

I tip my head to hear what she hears. I've got nothing. "What's going on in your barn?" I pull back the sheer curtain to get a better look outside the three-paneled window, but Beverly rocks forward and tugs the material out of my hand.

"Don't be so obvious," she growls. Her expression turns stern. Then her eyes shift to me. With a dismissive wave, she remarks, "That's Jedd."

I squint, trying to see through the transparent material, and get a glimpse of said Jedd, but still don't see anyone.

"Jedd Flemming," she clarifies. There's something in the way my sister rolls over his name which catches my attention and I turn back to her.

"Who is Jedd Flemming and why is he laying wood in your barn?" I bite the corner of my lip at the innuendo. Her expression softens and something like a spark briefly flickers in her eyes. Her lip twitches. *Is she fighting a smile?*

"He's renting space from me, so to speak," she defends. I stare at her, waiting out an explanation. "He wanted a place to train horses and offered to fix up the barn in exchange for the use of the space. It's nothing."

Nothing, my sweet backside. My sister's eyes pinch before she tugs her lip with her teeth.

"Does he stay here? In the house?"

She shrugs noncommittally. "He sleeps in the barn."

"What?"

"He's made himself a room out there."

"Beverly, there's plenty of space in the house." The old farmhouse has four bedrooms upstairs. There's more than enough space for the man to have a room inside.

"He says he doesn't mind sleeping outside. He's used to it from being in the military. Besides, I can't have a strange man sleeping under my roof with my daughter here." She picks at lint which doesn't exist on her pants. Sometimes, I think my sister is jealous of her daughter, showing off her young body for other's pleasure while her own withers away from her decisions. She used to be so pretty, but life has worn her down.

I'm surprised my sister is allowing a strange male to even sleep under the roof of her barn. Then, out of the corner of my eye, I catch movement and I notice my sister sit forward. I turn toward the curtain and see a large, solid man with a military haircut exit the barn. Sweat stains the front of his T-shirt despite the cool fall temps. He rounds his truck and I can't help but notice the spread of the tee over his broad back and the hug of his pants against his backside. Two perfect moons point at us as he bends forward to lug boards from the bed of his truck. He hefts the planks over his shoulder, and heads back toward the barn. It's then that I notice his left arm. The entire thing is a prosthetic.

My eyes flit back to Bev who watches intently as Jedd passes from the daylight into the dark barn. When he disappears, she sits back as if leaning forward and watching him took all her energy. Her face flushes.

"Bev, his arm?" I question.

Her sour face returns. "It's nothing. Take me to the store."

After our trip to the Piggly Wiggly, Beverly wants to return home instead of stopping at Daisy's. I can't believe Bev's skipping our weekly doughnut, but when we pull into her driveway and I see the silver truck, I understand her haste to return to the farm. Jedd.

Which reminds me of Nathan and my secondary purpose in visiting my sister today.

Beverly seems especially out of sorts though, and snaps at me once I assist her into the living room. "Help me back to my room."

I could argue with her that she's more than capable of tending to herself. Then I remember the farmhouse isn't necessarily handi-capable. The halls are narrow. The doorways slim. Support bars and railings were added to the downstairs bathroom for her. Attachments to appliances were added to assist her in the kitchen, but Bev typically waits for Hannah to cook or the community outreach to bring meals. Based on how thin she is, she isn't eating either way.

"I'll get the groceries," I mutter, wondering why I continue this farce of forcing my sister to town when she doesn't cook or eat. As I stalk down the hallway, I stop. I've passed this wall for years and hardly notice the images anymore, but something stands out to me today.

The three Winters sisters in a photograph.

Were we ever as close as the picture makes us appear? My oldest sister Scotia—now Scotia Simmons—stands in the middle, ever the attention seeker. She holds me in front of her, laughing at something over my shoulder. Probably my father who loved her the most, and who was taking the picture. Beverly leans her head on Scotia's shoulder, her face softer, sad even, as the middle sister. She stares into the distance, as if looking past our father, past anything behind him. *What was she longing for?*

Beverly knows all my secrets and didn't judge me when I first came to her place, all those years ago, but she also wasn't willing to let me stay.

"I need to keep Howard satisfied. You'd be in the way. Do you understand?" In hindsight, she might have been worried Howard would come on to me. I shiver with the thought. She knew of my guilty feelings, though. Both sisters did. At least, Beverly looked at me sympathetically when I first came to her, understanding my torment. I'd given myself to a man with false promises. She'd wanted Howard something fierce at first. She didn't realize keeping him satisfied wasn't her problem, but his. Nothing satisfied him, and she suffered her own false ideals married to Howard.

My oldest sister, Scotia, on the other hand, handed out judgment like a woman generously passing out Halloween candy. *As if her life turned out so prudent.* At first, Scotia blamed me almost as much as my parents for what happened, accusing me of tarnishing the good Winters name. *Did she even know our brother Jebediah?* He was a rebel his entire life. Drugs. Alcohol. Thievery. Women. And I loved him through it all. Scotia didn't have a clue, but she had plenty to say when I arrived in Green Valley.

"Don't be dragging your mud into my garden," she warned as if she owned the valley. She'd adopted the area as her home as if she was a member of high society. Karl Simmons was valley-bred and raised. The Simmons name meant status—along with Donner and Oliver and Payton—and that's what Scotia craved. Attention. Propriety. Prestige. With her self-righteous attitude, she would be the last to appreciate me finding Nathan after all this time.

"Naomi, bring me an apple," my sister's sharp voice snaps me out of my memories.

"Would a little *please* hurt you?" I mutter, continuing down the hall to the front door. Her tone decides things for me. I'm not ready to share Nathan with anyone yet.

Besides, there's nothing to share.

I return to the car for the groceries. The minimal amount of food my sister needs could be delivered, but I think it's important she get out of the house at least for a few hours every week.

You've become a pain in the ass, she often tells me. Yes, well, I miss you too, big sister.

As I lean over my trunk, a deep voice startles me. "Let me help you." The command runs from the tip of my head down my spine. I stand upright and nearly salute. I imagine the man before me was a sergeant in another life and I stare as warm chocolate eyes set deep in a severe face meet mine. His cheeks prickle with silver scruff, as if he shaved only this morning and it's regrown. His hair gleams white under the sun.

"Didn't mean to startle you. Can't hear myself speak sometimes."

He lifts his prosthetic hand which is actually a claw to motion toward his left ear. "I'm louder than I intend to be."

I simply smile in return and extend a hand. "I'm Naomi. Naomi Winters, Bev's younger sister."

His right hand reaches for mine and we shake. His palm is hot, fingers callused from working with the wood. His grasp is firm and delivers instant protection and comfort.

"Beverly tells me you're fixing up the barn. Going to raise horses here."

His grin grows, and his hard-edged expression softens. "It's beautiful land and the perfect space for a couple of thoroughbreds. It needs some TLC, but I'm not opposed to the hard work."

My eyes leap to his arm and away. I don't want to stare or make him uncomfortable.

"So Bee let you take her to the store."

Bee? He has a nickname for her. I bet she hates it.

"Every Wednesday, if I can."

"Huh," he snorts as he looks over in the direction of Beverly's bedroom window. The curtain shifts over the glass, and I watch his expression harden once again.

Huh, indeed.

Just what is going on here with my sister and this man?

I pick up a night shift at the library and enter with wandering thoughts of my sister and this new man, along with continued confusion over Nathan and the failed kiss. Julianne greets me without her usual cheer.

"Everything okay?" I ask, hanging my coat on a hook before turning back to the matron of our library. Mrs. Julianne MacIntyre is practically an icon in this community for her dedication and book love. Her motto is: *if you don't have anything nice to say, come to the library where you aren't allowed to speak.* We had that printed on a sign, resting on our front counter, for the longest time.

"I ..." her mouth opens and then snaps shut as she spins to face me from the swivel desk chair where she sits. Her hands come to her skirt-covered knees and she takes a deep breath. Inhale. Exhale. The exaggeration concerns me. Is she ill?

"We've had some distressing news, Naomi. It's about the library."

CHAPTER EIGHT

DEWEY DECIMAL CLASSIFICATION: 100
PHILOSOPHY AND PSYCHOLOGY

[Nathan]

A few days after the night I dub the failed kissed fiasco, I need to pick up Clementine from the library. Usually, my mother takes care of these things, or I ask Dahlia to fetch Clem but as I'm so close with the Bickerton job, I volunteer. The library is the last place I want to go, since I haven't been able to shake the disastrous lip-lock with one particular librarian. Yet, something ripples through my chest at the thought of entering the building and finding Naomi—despite her rejection.

It's been a rough few days trying to cover some mishaps with Dwight on the build. Then there's Dahlia lipping off at me again. I swear I'll never understand seventeen-year-old females. Even when I was seventeen, I didn't understand them.

My underaged daughter can't comprehend why I won't allow her to date a college man. First of all, I don't want her hurt. A man at a university chasing the skirt of a high schooler only wants one thing— the one thing he's not fortunate to get at said college. Secondly, I don't know this guy and letting her go off to visit him doesn't seem like sound parenting.

"It's a college visit," she argued.

"Uh-huh." I might not have gone to college, but I wasn't born yesterday. I know what guys want. And from what she wears some days, she knows they want her.

Please let Clem stay a child a little longer, I silently pray, as I approach the library doors and take in the front windows decorated in a fall motif. Immediately upon entering the building, I find Clem speaking with Naomi in the lobby.

"It's our secret, right?" Clem says to Naomi. My chest squeezes when I see Naomi brush back Clem's bushy blonde curls.

"Our secret." She winks.

I don't recall Margie being tender with Clem. I don't know how well she does at mothering the two times a year when Clem visits. I do know Clem is old enough to become more vocal about visitations —and her lack of desire for them. Margie likes things neat and tidy. Clem tells me the inside of her house is like a museum. She and her lawyer-husband have filled their house with expensive things and worries that Clem will break, or spill, or soil something. She's isn't a dog, though. She's a child.

I'm not allowed to eat on the couch. Or in the guest room. Clem doesn't even have an official bedroom she can call her own at her mother's home. Margie also doesn't offer much age-appropriate support for her daughter, which is the reason why I'm the one to check out books about menstruation.

I don't know what you ever saw in her, Dahlia once said to me after Clem told her sister about the expectations for her behavior at her mother's house. I didn't see then. I'd been led by my one-eyed monster. I got Margie pregnant shortly after meeting her. It's a trend.

Still.

"What's a secret?" I ask stepping up to Clem and Naomi. When Naomi's silvery eyes look up at me, I find my breath catching. Her hair is woven into some intricate braid, hanging long and twisted over her shoulder. She looks a little otherworldly and I want to give it a pull, yank her head back, and kiss the crap out of her until she responds to me. I swallow back the moisture in my mouth and lick my lips while I wait for an answer.

Her eyes follow the line of my tongue over my bottom lip and then her brows pinch as she glances between Clem and me.

"Clementine is your daughter?" Was I not clear about this when I checked out the books? "The books for …" The books I needed for my daughter. My daughter Clementine. It's as if Naomi is slowing piecing things together. She looks down at Clem and then back up at me, only her eyes roam the length of my body, taking me in as she bites the corner of her lip.

I want those teeth on me. I want those lips on mine.

I nod once to acknowledge the family tree. "Emma Rae is my mother. Clem here is my Dandelion, and my other daughter is named Dahlia."

"Dad," Clem groans as if I've embarrassed her while Naomi stares at me, processing my family.

"And you're not married?" she blurts as if she forgot, and I chuckle.

"No wives. Ever." My eyes narrow on her and a strange thought fills my head. I wonder what Naomi would look like dressed in white with that braid over her shoulder. Immediately, I erase the thought and focus on another.

"What secret?" I ask, shifting my gaze from Naomi to Clem and back.

"Girl things," Naomi clarifies, shaking her head as if clearing it. She slips an arm around Clem, and my heart skips a beat. It's such a motherly gesture. "I'm so happy you came to see me today." She stares down at my child before she swipes a finger under her eye and blinks several times. Then she sniffs and offers Clem a weak smile with an extra squeeze of her shoulder.

Something isn't right.

"Hey Dandelion, check out all your books?"

"I'm all set."

"Can you give Miss Naomi and me a second?" I riffle through my pocket for some change and point her to a box of fundraiser candy on the counter. Clem takes the money and skips away.

"What's wrong?" I ask stepping forward, drawing closer to Naomi. I inhale. She smells like honey today and I want a lick, but something tells me she won't play along. Glistening eyes look up at me and then away.

"Naomi," I plea, cupping her elbow. She wears a deep purple, long-sleeve T-shirt dress with thick leggings and her black lace-up boots. She looks a little sexier than the previous times I've seen her, and I'm distracted. *She has legs*, my brain screams. "Was it something with Clem? Did something happen?"

"No, no. Clementine is great." She pauses, avoiding my face with a few more rapid blinks. "It's nothing," she says, but it's not true as she swipes at the corner of her eye. I press her back until her backside hits the check-out counter.

"Speak to me."

Her eyes shift around my shoulder to Clem who found a seat near the front windows and shuffles through a book.

"We got word on Monday from the state that library funds have been cut." Naomi's lip trembles and she bites down hard. She deeply inhales. "We don't know exactly what that means yet, but Julianne … Mrs. MacIntyre says we should prepare for the worst. She'd recently read how the state is closing small town libraries to save money. They're reallocating funds to improve larger ones in bigger cities instead."

I stare at her. This doesn't sound good. In fact, it sounds down-right unfair. We don't have a local bookstore. Without the library, we'd have to drive to Knoxville for reading material. Not to mention, the library has programs for local kids, like my Clem, who struggles making friends outside of places like this.

"What will you do?" I ask, suddenly realizing the gravity of budget cuts. Naomi could lose her job. She doesn't dismiss me like I thought she would. Instead, a tear fills her eye. Briskly, she pulls at the corner of her eye, forcing the tear to disappear.

"I'm not sure yet." She pauses a moment, her eyes flitting back and forth between mine, and then her breath hitches. Slowly, she pulls back as if something occurred to her. Some thought. Her breath becomes more exaggerated. Is she going to hyperventilate?

"Naomi?" My hands cover her shoulders, holding her steady.

"This is all my fault." Her eyes widen, the widest I've ever seen. Panic fills them.

"What do you mean?"

"I ... I can't believe this happened again." Her hands come to my chest, and she gently pushes at me. "You have to get out of here."

"What?" My brows pinch at the harsh tone.

"You need to go. I can't be near you." Her voice struggles to stay level.

Ouch. That stings a little.

"Why?" I take one step back under the force of her hands.

"I can't be around you. This can't happen."

"Lady, what are you talking about?" My voice roughens.

"Bad things always happen after I'm with you."

I stiffen, straightening to my full height. My arms cross and I glare down at her. Saying such a thing is just downright mean. Her head shakes as her fingers curl along the open edges of my work jacket. Suddenly, I feel like she's tugging me to her instead of pressing me away.

What the ...

"When I'm with you, something happens. Something bad." Her breath catches. "Because we kissed, the library is closing."

I stare at her. She can't be serious, but I see the hysteria in her eyes, like a rabid, trapped animal. She actually believes what she says.

"Well, we didn't kiss," I remind her, my tone stern and condescending. "I kissed you, remember? And you didn't kiss me back, so I don't think it counts."

She glares up at me, her fingers still gripping my open jacket. Her shoulders fall, her head lowers, and it's as if I can visibly see her relax, like water cascading down a building, washing over her.

Exhale. Settle.

Exhale. Calm.

"I didn't kiss you back?" she questions and then her head pops up

67

again. She nearly shrieks with the hesitant realization. Commence inhaling, like she's winding up again. Full steam ahead.

"I didn't kiss you back," she repeats, her excitement growing. Another exaggerated inhale.

"I didn't kiss you back!" Now, she's just downright gloating, and the engine's ready to blow.

"You don't have to sound so pleased," I murmur. I glance up and notice Mrs. MacIntyre watching us through the window of the librarian's office behind the check-out counter. Her eyes narrow and I'm certain we're making too much noise for her liking.

"I … I'm so relieved," Naomi admits, her head falling forward, her fingers loosening on my jacket. Then her face turns up again. Her lids lift, slow and lazy. Her mouth curls in sweet relief, and she pulls herself up on her toes by the open edge of my jacket and does the damnedest thing. *She* kisses me.

CHAPTER NINE

DEWEY DECIMAL CLASSIFICATION: 306.7
INSTITUTIONS PERTAINING TO
RELATIONS OF THE SEXES

[Naomi]

Nathan Ryder has the best lips in the universe.

If Litha, the summer solstice, consummated with the winter god named Yule, they'd have bright shiny baby solstices flitting through the sky like glitter in a snow globe, and that's how my belly feels as my mouth collides with Nathan's. His lips are soft, smooth, experienced, and within seconds he drags me into him. A tug of the bottom lip. A suck of the top. Our mouths open for one another and then … a throat clears behind us.

"Mrs. MacIntyre is watching us." Nathan chuckles against my mouth.

"Sweet Goddess," I mutter, pushing off him. Hands flatten on the firmness of his chest I'm becoming too acquainted with. I attempt a giant step back but kick the counter behind me. Shaky fingers swipe at my lips, which tingle with the pressure from his.

Mother Earth, what have I done? I just sealed the fate of the library— with a kiss.

"I'm so sorry."

"I'm definitely not," he says, his mouth curving and that damn dimple becomes a beacon within his silver scruff. "But making out with you in the library lobby probably isn't permissible." He nods, and I close my eyes. Julianne just watched me throw myself at Nathan. Nathan! Of all people.

This is bad. *This is so bad.*

Then I peek up at him.

He tasted so good. Cinnamony and hungry for me, and just yummy, yummy, *yummy.* My cookie crumble center is all gooey and soft, like fresh out of the oven, pipin' hot. *Why do I want him so much?*

"That shouldn't have happened," I admit, waving a hand between us.

"But it did," he reminds me, a smug expression gracing his face. My eyes flit to Clementine. Thankfully, she isn't looking at us and I can only pray she didn't witness what just happened. I kissed her father! Thank the Goddess for the concept of stuck in a good book. Julianne, on the other hand, will probably be making a sign about kissing in the library.

No fraternizing with the patrons.

No cavorting with the librarians.

No snoozling in the lobby.

Don't make kissing a hobby.

I'd like to make Nathan a hobby, though.

Deny.

"I need to get back to my job, as long as I still have one." I hastily excuse myself from him as the severity of the situation hits me again. The last time I was with this man something happened. My brother flits through my head but I quickly dust back thoughts of him. I need to focus.

The state of Tennessee was working its way through budgets cuts. One area they'd decided to snip-snip was small-town libraries. *Why would us mountain people need books?* I can almost hear some ill-educated yuppie sitting in a mid-state office asking this question. I pay taxes, though. This is where I want my money spent.

I've worked at the library since I was twenty-one and had nowhere else to go. Bethany Winston welcomed me with open arms though I didn't have an education. After eighteen years of employment, I don't have any other skills. I don't just shelve books. I open the window of possibility to people.

Through books.

Adventure. Intrigue. Romance. Information.

In this fast-paced world we live in, people find answers at the drop of a fingertip. Yet books can still lead you to a valley, and over hills and dales, and into another dimension, and through the parallels of love.

I look up to watch Nathan exit the library with his daughter. He doesn't look back at me. Like he didn't look back the last time I was with him. My heart crashes to my feminine combat boots.

I've sold my soul to the devil again all for the taste of him.

And when I lose my job, and don't know what to do with myself, Nathan won't be around to Humpty-Dumpty me back together again. He'll disappear like he did before.

That's why I love books. Books are stable and steadfast. Reliable. Books are comfort from heartache and hope from despair. Maybe Julianne should put that on one of her signs.

I sigh. *What will I do without my books?*

After Nathan leaves, I hold my head high as I pass Julianne and collapse in the office.

Why did I kiss him?

"That was quite the display," Julianne comments. She's judging me, but lovingly, like the matriarchal figure she is. Twenty-plus years older than me, she welcomed me into the library but not quite as quickly as Bethany did. I had to prove myself to Mrs. MacIntyre—head librarian of the Green Valley Public Library.

Keep quiet.

Be diligent.

Stay orderly.

Not dissimilar from my parents' rules growing up, and yet,

completely different. Julianne MacIntyre takes her reign as queen librarian very seriously.

"I don't know what came over me," I say, as a shaking hand strokes down my single braid. Nathan stood so close. The concern in his eyes. The nearness of his body. The scent of cinnamon and sawdust. I latched onto him—and went a bit wild.

"It seems the Horned God gotcha." She winks. Bless her heart, she's trying to be funny. The Horned God is the counterbalance to my Goddess, as lord of the forest and god of fertility. I shouldn't think of the implications of a fertile Nathan. Instead, I think it's a case of just plain horny … on my part. Or maybe it was in desperation at potentially losing another piece of my life.

My brother.

My parents.

Nathan.

The library.

The list cannot get any longer.

"That was a bit embarrassing." Heat courses up my neck and over my cheeks. I should tell Julianne my feelings, my frustration. Kissing Nathan could lead to the demise of the library. Being with him once before led to deadly things. I sigh with my own melodramatics. Maybe I should open up to her and ask her advice. *Is kissing Nathan so wrong of me?*

I don't know what came over me.

"Why don't you let me close up tonight?" I offer instead, knowing Julianne feels the sting of possibly losing the library as much as I do. She's old school librarian, around since the days of wooden card catalogs with typewritten library cards and hand-stamps for due dates. Over the years, she's rolled with the technological advances as best she could, but her black and white copy paper signs are her attempt at controlling a spiraling climate change when it comes to libraries.

The internet is still a net. Don't get caught up in it, one of her signs read.

No longer a place of quiet solitude, some people want the library to be more like a coffee shop. A place to hang out for meetings. A spot for teens to stay out of trouble. A haven for children to discover a love of reading. The struggle has been real for Julianne, and as she nears retirement age, the idea of shutting down a place she's devoted her life to is a hard pill to swallow.

"I refuse to think it's all been for naught," she says as if reading my thoughts. "We'll find a way. Sister Bethany will look out for us."

Julianne holds different beliefs than me, but when she wants to call on a higher power, she calls on the deceased Bethany—our personal patron saint of the library. I always considered Bethany more of a fairy godmother. We hung a picture of her in tribute over the drinking fountain where a sign once hung on how to properly use the fountain, complete with Julianne's detailed description on how to hold the handle at a forty-five-degree angle to obtain the perfect water arch. *You know the drill, so you don't spill,* one sign read. Bethany's picture is a definite improvement to the alcove but hanging outside the bathrooms doesn't seem like a place of honor. Either way, I know what Julianne means. *Where there's a will, there's a way.* Somehow. Maybe.

"Maybe it won't happen to us," Julianne adds, and I appreciate her positivity. It's wishful thinking that we won't be one of the libraries to close. *A little niche in a valley, the state wouldn't possibly shut us down.* Sarcasm drips inside me. However, the initial announcement we received listed a rather large number of cuts coming without naming any specific libraries. Yet. *More good times to come.*

"I'll close up," I say standing. She deserves to go home and spend time with Seamus, her husband. Maybe being away from here will take her mind off our potential predicament.

"What I need to do is shelve those books," she states in her this-conversation-is-over voice.

"I can do it."

"Are you sure?" A hint of teasing judgment falls in her tone.

"I'm positive."

"You'll be okay?" Julianne lowers her head, eyeing me over the rim of her glasses. I wave her off with a flick of my wrist.

"I'll be perfect," I lie. Once I close the library for the night, I might be. In the solitude of dimmed lights and lined shelves, I'll wander the stacks, touching the spines as if reaching out to old friends. *Which one of you will go home with me tonight?* I'll ask as if I'm picking up a one-night stand. Eeny, meeny, miny, moe, this one will make a lover so ... I'll scan the shelves, my fingers tip-toeing over the spines.

Julianne does go home a few minutes early, and I close promptly at nine. I'm walking back to the shelving cart, thinking I'll just finish up the last returns, when a knock comes to the glass front door.

"We're closed," I mutter aloud although I'm alone in the library. The doors rattle and for a moment my heart stops. I stand still at the endcap of a shelf, using it to hide me. I might have wanted to play girl spy a few times in my life, but I'm not certain I like the adrenaline rush as I worry someone's going to break into the library and take me.

Capture the witch. Teasing, taunting voices skitter through my head. I close my eyes and concentrate. *It will never happen again.*

Craning my head to the side, sleuth-like, my heart roars back to life, thudding against my chest. My eyes narrow on a large man in a camel-brown construction jacket shielding his eyes with his hands peering through the window.

Nathan?

I turn and roll off the shelf endcap at my back and rub my hands down the skirt of my dress. Taking a deep breath, I walk toward the glass barrier.

"We're closed." I point to the sign which says such.

"Let me in." Surprisingly, I hear him through the panels. His eyes meet mine and I can't turn away. *Let him in*, my heart whispers and my chest heaves with excitement. We have cameras and I could lose my job for allowing him entrance after hours. Then I stop. I might lose my job anyway. I step forward and twist the lock.

"What are you doing here?" I ask, as I wave him past and then promptly lock the door again.

"I wanted to check on you." He pauses as he turns to face me. A whiff of freshly showered and cinnamon catches my nose and tickles it. "You seemed shaken earlier."

Shaken is hardly the word. Stirred up and left to froth is more like it.

"I'm doing better now," I say, the truth melding with the falseness. I am better. There's nothing I can do about the library at the moment, and strangely, his presence gives me instant comfort. "It was just a shock, is all. Getting the notice and then seeing Clementine. She's one of my favorites and thinking I might have to say goodbye ... well, it stung a little. I never put two and two together that she was your daughter." I hadn't made any connection between Clementine Ryder, granddaughter to Emma Rae, and Nathan. In my head, he was always reckless, single, and twenty-three.

"It seems you two have a secret," he hints, his expression softening at the mention of his child.

"I'm not supposed to tell you, but she's already read those books you got for her. Two years ago. The ones about ..." I don't think I can repeat the title to him. *I Have a Vagina*. He knows—*he knows*—my vagina screams.

"Oh. *Oh*," he chuckles, rubbing under his chin. "She's my precocious one. Curious to learn everything. Dahlia's the one who hates to read. I guess she takes after her father in that respect." That's right, he mentioned his other daughter earlier. I vaguely remember young Dahlia Ryder—shy, vulnerable, clinging to her grandmother. *That was so long ago*, and I feel foolish I hadn't known young Dahlia was his. Did he have a girlfriend when I met him? Is that why he didn't call? I feel slightly sick with the possibility. He's already told me he's never been married, so at least there is that.

The corner of his lip hitches as he walks farther into the library, noting the darkness as most of the lights have been turned off. "It's quiet in here."

"It should be. It's a library."

He chuckles. "Library humor?"

I weakly smile in return.

"You always close by yourself?" he asks.

"Sometimes. Tonight, I told Mrs. MacIntyre to go home early. She needed her husband, Seamus." Like I need someone.

Deny. *Deny*. You do not need a man for comfort, Vilma Louise would tell me.

"What do you do after hours?"

"I shelve books." The corner of his lip crooks higher as he huffs a laugh. Somehow, I don't think this is what he meant, but I dismiss reading more into his huffs, or puffs, or any other sounds he might make.

Just like that, Nae, his voice from long ago, mixed with a deep groan, whispers through my head.

"Speaking of, I need to finish emptying the cart." I point in the direction of my unfinished business.

"Lead the way."

My head tilts but I step toward the 300 section to complete the shelving. Nathan follows me as I scan the book labels for proper placement.

"So you love books, huh?" he asks, squinting to read titles.

"I do," I say as if that's enough explanation. "What about you? You don't read?" I've never seen him in the library in all these years. He pulls a book from the shelf and thumbs through it.

"Too many words," he says, a smile growing on his face and unleashing the wicked dimple. He turns the book sideways, holding it by the front cover. "I prefer pictures." He chuckles and it takes me a moment to realize he's referring to magazines—girly-magazines as my father used to call them. I snort in disgust.

"I'm kidding actually." He replaces the book, thankfully to its proper place. "The letters always ran together for me, and my brain had a hard time concentrating."

"Maybe you needed glasses," I suggest. Was he dyslexic? It breaks my heart to think he's missing the pleasure of the written word. He shrugs to respond.

"So, tell me more about the library closure." He casually leans against the bookshelf, watching me.

"We don't know anything for certain, but the news is unsettling."

He nods as if he understands and I hope he does. He's a little older than me, so I like to think he realizes losing a job at any age would be tough, but when you're older, with say a mortgage or bills, well …

"When will you know?"

"We don't know," I say, my voice falling in frustration. Nathan scans the shelves as I place another book in the correct sequence.

"Can you explain something else to me, then?" His smoky voice lowers as his eyes pinch to read a title.

Oh no.

"Why'd you kiss me?" The question seems to echo in the library like a judge's mallet on a podium. "Or better yet, why were you so happy you *hadn't* kissed me and then you laid one on me?"

I grip the shelf before me to steady my suddenly shaking legs. "I'm having trouble understanding it myself."

"Try to explain." His voice remains low, encouraging, and I risk a glance at his eyes. Earnest and questioning, he wants to understand me. I return my eyes to blindly focus on the book spines before me.

"At first, I think I didn't kiss you back because I was shocked you kissed me." And the fact that kissing you might lead to something bad. On a grand scale. "Today, I think I kissed you in my relief that I hadn't kissed you, which makes no sense, right?" *Nothing does when I'm around you*, I think, as I risk a side glance in his direction.

"The universe works in mysterious ways," I mutter. Why can't it send me a sign of what to do with this man?

"Meaning?" His forehead furrows and I take a breath before answering, holding it like I'm about to plunge into the depths of a lake.

"It seems bad things happen to me after I've been with you." *Jebediah.*

His face pulls back in a horrified expression. "Ouch."

"I don't mean it as harsh as it sounds. I don't think it's *you* directly. It's just … the universe, it sends out vibes. Positive. Negative. It's more like a reaction to an action. I do something, and the universe responds. I believe in these things. I'm a Wiccan."

Nathan pauses, his eyes focusing on a book spine. "I'm a Kama Sutran."

What? "Is that even a thing?" I ask with a nervous giggle as he pulls a book off the shelf. *The Kama Sutra* by Vātsyāyana.

"I don't know, but I'd like to find out." He holds the book up just below his nose, the cover facing me, and he wiggles a single eyebrow. He's too cheeky for his own good. "What's a Wiccan?"

"The official definition would be a neo-pagan religion reviving old practices in nature-worship, sometimes misinterpreted as witchcraft."

"That's where the rumors come from." He pauses in thought. "And your definition?"

"I have mad respect for nature. Trees. Earth. Water. We are a system of inter-related oneness. The Goddess is my supreme."

The same cheeky eyebrow raises again. "Meaning?"

Does he want every detail of following the moon cycle and celebrating the solar seasons? The triquetra and the balance of body, mind, and spirit? I doubt it, so I try to explain. I brush my hand forward. "It's like a wave. My energy goes out collecting..." I bring my hand slowly back to me. "... returning energy to me. The vibe I give out is the vibe I will receive back." It's not really an uncommon thought process. "The positive you make is the positive you take, but the same goes for negative stuff. For me, it's more a belief in my *self*, my inner goddess." I pause, turning to blankly stare at the books before me again. It makes sense to me and yet I find it difficult to describe. I chew my lip, thinking he'll laugh at me.

"You mentioned something bad happened the last time we were together. What? What happened?"

I turn to face him, preparing to tell him, but his brows wiggle as if he's taunting me, and because of his joking manner, I don't feel quite comfortable dropping the bomb. In fact, I don't want to discuss my brother right now.

Nathan's teasing brows lower and his forehead furrows, sensing my reason is something serious but also something I'm not about to share. I look away from him.

"So, we kiss and catastrophe," he says, throwing his voice to sound spooky. My head turns in his direction again. His lips twist as if he's thinking.

"You're making fun of me." I'm as hurt as I sound. While he claims I didn't kiss him back that first time, we technically did kiss, and thus the library news. The universe spoke. It's hard for people to comprehend because it doesn't fit their norms of religion. There isn't a formal system to follow, and what people don't understand frightens them. It isn't witchcraft but a oneness with nature, an understanding of our role in the wider world. A connection with the universe. People think it's hokey. I've heard that said.

"Maybe we should test this out." He steps closer to me, and I tighten my grasp on the shelf.

Don't touch him, my brain warns while my breasts tingle. Keep your hands and lips to yourself, my mind cautions without conviction even as my heart races and a part of me awakens like the thump of a drumline. Arms and legs should remain in the vehicle at all times.

"Kiss me," he suggests, his voice lowering as his head leans down toward mine. "If the building falls down around us, I'll believe you."

I should be put off by his teasing, but his nearness muddles my thoughts. "It doesn't exactly work like that," I mutter, my voice shaky. I swallow.

"Prove it," he whispers, drawing me into the flames of his smoky sound. I throw the proverbial gauntlet down, and meet him halfway, allowing my lips to brush over his. Tender. Cautious. Experimenting. This is not the attack of earlier, but a gentler discovery. My fingers tighten on the shelf. My nails dig into the wood. I will myself to hold on, but my mouth has its own agenda. *Take him.*

I submit to Nathan's lead as he guides my lips to follow his. Suck the lower one. Nip at the corner. Slip the tip of my tongue along the seam of his.

Like a butterfly released from a cocoon, I open for him.

My shoulders relax, and my grip slips from the shelf. I shift to face him, without breaking the kiss. A hand comes to my lower back, and the other dips under the braid at my neck. I lean into Nathan, gripping his open jacket like I did earlier and melting under his lips. How long has it been since I've felt like this?

Tingling.

Tempted.

Tortured.

And free.

I'm spun so my back braces against the shelves and Nathan's hands wander. My backside is gripped, and I'm pressed toward him. My breasts crush against his chest. I slide my hands upward, outlining his chest until I wrap them around his neck. My fingertips gently scratch the hair above his nape while he tilts my head to deepen the kiss. Sucking sounds echo around us as our mouths tangle. I'm lost in a spinning vortex of swirling stars and hazy darkness, and then I come to my senses.

Abruptly, I pull back.

Shaking fingers release Nathan and cover my swollen lips. *I shouldn't have done that.* But it was so nice, my traitorous lips mumble. So yummy. So cookie-crumble sweet. My eyes shift left and then right, waiting for the library to crash like he suggested. He chuckles as he leans forward to kiss my temple.

"See? Nothing happened."

Oh, something happened alright. My knees shake. My lips sting. My heart races. And another part of me is zinging like a comet—an aimless, inexperienced comet zig-zagging across the Milky Way.

"Let's make another deal," Nathan offers, and I stare blankly up at him.

"I'm not really a gambler."

He chuckles softly. "Take a risk. Give me a number."

Without questioning his motives, I blurt out, "Eighteen." The number of years I've been waiting to be kissed like that again.

"Too large. Try one to ten. Please say one." That grin. Dimple alert.

"Three," I snap. The Goddess number. The law of return.

"Okay. Three." He smirks. "Go out with me three times. If something catastrophic happens, we stop. If not ..." He shrugs.

"Sex?" I sputter, and his brows rise.

"Um ... not what I meant but I won't dismiss it." His brows lower, and the grin grows. Dimple sighting.

"No sex," I say although suddenly sex is all I can think about. *I have a vagina.* Take me up against this shelf, it screams.

"Kissing?" He tilts his head, and a single brow arches. Category five dimple. *Evacuate.*

"No promises," I tease. *Am I flirting with him? Would things really fall apart if I did kiss him again?* When I consider his lips on mine, I'm willing to risk heaven collapsing if Nathan will keep kissing the hell out of me. Then I worry. Kissing him gives me anxiety. Heart racing. Knees shaking. Sweating palms. Or is that just the result of his mouth on mine? I'm so confused.

His forehead wrinkles in surprise, and he rewards me with a full-wattage smile, dimple and all. "But dates?"

Should I do this? Could I do this? I'm two ends of a tug-of-war again when it comes to Nathan Ryder. One part of me wants to move forward and let go. The other holds too tightly to the past. An image of my brother crosses my mind, guilt riding along with it, but it quickly vanishes, as if blown like dandelion seeds into the wind.

"Okay."

CHAPTER TEN

DEWEY DECIMAL CLASSIFICATION: 303.6 CONFLICT

[Nathan]

"Okay."

I can't believe she agreed to this after her harebrained ideas about the universe. Okay, not harebrained, just different. Different is good. I like different. I like her, and I want to know her better. I want to understand her. I want more of this strange magnetic pull I feel toward her. The energy she's putting out that's drawing me into her.

"So, Friday." I don't know where I'll take her, but unpredictable is the plan. Someplace unique. I want to know if I can find the girl she once was, inside the woman she is now. She still seems a little uptight despite the enthusiasm with which she kissed me moments ago.

"Friday." She sets the last book on the shelf and I tell her I'll wait in the lobby while she does a final check of doors and shuts off the lights. I stand by the front door, noticing her car is parked under the singular light in the lot. It's too dark out here.

"That doesn't look safe," I tell her as I escort her out of the library. She remains silent and I'm worried she's rethinking our date until we near the VW Bug. "What the hell?"

Her taillight has been shattered, but as I inspect the ground, I notice there aren't shards of plastic.

"My car was vandalized."

"What? When?"

"Last night. I haven't been able to get to the Winston Brothers shop for a repair."

Winston Brothers Auto Shop is the local garage owned and operated by Cletus Winston and his younger brother Beau. They could fix this up in an hour or two. Why did she delay? I decide to survey her car and note a missing headlight as well. She's been targeted, and the broken lights mark her even more—especially on a dark mountain road. The lopsided beams would tip off anyone who is watching for her.

"I'm driving you home," I demand. Her eyes spark despite the darkness of the lot.

"You don't need to do that."

"We are not discussing this." *So help me, if I find out Dwight did this, I'll kick his ass.*

"I can't have you drive me home. I need my car tomorrow. I promise I'll take it to the Winston's when I'm done."

"I'll take the day off. Drive you where you need to go. I'll take your car to the shop. I can—" Her thin fingers lift close to my mouth to stop my panic-mode ramble, listing off all the things I can do to help her, all the ways I want to take care of her. The thought hits me hard in the chest and I reach for her fingers, quickly pressing them to my lips.

"That isn't necessary. I'll figure it out." She's a stubborn thing when she wants to be, and cupping her jaw, I step up to face off with her.

"It is necessary, but I'll let it go for now. I'm following you home, though. No argument tonight."

Her mouth pops open but my thumb touches her bottom lip. I trace over the swollen curve and I swear she sighs. I want to take her mouth again, swallow the sass she's giving me, press her up against this damaged car, but something tells me she's being watched, and I want to see her safely home.

"You have a truck," she states, glancing behind me and noting the mammoth black F-150 next to her cupcake-sized vehicle.

"I need it for construction work. Can't ride my bike everywhere."

"You're in construction?" It's as if she doesn't know me, and then I remember she doesn't. We don't really know anything about each other. We might have consensual carnal knowledge of one another from years ago, but we don't know-*know* each other.

"I work for Monroe & Sons Construction."

"As in Wyatt Monroe's family?"

"The same one, but he's with the sheriff's department. He didn't wish to follow the blueprints of his family."

Her eyes narrow as her mouth twists. "Is that construction humor?"

I wink and lead her to the driver side of her car. Before I reach for the handle, I squeeze her hip. "You aren't going to flake out on me and cancel on Friday, right?"

I don't know why I'm acting all insecure. If she didn't show, I'd hit up Charlese. On second thought, I wouldn't. I'd grow pissed off and then head to the Fugitive.

Her brow furrows and her lips pinch.

"When I make a promise, I stick to it," she says a little tartly before slipping into her car. As I follow her down the road, I wonder the entire time what she means.

Dwight Henderson is a womanizer with a capital W. He's a noted sleazebag from his frequent visits to the Pink Pony and his never-ending cycle of hitting on women in The Wooden Plank, a good bar if you're looking to get laid. The more I think about it, the more I'm convinced there's some history between Naomi and him, and I don't like it. There was an evil desire in his eyes. After the comments he made the other night, and the way he looked at her, I have a strong suspicion he vandalized her car.

When I finally see Dwight on the construction site the next day, I corner him.

"What's your deal with Naomi Winters?"

"I ain't got no deal with that bitch."

"Excuse me." My palm finds his throat, and in an instant, he's pressed up against the two-by-four studs framing out a wall at the Bickerton's project.

"Witch, I meant witch."

I squeeze. "Try again."

"I don't have anything against her." He speaks through gritted teeth.

"What did you do to her?"

"Why's it got to be I did something to her?" His face flushes bright red. Loosening my hold only enough so he can breathe, I'm not stepping back until I hear his explanation.

"Well?"

"She's the one who cursed me, telling me she hoped my penis would shrivel up and fall off."

My eyes narrow. *What the fuck?* Is he suggesting she put a spell on him? I'm cursing him myself, thinking the same thing about his limp body part. That doesn't mean I'm a witch. "Why?"

"She was jealous. She wanted me." He smirks and now I know he's lying.

"What. Did. You. Do?" My hand tightens again, pressing him back into the wood beams.

"Nothing. We only scared her a little. It was a joke. Jesus, it happened years ago." His voice squeaks like a pre-pubescent teen.

"You're leaving something out," I demand, knowing he isn't telling me everything.

"Capture the witch." He's smugly proud for someone pinned to a beam. I'd like to peg him to a stake and see how he likes it. How'd he feel, if unfairly judged? I release him and take half a step back. Then I wind up, haul my arm back, and belt him in the jaw. His head bobbles into the boards behind him before he straightens.

"Son of a bitch," he mutters, cupping his face with one hand while covering the back of his head with the other.

"I ever hear you speak ill of her again, you'll suffer more than a clocked jaw and a headache."

Dwight doesn't look up at me as he spits blood onto the plywood floorboard. "I think you loosened a tooth."

"I'd like to loosen a few other things, but you obviously have a few screws missing already. And a shriveled-up penis."

"My dick functions just fine," he snaps, standing taller even as he winces from the effort of speaking.

"Yeah. That's what she *didn't* say." It's childish, but I don't care. "Too bad you fell on your own face, tripping over false accusations." I point in the direction of his jaw, emphasizing what I'm not saying. *Don't even think of mentioning this to Bill, our boss.* Dwight's a tattletale, and a chronic complainer looking to get out of hard work. Bill will more than likely take my side although he might question my timing. He wouldn't mind Dwight getting knocked down a peg or two, but he also wouldn't be proud of me for socking someone, especially on the job. "Understood?"

Dwight looks away. I don't trust him to behave but I've said my piece for the moment. His idiocy changes everything for my Friday night plans. I need to do more than make a statement at the local doughnut shop. I need a grand gesture, declaring who Naomi is to me. Hell, I'm not even sure who she is to me, but I'm pulling her under my protection.

Speaking of grand gestures, the lady who owns the property next to the Bickerton project has declared her own war on the construction site. Signs on small wooden stakes line the outer edge of her property. I've yet to go exploring as I'm not concerned with who lives next door, but I am upset about the latest signage:

There's two Ps in property. Keep both of yours on your own.

I don't get it at first until one of the younger guys, obviously lacking maturity, explained how someone pissed in her yard. "He peed on her property. Get it? Two Ps. Penis and Pee." What the hell? We have port-o-cans for the crew's business and the behavior doesn't sit well with me. Whoever she is, she is rather creative, though. My favorite sign is: *How did the roofer end up doing such a bad job? He was always eavesdropping.* Construction humor. The thought makes me think of Naomi. Kind of reminds me of some of the signs I've seen hanging around ... *oh shit.* The library.

Hours later, Catfish arrives at the construction site with Dirty Dave. Curtis Hickson is two years younger than me, but it didn't stop us from becoming friends in high school. We were both a little lost back then. He lived a questionable life with the Iron Wraiths, and at one point, I wanted to join him. I prospected for the Wraiths. Dirty Dave, on the other hand, is both dirty in appearance and in action. He's an older man who's been around a bit, dating back to the originals in the MC like Razor, Repo, and Darrell Winston.

While Catfish could be here for any number of reasons, instinctively, I know they are here to see me.

"How's it going, Wolf?" The name drags up the distant past—my stealth getting in and out of a situation. There's also the matter of my skill on a bike, especially down one particular road. And then, there's the fact I didn't patch-in. Presently, the road nickname has a negative connotation with Catfish. Alphas travel alone.

"Same old, same old," I say ignoring them both as I load my tools into the back of my truck. Our foreman is Bill's son, Garrett, and he would have a heart attack to see Iron Wraiths at this project. We don't need any trouble. We have enough with the owner changing his mind every five seconds. *Move the front to the back and the back to the front, and while you're at it let's just reconfigure the staircase and redesign the second floor.*

"Haven't seen you at the Canyon lately," Catfish states, watching me as I close the tailgate with a loud snap.

"Not much of a gambling man," I say, although I've made my share of bets in the past. Taken too many unnecessary risks—the biggest one probably coming back to Green Valley. The dirt racetrack in an abandoned mine is where I ran into Catfish about six months back. It's where he asked me to consider patching in again. Rumor has it the Iron Wraiths are living in chaos and looking for new recruits.

You're a smart man, Wolf. I remember that about you. Not to mention, you owe me.

The Wraiths active recruitment is one reason Dwight Henderson stepped forward, but he'll never fit in with these guys. He's too much of a weasel.

"Consider my offer yet?" Catfish questions, although it wasn't really an offer. It was more a warning. *Join and we're even.* I don't consider that I owe him anything, but I know under the bylaws of the club, I do. Catfish took responsibility for me stepping away from the club. It was a big risk letting me leave—putting his faith in me and his life in danger with them.

I pause with my hands on the tailgate. "I ride alone," I remind him.

"I remember that about you. Like to go off on your own," Catfish speaks, and Dirty Dave smirks as if he knows a secret. "We can use a wolf like you again."

"Nope," I say quickly.

"You'll change your mind," Dirty Dave mutters. "Heard you're fickle like that." Here's where Dave's wrong and showing his ignorance. *Does he even know what a word like fickle means?* I changed my perspective—for the positive. Accidents tend to do that to a person. So does having an irate big brother and a bawling hungry baby.

"You can't be rogue forever," Catfish chimes in. Wrong again. I can, because I am. At times, I ride collectively with Todd and Big Poppy because we find safety in numbers. Sometimes, we ride out for a good cause, like toys for kids. But we belong to no one but ourselves and any open road willing to take us. We're just a group of guys who like to ride bikes, drink at the Fugitive, and get laid, but not with each other, of course. We're independents.

"Seems I can," I respond before turning back to them. "We good here? I got to pick up my kid." I don't want any trouble, so I try to be respectful, but also keep my distance. It's a miracle I avoided Catfish for as long as I did. We said our piece to each other upon my return when he warned me he'd be watching me, but I didn't worry as I don't have anything to hide. At least, nothing he doesn't already know. The Wraiths have bigger concerns than me.

"Until next time," Dirty Dave mutters, and an idea strikes me. It isn't one of my finer ones, but something I believe needs to be done.

CHAPTER ELEVEN

DEWEY DECIMAL CLASSIFICATION: 580
BOTANY

[Naomi]

S ome nights, I enjoy a little walk through the wooded area located to the side of the library. It's a short distance to the edge of the property and then a mile-stretch southeast to my home. Moonlight. Deep quiet. Just me and the trees. Each tree holds meaning and it's one reason I love Samhain bonfires so much. The burning of sacred wood restores energy to the spirit.

After the day I've had I'm in need of some restoration and peace.

Not to mention, I can't stop thinking about Nathan and our kiss— or our date. *Three dates*, actually. I haven't ever officially been on a date. I've led a life on the road less traveled for a woman, and it reminds me of a Robert Frost poem as I enter the space between the solid, dark trunks. No dates. No sex. No men. And I'm almost forty. I'm an anomaly among my religion which embraces the earthly nature of sex. The contradiction isn't lost on me, but the guilt my parents wrapped around me at the death of my brother built my resolve to deny myself pleasure from others. Guilt *and fear* held me back from being myself. I was afraid of being hurt like I was when Nathan never called, when he disappeared. But the more I think of Nathan, the more I want to hand him wire-cutters and beg him to snip the fences around my heart, or at least, around other sacred body parts. I'd like to experiment, be curious, maybe adventurous—with him.

But why him?

A snap of wood echoes behind me. My heart skips a beat, but I remind myself, the woods are not mine alone. Creatures live here. I've entered the realm of Nature and I respect the habitat of those within.

Another snap and then a hushed curse, and I realize the critters are not small and harmless, but human and potentially mean. I'd love to cast out a binding spell, but instead, I offer a prayer to Mother Nature to protect me, and I run.

It isn't a full moon but there's enough moonlight to filter through the trees bare from the changing season. My heart races. My skin turns cold. My boots crack fallen sticks as I race through the trees, and then I hear my name. I stop, hoping I didn't imagine the call. Hoping I am imagining someone following me.

"Where is she?" A male voice grumbles. I'm thankful for the dark color of my long, black cape-like coat, and I slip between the trees, hoping to blend in and disappear from whoever is behind me. The snap of twigs and the crunch of leaves echoes through the forest under heaving feet another minute or two and then they stop.

"Naomi." A deep voice bellows, no doubt frightening some creepy crawling critters of the night. The sound is also scary enough to keep away mountain lions, or worse, bears. It isn't unheard of for them to wander toward town as the season changes and food becomes scarce.

"Nae, hold up."

Nathan?

The woods fall silent around me. I no longer hear feet crushing the covered path and I still. Then a hesitant step or two ripples near me, and I peer around the tree where I've been hiding to see a large man in dark clothing stumbling slightly as he twists around to look behind him. Despite his broad shoulders and tall stature, his head cranks this way and that. He looks lost among the sparse trunks, dark space, and eerie quiet. The trees bring me comfort. For him, he looks … frightened.

"What do you want with me?" My voice rings soft and feminine, and I watch as Nathan's shoulders relax even as he spins away from me.

"Naomi?" Quiet follows the soft echo through the black night. His voice rings with concern and a strange sense of peace washes over me after the exhilarating run and fear of being hunted. I shift out from behind the tree, but still stand in the shadows.

"Nathan?"

He spins toward me and freezes. I've stepped into a patch of moonlight, revealing part of myself and Nathan observes me, his eyes fixated on my hair.

"You're so beautiful," he says as he exhales. His eyes roam down the length of my coat and I imagine most of me disappears with the dark outerwear. Then his eyes snap back up to my face. His expression morphs from a man on a mission to something softer, something puzzled. "You look otherworldly, Nae."

His voice is breathless, reverent even, and my body quivers under the seductive tone.

"No one calls me that anymore," I say, stiffening a little at the reminder of my brother.

"What are you doing in the woods?" His feet remain in place although his hand curls and uncurls at his side, as if he's fighting himself.

"I was walking home."

"Where's your car?"

"Winston Brothers Auto Shop. Beau needed to keep my car overnight, waiting on the replacement lights."

"I came to pick you up. Didn't you see me in the parking lot?"

My thoughts were so preoccupied, I hadn't even glanced up to the lot when I left, knowing my car wasn't there. That wasn't a safe decision, though.

"So, you decided to walk home in the dark?" Irritation laces his voice mixing with frustration.

I sigh. "It appears so." I tip back my head, taking in the peaceful surroundings. I love the dark woods.

"Is this witch humor?" The question cracks like a twig, and my head snaps back to face him.

"Do you think I'm a witch?" I ask, my voice dropping as I step toward him. He steps back.

Is he afraid of me?

"I've heard a few things."

"And you always believe what you hear?"

He hesitates by taking a deep breath before he speaks, as if he's collecting his thoughts. "Actually, I don't give two shits about rumors or gossip, but I am concerned about you. I don't care what you are."

"So, you believe that I am."

"Are you?"

Why are we playing this game? "Why do you want to go out with me?" It's something I've been thinking about all day. Why does Nathan want three dates with me? Why now?

"I feel like there's something between us. A missing puzzle piece. I want to put us together." He steps toward me with those words. I step back.

"So, I'm a mystery to you." Is that all I am? Some piece from his past, unresolved? Nathan's unsolved to me as well. Why didn't he call me like he promised he would after that night? Where did he disappear to and why is he back?

"Maybe." He pauses twisting to look left. Then he straightens and peers back at me, eyes full of wonder and awe and something more. "Definitely."

"You want to solve me."

"There're many things I want to do with you, Naomi. Solve you isn't one of them. I want to solve what you're doing to me." My breath hitches, and he takes another step closer to me, shortening the distance between us.

"What do I do to you?" I whisper, holding my breath.

Reaching for my cheek, he cups loose hair around my ear. "I'm all tangled up inside over you. I'm ... I'm stuck on you," he says, his smoky voice dropping. I don't even know what that means but before I can ask, he says, "Your face is freezing." The concern in his tone warms me from the inside out and I lean into the thick pad of his palm.

Am I stuck on him, too? Would it be so bad to give into this man?

"It's cold outside."

"I came to the library to give you a ride home."

"That wasn't necessary," I say, heating under the deepness of his voice. His thumb strokes over my cheek, down my jaw, and across my lower lip. Then he leans forward and kisses me, soft, delicate, too quick.

"Nothing's necessary, Nae. I just really wanted to see you again." His mouth finds mine again, brushing lightly over my lips. I reach for his wrist, craving more connection between us, but then I notice something about him.

"You're trembling."

"Not a fan of the dark woods." His ashen voice drifts and I don't recognize the tone while his head twists side to side as if he's searching for something. Is he afraid of the forest? Does being here trigger a memory? Did something happen to him? Sliding my fingers to his, I curl them together and step around him, not letting him go as I lead us back to the parking lot.

"Then let's get out of the dark."

Inside the heat of Nathan's truck, I remain quiet while Nathan drives me home. The entrance to my driveway is tucked under overgrown branches, and it's as if we enter an alternative universe as we pull into the drive. I am in another world as I don't know what I'm doing with this man, but I don't want to let him go.

Why him?

My house is detailed like a miniature French chalet—a white stucco structure with brown crossbeam accents—glowing brightly from lights within. It looks like something out of a fairy tale and it makes me smile to see it all lit up. As we pull to a stop, I notice Nathan focusing on the house, his brows pinching in question.

"The lights are on a timer. It's welcoming when I come home. It makes me feel like someone is waiting for me." My voice falls small. It sounds a little lonely, which I am. Since the return of Nathan, I've taken note of how alone I really am.

"I'm working on the Bickerton project next door. We're enjoying your signs."

Ah, the monstrosity going up on the old Coppersmiths' property.

"You're laughing at me."

"Not laughing," he says, swallowing back a chuckle I know he wants to release. "But they are original."

"Well, some of your men are rude. I'm just channeling my inner Mrs. MacIntyre." I say, smiling weakly, as I recall the man I caught with his hands in his pants, relieving himself on the edge of my land. They're lucky staking up warning signs is all I've done. Mrs. MacIntyre would have all kinds of things to say about their public indecency and urination. "Library humor."

I glance back at the house and Nathan's eyes follow the direction of my sight.

"The Coppersmiths rented their coach house to me when I first started working at the library. The monthly bill was affordable, and they treated me like the daughter they never had. They were unique people and Lodean taught me the ways of Wicca." *Believe in yourself, honey, and the universe will support you.*

"As my neighbors for sixteen years, I was heartbroken when they moved to an assisted living facility in Knoxville. Lodean had dementia." I shrug with the memory, although I'm not nearly as nonchalant about her disease. "She died a year after their move."

My vision blurs and I pause.

Lodean loved you like a child, Henry told me. *She would never rest in peace unless she knew you were provided for.*

"Henry wanted to gift me the coach house and its property. It was one of the most generous gifts I've ever been offered, but I never wanted to feel like I took advantage of these people who treated me better than my parents. I insisted Henry sell me the land. I paid one dollar for the house and another dollar for the acre around it." I smile when I recall the transaction. The shock on the lawyer's face but the insistence of Henry Coppersmith. He wanted it all legal and written, so no one could take anything else from me. I didn't have many reasons to remain in Green Valley. I could have gone anywhere after that first year of grief, but their kindness and acceptance gave me new roots. I bloomed where I was planted among the woods, their unconditional love, and a new religion centered around both. The Coppersmiths were family to me.

"Sadly, Henry died three weeks after his wife. Everyone believed it was one of those romantic moments where a couple couldn't live without each other. The date was their sixty-fifth wedding anniversary. Lodean would have found it ironic."

It's a sign the universe wanted us together for always.

I glance over at Nathan, finding him fixated on me. The look in his eyes brings heat to my cheeks and I realize I might be talking too much. He's a vision of calm and collected after our adventurous trek through the woods. His wrist rests on his steering wheel and his large hand dangles beyond it. I'm becoming obsessed with noticing his wrists and I want to reach over and trace the lines of it. The bony edge. The swollen vein. The tender skin underneath.

"Anyway," I add, dismissing my rambling and reach for the handle of the passenger door instead. "Thank you for the ride."

"Wait." Nathan hops out and rounds the hood faster than I can say *it's not necessary*. He stands outside my door and pops it open, holding it with one hand while he offers me the other. I step out but we don't move from beside his truck. In fact, keeping my hand in his, I'm pressed up against the side of the vehicle while his other hand curls over the edge of the bed, caging me in. Absentmindedly, he strokes his thumb over the back of my hand, his eyes concentrating on the movement.

"Can I ask you something? What's the story with Dwight Henderson?"

I shrug at first, but the squeeze of Nathan's hand tells me he isn't letting this go. I exhale before I relive another painful memory.

"Dwight is younger than me. He was seventeen; I was twenty-two, and the new librarian. He used to come into the library often to study. He was book smart and working toward a scholarship. He wanted to go to Notre Dame." I swallow back the images of a young student with big dreams. He was so full of himself. Charismatic and charming and a little dangerous. I had no interest in him. Naomi at twenty-two seemed a world older than a high school teenager.

I concentrate on the circle Nathan makes over my hand. "He was only in high school, and I think ..." It seems foolish to admit what I thought back then. "I helped him study. Worked on problems with him. I think he was attracted to my intelligence."

"He had a crush on you," Nathan says definitively.

"Maybe." I chew at the corner of my lip and his thumb strokes increase in pressure, the circling growing more intense and drawn out.

"Did he make advances? Ask you out?" Nathan's voice rolls with concern and hesitation.

"He did, but I didn't see it as anything more than him offering to buy me coffee to pay me back for studying with him. I said no."

Nathan nods, as if piecing together his own version of a rejected seventeen-year-old interested in a slightly older woman.

"Tell me what 'capture the witch' means."

I gasp. *How does he know about that?* "It was a long time ago."

Nathan releases his hand from the edge of his truck and tips up my chin, so I look at him. His eyes spark, telling me to trust him, asking me to open up to him.

"They were just kids," I tell him—tell myself—but my lip quivers with the memory and Nathan shakes his head, warning me that my explanation isn't enough. "Dwight and a group of his friends cornered me outside the community center before the annual Halloween party. I kicked and screamed and ..." My voice falters as I recall being gagged and tied and tossed into a back seat. I tremble with self-shame at my physical reaction. "They took me to Cooper's

Field where they released me. I might have said some mean things to them."

"Mean things?" Nathan snorts exasperated. "He kidnapped you. I think insulting his dick is the least you could do."

My head snaps up. "How did you know about that?"

"Dwight told me. They didn't … they didn't touch you." He looks ready to pummel someone.

I shake my head. "I don't know what they intended to do to me, but two men on motorcycles pulled into the field. They demanded the boys let me go. Told me to forget anything happened which I promised to do. I was told to run, and I held my breath until I realized no one was following me."

"Jesus." Nathan hisses, swiping a hand over his head in irritation. "Who were the men on bikes? Do you remember?"

"I don't know. Someone named T-bone, maybe."

"Repo?" Nathan's jaw clenches and his hand returns to the truck's edge, caging me back into his space.

"Could have been."

"Did you call the sheriff?" His forehead furrows with concern.

"Who would believe me against a group of popular kids? I was the new librarian that no one had heard of and I liked it that way." I shrug. I didn't need to be a spectacle in a new town. I'd already been kicked out of my old one. "The motorcycle guys told me not to talk and I didn't, thinking it was safer for me."

"I hate that Dwight did this to you. I hate the rumors about you. You should have …" His voice falters and his head lowers, resting against mine. "I'm so sorry. Holy God, you were lucky." He tugs me to him, wrapping both arms around me and tenderly holding me with a hand on the back of my head and another at my lower back. It's nice, comforting, safe.

Nathan can't stop stupid men from being evil or immature teens from acting dumb, but the person I need safeguarding from the most is Nathan himself. I'm at great risk of falling for him, and my heart is the part that needs protection.

"Holy God? Did you mean Horned God?" I question, wishing to

lighten the aura around us and not talk about what happened any longer.

"Who's a horny god?" He teases, pushing me from him and chuckling hesitantly.

"Witch humor," I tease in return, wiggling a brow at him. He laughs deeper, the revelations of the night dissipating for a moment, and he lifts my hand to his lips, kissing my knuckles.

"I'm so glad nothing happened to you. Well, nothing more extreme …" He tugs my hand to his chest, flattening the palm over his left pec and his heart races underneath the soft cotton of his Henley shirt. I stare at my hand, absorbing his heat and his relief. It's as if I can feel the tension slowly release from him. He leans forward and kisses me, cautious lips covering mine to reassure me I'm safe. It's sweet. He's sweet.

Please, universe, let me keep him.

His mouth on mine is all cookie dough in vanilla ice cream and we slowly grow more eager, more hungry, more let-me-get-to-the-chocolate-chip-center-of-you. His arms slip around me, tugging me into his chest and I grip his open jacket like I did the other day, tethering myself to him with my grasp. As the kiss heats, he pulls back, breathing heavily and holding me at arm's length, fingers digging into my shoulders.

Forget melting ice cream. The fire in his eyes is the color of charcoal, prepped and sizzling with desire.

"We need to …" He doesn't finish his thought but swallows hard. I feel the same. *Slow down.* I should ask him inside, but I don't know if I'm ready for this, ready for him. Allowing him into my home, my sanctuary, feels too soon, but there's no denying I want him. I want him like I've only ever wanted him because there's been no one else in between.

Yet, while my body says *yes, yes, yes,* my heart says take caution this time around.

"Does this count as date one?" I inquire, hoping he'll let us out of his experiment. It isn't that I don't want to date him, but I am frightened of what dating him might mean. I'm so drawn to him and I don't think I can take the heartbreak of three dates, which will only prove we aren't compatible because we aren't the Naomi and Nathan of then. We're us now.

"This is definitely not a date," he growls, staring down at me. "I'll be picking you up on Friday at seven. Wear something warm and comfortable. Casual for outdoors." His eyes rake down my long coat draped to the top of my boots. It's functional, not fashionable, but it keeps me warm.

"Friday then," I say, unable to fight the grin curling my lips. Nathan shakes his head with a soft chuckle.

"Witch or not, Naomi Winters, you've put a spell on me, and I don't want it broken."

CHAPTER TWELVE

DEWEY DECIMAL CLASSIFICATION: 367
GENERAL CLUBS

[Naomi]

When Friday arrives, I pace my living room, chanting words of encouragement and slipping my black tourmaline crystal up and down the leather strap around my neck to calm me. I also wear a bracelet of garnet spessartine—a set of orangish colored, polished stone-looking beads—which opens the sacral chakra, one of the seven which balances the energy in our systems. The sacral chakra is linked to our sexual health. In other words, I don't want anything holding me back from letting my inner goddess explore a bit with Nathan, should the opportunity arise.

Am I still concerned about a catastrophe if I'm with Nathan? Not quite as much.

I mean, the world won't end, but my heart might not survive him again.

On a night like tonight, I miss Bethany. I have so many questions. Because while Vilma's Videos have helped me discover myself, I don't know how to be with another person. *Be yourself*, Bethany would say.

She was surprisingly down to earth and open about things. Beautiful inside and out, smart, funny, kind, and full of sage advice, I'll never understand how she got mixed up with a wicked man like her husband Darrell or how she had seven children by him. Some days I'm grateful her soul rests with the angels even if she was taken too young from this earth. Other days, I miss her like crazy.

A knock on my door makes me jump out of my skin, even though I've been expecting him. After I open the door, his eyes roam my body, and for a second, I worry he's disappointed. I'm wearing an olive-colored dress with thick leggings. My traditional lace-up boots and a bulky scarf around my neck. I don't own skinny jeans, cute fashion booties, or anything of the sort. My long, loose clothing has been my armor, but in the last week, I find myself wearing a few more revealing pieces of my wardrobe.

"You look pretty," he says, and my feminist friends be damned. I'm not changing my appearance for a man, but let's be honest, when someone calls you pretty as a genuine compliment, you feel it, you own it a little. Let me clarify, a slow change has begun for me, not *for Nathan*, although Nathan plays a part because of how he makes me feel about myself.

I argue with myself as my eyes focus on his lips, and I watch as his mouth crooks up at the corner. Dimple alert. Caught staring, I don't even think I've said hello. My gaze shifts to his eyes, finding the gray crystallized with something bright and tummy-dropping. *Hunger* —for me.

"You look nice, but will you be warm enough in that if we hang outside a bit?"

I swipe a hand down my hip. The dress is sweatshirt material with a fuzzy inside. "I'll be fine." I reach for my long coat which will keep me extra warm, but Nathan stretches for it as well and then holds it open. I'm awkward in response to his gentlemanly attention. My brain struggles to mesh my memory of Nathan as the slick motorcycle man at the Fugitive, so sure in his appeal to women with this new considerate version.

He drags my hair from the collar of my coat. Pre-mature gray hasn't lessened the weight despite the coarser texture. "Your hair is so long and heavy." The rugged timbre of his voice at my ear sends a shiver down the back of my neck. My mouth waters as I imagine his lips kissing me at the nape. I'm a shaky mess and we haven't even left yet. The sexual aura-awakening bracelet might be overkill. I'm already awakened to him. To distract myself, I take a fistful of my hair and twist the curls until I can tuck the heaviness under a knit beanie.

"Where are we going?" I ask, my excitement growing a little bit. I haven't been anywhere other than library conventions in years.

"I hope you like it," he says, scratching at the scruff under his chin, a nervous habit I've noticed, which makes him sound hesitant about our plans.

The last thing I expect is where we end up.

The Canyon.

Generically named, it's where locals go for illegal car racing. Red clay and dirt walls are exposed on three sides of an abandoned mine. A dirt track fills the center of the canyon floor. Industrial lights highlight the oval. The air smells like wet dirt, gasoline, engine oil … and bonfires. Three moderate pyres burn at intervals along the side not lined with rock.

I've never been here before, only heard about it, and it's not a place I thought I'd ever visit. The atmosphere feels sinister, dangerous, and a bit rebellious. It's definitely a place I would have snuck off to as a teenager, if I had known about it. We were relatively secluded in Cedar Gap—additionally sequestered by our parents. Once Jebediah was old enough to rebel—stealing motorcycles or "borrowing" the car —I'd occasionally be sprung from our parental imprisonment Older than me, my brother sympathized with me on the cage we felt we lived in and he'd allow me to sneak off with him for what he deemed safe destinations. The Canyon wasn't one of those places, and I'm not the risk-taking girl I used to be. Presently, I'm sorely out of place here among the black leather and exposed skin.

"I don't think this is a good idea," I say almost immediately after exiting Nathan's truck. He wears a leather jacket and a dark look on his face as he reaches for my hand.

"Give it a chance. This place has everything. Good food. Lots of drinks. And heart-racing entertainment."

"Racetrack humor," I mutter, and Nathan squeezes my fingers. My lips twist in disbelief, but I note the food booths and the beer truck as we walk closer to the main crowd of people. This really isn't my type of entertainment but then again, I haven't had much adventure in eighteen years. *Open your mind*, I remind myself.

"Do me a favor? Just stick it out for a little bit. Hold my hand no matter what though." The last statement is a warning of sorts. Fortunately, I have no intention of letting him go.

Nathan leads me to a barbeque booth, and I admit the food smells divine. I decline a beer but don't judge when he orders one. We watch the first race and I find it surprisingly exhilarating. I'd love to let loose and speed through life, but fear holds me back from doing something so carefree as racing.

"Wolf, is that you?" A man dressed head to toe in leather approaches us and reaches out to shake Nathan's hand. Nathan hesitantly chuckles as he grips the offered hand but squeezes mine to remind me to stay attached to his.

"Catfish, long time no see." Nathan's tone suggests otherwise.

"I knew you'd come around," Catfish says before turning to an older gentleman next to him. "Dirty Dave, can you believe who snuck in?"

"Sneaking around always was his thing," the older man says, his eyes roaming over Nathan before leering at me. I shiver and step closer to Nathan's arm. "And who is this?" His nose wrinkles like he's smelled something bad, as if his own name doesn't suggest something which might stink.

"This is Naomi. She's with me." The way Nathan introduces me turns my head. The deep timbre of his voice speaks of possession and warning in volumes. My other hand reaches for his bicep and I stare at the twitch in his jaw. He's not only making a statement. He's telling them something. I swivel to face both men again.

"Okay," Dirty Dave says, his voice rough but accepting. His eyes narrow. "Do I know you?"

I shake my head as Nathan states, "Never seen her before." It's more a threat than a declaration of the truth.

"Come have a drink," Catfish mutters. He steps away, moving toward one of the bonfires, and Nathan leads me to follow. I want to ask what just happened—what all of this means—but I don't.

My nose registers scents from the bonfire we approach. Birch. Oak. Pine. The birch could be a sign of new beginnings, but my surroundings tell me the practice of racing here has been around a bit. Oak—a masculine tree—means money and good fortune. Obviously, money will be exchanged here in hopes of success. Pine is the scent which throws me off and I can only assume it's convenient for starting fires, as it ignites quickly. Then, I tell myself to quit reading into things. This isn't Beltane season, nor a Samhain celebration. The sudden roar of engines reminds me this is a racetrack with innocuous bonfires.

As another race begins, Nathan lowers to my ear and his nose traces the shell. An innocent observer would think he's whispering sweet things to me, or maybe even naughty thoughts. However, when he speaks, he's all cautionary.

"When I was young and stupid, I fell in with the wrong crowd. I wanted to be someone, belong to something, and I became a prospect of the Iron Wraiths." My breath hitches. I remember he rode a motorcycle that night long ago. Why else would he be at the Fugitive where we met? But I had no idea he wanted to be part of a motorcycle club, especially not one like the Wraiths. "I needed to do terrible things to be one of them, and I was prepared to do whatever was necessary, Naomi. Steal. Pillage. Deal. Then, one night I met a girl. I fell between her thighs where I wanted to stay all night."

Why is he telling me such things? I don't want to hear about his sexual escapades. Suddenly, I don't want to be near him, and I tug at his hand. He releases me only briefly, slipping his arm around my waist to catch me before I can walk away. He drags me before him, my back to his chest. His other palm cups the back of my hand and he dips our collective hands into my deep coat pocket. He lowers his head again, continuing his tale in my ear.

"As a prospect, when you get a call, you jump. You don't question. You don't whine. You just do what is asked. I couldn't disobey an order, but I didn't want to leave the girl. She was such a sweet thing. One more kiss. And I was gonna be late."

I hate him. I don't care about his lingering in bed with some girl.

"Late," he repeats. "And I knew there'd be hell to pay. And I paid. When I finally pulled myself away, Destiny, as you might say, or the universe, had other plans for me." His breath is warm as he explains all this to me. The heat does nothing to melt the ice slowly filling my insides at the thought of him as a member of the Iron Wraiths. I remember Darrell Winston and the way he treated his sweet wife, Bethany. *Ex-wife*. She finally divorced him, but it didn't seem to stop him. Then I recall Nathan's monstrous bike.

"You still ride?" Was he one of them?

"I never patched in. Sometimes I ride with others, like my brother Todd and his best friend, but no other shenanigans. I like to ride alone, mostly." This makes some sense to me. I'm considered a solitaire Wiccan, which means I practice as I please within standards I set for myself. I don't want to be ruled by confines. I've already lived that life with my parents and their religion, and it suffocated me. Still, I can't believe Nathan wanted to be an Iron Wraith or the fact he didn't become one because of some hussy in his sheets.

"Do you know who that girl was, Nae?" A shiver ripples down my spine.

"How would I know?" I snip.

"You."

The hussy in the sheets. Me? I try to twist and face him, as old feelings of guilt and waywardness conflict inside me. However, Nathan holds me still. My eyes leap to Dirty Dave and Catfish. Dirty Dave peers at me over his shoulder.

"You were part of the reason I didn't patch in, Naomi. A reaction to an action. A pretty girl. Dark hair on my pillow. Tempting lips on mine." I stiffen against him as I remember my younger self.

I don't understand why he's telling me all this, but I hold still when Catfish turns to look at me. Then Dwight Henderson comes into my peripheral view. My breath hitches and Nathan's cheek pulls back from mine.

"Get why our date is here, yet?" I think so. He blames me for not making it in the club. *Sweet Goddess, he hates me.* For a split second, I worry I'm about to be sacrificed on the flames. Then, I shake the thought.

You're being ridiculous, Naomi.

"Why didn't you just tell me you were upset? You didn't make it in the club because of me. You didn't have to throw me into this pit and show me all you've missed."

Nathan chuckles bitterly behind me, before kissing the side of my head and lingering on my temple. Something whispers over my skin and I stare at the flames of the bonfire. Protection. Security. Beginning.

"No, Naomi. You were a part of me *not* making one of the biggest mistakes of my life. I'm not sorry one bit I didn't patch in with them. But they want me back now, and you're here so they can all see you're with me. No one can touch you without getting through me first."

"What?" I choke.

"Bringing you here makes a statement to the Iron Wraiths and that dweeb Dwight who wants to be one of them. They need to stay the hell away from you or deal with me."

"I don't understand," I whisper.

"You're my girl in their eyes, sweetheart." He kisses my neck and then looks up at Catfish watching us. Nathan straightens behind my back and Catfish turns away. Dwight hasn't looked in our direction, but I sense his eyes shifting. He wants to gawk, but something stops him. I spin in Nathan's arms and grip the edge of his open leather jacket.

"Get me out of here," I whisper. I don't want to be anywhere near Dwight Henderson or any of these men with their leering glances.

"Kiss me first," he mutters. There is a reason for his soft command, and I'll do whatever he asks of me, if it gets us out of here. I trust him to keep me safe and draw courage from his presence. He leans forward, and I tip up on my toes, taking his mouth with mine like I remember doing eighteen years ago. I kiss him with all I know. My mouth demands he take my gratitude for his protection. My tongue sneaks forward to let him know I understand. My lips open wider, drawing him into me. His kiss is my oxygen, because I can't breathe with these men watching us.

Nathan pulls back first, and a mischievous smile graces his lips. He looks over my head and I twist in his arms enough to peek over my shoulder.

"You should patch in again," Catfish states. I grip Nathan's jacket tighter in my fists. "We need men like you." Catfish narrows his eyes. There is something he isn't saying, but Nathan understands. He chuckles softly as he shakes his head and I feel the vibration against my cheek at his chest.

"We don't need a witch on our side," Dwight smirks and Nathan is gone in a second. He slips from my grasp, stepping around me toward Dwight. Nathan grabs the collar of Dwight's jacket, yanking him forward.

"I wouldn't want to join your team if these are the types of players you recruit," Nathan hisses in Dwight's face, but he directs his condescension to Catfish. A guffaw from Dirty Dave hints at deviousness, while Catfish places a hand on Nathan's shoulder.

"It's nice to see a little fire in you again, Wolf. I remember that flame, old friend." Catfish states, and I swallow at the implication.

Nathan shoves Dwight away from him. "I already proved myself."

"You didn't," Catfish proclaims, narrowing his eyes at Nathan. "But I remember your conviction. And some serious"—his eyes shift to me, assessing my attire—"balls, especially showing up here like this." Catfish's gaze remains on me.

"Easy," Nathan warns, not liking the direction of the motorcycle man's tone.

Two men suddenly appear, flanking either side of me, and for a moment I think we are surrounded by Wraiths.

"You okay, Nathan?" One asks. He stands just as tall as Nathan, similar silver-white hair with a tease of facial scruff. The other man is taller—broad and buff—with a thick beard like a true mountain man.

They both wear leather jackets and dark jeans. With arms defensively crossed, they look like guardians at my sides.

Hands raised in surrender, Catfish speaks. "Toad," he addresses the white-haired man, and I assume that can't be his given name. "Big Poppy," he says to the mountain-sized one. "Just enjoying a night at the track."

The tension is thicker than my oldest sister's now famous fried pickle batter. The vibe around us is just as crisp, too.

"We don't need quitters," Dwight blurts as an afterthought. "He walked away."

Nathan's head swivels to glare at Catfish and a conversation seems to ensue between the men.

"Not that it's any of your concern," Nathan eventually addresses Dwight. "But I'll be walking away now, too." With that, Nathan steps back and wraps an arm around my shoulder. The two men standing guard next to me nod at Nathan and slip forward, blocking our retreat. They wait as Nathan spins me toward his truck.

"Don't look back," he warns me, but he doesn't have to worry. I don't want to look back on any of this.

CHAPTER THIRTEEN

DEWEY DECIMAL CLASSIFICATION: 646.77
DATING

[Nathan]

S hit. Shit. *Shit.*

That was bad.

So bad.

I lost my grip on the situation, probably making it worse instead of better. The Canyon is neutral territory. Skin-heads. Bikers. Mountaineers. It's a rough crowd but harmless. A promise of anonymity hovers over the property and I thought it would be a good place to present Naomi as under my protection. But instead, I think I made things worse for her.

I'm going to catch hell from my brother Todd, whose road name is Toad, and his best friend Big Poppy, for getting in the face of an Iron Wraiths prospect. Not to mention, Todd doesn't want me anywhere near the Wraiths again. He knows Catfish has been stalking me to re-up, holding over me what happened the first time. I gave Todd my word I wasn't going back.

There will be questions about the woman as well, and Todd will flip when he learns who Naomi is. Keeping her snug under my arm, I help her into my truck and then circle the bed. Once I enter the driver's side, I start the engine and take a deep breath. I need a second.

"I'm so sorry," I mutter, scrubbing two hands down my face. "I thought I was helping you, but I might have just made it worse." I turn to look at her. Her wide eyes—filled with question and surprise—focus on me.

"You're trembling," she softly says. I'm not actually. I'm vibrating with adrenaline, trying to regain my composure after nearly losing it on Dwight.

"I'm not a violent man by nature," I tell her, hoping she isn't frightened of me.

"I believe you," she says softly. She's leaning with one hand on the bench seat of my truck, her body positioned to face mine.

"I'll get us out of here," I add, but with the look she gives me, I just want her close. I reach for her, hoping to draw her near me. When I tug her upper arm, I catch her off guard, and she lunges forward with the force, face-planting into my chest.

"Ow." She pulls back, covering her nose with her fingers.

"Shit. I'm so sorry." I reach for her jaw while her fingers pinch the bridge of her nose.

I'm making a fucking mess of this night.

"I'well be oway," she says all nasal-blocked.

"Sweet Jesus," I murmur.

"I don't pray to him, but I'm alright." Releasing her nose, she continues to stare at me. In fact, she appears calmer than I feel. So much for date number one, I think. It really is turning into a catastrophe, and I turn back for the steering wheel, peering through the windshield until her hand brushes my arm.

"Nathan." There's something in her nasally voice and I face her again to see she has shifted on the seat. She slides closer to me. I watch as she crawls forward before lifting a leg as if she wishes to climb in my lap. There are several issues with this idea.

The distance between me and the steering wheel isn't wide enough for both of us.

Her long coat tangles in her leg.

Her knee hits the horn.

The screeching beep startles her and forces her knee downward. I separate my thighs with hardly an inch to spare from the family jewels as the loud honk echoes through the silence around the truck. Thankfully, I catch her at the waist before she face-plants on the steering wheel.

"Whatcha doing?" I can't help but chuckle through my frazzled nerves.

Her leg between my thighs retracts but not before her heel catches on the steering wheel. Her ankle slips into the opening.

"I think I'm stuck."

The statement draws more unexpected laughter from me. Maybe she's right. Maybe the universe is cursing me. Maybe the universe is trying to tell me I'm a major fuck up in all things concerning this woman.

I try to help her release her ankle from the slim opening between wheel and horn. The force I use tugs her knee forward and it catches me in the chest. It doesn't hurt but it startles me, and I huff, choking on oxygen and my guffaws.

"I'm so bad at this," she mutters, once her foot is free, and she scrambles back to the passenger side of the truck, plastering herself against the opposite door. She thumps back on the seat, straightens her coat, and folds her hands in her lap.

Yeah, things typically work a little better than this.

"Nae," I exhale, trying to rein in the hysteria rippling under my skin. She stiffens before lifting her arm to the passenger door and pinches at her forehead with her fingertips. Her gaze remains focused out the front window. I don't understand what just happened here. This woman is all kinds of contradictions. She acts like she's never been kissed but looks at me like she wants a lick. She seems like she's holding back and then the next minute she's ready to attack. I don't know what to do with her, but I need to get us out of this lot.

"I think you should take me home," she says. My heart drops. She won't even look at me. Without a word, I shift to reverse and exit the Canyon. We ride in silence until I can't take it anymore.

"I don't want to take you home yet." My head twists to momentarily peer at her, all buttoned up and stiff as a board in that damn long coat. We are almost halfway between the abandoned mine and Green Valley, and I pull into Cooper's Field.

"What's this?" she asks, eyes opening wide as she glances out the window. A few other drivers have a similar idea as me, tucking vehicles into nooks by trees or paths among the field. My truck jostles as we find a little privacy for ourselves among the scattered parked cars.

Naomi's head shoots back to me as I cut the engine and hang my wrist over the steering wheel. I turn to her while I lean the seat back as far as it will go.

"Let's try this again," I say, my voice rough with need. I won't press her. I just want to make up for earlier.

"Come here," I say, reaching for the front of her coat and gently forcing her attention to me.

"Do you really think this is a good idea?" I hear the concern in her voice. The worry of catastrophe. We just survived one though. Makes me almost want to celebrate. She shifts on the seat to face me, and I watch my fingers fumble with the large button at the collar of her long coat. I ignore her question.

"Let's start by loosening up a bit."

She doesn't say anything but her breathing increases. With each button dragged through another hole, a deep exhale releases from her. Her breasts heave, and my fingers twitch to cup her, feel their weight and squeeze. How would she respond to me?

When the coat opens, I slowly remove it from her shoulders. There's too much bulk to this thing and I want her close without the barrier. I curl an arm around her back.

"Come to me," I groan, tugging her toward me and guiding her onto my lap. She follows my direction and slips her leg over both of mine. We move slowly this time, and I've suddenly become appreciative of her dress which slips up to her hips as she balances on my thighs. Her hands rest on my shoulders and I reach for her hat, freeing her silvery hair. I like how it glows in the dark night. Her lips twist as

I comb through the heavy strands, loving the way they spring back to a kinky wave when I reach the end.

"Are you cold?" I ask. It isn't wintery outside, but the air holds a chill, hinting at the next season. The heat in the truck cab is rising with our warm breaths, but I still want her to be comfortable. Naomi shivers as she says no, her tremors having nothing to do with the temperature. I rub my hands up and down her arms.

For a moment, I'm a teenager again, all hot and bothered. Eager, yet holding back. On the verge of bursting in my pants. I tug at the scarf covering her neck, unwrapping her like a present to reveal the curve of her throat and the line of her jaw. I want her undressed—open and exposed to me—but not in my truck. Not this night. This night will be a teaser of what we could be together.

Tossing the heavy material to the side, I return my hands to her hips, climbing up her sides until my palms settle near her breasts. My thumbs draw up under each swell and her breathing exaggerates, forcing them to rise and fall in a way that makes my mouth water. With the size of them, I know one would fill my thirsty mouth.

"You almost got in a fight back there." Her voice remains quiet and low as if others might hear her. She exhales, and the weight of her breasts under the thick pads of my thumbs feels amazing. I press upward, desperate to cup their fullness. "No one's ever stood up for me like that before." Her hands cover my scruff-covered jaw and my eyes focus on her lips as she licks them. Then she leans forward, hesitant and patient. I don't have as much restraint and meet her halfway. My mouth takes hers as I wrap my arms firmly around her back and draw her down my lap. She moans into my mouth as her hips wiggle until she settles right where I want her most. I squeeze at her spine and she rocks forward.

"There she is ..." I mutter between kisses. "The girl I remember." Past images slowly drift back to me. A girl who took her time although she was in a rush. Movements like a slow dance. Unbearable anticipation and incredible patience. She pulls back from my lips, bites the corner of hers, and then something unleashes. Her fingertips tenderly scratch at my scruffy jaw before her mouth crashes with mine. Teeth clash. Tongues collide. It isn't pretty and yet I want it all. She settles into a rhythm with my lips, allowing me to lead and then she rocks against me again.

"Nae," I whisper as I trace kisses to her jaw. I haven't made out with a woman since I was a boy but I'm enjoying her mouth and her movements. Her fingers grip my jaw and her undulating increases in my lap. Her breath hitches on my name and if I didn't know better, I'd think ...

"Sweet Jesus," I groan, pulling back to look up at her. Her head tilts back. Her eyes close. She's set a pace at the seam of my zipper and I know what she's going for.

"Sweet Goddess," she murmurs, without a break in her stride. Her hips swivel and roll, and my hands clutch her backside.

"Yeah, her too," I reply under my breath, and a small grin crosses Naomi's lips. I want that grin, and her full smile, and her gentle laugh. I want it all but first, I want her orgasm.

"Nae, I'm gonna—" I'm about to have a problem in my pants. Her eyes open and silver beams silence my tongue. The mercurial gleam in them holds me prisoner as her body continues to work at coming undone over mine.

"Please," she whispers. "Don't make me stop." With her begging eyes locked on me, I can't deny her. *As if.* I shift under her and she squeaks without losing her pace. Her steadiness increases, the pressure building. I'm not going to last, and then she stills, her lips covering mine. Her body tenses as her nails scratch over my beard. Her knees dig against my outer thighs while a moan fills my mouth and I know what she's done.

I'm on the edge, teetering with an achy need, but I'll let her have this one. She releases my lips and rests her forehead on mine.

"I was bad at that, wasn't I?"

"Seemed pretty good to me." I chuckle lightly, kissing her nose.

"So good," she whispers. "It's been so long." I want to think she's talking about me and the firm ridge screaming under her, but I'm sensing something else.

"How long has it been?"

"Eighteen years," she says pulling back. Her hands slipping down to my shoulders. She's drawing away from me, and it's more than physically.

"Eighteen years since you orgasmed?" That can't be correct.

Slowly, she shakes her head. "There was this boy in a bar. No, a man on the edge. He was dangerous and sweet, a heady combination for me, and I thought he was into me."

I swallow at the hollowness in her voice. This doesn't sound like a good story, and why the fuck do I care about some dude she screwed around with so long ago.

"I felt special that night. Maybe it was him. Maybe it was because it was my birthday."

Oh shit.

"I was dancing, and I'd been drinking, but I wasn't drunk. I knew what I was doing and what I wanted to be done." Her fingers slip down my leather jacket. "He peppered me with flattering words and covered me in kisses." Her voice turns edgier. "And I gave him everything of me."

I stare at her until I think I understand. "Were you a—" I can't get out the word.

"Couldn't you tell?" It takes me a moment to register what she asked. *You.* It's hard to answer the question but it's equally difficult to dismiss. We were drinking. She was cute. Did I take advantage of her? Did I push her too far? Then understanding occurs.

You're giving me something sacred.

"You were a virgin," I choke, surprised and disappointed in myself. How did I miss that? How did I not know this detail? The rest of the night flashes before me—*the after*—like a flip book you make as a kid in the edge of a textbook. The *after* clouded everything and I realize how it's possible I forgot this precious detail, but I don't think so. An additional comment she just mentioned becomes a red flag.

Eighteen years.

"And you haven't been with anyone else since then? Since me?" I swallow hard, uncertain how to feel about this revelation other than an ass for not recognizing her condition.

Her head shakes once. "We'd see each other again. He promised. He said he'd call." She shrugs as her lips twist. "He never did."

Fuck me.

I swallow again. I can explain what happened but now isn't the time. The accident. The Wraiths. The conditions. I'll never forget that night—it haunts me in more ways than one—and I try not to remember the smallest details. But a memory taps my brain. My phone. I'd left it behind.

Put your digits in here, I said as I tossed my phone to her in my haste. I was going to be late, so late. And I was going to be in trouble with Catfish. Being a prospect of the Iron Wraiths was fucking punk work, and I hated it most days, but I'd pay my time to be part of something greater, to belong to something. I'd forgotten my phone on the bed after one more kiss. I rushed out of the Fugitive, leaving the girl behind as well. I can't believe I forgot my phone, as my leaving it behind would play a crucial role later in the night.

"Do you know who that person was now? The one who didn't call." Her words remind me of my confession earlier this evening about her. I don't need to answer her. "I'm still waiting for him."

CHAPTER FOURTEEN

DEWEY DECIMAL CLASSIFICATION: 386.4
TELEPHONE

[Naomi]

I have no idea what I've just done. I mean, I know what I've just done. I've given myself an orgasm on Nathan Ryder. I rode his lap, like a mechanical bull where I control the speed, but now is not the time for joking. There's nothing funny about what I've just told him. I've just admitted one of my deepest secrets and biggest regrets. I gave my virginity to a man with false promises. And I'm still waiting for the man I'll never have. He's a memory that's lived in my head for too long. He's lived a lifetime in the eighteen years since I've seen him, and I'm sitting on his lap like the hussy I was at twenty-one, taking orgasms from him.

I slip off his thighs.

"Nae?" His voice drips with hesitation.

"I got carried away," I whisper, my voice trembling. *You have this effect on me.*

"You must hate me," he says, and my head turns toward him.

"Hate is a strong word, Nathan. One of the deadliest. I don't feel that strongly toward you." I feel something else entirely, when I shouldn't.

Deny.

"So why didn't you call?" I ask as the tension and silence thickens.

"I had my reasons, Naomi, but I swear it had nothing to do with you. Nothing. I wanted to see you again, but I ... I just couldn't." The sorrow in his eyes as he stares at me tells me to believe him. Something happened to him, but he isn't trusting me enough to tell me what.

"Can I ask you a question?" The hesitation in his voice concerns me but I nod. "Why weren't you with anyone else? I mean, it's been eighteen years."

I want to believe he isn't judging me, and in some ways, I want to rail at him, and remind him again he said he'd call. I want to fault him in some ways but after Nathan, my avoidance of sex came from something deeper. The shame my parents placed on me at the death of my brother. Once I learned Wiccan practices, I accepted my responsibility even more—a reaction to an action—instead of freeing myself completely, which my religion would encourage. My actions with Nathan resulted in the reaction of my brother's death. Since then, I've worked hard to put out positives in order to receive them, avoiding anything negative ... which included sex.

"I've just been waiting for the right person to be next." And I've been afraid it would happen again. Someone wouldn't call, wouldn't keep their promises. I didn't seek out men and they didn't seek out me. I mean, I've been attracted to some but avoided the desire, denied myself.

So, why Nathan? Why now do I feel this need to release the inner goddess and stop denying myself?

An unsolved puzzle, like he said.

His shoulders fall and he scrubs at the underside of his chin, the scratchy sound of his stubble filling the truck cab. He shakes his head and starts the engine. *Guess the night is over.* Date number one—fail. All that is left now is to go home and wait for the catastrophe that will inevitably follow tonight, despite my rational mind believing there won't be a disaster. Yet as I gaze out the window while we finish the drive back to Green Valley, the trees remain upright, the fields billow in the evening breeze, and my house still stands when we pull into my driveway. It's my heart which won't be able to handle the aftermath of this evening.

Once we park, I open the truck door but find Nathan already standing beside me.

"This didn't really go as planned," he mutters, more apologies filling his tone. His eyes still hold a sympathetic twinge and blood ripples through my veins. I don't want him to feel sorry for me. I want an explanation. If it wasn't me, what was it?

"No plan," I say instead, weakly grinning up at him, repeating the words he said to me when I saw him at the Stop-and-Pump, and he asked me to join him for a drink. A thick hand palms my cheek and then slips under my chin for a second. He stares at me for a long moment and I can't read all those silver eyes are trying to say. Releasing me, he reaches for my hand and walks me to my front door.

"Hand me your phone," he commands, when we near the door and I reach in my pocket.

My head shoots upward and I blink. "Why?"

"I want to call you." My heart drops—caught between the possibility he could be mocking me and his potential sincerity. I hand him my phone, and he gasps. "What is this?" I glance down at the device in his thick fingers as he flips open the cover.

"It's my phone."

He chuckles, genuine and refreshing after the tense car ride. "We need to move you to the modern era."

"You want to change me?" I sarcastically mock, although in some ways I'm not certain it's a joke. Maybe it's more of my own insecurity. I don't think I can satisfy Nathan. I'm not a modern woman, not by his standards. I'm not leather and skin like the girls at the track. I'm not carefree, casual sex either.

"Not change you, sweetheart. Just want to find the girl I believe still lives inside you."

"That girl isn't who you thought she was, Nathan, and most of the time I try to forget her."

"Why?"

I shake my head. "Because she just doesn't exist anymore." She couldn't exist. She caused too much suffering.

"What happened to the carefree spirit of that girl?"

I'm not ready to tell him, not tonight. "She disappeared," I whisper. "She had to go."

He stares down at me, his brows severely pinched. "She's just holding back." He leans forward and tweaks my nose. "She's waiting, but the wait is over."

His thumb caresses my lips and then he glances back at my phone and adds his number.

"Hello?" The ringing of my cell phone catches me off guard. I've hardly made it inside my door.

I had an orgasm. On Nathan Ryder. With shaky legs, I'm sliding to the floor against the wooden barrier as I answer.

"Hey," a thick smoky voice fills the line.

"Who is this?" Trembling fingers come to my forehead and squeeze.

"It's Nathan." He chuckles.

Oh, *oh*.

"I know I'm about eighteen years late, but I wanted to call and say I had a nice night."

"You did not." I laugh, mocking his sentiment. "It was awkward and weird." .

"And too short." Silence falls between us.

"You just left," I say, stating the obvious as I thump my head against the door behind me. Laughter fills my voice as I ask, "Why are you calling me already?"

"I didn't want to break any promises this time." He pauses. "And I didn't leave yet."

I spin to my knees and then knee-walk to my front window. Peeking through the curtains, I see his truck still in my yard.

"What are you doing?" I hush-whisper.

"Keeping my promise."

I. Can't. Breathe.

"I don't want the night to end yet, so I figured calling you would prolong things."

I should ask him in, but then again, I want to play this game with him. "I haven't really talked on the phone in a long time. I mean, who chats by this mode of communication anymore."

"I know, kids these days. Always their nose in a phone and thumbs moving on the screen but not speaking." He chuckles again.

"Guess it's just us old-timers who talk on the phone."

"I'm not old," he laughs. "I'm seasoned." He's definitely seasoned. His mouth. His scruff. My thoughts wander to the thick length pressed at my center about thirty minutes prior. *So seasoned.*

"So, is this like a phone date? Date number two."

"This is not date number two. I'll do better next time. And as for a phone date … well, unless you'd prefer phone sex …"

I gasp. I've never had phone sex or any other kind of sex other than the one time with him, and he knows that now. My cheeks heat with the thought and I'm grateful he didn't judge me for my lack of experience. He's right, though. I need to join the modern era. But that's what Vilma's Discovery Videos are all about. The modern woman doesn't need a man to complete her.

You are your own center.

"I …" I don't know how to respond.

"Forget that." He chuckles. "Let's just talk."

"Okay. What's your favorite book?" I'm not good at small talk. I mean, I can do small talk. I do it all day with children at the library, and occasionally adults, but that's because books are the main topic. I don't know how to start a conversation with someone I hardly know other than asking about their favorite book. I'm also thinking we need to calm things down before I do another thing I've never done before —like give a man a personal lap dance to get myself off—and invite him into my home. To my room. To my bed. *Mother Earth, what came over me?*

Nathan chuckles. "Would you hate me if I said I don't read? Remember I already mentioned I'm not good at it."

Not hate, I think. Definitely don't hate him.

"Well, what are you good at?" He chokes a cough through the phone and my cheeks heat again. *Okay, then ...*

"How about your favorite song?" We play twenty-questions for several minutes, exchanging random information about ourselves until the conversation shifts to his daughters. Nathan explains how he got some girl pregnant, resulting in Dahlia. The timing of things seems strangely close to when we were together, but I don't ask.

"I was living in Nashville for a short time before I went to Florida. Her mother, Becca, didn't want to be a mother by the time Dahlia was one. Most days I don't feel I've done much better at parenting. I didn't do right by her, sending her off to my mother when she was so young, then claiming her back when she was six, and moving us back here when she was sixteen. She hates me on a good day."

I'm saddened to learn the tale of Dahlia. It certainly explains the girl who didn't leave her grandmother's side when she was a child.

"She certainly has changed," I say, not meaning to insult her but recognizing the difference from the shy child she once was.

"Yeah, she's a handful lately. I think God's punishing me by giving me girls." He huffs, and I smile to myself.

"Why punish?" The line goes quiet and I wonder if I've struck a nerve.

"Maybe punish is too strong a word. The big man is waiting for me to get it right with women." I'm reflective for a moment. What does he mean? There's so much I want to ask, but I'm worried forcing the conversation deeper will scare him off.

"Well, I adore Clementine," I interject, clearing my throat, shifting the topic. "She's so sweet."

"She seems to adore you as well." Pride fills his voice, and he tells me more about his second daughter. "I call her Dandelion because of that crazy fuzzy hair. I'm sure she'll hate it as she gets older, but I can't stop myself. My two flower girls." He chuckles. "I'm not sure I'm doing much better by her either, but she's been with me her entire eleven years and I don't plan on that changing. Her mother, Margie, didn't want to keep her once she found her fancy attorney husband." There's a pinch of bitterness at the mention of Clementine's mother.

"And you never married either woman?" I hear Nathan sigh, but I need this answered.

"Becca wasn't a smart move on my part. Like literally, my head wasn't in the right place with her and being with her I blame on my faulty wiring at the time." He chuckles without humor. "Margie. Well, I thought she'd be different but turns out she didn't want a man with another daughter, a lingering mother, and only a construction working future." *I do*, I think but I'd never say this to Nathan. The words sound significant. I. Do. Words I'll never say to a man.

When I think of his children, my heart swells. I don't have children of my own, obviously. I have two nieces, but it's never been the same thing. The children at the library are all my children. Some I'm happy to return to their parents, while others I'd like to hold onto a little longer, like the Harrys and the Clementines of the valley.

"You and Dahlia will find your way," I offer, drawing away from the bitter tone of Clementine's mother. "And Clementine. She's going to be a beautiful swan one day."

"What do you mean?"

"She's all fuzzy, right now, with that light, yellow hair. An ugly duckling, she says." Clem has large glasses which magnify her eyes and with the flyaway ringlets, she looks a little disheveled most days. "But I tell her ducklings aren't ugly. They're sweet, and fluffy, and spread joy. And one day, she'll grow into a beautiful swan." She was cute when she asked if she will be a swan like me, curling my white hair around her finger when she questioned her future. "Of course, then she had to correct me, telling me swans don't have ducklings. Ducks do."

Nathan chuckles, but something remains stuck in his throat. "Sounds like her. She's so smart."

"Precocious," I tease. "But she's sweet."

"You're sweet," he says, and my heart skips a beat.

"Thank you, I think." I mean, ducklings are sweet. Swans are more regal and refined, but ... oh, never mind.

"When can I see you again?" He's still sitting in my driveway, and if I had the courage, I'd ask him in right now.

"Maybe sometime this week?"

"Perfect. That means I need to call you again to set a date." His voice teases, but my insides warm with the humor in him. I shake my head. I'm sitting on the floor against the wall between the window and my front door. I haven't taken off my coat as it smells like bonfire and Nathan. I'd sleep in it if I thought I'd be comfortable.

"I guess I should let you go, so you can finally go home."

"Don't let me go, Naomi. But yeah, I probably should get out of your driveway."

We're silent for a second and I remember phone calls like this as a kid to other boys I had a crush on. The calls where you didn't want to be the first to cut the connection.

You're a hellion, Naomi. God will take care of the devil in you.

I shiver with the memory of my mother's voice.

"Talk soon?" He questions, and I smile at the vulnerability.

"Talk soon."

CHAPTER FIFTEEN

DEWEY DECIMAL CLASSIFICATION: 152
PERCEPTION, MOTIVATION, EMOTIONS, DRIVES

[Nathan]

As soon as I enter the library on my lunch break on Monday, I know something's wrong. My first hint—a new sign on the counter reads: *Save Our Library*. In a second plastic sheet display stands the official letter from the state formally announcing the closure of the library by the end of the calendar year.

"Where's Naomi?" I ask the second I read the announcement. Something in my eyes frightens the meek librarian behind the counter and she squeaks. Mrs. MacIntyre steps up instead and I repeat myself.

"She took off about half an hour ago. We had just read the letter." Mrs. MacIntyre frowns and I'm certain she's disappointed in Naomi's disappearance.

"She couldn't breathe," the younger librarian stammers, her eyes wide as she speaks to me. She glances toward the back of the library and I turn for the corner, but I don't see anything other than shelves of books, something Naomi loves. Books are her life, she told me when we spoke on the phone the other night. Our phone date.

Date one point five.

As I spin around, the quiet girl points at a security door.

The woods, I think as I take off through the door ignoring the emergency alarm which begins pealing at my departure.

"Naomi," I yell before I've even reached the trees, as if she can hear me. I don't know how deep she's gone in thirty minutes but if it's anything like the night I followed her, she can get pretty far, pretty quickly.

Thankfully, I find her within a few yards, crouched down in a squat. Her forehead presses to a thick trunk. Her hands brace the sides like she's holding on for dear life.

"Sweetheart," I say, my voice cracking. Her head picks up and then she shakes it without looking back at me.

"Go away, Nathan." Her voice is hardly more than a whisper, but I can hear the pain loud as the geese overhead. I ignore her request and step closer.

She shivers, and I quickly remove my jacket. I wore it only to ward off the chill on my Harley. It's another beautiful fall day and I didn't want to waste it in my truck when I could get away with the bike. I slip the coat around her shoulders and her head falls forward again.

"Speak to me," I command softly, squatting down behind her. "What are you doing out here?"

"I just needed some air." Her voice lowers. "I needed the trees." Her cheek presses against the base and her arms wrap farther around the massive trunk.

"What happened?" I want to reach for her. I want to pull her close to me, but she seems delicate, like if I make the wrong move, she'll break.

"The library is closing effective December thirty-first and I can't shake the feeling it's my fault somehow."

"How could it be your fault?"

"I gave into you again."

"Naomi," I warn gently as her spirit seems fragile.

"I shouldn't have done it, but I couldn't help myself." Without meaning to, she's made me smile and I lower my eyes to look at the crushed, dead leaves under my feet.

"Where do you come up with these things? These thoughts that being with me will make the world crumble?"

"You won't understand."

"Try me," I say, knowing there's nothing she can say which will be stranger than her thinking an orgasm closed a library.

"My parents." She shivers despite my warm jacket. "My father was a pastor of a very small church. My mother wanted to be a nun but left her religious studies to be with him. She blamed me for everything. I was too forward. I was too brash. I was too affectionate. She said my sexuality would be my undoing. Anything bad that happened was because of my promiscuousness. They called me a slut."

Who says such a thing to their child?

"That can't be true." The label does not fit her. She told me she's only been with me and I believe her, but I remember a girl who looked like she had a wild streak to her. I'm not judging her, though. I'd be the last to judge anyone.

"They said it," she whimpers.

"I'm not doubting what you're saying about them, sweetheart. I mean, it can't be true *about* you. I don't believe acting in any particular way causes bad things to happen. Life isn't like that. God isn't like that."

"I don't believe in God."

Okay. "What about your Goddess? Would she think such a thing?"

Naomi's quiet for a moment and shakes her head. "She believes in the power of three. Whatever I do, whatever energy I send out into the world, will come back to me threefold. A reaction to an action."

"So you have an orgasm and the library closes? Come on, sweetheart. That's not apples to apples. Your sexuality doesn't equate to the states' ignorance or their business practices. If it does, that's pretty powerful stuff."

She shifts to look at me over her shoulder. Sad eyes find mine and then lower to the forest floor. Her fingers dig into the trunk, the bark crackling under the pressure. "You're mocking me."

"I'm not. I'm saying that's one powerful vagina." She glares up at me, without a blink. Then she breaks into choking laughter.

"Vagina humor?" she mocks, twisting her body to slump against the tree's base.

"Heard laughter is the best medicine." I smile weakly at her, pain in my own chest at her sadness. With my words, she breaks into a sob. Her hands cover her face and the tears fall in earnest.

"Oh, baby," I say, scooting up next to her and pulling her into me. "It will be okay. If you believe in the power of three, then three good things can happen just as well as three bad."

"I know this," she mutters against me, sounding unconvinced. "I know."

"Well, unless you think your orgasm sucked, then you deserve something good, right? And good multiplies to more good." *Jesus*, I shouldn't have said multiplies because now I'm thinking of giving her multiple orgasms in order to spread the positive energy she needs. Then again ...

"Nathan," she admonishes with a chuckle. "This isn't the same thing."

"And neither is the library closing because you were with me." Her shoulders rise and fall, and she settles into me. Her tears have stopped, and I kiss her temple.

"I know," she whispers again, not very convincingly. "I'm just looking for answers in places they don't exist."

"I don't want us, or anything we do, to be your answer." I place a hand on her cheek and force her to look up at me. She nods to acknowledge what I've said. "And your parents were wrong about you, Naomi. They just were. No one understands guilt and blame like I do, but eventually, you have to release it." I pause, taking a breath to calm my irritation. I'd like to admonish her for taking their words to heart for so many years, but I understand the power of shame. "You love the library. You'd never do anything to harm it, including being with me if it really meant us being together would take down the library." I swallow hard at the thought of losing her. "Tell me more about the library closing."

"Julianne received the official email this morning. I couldn't breathe. My chest felt like it was caving in, crushing me. I mean, what am I going to do?" Her voice falls so soft, so worrisome. "I have no other skills. I've been grandfathered in as a lead librarian where the states now require a degree in library science to work in a library. I got my current position by default—my friend died. Prior to that, I was only an associate which is now Sabrina's title. There aren't other libraries in the immediate area. But that's the point. The state wants to force patrons to bigger cities with high-traffic branches and more resources." She exhales.

"I don't know what I'd do without the library. It's the only job I've ever had." Her head shifts, and she looks up at me, and stormy eyes beg me to understand.

"Okay." I breathe out. Construction work is all I've known so I can relate. "Okay, we can figure this out. Are there other libraries? Knoxville, maybe?" It's only about twenty minutes away.

"I don't want to move. When I think of my house ..." She trembles in my arms. "It's important to me. I've had so few things that were truly mine without conditions on them." Her eyes glance up to me. "It's also the principle of this closure. The injustice. I don't want another library. I want mine."

I admire her conviction and smile at the dedication and determination in her tone. She's been a survivor for a long time, and she'll weather this storm with grace.

"No one's moving," I tell her. "What about the local schools? Or maybe there's something to be done about the closing. A committee or a politician who can help."

Naomi presses upward, a hand on my chest as she straightens. Her eyes not leaving mine.

"Billy Winston is a congressman." Those Winstons cover everything. Auto repair. Scientist. Stay-at-home dad. Veterinarian. Politician. And their mother hired Naomi. They had been friends.

"See, we have our own congressman right here in Green Valley. We voted for him. Surely he can do something."

Her arms come around my neck, and she pulls herself up against me. I like this feeling. Her wrapping around me and holding tight. I like her needing me.

"Thank you," she says pulling back but not releasing my neck. Her eyes are crisp and grateful. Then they shift and drift down to my chest. "I must look a mess. I'm an ugly crier." She swipes at her cheeks, brushing at non-existent tears.

"You can cry if you want to, sweetheart. You're hurtin'. I get it. And you still look beautiful."

She gives me a curious glance again—the one where she doesn't blink—and then her mouth brushes mine. I follow her lead a second before taking over and dragging her into my lap. I'm liking this position, only I wish we were naked and not sitting up against a hard tree. Then again, I'd take her here if she'd give up her notion of catastrophe resulting from us being together.

Suddenly, my phone alarm rings. I have ten minutes to get back to work which isn't enough time to have my way with her, not the way I want, which will be salacious, but slow and full of rediscovery.

"It's your lunch break," she states pulling back to look down at me.

"It is."

"And you came to see me?" Her now-bright eyes widen.

"That I did," I say, my lip curling. Her fingertip draws a curve around the corner.

"That was sweet."

"So are you," I remind her, taking her mouth one last time, wanting more but pulling back quickly so as not to take her under the tree. "Feel better, baby?"

"I do. Thank you. Thank you for listening to me and giving me suggestions and just everything."

"I'll give you everything," I say, and it's a promise I intend to keep, along with proving us together will not be a catastrophe. "But first, I need to get back to work."

I lift her off me and stand, brushing at the seat of my pants. Offering her a hand, I tug her upward. "And you, my beautiful booklover, have a library to save."

The next evening, I take a ride. It's been a long day. Dwight messed up something again on the site and a building inspector read Garrett the riot act. I waited out the delay although my mind wasn't on the project. Naomi has me all twisted up after my visit to her at the library. I hate to see my girl crying and I feel helpless without solutions. *My girl.* How quickly I'm thinking of her in such a manner.

I can see how losing the only job she ever had would be devastating.

I can't see how anything she does sexually plays a part in losing everything.

Her parents did a real head job on her and I decide it will be my mission to correct those negative thoughts.

I'm pondering these things as I head to the Fugitive. The bar is an epicenter for motorcyclists risking a ride south down the Tail of the Dragon. This strip of road isn't a strip but curves and swerves some twelve miles long. The road holds ghosts for me, and I don't take traveling down it lightly. In fact, I love the thrill of racing down it, as if I can outrun my demons which lived and died on this road. The memories haunt me each time I hit a certain curl and I hold my breath.

I'm sorry, I whisper for the millionth time as I buzz past the spot that changed my life. I understand guilt. It's one reason I understand Naomi's predicament. I also know shame is a disease which can eat at your soul if you let it. It ate at mine for years until I finally accepted there wasn't anything else I could do. Coming home to Green Valley, I knew I'd have to face my sins, my fear of retribution, and this godforsaken road. But like so many times before, I ride without incident. Each time I survive the Dragon Tail I remind myself there must be a reason I lived, when someone else didn't.

Then I think of Naomi, and I realize for the first time, she might be another reason I returned to the Valley.

I'm stuck on you.

A reaction to an unresolved action.

She's unfinished business and the universe, her Goddess, or whomever, is giving me another chance to make it right.

Maybe.

As I near the Fugitive, my thoughts turn less morbid. Attached to the bar is a motel, nothing classy, but clean and well-kept. I park alongside a long line of motorcycles from various states. The foliage change in the fall is a big draw to the mountains this time of year.

When I enter the bar, I'm prepared for the grilling I'm about to receive from my brother standing behind the wood counter like he owns the place—which he doesn't. His best friend Big Poppy does. Todd is an unofficial bouncer, manager, knower-of-all things man, who keeps his eyes on the visiting MCs, making sure everyone minds their manners.

I slip onto a stool and Todd hands me a beer.

"Who is she?" Todd steps back, leaning against the inner counter of the bar, the one with a wall of glass shelves and colorful bottles of liquor above it. His road name is Toad. He claims it's because his tongue can reach a great distance and be creative in all sorts of ways pertaining to the female anatomy. The truth is our dad called us Frog and Toad from those kid's books. *Two opposite and yet similar boys*, Pop would say. Todd was chubby as a kid. I was the lean one. We've both bulked up and our stature is similar, but three years older, and my brother's hair isn't nearly as white as mine. A strong salt-and-pepper mix covers his head, and he has a beard to match. Cold blue eyes narrow at me. He isn't pissed. It's just his natural expression.

"Her name is Naomi Winters. She's the one from that night."

My brother's brows rise as his hands fall to the counter behind him. He whistles low, knowing which night I reference. The night I didn't patch-in. Todd teased me afterward, trying to make light of a difficult time in my life.

She must have been an angel in bed, he said. He knows the details. There was a call to fulfill my prospect duty, playing bitch to the club. There was a girl I couldn't quite resist, making me late.

"How the hell did you find her?"

"At the Piggly Wiggly."

He snorts with a gruff chuckle. "You have the damnedest luck." His arms cross his barrel chest again. In some ways, he's right. I feel lucky that I found this girl from my memory but also strangely out of sorts over her.

"So, it isn't ironic you almost threw down against the Wraiths for the same woman."

I take a gulp of my beer and eye my older brother over the bottleneck. It is weird. I feel protective of her and worry I made it even worse threatening an IW prospect in front of the clubs' unspoken leader. If I know Catfish, he's only biding his time until he can become prez. With the current president in the Knoxville State Penitentiary, the second-in-command in the hospital, and another key leader missing for years, the Wraiths are struggling. Then again, I like to think Catfish has enough sense not to judge me based on Dwight being a dimwit.

"It wasn't an ultimatum."

"Pretty damn close. If you'd pissed a circle around her, it might have completed the statement."

Jesus. It wasn't that bad, was it? I just wanted the Wraiths to understand who she was and Dwight to see that she's mine.

The thought makes me choke on the next sip. She isn't really mine. I feel like I hardly know her, but something in my chest tells me I actually do. We're linked somehow. She was special all right, and I knew that night was important. I surmise that must be the connection. *That* night.

You're giving me something special.

How could I not know she was a virgin? Then I think of my reasons for not patching in and remember the rest of the night was a dose of biker reality.

Still. I curse myself for not remembering the smallest of details.

Did I hurt her?

Did she enjoy us?

What is it that draws me to her?

I'll call you, I remember telling her after I got the call from Catfish and had to split too quickly. I never came back for the phone and had no way to find her again.

"Must have been something special under that long coat to haul your ass out of the Canyon without introducing her." His drawl grows heavier, the accusation deep. It's not like we're high society, but Todd prides himself on introductions and knowing people. "Just wanted to meet the lady who I was willing to fight for next to my brother." *Ah, there's his reason.* He will go to hell and back for me if I need him, but he also wants a reason other than loving me as his kid brother.

"Don't talk about her like she's some barfly. She's not."

One brow rises and then the corner of his lip curls upward. "Based on her outfit, I could see that."

So her coat was long and her hat homemade. She isn't like the regular girls who attracted me before—younger, darker, more leather, and all lace, but I find I'm liking the taste of someone more my age, refined, and a little on the innocent side. "She's … sweet." Hesitating after the word, I wait for Todd's scoff.

"Pussy is sweet, Nathan. She is—"

"Choose your words carefully," I warn, suddenly feeling like I need to defend Naomi's honor to my brother of all people.

"Interesting." He smirks. So what if she was different than my usual flavor? Perhaps it was time to expand my palate.

"Ever think the universe is working against you?" I ask of my big brother, expecting his sideways glance and narrowed eyes.

"I think everything happens for a reason." I can't find the reasoning in a person senselessly dying. I can't find the reasoning in losing Becca or Margie. Then Naomi moves forward in my thoughts. "Could it be the universe is working *for* you for once, Frog?" The soft tone he uses to call me my childhood nickname lets me know he isn't teasing me. I've never doubted my brother wants what's best for me, and he knows a thing or two about losing people. He lost Meldee, and I know it still hurts him.

"How so?" I ask.

"Maybe she's another reason you were meant to come home." Todd knows I shouldn't have returned, but he missed me, Ma missed the mountains, and I needed more security than the transient work in Florida. "She's unfinished business for you."

I nod. Could it be? Could Destiny or Fate or Naomi's Goddess have pulled me back to the valley for one of those reasons? Then I consider our first date and the phone call. Her tears when she spoke about her fears with the library and her kisses when she latched onto me. She's more than business I want finished. I'm not sure I ever want to be done with her.

I'm stuck on you.

"What about Charlese?" Todd asks.

Shit. I haven't thought of her in the last week since missing our night when I took Naomi to the Nut House. I called to cancel. A simple *something came up* was all she needed. That's how the relationship went between us. Uncomplicated. But I'm finding I like some complication in my life, especially if it comes wrapped in a little awkwardness and lick-me eyes.

"Guess we're over." I drink down the rest of my beer. One is plenty before I ride home. I stand from the stool, feeling Todd's eyes on me.

"You really dig this Naomi chick." He's questioning me, and I nod. I'm definitely getting buried in the possibility of her and me.

Date number two needs to happen sooner rather than later, but unfortunately, Naomi works the remainder of the week and has plans for her day off on Wednesday. I never knew Beverly Townsen and Scotia Simmons were her sisters.

"Scotia is the oldest." Naomi teases, exaggerating a drawl as we speak on the phone later that evening. "She's a peach. And she married a Simmons, so don't you know that makes her someone." Sarcasm drips in her voice and I like her snarky.

"Then comes Beverly, and I'm sure the whole town knows her story. Drunk driving accident. Lost the use of her legs, not to mention her driver's license and her pride. Became a self-proclaimed shut-in."

"Actually, I hadn't heard the story. I've only been back here for about eighteen months."

"Oh, well, this happened ten years ago. None of us are from Green

Valley in the first place. We're from Cedar Gap. I'm the baby of the family."

"Me too I guess, seeing as there is only me and Toad."

"He's one of the men from the other night, right?"

Right. The two men who flanked her as I lipped off with Dwight. "Yeah, about that. Again, I'm sorry for losing my temper in front of you. I don't want Dwight speaking ill of you. Hell, I don't want anyone talking about you, but I should have taken a second to introduce you to my big brother."

"Maybe another time," she hesitates as she offers, a question lingering in her voice.

"So, speaking of another time ... I want our second date." I wish I could see her face, see those lick-me eyes I like so much. As I sit against my pillows, legs stretched out and crossed at the ankles, I wonder how she'd respond to me in this bed. Thinking of her in these sheets prompted me to give in and call her.

She clears her throat. "I host the Thursday night poetry reading at seven. Ever been to a poetry reading?"

"Can't say I've ever done something like that."

She giggles. "Well, I've never been to a racetrack."

Oh no. I'd never live that down if the guys found out. Todd would have a heyday with that one.

Rose are red,

Violets are blue.

Nathan's crazy for some chick,

And lost his balls too.

Then again, Naomi isn't a chick. She's different ... to me.

"How about Saturday?" I suggest brushing off the poetry reading.

"Sure." Her voice betrays her, but I can't do it. No to poetry.

"So, Saturday," I continue. "Genie's?" Genie's Country Western Bar is known for dancing and drinking. It's a little less rambunctious than The Wooden Plank or The Fugitive.

"I don't dance," she says, her voice lowering. *Okay then.* "I mean, I don't know how."

How hard is it to dance? I lead. She follows. But then I remember something. "I don't believe that's true." A vision of her dancing around me when we met and leading her slender, wiggling body to a room off the Fugitive fills my head.

"I don't anymore," she clarifies, and I realize this is all tied up in more bullshit from her parents. She's carrying some strong guilt linked to their words and I wonder if it's connected to something she did. I can't imagine what she could have done to inspire such reproach, but then again, I know how guilt works.

"Maybe it's time to try again," I offer, my voice teasing. She holds back from me, but she's like a rubber band, springing forward without warning after you tug and tug and tug.

When she doesn't answer me, I ask another question. "Well, what else do you do?"

"I make soap. I knit. I work at the library." *That's all?* She sounds eighty instead of thirty-nine. Next, she'll tell me she has sixteen cats. We need to find her some fun.

"I'm not good at *things*, Nathan." She speaks as if she's read my mind.

"Maybe we just need to reintroduce you to *things*."

"To drinking, dancing, and cavorting?" I can tell she's trying to be funny but her voice is tight and I'm not joking anymore.

"Let's talk about cavorting. What does that even mean?" I think I know, but I want to hear it from her. If she whispers one four-letter word rhyming with *truck* I'm going to have a night's worth of fantasy just from the sound of her voice.

"You know," her voice deepens, and I smile at the hesitation.

"I want to hear you say it. Call it what it is."

"Sex," she blurts like she did when I asked her to agree to three dates, only this time her breath exhales in a pleasant sigh around the word. *There's my girl*, I think as I slip lower on the bed. My hand rubs over my belly as a part of me twitches to life.

"Hmm ... say that again," I tease.

"Sex," she purrs, and my fingers loosen the button of my jeans. I hear her shift through the phone and I wonder where she is and what she's wearing, which makes me sound like a creeper, but I need to know, so I ask.

"I'm in my bed, in a nightgown."

I have girls, so I know what a nightgown can be. Frilly ruffled material tight to the neck. Flannel down to the wrist. Dragging on the floor. With a giant Cinderella on it. For my purposes, I'm imagining her in a silk nightie. Deep black.

"Naomi Winters, are you trying to have phone sex with me?" I flirt, slipping my fingers inside my jeans.

"Is phone sex simply saying sex through the phone?"

"You're teasing me, right?" I want to chuckle, but I hear the reluctance in her question. "No, sweetheart. You touch yourself, while I touch myself, and we describe what we're doing." The idea has me hard in a heartbeat, and I curl my fingers around my warm shaft, giving myself a quick tug. "Do you do that? Touch yourself?"

"I might not have sex, Nathan, but I don't deny myself completely." Her voice sounds stern, almost like she's reprimanding me. *She can spank me if she wants.* But her comment reminds me of what she told me the other night. She's been waiting—eighteen years—and she hasn't had sex. I find it hard to believe, but a strange sense of pride fills me. She's been waiting on me.

Then I think of her alone—an image of her slipping her fingers between her thighs—and I'm squeezing myself harder.

"Why did you hold out, sweetheart?" I can't help asking although the serious question could dampen the hard-on I'm working. I don't want to think about other guys with her. I kind of like the fact it's been only me.

"Besides the guilt my parents put on me, and the fact I didn't want something terrible to happen?" Her tone lowers, and she pauses a moment. I frown at her response. She's hinted before at an incident resulting from our first encounter, but she hasn't explained it. I figure when she's ready, she'll tell me. Tonight, I want to know more about her sexual history. "I guess I've also just waited. I wanted it to be right. I didn't want to be hurt again." Something stabs at my chest as I'm the one who hurt her before. "I want it to be special, if it happens again." Her final statement conveys her vulnerability.

She was special to me.

"I want to be special to you," I whisper, closing my eyes with thoughts of how we could be. "Would you ever let someone touch you?" It's an intimate question, a sensitive one, but I want her secrets and her fantasies.

"If someone were to touch me again, I want it to mean something." Her voice remains quiet, husky and deep. *If?* Oh, there's definitely going to be touching in our future, and I'll make it as special as she needs.

"So you aren't totally opposed to my wand in your cauldron?" I flirtatiously tease.

She lightly laughs, but then admonishes me. "Don't tease."

"I get it. You want intimacy and meaningfulness. That's what fore-play is for. A little practice. A lot of warm-up."

"Foreplay?" She chokes, but there's a hint of curiosity in her voice. I'm so damn attracted to this vulnerable piece of her. I imagine it's what drew me to her the first time. My fingers tighten over my thick length which wants her innocence again.

"Touch yourself, sweetheart." My voice drops an octave. It's so rough and deep I don't recognize myself, but I want her to trust me. I want her to give me this moment.

"I don't know if I can." Her voice lowers to a whisper, but there's something in her tone suggesting she's willing to try, she just needs me to lead.

"Just a little stroke," I plead. In my mind's eye, I see her expressive eyes and her wild hair spilling everywhere. "Pretend it's me. You're safe with me," I assure her, pausing a beat as her breath hitches through the phone. "It feels good, doesn't it?"

"Oh." She breathes out. "*Oh.*" The sweet breathiness stiffens me further.

You're giving me something sacred. The words trickle through my memory, finally making sense to me. Her original innocence. Her current vulnerability. I don't want just her body; I want her faith in me. I won't disappoint her again.

"Yeah, Nae." I exhale, gripping myself tighter. "I'm thinking of touching you while I touch myself."

There's more shifting, and then the soft hitch of her breath.

"I wish I could see you right now," I say, my voice lowering as my arousal rises. "You give me these eyes …"

"What eyes?" Her voice catches.

"Eyes like you want me to lick you all over." Another sharp hitch and I'm ready to crest the hill. "Lick-me eyes."

"Nathan …" she warns on a low moan.

Sweet Mother. I want to say nasty things to her, swirl my tongue over her essence, and part her like the Red Sea. I want to fill her with all of me and hear the husky groan of my name.

"Nathan," she breathes out like she did riding me in my truck. My name is a spell on her lips, and I drink in the potency of it.

"Goddess," I whisper as I hear her unfold and I make a mess of myself.

What is this strange woman doing to me?

Her breath shudders through the phone.

"You okay, sweetheart?" A soft purr is her response. Coming down from my high, I stare up at the ceiling, sensing I crossed into a protective circle around her and liking that she let me pass. "See you Saturday, baby."

"Good night, magic wand," she whispers with a pleasure-filled voice and a smile clearly on her unseen face. I send up an enchanted request to hear that sweet tone every night before I sleep.

"Good night, my little cauldron."

CHAPTER SIXTEEN

DEWEY DECIMAL CLASSIFICATION: 808.81
COLLECTIONS OF POETRY

[Naomi]

"Ladies, we're so pleased you could join us for another evening of poetry." Julianne greets our poetry reading regulars. Our Thursday evening gatherings have dwindled and shifted over the years. Bethany Winston started this themed night. Diane Donner-Sylvester was one of the biggest patrons. She was the one who introduced me to Vilma Louise and her self-discovery videos. Surprisingly, I miss her at this weekly event.

Some nights people read classics. Other nights originals are presented. We told those present about the plight of the library prior to this evening, and Julianne requested it be our theme, so I find Julianne's reading of "Still I Rise" by Maya Angelou profoundly appropriate. She wants to believe we will overcome the injustice of the closing and she's even made a new sign for the front counter.

Books have been oppressed, suppressed, and addressed for years. Don't deny our access. Use your right to express Freedom of the Press.

I wanted to remind her that the state isn't burning books, but when she becomes passionate about something, look out ...

When it is my turn, I read "Little Red Cap" by Carol Ann Duffy about seduction by a wolf. From the wolf's poetic words, he lures his prey to his den. It is graphic and intense while beautiful and sad, and as I finish, I look up to find Nathan watching me over the low shelf at the back of the gathered audience. Our eyes lock and the hunger in them makes me shiver. I'd let *that* wolf eat me.

I still can't believe I did what I did with Nathan the other night. It felt wicked and salacious and freeing. There's something about him which calls to me and draws the inner goddess out. I wanted to feel guilty afterward. I should have felt guilty after what we did. But I didn't, and I said a chant, dispelling the negative thoughts and calling on the Goddess to make me whole again. Strangely, Nathan is contributing to this sensation of wholeness, which goes against what Vilma teaches, but I'd like to believe there's room for personal inter-pretation with her videos. He serves a greater purpose in my life—although I'm not quite sure what that is yet.

Mabel Murphy is up next, and I excuse myself to walk to Nathan.

"What are you doing here?" I whisper with a sheepish grin on my face, as I round the shelf to stand next to him.

"I wanted to see what this is all about." He smiles slowly, the dimple peeking out and I want to tackle him to the floor behind the bookshelf. *Nathan came to poetry night.* My body heats everywhere. This isn't a hot flash but the nearness of him and the memory of what we did. Quickly, I look away, catching the tail end of Mabel's reading of "Interview" by Dorothy Parker which I can never interpret. Does the poet mean staying home is the way of a woman or going out is?

"Would it upset you if I also said I wanted to see you?" he softly asks and my insides warm from my toes to the tip of my hairline. I want to giggle like a schoolgirl.

"I thought you didn't do poetry," I hush-whisper without looking at him.

Nathan moves his arm and I know he's going to scratch under his neck. "I was chicken."

I softly chuckle, and then try to cover it as a cough. "What do you mean?" I keep my voice low as Julianne has already given me a glaring, silencing look. She's perfected that stare.

"I didn't think I could handle some boring poetry reading, mainly because I knew I wouldn't understand any of the poems." He shrugs. "But then I thought about the other night and how you might have been nervous to go to the racetrack. You still came."

My head swivels to him. Is he being funny? Punny? His lip slowly curls, and forget the innuendo, I want to kiss him silly.

"I decided if you could trust me, I should trust you. It won't be boring." He winks. I blink.

The poem I read comes to mind. *You frighten me in the best of ways.*

"I do trust you," I say, offering a piece of myself to him. I realize I do, or I wouldn't have given him the experience we shared the other night. The curve of his mouth deepens, and I want a sip of him. He'd be hot cocoa on this cool evening—sweet and filling.

"Anyway, I figured I wasn't giving it a fair chance. Besides, you were right. So far, it isn't boring."

I bite my lip, pleased that he's trying to meet me on my turf like I went to his. In fact, I find his open-mindedness kind of endearing.

"But this isn't a date," he clarifies, holding up a finger. "We still have Saturday."

I stand straighter, inhaling deeply. "Okay."

"I'll take you out for ice cream or tea or whatever after this, but I don't want it as a strike against our date count."

My brows pinch. "Why not?"

"Because this is where you work, so it shouldn't count." I don't know that I agree with his reasoning, and I think he's only trying to finagle another date out of me, but I'm also thinking I might not mind more than three outings with him.

For the remainder of the readings, I stand by Nathan. Our bodies press close, and I'm thankful the low bookshelf blocks our bodies. He leans his elbows on the bookcase, his hands clasped together. Then he shifts on his feet, dragging his arm sideways to brush against mine. His knuckles trail along my forearm. My eyes dart to him but I don't move. My legs tremble. My body hums.

His hand swipes across my backside, slipping to my opposite hip, and I clamp my lips, holding in the gasp desperate to escape at such a bold move. Instead, I grip the top edge of the wooden shelf and slip my foot around his. I shift so his leg wedges between both of mine.

"What are you doing?" he hisses near my ear, but he doesn't prevent the slow torture of our bodies coming together. He draws his knee upward, forcing my thighs apart and my core pulses in iambic pentameter.

Ba-dum, ba-dum, ba-dum, ba-dum, ba-dum.

I want to write poetry over his skin.

The hand at my hip remains, while the other rests on the top of the low bookcase, next to mine. His thumb stretches out and strokes at my pinky. I'm concentrating so hard on the tender touch, I almost miss his body shifting, drawing flush behind me. The seam of his front presses into my lower back. I stand straighter and lean against him. My back melts at his chest and his breath tickles along my neck.

The wolf inhales my scent and I close my eyes.

"You smell good enough to eat," he whispers, and I lick my lips. I'm the one who wants a taste of him. My palms flatten on the bookcase and his fingers crawl forward to entwine with mine. The movement brings him tighter against my body from behind. My backside presses against him.

"Don't tease, Goddess, or I'll bend you over this wood."

More puns? My breath hitches. Do I want him to do that to me? I've never ... *but I might.* With the pulse between my thighs ratcheting up a beat, I begin to wonder what it would be like to be taken against this shelf.

Roses are red,

Violets are blue.

How I want you to fill me,

I do, I do, I do.

I lean forward but his body follows, pinning me against the bookcase. His fingers release my hand and skim up my arm before dropping behind the stacks to clutch the material of my dress. The fabric rises along my outer thigh.

He wouldn't ...

"What are you doing?" I hiss, my eyes forward, my mind unable to concentrate on Hazel Cumberstone, Mabel's twin sister, reading a poem. His palm flattens on my outer thigh over my tights and massages downward.

"I like this dress," he whispers. "It's a little easier to access than the rest." I'm wearing a deep purple one which comes to my knees. It's the same one I had on the night I kissed him in the library the first time. It is shorter than most of the dresses or skirts in my wardrobe, and I always feel a bit risqué when I wear it. I feel especially risqué with his hand rubbing my outer thigh and my dress riding higher and higher to my hip.

"You have thick hands," I say, disregarding his comment about my dress. I want to tip my head back for some reason, give him access to my neck and feel his lips suck at my skin. But I don't dare move with an audience before us.

"All the better to touch you with," he murmurs near my ear. My knees buckle, and my flattened palms squeak with sweat against the smooth surface of the shelf. He catches me with his knee between my thighs and a sudden heat envelops me. This isn't a hot flash. This is an inferno of desire.

"What time does this end?" He exhales at my ear, squeezing at my thigh, his fingers slipping forward, rounding my leg to the front. My core clenches, pulse accelerating. He's going to make me embarrass myself with just the brush of his fingers.

"I have to close tonight, so nine."

He groans and the sound ripples over my skin. His hand stills, and his forehead lowers to my shoulder. A strangled grunt resounds against my bone.

"I can't keep this up for another hour and a half. You'll make me lose my mind." He straightens, releasing my dress to fall back into place and returns his hand to the top of the bookcase near mine, only this time it's a fist for control. I slump against him, a little disappointed but also a bit relieved. I can't have an orgasm in the midst of poetry night. That would be poetically inappropriate, right?

An hour and a half later, I feel differently. My skin tingles. My underwear is wet. I need relief like I've never needed anything in my life. Julianne gives me another reproachful look as Nathan remains inside the library doors when I tell her I'll lock up.

"After hours visitors are not permitted," she reminds me.

"I understand. He's only waiting for me. Once I lock up, we'll be leaving," I promise her. She gives me a scathing look of disbelief and I'd like to think I don't deserve it, but I do. The second the door clicks to lock, I spin and lean against the cool surface to face Nathan. His eyes roam my body in the dress he says he likes, and I feel that look like a teasing paintbrush on the canvas of my skin.

I want him to touch me. Not just over the tights on my thighs, but deep to the core—bare, raw, unfamiliar.

"I was wondering where to find poetry in the library. In case I'm interested in reading more." He tries to keep his voice even, sounding studiously serious, but there's a tease in his tone. The corner of his lip tweaks upward and I shake my head at the smirky dimple. Pressing off the door, I lead him to the 800s—the Literature section. My fingers comb the spines until I get to the first section of poetry.

"Are you interested in writing it or reading it?" I pause and glance at him over my shoulder. He's followed particularly close to me as we saunter down this aisle. He removed his jacket an hour ago, settling into the readings, the critiques which followed, and the short social hour. Mabel and Hazel, forty-something twins, were hitting on him, and twinges of jealousy surged through me. I have no claim on Nathan, so I tried to keep my kitty cat claws in check. I don't even like cats, but I like Nathan. Too much.

"Writing it," he says, and I spin to face him. He leans against the shelves, which stand taller in this section, and holds something in his hand.

"What's that?"

His eyes remain lowered as he unfolds a piece of paper. His hands tremble and my curiosity piques.

"I thought poetry night meant you had to write your own poem and then perform it."

I smile before I explain. "That's more like a coffee house poetry reading. Maybe we should consider it for the library." We've started a list of new ways to attract patrons in hopes to keep the library open.

He begins to refold the paper, but I reach for his wrist. "What is this?"

"It's silly." He shrugs, his body shifting against the shelf so his back leans against it. My brows pinch until he cups my hand in his and brings it to his lips.

"Did you write a poem?" My eyebrow rises as he glances sideways at me and then gazes down at his booted feet. He looks like a guilty child, so I lower my voice like I would talk to Sabrina's nephew, Harry. "Will you read it to me?"

Now, I'm trembling. *Nathan wrote a poem.* Could I like this man any more?

"That would be a firm no-can-do. I'm no poet, and I'm bad at reading aloud."

"But you already wrote it. You already know the words."

"It's doesn't really rhyme or anything."

"Most poems don't. It doesn't have to."

"It doesn't make much sense." My heart races in my chest as his fingers tighten around mine. The paper in his other hand shakes.

"I won't laugh." With my free hand, I cross over my heart. Then, I promise the Goddess and Mother Earth and any other deity who wants to listen that I will not chuckle at a single word.

He wrote a poem.

I reach for his jaw and spread my fingers, loving the prickle of his chin hair against my palm. "You can do this, Nathan. I believe in you." I don't know why I say it. Maybe because I feel stronger when he's near me. Maybe because I gave into him, and nothing happened to me. Nothing happened to the universe around us.

He grins and that darn dimple peeks out again. "Those eyes," he warns, and I stare back at him. *Lick-me eyes?*

"I won't look at you. I'll just listen." Closing my eyes, he clears his throat. His voice trembles as he begins:

. . .

151

Tis the time of year for changing leaves
  And howling winds in the shifting air.
  Wolves bay at the round moon.
  Ghosts roam the circular earth,
  And witches rule the dark woods.
  I met one such ruler among the trees.
  She whispered my name like a kiss.
  I responded with one of my own,
  And so I am bewitched.
  Onto her lips, she adds my name to her spells
  And find I'm stuck on the thought of her.

When Nathan finishes, I can't breathe. My lids slowly open, and I stare up at him. He isn't looking at me, but keeps his eyes focused on the trembling paper.

"It sucked, right?"

"It was perfect." The words fall from my mouth, breathless and seductive.

His lips twist as his eyes drift to mine and then back to the parchment. "It wasn't very good."

"Was that about …" I swallow the lump in my throat. "Was that for me?"

Nathan Ryder wrote a poem. For me.

He nods once.

"May I keep it?" My voice shakes as I ask. If he says no, it won't matter. I've memorized it in seconds and emblazed it on my heart. I'll have it tattooed on my side and I don't have any tattoos. He hands the paper to me and I fold it into squares like he had it. I don't have any pockets, so I place it in the palm of my hand like a revered gift, covering it with my other hand. It is a gift.

"This is very special to me." My voice comes out hardly more than a whisper. "You're special to me." I know I'm offering him yet another piece of my soul, but writing me a poem? It's just so much.

He peers up. "Damn it, Nae. Those eyes." His voice roughens as he speaks quietly, and he shifts his body to face me.

"What do my eyes say, Nathan?" My breathing increases and my chest rises and falls. I don't recognize myself. He turns me on like a light switch, the hum of electrical energy buzzing through me.

He wrote me a poem.

His head is shaking in response to the question I asked, so I answer for him.

"Nathan Ryder, I very much do want to lick you."

I don't have time to contemplate my admission because his hands delve into my hair and his mouth covers mine. I'm pressed back into the opposite stacks as his lips devour mine. Open mouth kisses and searching tongue, Nathan acts like he could eat me up, and I'm reminded of the poem I read about the wolf and the girl who followed him.

"Mmm, your lips. You taste like honey and almonds and everything sweet," he says against my mouth, and I melt a little more at his slow tenderness. "I want to punish you for teasing me earlier and yet take my time to savor every kiss."

Punish me? What did I do? Instantly, I recall pressing against him, the length of him rubbing at my backside. His mouth continues his hungry attention before lowering to my neck. I tip my head like I wanted to do earlier, allowing him access to my skin. His hand slides from my hair down my front and lands on one breast. Squeezing, I arch into his touch as my fingers claw down his back.

He pulls away abruptly, maybe shocked that I've allowed him to touch me in such a manner. Maybe equally surprised at my response. It isn't enough.

Sweet Goddess.

"I'll never do anything you don't want me to. We can take it slow, but I still want more of you." He's telling me something with his searing gaze, but I can't read him. The only thing I understand is the throbbing ache at my core and the hard length of him pressed against my hip.

His hand releases my breast and I whimper as he leaves me.

Another sly grin graces his lips and his hand falls to my outer thigh. Once again, my dress lifts while his eyes stay trained on mine.

"I want to touch you," he whispers, his mouth less than an inch away. "I want to know how wet you get for me."

My eyes close and I don't recognize myself as I answer, "Very wet."

Catastrophe may be written in the stars but the only thing I want printed is his fingers on me. My dress rises to my hip and his hand dips into my tights. The first brush comes over my underwear and I moan at the tenderness.

"Nae," he exhales, finding the answer to how wet he makes me. His finger nudges the cotton to the side and the tip of a thick digit slices through my core. I flinch forward, surprised and eager for more. One stroke isn't enough.

"Again," I encourage.

"Oh, sweetheart, it's going to be again and again ..." His words drift as his fingers sift through slick folds, finding the sweet spot, forcing me to gasp. I rock forward with his touch, my body begging for more. I exhale his name like an enchantment and Nathan begins to speak as he rubs circles over my sensitive skin.

"She whispered my name like a kiss." His finger enters me, and I buck forward. My arms stretch for the edge of the shelves to hold me upright. His middle finger slides in and out, the slick sound mixing with our heated breaths.

"I responded with one of my own." His mouth crashes against mine as a second finger enters me. I grunt at the intrusion and he pulls back, concern on his face, but I don't want him to release me.

"It feels so good," I whisper, swallowing the emotion in my throat. My eyes close as his nose skims up my neck and his fingers continue to drag in my depths.

"And so I am bewitched," he murmurs into my skin. His thumb flicks over the sweet spot, and my breath hitches in combination with his name.

"Onto *his* lips, I add my name as a spell." I struggle to speak, imposing myself in his poem. He groans before kissing me once again. My toes curl in my boots and my belly flutters. My hands come to his biceps, digging into his cotton-covered flesh. I pull back to whisper another line.

"And find I'm stuck on the thought of him." My voice rises an octave as my body can no longer contain the pleasure. I collapse into sweet release, slowly melting against the hard shelves at my back. My knees buckle. Nathan keeps me upright with his hand at my core until I can't take anymore. His lips come to my forehead until I've settled from the stars dancing before my eyes. He withdraws from me and strangely, I find I miss the warmth.

"Sweet Goddess," I whisper as he rights my clothing.

With a kiss to my temple, he mutters, "You're a goddess."

CHAPTER SEVENTEEN

DEWEY DECIMAL CLASSIFICATION: 612
HUMAN PHYSIOLOGY

[Nathan]

She is a goddess, and I'm flattered that she let me in a little more. The raising and lowering of her chest slows as her hands coast over my pecs. I like her touching me, exploring me, and a flashback comes to my memory of her doing the same thing when we were younger. Only we were naked, and she was on top of me.

How did that wildfire girl turn into this smoldering woman? Who hurt her so badly? Was it me for not calling? Was it her parents for what they said? What happened to turn her into herself and not allow the pleasure of others? Whatever her situation, I'm honored at being the one to reignite her a little bit.

Her hands continue to rub at my chest, lowering inch by inch. Her fingertips scrape at my abdomen and my belly flinches.

"Are you ticklish?"

I might be, but I won't give her an answer. I don't want her to stop. Her eyes watch her hands as she tugs my shirt from my jeans and ducks under the material. Hesitant fingers brush over my skin and my abs suck inward again.

"You are ticklish," she teases, but it's more her tenderness, her hesi-

157

tancy. Her palms flatten, caressing the ridges and ripples above my waist. Does she even know how she's torturing me? She leans forward to sip at my neck. An open mouth kiss sucks at my skin.

Sweet Goddess, as she would say. That feels nice. So nice. As if reading my thoughts, she does it again. My spine prickles from the sensation. She's slow and focused, and it's driving me crazy. Her fingers come to the waist of my jeans, tips curling into the denim.

"Naomi?" I lower a hand from its resting position braced on a shelf behind her head. "This isn't necessary." My heart races in my chest. Things are progressing so much faster than I expected, but determined eyes look up at me. Their silvery shimmer blazes while she unbuckles my belt.

"Nothing's necessary," she states repeating my line when she throws the phrase out to me. "Except actually, air is necessary. So is food and water. Then there's—"

"Naomi," I say, placing a hand on her wrist to stop her rambling.

"I'm just nervous." She pauses, sucking in her lips. "Please, Nathan. Let me do this with you." *Damn it, there's the girl.* The one from years ago, begging sweetly for things she didn't even know she wanted.

The unzipping of my jeans slices through the silence of the books around us. My belt clatters as my jeans spread open and then her hand dips into my boxers.

"Sweet Mother," I hiss as her curious fingers eagerly curl around the heat of me, which is hard and firm and desperate for her. She tugs, and my forehead falls forward. "What are you doing to me?"

"Casting a spell." She giggles but she's not joking. I don't care. As long as she keeps touching me like she is, she can be anyone she wants to be.

"You don't have to do this," I warn again, although I'm silently praying she won't stop. My hips buck forward, her touch too gentle, too safe. She's going to kill me with her hesitancy.

"Grip harder," I explain, and when she does, I nearly come out of my skin.

"Like this?" My arm shakes to support me, and my knees give a little.

"You're perfect," I lie as she fumbles at first, then she shucks my jeans a little lower, releasing me and I can't look. I'm going to blow too soon if I watch her examine me with curious fingers. Her pace increases. Her rhythm intensifies.

"Nae," I choke, not knowing if I'm warning her, telling her to stop, or begging her to keep going.

"I want to do this," she says, those innocent eyes sheepishly looking up at me. "But I'm going to be bad."

Sweet Goddess, she has no idea how that sounds in the low rumble of her voice. My dick leaps and her grip tightens, tugging and stroking harder. With my hands supporting me on the shelf above her head again, I hold back from thrusting forward too fast. Still, my hips buck.

Keep it slow, Nathan. Let her lead this dance.

"You don't owe me anything, sweetheart. I enjoy giving you pleasure."

Shut up, my dick weeps. Why are you trying to talk her out of this? I don't want her to stop but I also don't want her to do something she'll regret ten minutes after we finish. We've moved like a rocket shooting off, which is going to be me if she keeps this up.

Who knew poetry could inspire such sensuality?

"Just like that, Nae," I whisper, rocking into her squeezing fist. It's been a long while since I've had a hand job, but *fuck, that's nice*, my brain sputters as her hold increases.

"Nae," I warn, as my hip movements are beyond my control. She grasps me with inexperience and determination, a combination that makes me see stars within seconds. I unfurl, waving a flag of surrender. Tendons tighten, and invisible fingernails crawl up my back as the orgasm races to the forefront. With my fingers suddenly in her hair, I warn her again. Her name is a spell hissing from my lips.

With determination, her pressure intensifies, and I spill into her fist, releasing a build-up of denial. My forehead falls to hers as she watches my body react to her touch. It doesn't take long before I can't take the sensation. It tickles in a torturous way.

My hand covers her wrist to stop her movements.

"I was bad at that, wasn't I?" she whispers and closes her eyes. Cupping her chin, I tip her face upward, but she refuses to open her lids. I kiss her, slow and grateful for what she's given me.

Trust. Her trust in this experience.

"You're perfect," I remind her, pulling back as the tenderness of the kiss fills me with an ache in the pit of my stomach. I pull a bandana tucked in the back of my jeans' pocket out and wipe off her hand. She stares down at her fingers as I swipe between them. We need a little better clean-up but the furrow to her brow has me concerned. "What's going on in that pretty head of yours?"

Her lingering eyes close. "I don't understand myself when it comes to you," she whispers, her head lowers, and her wild hair curtains her cheeks.

"Try to explain it to me," I say, stroking back her hair, brushing it behind her ear.

"I don't want to want you like I do." Like a sucker punch to the gut, the comment hurts. Then she looks up me, intense silver eyes gleaming. "But I think about you all the time. I don't want to get caught up in you again and yet I'm already caught. I don't understand why you want to date me, but I very much like you."

Her ramblings remind me I asked for an explanation, and while slightly juvenile, I find I like what she says.

"I've experienced this out of control feeling one other time, with you, and I keep waiting for the other shoe to drop. Heck, I'm thinking a whole house might be falling on me soon, but I'm hoping to outrace it and get what I want before it happens."

"And what do you want, sweetheart?"

"I want you," she whispers, her voice so full of desire and confusion. "Why do I want you so much?"

I can't directly answer her any more than I can explain the attraction I have to her. But I'd like to beat my chest with pride at her admission. *She wants me.*

"Maybe it's the universe telling us something."

She shakes her head, her lips pursing as if I'm teasing her.

"Just hear me out, what if I'm right. What if somehow, we're meant to come back together. A cataclysmic force reunited. Or unfinished business." She just stares at me like I've sprung two heads and I'm painfully aware I'm still sticking out of my jeans. Hastily, I tuck myself in. "Listen, I'm not opposed to discovering what this is. Are you using my body to prove something ... to yourself or to me?" She opens her mouth to interrupt me, but I continue. "I don't care if that's what this is. I just don't want you to regret anything." I already regret not calling her, but I had my reasons, and once again, the timing isn't right to explain myself.

"I'm not using you," she says a bit sharply. "What about you? Are you trying to make up for something? Unfinished business, like you said." The ache in my stomach grows. That isn't what I meant.

"I'm not trying to do anything other than get to know you better. I very much like you as well. I want to know more of you ... who you are, what you like, where we'll go next."

Her mouth pops open but I cover her lips with two fingers.

"Don't give up yet, sweetheart." My fingers stroke back her hair and then gently tug, forcing her to meet my eyes. "I'm stuck on you."

Her eyes widen. "In my hair again?" She tries to twist thinking we're back to jewelry malfunction, but I hold her head in place, keeping her focused on my eyes.

"No, Naomi. Me. *I'm* stuck on you."

Her expression softens and her lips twitch as she fights a smile.

"You've put a spell on me, and I don't want it broken." *Ever*, I think, but I can't tell her that yet. My mouth comes to hers, the whisper of her name imprinted on my lips. What if I'm stuck on her until I get it right with the universe? But I find I don't seem to mind. I don't want to be stuck anywhere else.

"Ready for the not-official-date ice cream I promised earlier?"

"I could use a vanilla swirl dip," she teases, her mood lightening, as she has no idea how much I'd like to dip her in a little vanilla swirl.

On Saturday night, I pick Naomi up at her house, and I'm a bundle of nerves. When I surprised her on Thursday at the poetry reading, I never expected the surprises she gave me in return. Allowing me to touch her. Her fingers touching me. I'm still on a high from the experience when I knock on her front door.

When she opens the door, her smile takes my breath away, but in her hands is a pile of fur.

"What the heck is that?" I chuckle as she steps back and allows me in.

"This is Dewey," she says, purring at the pile in her palm. "He's a hedgehog."

"Dewey?" I question.

"As is in the Dewey Decimal Classification." Her head pops up, widening in pleasure at the reference. "He looks like a decimal point when he balls up."

"Library humor?" I tease and she chuckles as she strokes his underbelly. He doesn't look very cuddly but he's cute. "Is he legal?"

"In most states." She holds him higher to bring him eye level.

"In Tennessee?"

She shrugs in response. "I suppose I should have a better therapy pet, but he was too cute to pass up when I was in Louisville at a library convention."

"What about a cat?" I can't help myself, and I scan the floor looking for additional animals.

"Witch humor?" she snarks. "I suppose a cat would be stereotypical, even more so as a librarian, but I don't like cats. I wanted a sea otter but there aren't any saltwater reservoirs in the mountains, and I read they are actually mean creatures." She makes her statement so matter of fact, I laugh.

"You look beautiful, by the way." She does. Her hair is in a fancy braid again and her dress is short and black. She doesn't wear tights tonight but knee-high black boots, hinting at skin on her thighs. I wonder what she'd look like naked and I'm ready to skip dinner to find out, but I promised three dates, and this is officially date two. Dinner. Dancing. Maybe some pseudo-cavorting.

I've been inside her house before, when I picked her up for date one, but I take a moment to look around her place while I wait for her to return the hedgehog to a cage upstairs. The front room has a small couch, an overstuffed chair with a matching ottoman, and a large rocking chair in a corner. Her furnishings are primarily blue, including the rocking chair. Stacks of books rest next to the couch as does a basket with balls of yarn. A braided rug over light-gray hardwood floors centers the room, giving the space a French cottage feel.

"Bill Monroe was right. This place is like a gingerbread house." I say to her when she returns downstairs. I'm a large man and I feel like I'm taking up a lot of space in this quaint room. "I like it. It suits you."

"Thank you."

I reach for her long coat and she gives me her back to help her slip it on. I lift the thick braid and free it from the coat, laying it over her shoulder.

"I love your hair." My voice lowers and I notice her shiver. I can't help myself and I kiss her neck which she tips to the side, allowing me more skin. "You offering me your neck like this will lead to us never leaving this room, which I'm not opposed to doing, but I promised you date number two."

She quickly spins to face me, embarrassed by my hint of wanting more. Those eyes stare up at me.

"Naomi, I'm warning you. You're doing that thing."

"What thing?"

"The lick-me eyes thing."

"Oh yes, remind me again what that is." She's teasing me, right? Is she flirting with me? I like this side of her.

"The look you give me, like you want to lick me or want me to lick you. I'm game either way, but I think we should have dinner first."

Her mouth pops open and it's even more tempting to consider what she could do with those lips.

"Yes, dinner," she says, breathless and wanton, and suddenly, I'm only hungry for her.

"Naomi," I groan. "You want special and meaningful and I want to give it to you." I choke on the words and then clarify. "You have to let me take you out on dates."

She nods like she understands but she still doesn't speak. I place a hand on her lower back and guide her to the door. No more licking discussion. Dinner.

Genie's is packed for a Saturday night, but we're able to secure a booth. The music is loud, and I don't want to have to shout so I sit next to her.

"What are you doing?" she asks, eyeing me as I settle in next to her.

"I don't want to I feel like I'm yelling at you, and I want to hold your hand." I reach for her fingers, which are gripping the skirt of her dress. Slipping my digits between hers, I lift her hand to my mouth and press a kiss to her knuckles before lowering our collective hands to my thigh. "Better."

I order a beer while Naomi gets a water.

"Do you never drink?" I ask, just curious about her.

"I will on Samhain and maybe Beltane."

My brows pinch as she tells me about the two holidays relating to Fall and Spring. It's fascinating to hear her explain her religion. My elbow rests on the table blocking out the rest of the crowd. I took her to a public place so I'd behave myself and yet my position makes me feel like we're the only two people in the room.

Her explanation is interrupted when a waitress comes to take our dinner order. I get a giant cheeseburger while she orders a salad. I don't want her to be one of those women—cautious and all *I'm fat*—on a date, but she quickly reassures me that she tries not to eat processed foods.

"Which is almost hypocritical of me, as I love a good brownie or cookie." Note to self, I decide.

When the waitress walks away, we talk a few minutes about the Bickerton build, as it's next to her home. Somehow this leads to the fact she didn't grow up in Green Valley, but Cedar Gap, and then she mentions a brother, who she hasn't spoken of before.

"He wasn't a bad person, just did bad things. Stole motorcycles for one thing, but then he took me on rides with him. It was very freeing."

My thumb reaches out for her lower lip, tracing over the sad smile she gives me. "I'd like to give you freeing experiences."

She surprises me by leaning forward, quickly kissing me. It's short and sweet, but it grounds me. My eyes remain closed a second longer as she pulls back.

"I like to think you are," she whispers.

"Just make sure I'm the only one," I tease but I'm totally serious. I don't want her with other guys. I want to be the only one.

The food arrives and I order a second beer. We continue our casual talk while we eat, chatting as we have many nights the past week on the phone. When a slow song comes on, I ask her to dance. I slip out of the booth, tugging on her hand still linked with mine.

"Just follow my lead," I assure her. I just want to hold her, but her eyes look so hesitant, so panicked. I'm about to give up when Jackson James stops at the table. Jackson is a deputy sheriff, working under his father who is the sheriff. His dad is a decent man while Jackson can be a bit of a pain in the ass.

"Miss Winters, you doing all right this evening?" Jackson hitches his waistband as if he's wearing his uniform instead of regular blue jeans. There's something in his tone that disconcerts me, and my eyes jump to Naomi's, which have switched from frantic to paranoid.

"Why wouldn't she be all right?" I ask defensively, shifting my gaze from Naomi to Jackson. He's younger and shorter than me, yet he straightens as if to exert authority. He clearly knows something I don't, and the protective hackles rise on the back of my neck.

"Just checking in after the other night." Jackson winks at Naomi, insinuating something I don't like. I drop Naomi's hand and swivel my head to look at her.

"What's he talking about?"

"In her yard the other night." My eyes narrow at Jackson's vagueness, remaining on Naomi, who lowers her face.

"Something you want to tell me, Nae?" The nickname mixed with the accusation could be insulting but the jealousy in my head is near exploding. Does she have a thing for Jackson? I know some women like a man in a uniform.

"Not really," she says, her voice dropping as she avoids my icy glare.

"Want to clarify what the hell you're talking about?" I address Jackson.

"The fire. Just want to make certain everything was taken care of."

"What fire?" I turn back to Naomi feeling like a pinball wacked around in a machine.

"Um …" She glances at Jackson, but he interjects. "The one set in her yard. Don't you worry, Miss Winters, we'll continue to do our drive-bys until we catch whoever did it."

"What the …" I swing my attention from Naomi to Jackson, dismissing him by saying, "Thanks for checking on her, Jackson."

"Deputy James," Jackson corrects me, and I tip my chin to acknowledge the title before I decide to punch him. Blindly, I reach into my jeans for my wallet, drop some bills on the table, and pick up our coats. I'm too worked up to address this issue in front of half of Green Valley, and Naomi doesn't speak as she follows me out of the bar.

A fire? In her yard? What the hell? Who the hell?

Without a word, I open the driver's door to my truck and help her up, then I slip in after her, forcing her to the center of the bench seat.

"Naomi, why didn't you tell me this happened?"

"It's nothing," she lies, and the vibration rolling off me tells her she needs to start talking. "When I got home on Thursday evening the fire was in my driveway," she explains but the shake to her voice tells me she knows it's something.

"Why didn't you call me?"

"I didn't think it was a big deal."

Her nonchalance bothers me, and I exhale, dragging both hands down my face. Dangling one wrist over the steering wheel, I drape my other arm over the seat.

"Naomi, I like you. We've established this, so I worry about you. You're free to be who you want to be, but I don't like you dismissing this as if it's nothing but kid's playing around. As if it's even okay. I think Dwight is up to something, and I don't like it. At least you called the sheriff this time," I huff.

"Actually, I called the fire department as I couldn't get the fire out with just my kitchen extinguisher. Jackson arrived as well."

"Naomi," I groan, reaching for a twist of her hair and curling it around my finger.

"Don't you think Dwight might be a little old to set Halloween decorations on fire?" she mocks. "It was probably just some kids."

I'm not satisfied with this answer. "What do you mean?"

"It was one of those witches that look like they flew into a tree ..." Her voice drifts as I stare at her. She doesn't have anything like that in her yard which means it was purposefully brought to her home and set on fire. I hate that this happened to her, and I hate that it might be my fault.

"Regardless, Dwight's not too old to threaten you. He's a dick like that."

Silence fills the truck, weighing thicker than the mountain mist around us.

"Come here," I quietly command, slipping my arm from the back of the seat around her shoulders and tugging her into my chest. "I'm glad you called the fire department. Hell, I'm even glad that dweeb Jackson came to your rescue. For a moment there, I thought something else happened with him. But most of all, I'm glad you're safe."

"What could possibly happen with Jackson?" She scoffs into my chest, ignorant to the fact Jackson could be attracted to her. She pulls back but I don't release her.

"Like you getting with Jackson. Shithead made it sound like that for a minute there."

Naomi chuckles harder. "Be serious, Nathan. He's too young for me."

"Well, some guys go for older women. Obviously, you have a track record of this," I suggest, implying Dwight's youthful obsession. "And the way Jack*shit* was looking at you—"

"That's just Jackson."

"I don't like it."

"Are you jealous?" she asks, incredulous.

"Damn straight I am. You're my girl, Naomi, and I don't want anyone thinking they can have you." I sound like a caveman calling her *mine* and *girl* and making demands, but dammit I don't want her with someone else.

"Does this mean we're going steady?" She teases.

"This means we have one more date before decision time and I need to take you somewhere to show you why you should consider more dates after number three." My mouth presses into hers, passing all my energy into her lips beneath mine. Her hand cups the back of my head, combing at the hairs on the nape of my neck and my spine shivers with the tender touch. The heat of her lips matches mine, and if I don't get us out of this parking lot in another half-second, I'm going to have her on her back in the front seat.

Then I decide to kiss her a little longer and remember that this was how all the trouble for me started in the first place. *One more kiss.*

CHAPTER EIGHTEEN

DEWEY DECIMAL CLASSIFICATION: 152.5
PHYSIOLOGICAL DRIVES

[Naomi]

"I don't want to take you home yet," he says breaking off the vanilla swirl melting kiss.

"We could go to my house and you could come inside for a bit?" The invitation rushes out before I realize what I'm saying, although I shouldn't be surprised. Before Nathan knocked on my door earlier tonight, I was a hot mess imagining him without clothing. He is the horned god to my inner goddess, which might be another reason I've held out so long with other men. I've been waiting for him.

Nathan starts his truck engine and my mind roars to life. I don't have coffee. I don't even have alcohol other than a bottle of wine which I am saving for Samhain. I don't know what I'm going to do with him, but I also know I can't deny myself any longer. Despite us not talking while he drives, I hear his voice in my head. The seductive timbre even when he isn't trying to seduce me. His laughter, hearty and rich, when he thinks I'm being funny and I'm actually serious. His lips still linger on mine after our kiss—kisses telling me he wants me. *Me*. And when he puts his hands on me—strong, warm, comforting—

and brings me pleasure I've never known, I don't want anyone but him.

He wants to know me, and it's been so long since someone tried to understand who I am, how I feel. I'm practically a virgin, and I know that makes me different, unique even. If I can't convince myself to take the next step with Nathan, I'll be a forty-year-old-virgin cliché. However, Nathan is lowering my guard and I'm *so* close to rewriting my story.

Everything sounds louder in my ears as we pull into my driveway. The gravel under the tires. The evening rustle of leaves. The racing of my heart. Suddenly, I'm not as confident as I was on the ride home. *What am I doing?* I exhale as my fingers curl around the passenger door handle.

Freeing the inner goddess, my inner goddess whispers. *You can do this.*

I nearly jump out of my skin when knuckles rap on my closed window.

"Coming out?" Nathan teases and I nervously chuckle as he opens the door for me. I lead him up the flagstone path to my front door. Shaky fingers place my key in the lock and twist, and I press open the door. Stepping forward, I release another deep breath.

"Come inside?" I question when I turn to face Nathan, and a cautious grin graces his face. He steps over the threshold and closes the door himself. With the soft click of the latch, my heart realizes, *This is it.*

Nathan looks like a giant in my small-scale home and I watch him remove his leather jacket as I unbutton my coat. Hanging it on a peg near the door, I offer to take his. When I hang it next to mine, I take a moment to stare at the combination of our outerwear.

The wait is over. Did he mean what he said that night after the Canyon?

When I turn around, Nathan has helped himself to the couch.

"Would you like something to drink? I don't have any beer. But I—"

"Come sit next to me," Nathan pats the cushion beside him. Sitting there would be a very bad idea, but the goddess inside wants comfort, and Nathan's nearness provides it. I step around him and settle on the seat, which is not made for such a big man. He sits forward, elbows on his knees, and I awkwardly press at the skirt of my dress. The room feels too small with him in it. The lights are too bright. I like all my lamps. As I told him, it makes me feel welcome when I come home at night, but right now it's too much.

"Can you give me a second?" I ask, nerves catching up to me as I stand and quickly excuse myself. I walk into my kitchen and fall against the wall hiding me from his sight. My head tips back on the plaster.

I have no idea what I'm doing with a man like him.

His intense eyes. His thick hands. His dimpled smile.

I wonder once again what he'd look like naked as the man he is now.

The thought makes me wonder what I'm doing hiding out in my kitchen.

I press off the wall, shake out my fingers, and then stroke down my braid. I circle back into the living room, and the first thing I notice is most of the lights have been turned off. The space suddenly has a subtle romantic ambiance. Then I notice Nathan holding a video case in his hand as he stands in the middle of the room.

"What's this?" he asks.

Vilma's Discovery Videos.

I don't need to see the cover to know which one he reads. A pink petalled flower and two fingers making a V around the floral photograph. This one is *Vilma's Vagina Video.*

"It's a DVD," I state the obvious, an anxious chuckle in my throat as my fingers twist together and my face heats. I stand across the room from him. Sweet Goddess, he's going to think I'm a pervert.

"Looks like a VDV, actually," he mutters. "Or better yet a VVV." I shouldn't laugh, but a nervous giggle escapes. He's trying to add humor to an awkward situation and his face lifts to look at me. "A triple V?" he questions, raising a brow.

I step forward and reach out for the video, but he lifts it above his head. As if I'm not already embarrassed enough, I jump up like I can rip it from his fingers, but I land on his foot, slipping off his boot. As my hands reach for anything to catch me from completely tumbling to the floor, they slide down his cotton-covered chest and my wrist hits his belt. I curl my fingers inward and latch onto his waistband. He wraps one strong arm around my back and holds me pressed to his abdomen. I bury my forehead against his firm upper chest as he begins to read the box aloud.

"Discover how you are the center of your own universe. Self-guided video instruction on the art of finding pleasure within your-self." Even though my fingers are tucked into the edge of his pants, I don't release him, afraid I'll melt on the spot. I'm going to expire from embarrassment, even though Vilma professes there is nothing to be ashamed of. It's personal discovery and pleasure seeking.

"Do you use these often?" His voice deepens, ashen and rough.

Sometimes.

Too often lately.

Because of him.

"Diane Donner-Sylvester gave them to me."

"Who?"

"Never mind." It's too complicated to explain Diane's story.

"Hey," he murmurs, slipping his fingers along the length of my braid to curl around his fist. He gently tugs my head back, so I'm forced to look up at him. "Tell me about this."

My face heats again even though I didn't think I could get any redder. I'm certain I'm more than cherry red, which has me thinking about cherries as a body part and not a fruity delicacy.

Could the earth just open and swallow me whole, please?

"I ... I mentioned how I haven't ... you know...but I don't deny ... I mean, obviously, I've done things ... to myself."

"So alone is good. With a man equals disaster." Nathan's voice remains light, teasing, controlled. I remind myself he wants to under-stand me. He blinks. I swallow. "You still haven't told me what the disaster was?"

Mentioning my brother would end this night.

I tug back to release his hold on my neck, but his fingers tighten, giving me a subtle yank. I should find it forceful, domineering, threatening, but I don't. I like it. My eyes close and I lick my lips. When I open again, the gray of Nathan's eyes has shifted to fiery steel.

"Naomi Winters, when you're giving me those eyes, I find I have discovery plans of my own." I close my eyes but Nathan squeezes at my neck. "Don't hide from me, Nae." His voice dips as it softens.

"I think we should test the theory, though, about disaster and being with me."

His fingers release the braid, stroking down it until he reaches the tip which he strategically places over my breast. Then his mouth collides with mine, drinking in my embarrassment. His eager lips make me forget my fears. *This is Nathan.* We stand for several seconds, lips tracing lips, tongue finding tongue, until my body shifts. I pull back in hopes of leading him to the couch when I realize I can't move my wrist.

My garnet spessartine bracelet is caught on something.

"I'm stuck on you," I mutter, mortified at another jewelry malfunction, but Nathan chuckles, the deep sound near my ear.

"I'm stuck on you too, sweetheart." He reaches for the bracelet and rubs his fingers over the beads. "I noticed this the other night. Is it something special?"

Sexual courage? "Our bodies have something called the seven chakras. It's popular in yoga. These beads, crystals actually, are known to help open the sacral chakra."

Nathan swallows as if he knows what I'm saying but then he asks, "What's a sacral chakra?"

"Sexual health." My voice is so low I'm not certain Nathan hears me but then he tugs at my wrist and the bracelet explodes, sending beads raining to the floor. I'm not as upset about the broken bracelet as I'm surprised at the fireworks of orange crystals around us.

"Now there's sacral chakra all around us." He isn't exactly correct, but my heart races in my chest at the innuendo. My sexual energy is definitely open to him. He pauses a moment, rubbing his other hand up and down my spine in a soothing motion. "Want me to clean that up?"

"Not yet," I say and step away from him to guide him to the couch. I expect him to sit next to me but instead, he kneels before me, pushing a small table out of his way.

He separates my legs with the bulk of his body, his forearms on either side of my thighs while his hands wrap around my hips.

"Let me discover you, Naomi." He leans forward for a soft kiss, telling me he wants me with his lips, but also telling me I'm safe with him. He'll take care of me. At least, he'll take care of my sacral chakra. He slips to the corner of my mouth and then lowers to my jaw before skimming down my neck for my shoulder. *Right there*, I think. If he nips me right near my clavicle, I'm going to explode for him like my bracelet. Nathan does not disappoint. The tender bite releases a groan-gasp and my legs tremble.

His hands make quick work of pressing the hem of my dress upward and slipping his warm palms under the material, exposing more leg to him. More skin.

"You're not wearing tights tonight?" He mutters as we both watch his hands massage my outer thighs, curling around the muscle until his thumbs press on the inner part and force me to spread open a little wider. "Did you do that on purpose?"

My face heats, mortified at being caught. Was it wishful thinking that he'd touch me again if I didn't wear them? Unconscious dressing? *I think not.* My inner goddess might have had a plan. A hope. A wish.

Nathan pulls back, his eyes searching my face. "You can stop me at any point, but when you give me those eyes ..." His voice settles in a deep appreciative rumble.

"Lick-me ... eyes." My throat clogs, separating the words when I swallow the nervous lump in my throat. A wicked grin curls Nathan's lips as his fingers finish their upward journey. His eyes watch mine as his knuckles rub against the cotton over my core.

What is he doing to me? My heart races. My sex pulses, and yet I know the answer. He's going to touch me in a way I haven't been touched. Discover me in a way I can't discover alone. Spread as I am, I can't shy away from him unless I tell him to stop.

I won't stop him.

"You doing okay?" he asks, heat in his question. When I nod, his fingers reach for the side of my underwear and he tugs, drawing the material down my thighs, slipping over my knees to my ankles. I'm still wearing my boots, and he stretches the cotton to be free of me.

Am I really going to let him do this?

He lowers a little and rubs his nose inside my leg, pushing my dress upward.

"You smell delicious. Honey and almonds." His voice holds its own drip of honey. He's naughty and sweet mixed together. A decadent treat. "Wonder if you taste as sweet."

Is he going to ...

His face goes between my thighs and he inhales once more, his nose dragging across my core. My dress is bunched up to my hips and he draws back. His eyes focus on mine once again, judging my comfort with this position, asking my permission. He leans up to kiss my lips one more time before lowering between my thighs.

Sweet Goddess.

The air whooshes out of me as his tongue licks my seam. My hips buck up at the tender touch, but his hands quickly pin me to the cushions.

"Relax, sweetheart. Your videos can't teach you this kind of pleasure. Please allow me to be the instructor."

Mother Earth, I volunteer as a student experiment. Words escape me. I nod because I can't say anything else. He's correct. The pleasure he's offering is something I haven't experienced in a long, long, *long* time ... and I want it.

A lick. A lap. A kiss. I've never felt anything like this, and I melt under his tongue. My fingers hesitantly come to his hair and I comb the short locks with my fingertips. He moans against me, the vibration traveling upward and inward, and my head falls back. Nothing I have ever done by myself compares to this pleasure. No video could teach me such things.

"Nathan," I whimper, recognizing the flutters in my lower belly and yet not altogether familiar with the growing sensation. Like a swirling tornado, twisting and twirling, collecting fragments of me and tugging them together until I tingle from my toes to the tip of my head, sensation whirls through me, until I groan his name in wonder. I fold forward, releasing the cyclone of all orgasms.

My hands clamp over his ears, willing him to stop but he continues, sucking every last spiraling drop from me before slowly pulling back and kissing my inner thigh. I collapse back to the cushions as he rests on his ankles. Slowly, my eyelids lift, and I find him watching me.

"I'm so stuck on you," he whispers, a slow, satisfied smile curling his wet lips.

"What does that even mean?" I ask.

"For now, it's my way of saying how I feel about you. I'm stuck and I don't want to be unstuck."

CHAPTER NINETEEN

DEWEY DECIMAL CLASSIFICATION: 612.4
SECRETIONS, EXCRETIONS, RELATED
FUNCTIONS

[Nathan]

I f I thought her lick-me eyes were intriguing, nothing can explain the look she gives me after my explanation of being stuck. She leans forward and within seconds, I'm on my back.

"Oof." The air whooshes out of me as she falls over me and my spine hits the thin rug-covered floor.

"Did I hurt you?" Her voice is both eager and concerned as she pops up, pressing on my chest with an elbow that's digging into my sternum.

"No, but whatcha doing, sweetheart?" I ask, straining as her thin elbow digs into the hard bone in the center of my chest. She slips her arm off me and settles each hand on either side of my biceps, pressing herself upward. It takes effort to raise my hand and stroke up her lower back, and I need a second to catch my breath. This is what she does to me. She knocks the wind out of me, taking my breath away.

With that innocent, anxious look she's giving me.

With that intricate, sexy braid dangling down to tease me.

With the collection of orange beads under my back.

I shift a little, hoping to release a few of them from the pressure points below my shoulder blade and beneath my lower spine.

"Sweet Goddess," she mutters. "I'm so bad at this." She attempts to sit up but my hand on her back keeps her in place. Her legs fall between mine. I don't know what her plan is, but I don't want her to move yet.

"Where you going?" I ask, a weak chuckle as my breath slowly comes back to me. Then I choke as air whirls out of me again. She's at my belt buckle, hastily unbuckling. My head lifts and her fingers shake as she lowers my zipper. "Goddess?" This lifts her head but does not stop her intention. Her fingers dip into the sides of my jeans.

"Please don't deny me, Nathan." She's practically begging me, her eyes filling with a question, as if I'd tell her no. She can have anything she wants from me. My body. My heart. My soul.

When she tugs at the sides of my pants, I lift my hips, aiding her. Still, I worry she's moving too fast.

"Naomi, whatcha doing?" I ask again, concerned for her while my dick curses me to shut up.

"I want to do this. I want to discover you, too. You make me bold, even though I know I'll be bad."

Sweet goddess or any other deity that wants to listen, when she says those words to me, she has no idea. I want her to be bad with me in a million ways although I know she's too good. Inside, she's still so innocent, but when her fingers wrap about my stiff shaft and then the tip of her hesitant tongue swipes over the smooth head, I fall back, surrendering to her. She can be as bad as she wants with me.

Her mouth opens and she draws me in, taking her time to experiment. The slow pace makes my leg shake and invisible fingers tickle up my spine. Eventually, she lowers, taking me deeper. My fingers find the thick braid hanging over her shoulder and I stroke the intricate design. Her head bops, her cheeks hollow and she grips the part of me which won't fit in her mouth. My eyes roll back in my head. If she thinks she doesn't know what she's doing, she's wrong. *So wrong.* Then she draws back.

"It's messier than I remember."

Sweetmothertruckercheeseontoastbuckler. "Be messy," I whisper-choke with a desperate chuckle. Her mouth returns to me, sucking with more vigor. Her tongue swirls, licking up the side before swallowing me in again. My fingers turn to a fist on her braid, holding myself in place.

Let her lead, Nathan, I warn myself as my hips want to thrust upward, seeing how far she can take me. When she surprises me, and swallows me to the back of her throat, I groan out a warning. We should have talked about this first.

"Naomi, you don't have to—"

Her free hand comes to my lower abs, drawing her short nails down my skin. I buck upward under the tickling sensation, and just when I think I'm going to lose her, she redoubles her efforts. I'm taken to the back of her throat again, and my body unleashes.

Christdrivingatractor. She holds onto me, drinking me in. My eyes roll back again as my lower spine tingles until I can't take it anymore and I'm empty. My hands come to either side of her head and I gently push her upward. She releases me with a sloppy pop. Sitting up, her lips are wet and swollen, and my brows pinch. Sheepishly, she grins down at me.

"That was very bold of you," I tell her, hoping she'll understand I'm proud of her for taking what she wanted from me.

"It's easy with you," she tells me, and I understand better what *I'm stuck on you* really means to me. I'm falling for this woman. Falling hard. The universe and its energy be damned if it tries to take me from her again.

"Can you kiss me after what we did?" The comment surprises me and I cup her cheeks.

"I'll do anything you ever ask." And then I kiss her to let her know I mean every word.

As I'm leaving her house later in the evening, still on a high from what we did, I hear voices through the thin brush and bramble hedges between Naomi's home and the Bickerton build. The night silence and the foliage-thinned trunks carry the voices subtly to her yard. I pause in my tracks, drawing closer to the rough male tones.

"You sure we won't get caught?"

"Naw, my pop don't pay attention to me other than to smack me around. He'll never know it's us." The second voice sounds too familiar and the hairs on the back of my neck rise. "Besides, no one checks this place at night. It's the perfect spot."

I lower behind the thin saplings, hoping the darkness hides me while I creep closer to the voices.

The wolf returns.

"What about that woman next door?"

"The witch? She's too busy brewing potions or casting spells to hear us." Sickened, I straighten knowing they refer to Naomi without understanding a thing about her. She's not brewing or chanting, but I bristle further with the realization that they know she lives next door.

"You think we can pull this off?" the first voice questions again, sounding too young, too uncertain of whatever mission is planned. The shape of both males is more man than boy, but the tenor of their voices gives away their youth. "I don't trust the deputy. He keeps driving by."

"He only passes once. Quit your worryin'." The second voice scoffs and the guffaw tips me off. Junior Henderson.

Ready to stalk through the bushes and give those boys a piece of my mind before kicking them off the private property, I'm stopped by the sound of approaching motorcycles. I stiffen as I watch two bikes pull into the drive. The gravel softly crunches and then the bikes die. I don't have to see him to recognize the outline of a man I once knew well. Catfish hikes off his bike and walks heavily to the boys, not an ounce of stealth in his steps.

"Boys," he addresses them.

"Men," Junior corrects.

A deep, smoky laugh follows the correction and I notice Dirty Dave still perched on his bike.

"Whatcha got?" Catfish asks and I squint in the darkness, as something passes from one hand to the other. Drugs? A gun? Cash? It's too hard to tell, but whatever it is, is most likely not legal. After a brief inspection from Catfish, he pockets the treasure and speaks again. "How you doing on that other thing?"

I recognize this tactic. As if by keeping their words vague, it lessens the seriousness of whatever illegal action is planned.

"Still working on it," Junior replies, standing taller against a man twice his size. I can't even surmise what Catfish would want with two seventeen-year-olds, but knowing we patched in at roughly the same age, I can only imagine none of it is good.

"And the girl?" Catfish asks, and my breath catches.

"Won't be an issue." Junior pauses. "What about the wolf?"

"He's not your concern." There's an edge to Catfish's response and I wonder what he's got planned for me. "I'm damn proud of you," he adds, lowering his tone to prove his point. The depth of Catfish's words is not lost on me. Pride was something he desperately wanted as a young man after his parent's death and he was forced to live with his miserable uncle. Recognizing Curtis as easy prey, the club provided the admiration. I don't know Junior's story, but from what I just heard, Dwight smacking around his kid doesn't sit well with me. Junior Henderson's story could too easily match Curtis Hickson's history and that worries me for the younger man.

I'm roused by a heavy smack of leather as Catfish claps a hand on Junior's shoulder.

Don't shuck it off, kid, I mutter in my thoughts. If his dad roughs him up, he'll hate that touch, but if he wants Catfish's approval, he'll hold firm. For a moment, I'm that kid, desperate to belong to a group, to find approval, and I'm propelled back to the things I did to be a part of the Iron Wraiths. Theft. Deals. Alliances. It was all only a stepping-stone to something larger and something I'd never considered. Taking a man's life was never my plan. I shiver with the memory, crossing my arms as I watch Catfish return to his bike, the roar of his engine cracking open the night like an ax splitting wood. My eyes trail after the retreat of Catfish and Dirty Dave, drifting down the switchback road, and then quickly I return my attention to the two teens.

"You're gonna be one of them soon," the first boy says with excitement to Junior, clapping him on the back.

"Don't touch me," Junior warns, shrugging off the enthusiastic smack. *Ah, there he is.* The tough guy holding it together under pressure around a bigger man and then exerting his authority over a lesser one. He'll make a good Wraith one day and my chest aches for the future of a kid I really don't know.

As the two disappear behind the opposite side of the construction site, I wait until a car appears, slowly coasting down the gravel drive. It appears they want to remain invisible as best they can, keeping the lights off until they hit the road. Headlights flicker to life a few feet away from the drive, and then they pick up speed, blending into the night. I shake my head and turn to look back at Naomi's dim house.

Should have hung out at the library, kid. Maybe reading a book would've prevented him from wanting to deal shit.

CHAPTER TWENTY

DEWEY DECIMAL CLASSIFICATION: 127
THE UNCONSCIOUS AND THE
SUBCONSCIOUS

[Nathan]

Our next date is the official number three, although I don't know why we're counting any longer. Unfortunately, we can't get together until Saturday and strangely, I miss her all week. After the interchange I witnessed at the construction site, I'll feel better once Naomi and I spend more time together. Saturday is one of those lingering Indian summer afternoons with a last shot of warm sunshine before fall truly sets in and winter arrives. Seeing as Naomi loves trees, I thought she might like a trek through the woods. I'll appreciate the hike as long as it's daylight. Cooper Road Trail is off the beaten track, and I want something unique for our final date, because I don't want it to be final. I'm hoping date three is *the* date.

"Each tree has meaning," she states as we begin our short hike. She's jabbering about pines and hazelnuts, and it makes me smile how she's so animated about each tree, like they are old friends.

"Recognizing our purpose within Nature and how it is connected to us, is one of my favorite things about being a Wiccan. Trees. Flowers. Herbs. It's all part of something bigger."

Naomi isn't like any woman I've known with her philosophies on life and her being one-with-nature-ness, but I enjoy the difference. There is a lightness to her steps as she admires each solid oak and river birch we pass. Her hands fondly touch trunks as she explains the deeper purpose behind the wood. As we walk, she gathers the biggest leaves fallen to the forest floor, making a brightly colored fall bouquet. A real inner peace seems to surround her today, and I'm hopeful she can finally release the certainty that doom-and-gloom will follow us being together. Nothing major has happened to her since the last orgasm and while it might seem silly to keep track, I'm counting the orgasms as proof her vagina doesn't rule the universe.

I can't believe I'm thinking these things.

Eventually, I chuckle. "I've never known anyone like you."

"You're laughing at me," she teases, but something shuts down in her eyes.

"No. I'm delighted by you. You see things so differently. It's like you belong here among these trees. I wish I had a place that made me feel so ... calm. So peaceful." I'd had another blowout with Dahlia. She wants to attend a Halloween party some three towns over.

"You never let me do anything," she screamed.

"I let you do plenty of things. Go to school. Live in my house."

"Gah, I can't wait until I move out. Lexie and I are already looking for apartments."

Heaven help me. I don't need her falling into the wrong crowd, and I have no idea who this Lexie person is. Somedays, I think I'm not going to survive her seventeenth year. Dahlia's rebellion makes me think of Junior and his choices. The exchange I saw still haunts me. I have no idea how to save him from a decision that could change his life forever.

"What about building? Creating something with your hands? Doesn't that bring you a sense of accomplishment? I would think completing a project and seeing a job well done would bring a certain satisfaction."

I snort. "Not exactly. Especially not when I'm correcting the mistakes of others." Dwight comes to mind, but then I think about what she says. At the end of a project, with a build finished, it does feel like I've created something—someplace special.

"I guess I never thought about it," I admit after a moment.

"When you build someone a house, the wood has purpose. It will provide comfort and warmth and love inside the walls you created."

A place where someone will be waiting.

When we find a spot near a stream, I spread out a blanket I keep in the truck and we settle on the ground for sandwiches. I'm not really a gourmet cook, but I've perfected the art of sandwich making. The sandwich roll can't be too thick. It's the meat layered in curls, plus cheese, that makes the flavor. I prefer an oil-and-vinegar spread with extra pepper sprinkled on mine. I confirmed with Naomi her preference and had to swallow back my comments when she asked for only veggies.

"I try not to eat processed meats and cheeses." But she'll eat a doughnut?

She's worn a dress again with another pair of thick leggings. Sitting cross-legged, she spreads her dress to cover her legs. Now that we've sat, she seems fidgety. Her fingers twist and untwist within her skirt.

"You okay?"

"I have something for you."

I stare at her in wonder. "You brought me a gift?"

"Well, I don't know if I'd go that far," she states, shrugging and blushing. "But this is date number three ..."

Does she think we're over? I thought bringing her to this place would be the perfect time to discuss what's next—*us.*

"The number is not relative at this point, Goddess," I softly warn, my voice low as I scoot toward her and lift a knee, draping my arm over it. "What do you have for me?"

My voice drips with innuendo, and she chuckles before pulling something from her pocket. In the palm of her hand is a bead bracelet and I stare at the masculine combination of browns, greens, and copper.

"It's called a gratitude bracelet. The wood beads connect you to nature and the copper is a metal. It's a conductor making the beads work together. The green-toned beads are rhyolite which connects you to the life force in nature, giving joy, and the cream-colored beads are picture jasper which keeps you grounded and reminds you to love." Her voice falters on the last word and her eyes return to her lap. I stare in wonder until she looks up again.

"You think it's silly, don't you?" she asks, lowering the bracelet. "I just thought it looked manly. It reminded me of you, and I thought you could use the energy—"

She abruptly stops when my palm covers her cheek. I lean forward and kiss her, drawing her mouth into mine, tugging and teasing until she opens wider, allowing my tongue to search for hers. Her hand comes to the side of my head, curling around the back as the kiss deepens. My fingers delve into her hair, twisting a fistful to turn her head and allow me better access to her mouth before I slowly draw back from her and reach for the bracelet clutched in her hand.

"This *is* a gift, and I'm honored." My insides feel strange, warm and ripple-y. She gave me something. Something which reminds her of me, and yet the entire collection will make me think of her—her love of nature, her groundedness, and her energy force. I'm not opposed to male accessories. I wear leather straps and the occasional silver rings, so I easily slip it on my wrist and admire the colorful combination of wood tones and copper beads. "This might be one of the most thoughtful gifts I've ever received. Thank you." It's a gratitude bracelet and I'm thankful for her, thankful for the second chance with her.

I hold up my wrist to show her how it fits, and she surprises me again by leaning forward and kissing my pulse point. "Thank you," she mouths, and with her eyes locked on mine, she kisses me there again, only this time she opens her mouth, sucking at my skin a second. My breath catches as I watch her. Then she does it again, adding the tip of her tongue to draw along the vein under sensitive skin.

"Naomi," I groan, cupping her face with both my hands and crushing her mouth with mine. I can't get enough of this woman and each time she surprises me … I'm surprised. She's unexpected, just like the first time we met.

"I'm stuck on you," I say, looking deeply into her eyes for a moment. While I want to take her on the blanket, underneath her beloved trees, I also want to spend time with her on this beautiful day, so I pull back and tug at her necklace, the one I never see her without.

"Explain this to me," I ask, holding the black crystal in my palm.

"It's a black tourmaline," she explains, scooping the gem into her own. "It's a protection crystal to cleanse the negative and soothe anxiety. My sister gave it to me, which is a bit surprising."

"Is it magical?" I ask. I'm curious. She's really into this stuff and I want to understand.

"Not exactly. It's more a mindset. I believe in these things," she says with conviction.

"That's cool." I smile with a nod and offer her a sandwich. Scooting back just a little bit, I fall back on one elbow and stretch out my legs. I take a bite of my mine and then ask another question.

"Speaking of mindsets, you mentioned your family was ultra-religious. No offense, but what god says your sex life causes a catastrophe." I'm joking to lessen what I really want to know. "What happened?" It's a sensitive question but I'd like to know what caused her to believe her sexual relations could directly cause some travesty, particularly if connected to me.

Thankfully, she giggles, as she unwraps her sandwich. I don't want to insult her, but she hasn't mentioned being close to her parents, just their accusations. "The religion according to Winifred and Willard Winters."

"Whoa, that's a lot of *Ws*."

"That it is," she says, smiling good naturedly. "But seriously, my parents ran their own church and they were strict. No funny business. No dancing. No drinking. No cavorting."

"Cavorting." I snort.

"Of course, they cavorted at one point as there were four of us."

"Four?" *Right*, her brother. She hasn't mentioned him much.

"Scotia, Beverly, Jebediah, and then me. He was three years older than me." Her sandwich rests in her hands as she picks at the bun.

"Was?" I don't miss the past tense.

"He died when I was twenty-one. We were close." We sit in silence a moment. I've set my sandwich on the paper wrapper, waiting for her to tell me more. "The night I was at the Fugitive. The night we met. He was killed in a motorcycle accident."

A lump immediately forms in my throat. I think I stopped breathing. I don't move though my body screams for me to sit up.

"I was there for my birthday. I don't know if you remember that part."

You're giving me something sacred.

"Anyway, you kind of quickly disappeared after we ... you know ..." She waves between us. I bite the inside of my cheek. "So, I called my brother. He was so pissed off that I was at the Fugitive." She shrugs as a sheepish grin crosses her lips. Then, her voice lowers. "He had no business being on the Tail of the Dragon between Green Valley and the bar."

I'm all too familiar with the danger of that road.

"He crashed on his way to pick me up."

Fuck. Fuck. Fuckity-*fuck.*

I slowly press myself upward, my arms shaking from the effort. My sandwich feels like a brick in my stomach.

"When he didn't show up, I didn't know what to do. I didn't have anyone else to call, so I got a ride home from some guy. I didn't know what happened until later. Jebediah was declared dead at the scene of the accident. It's a bit of a mystery how it happened but considering the posted warnings about the danger of the Dragon, well ... Regardless, my parents blamed me."

Can't. Breathe.

"They demanded to know where I'd been. It was bad enough I came home on a motorcycle at three in the morning. They had just learned the news of their son. I confessed everything to them, and I mean *everything.* My father called me a sinner. My mother said Jebediah's death was on my conscience. I was going to hell for what I'd done."

She looks off to the trees and I'm relieved. I can't look her in the eyes. The pain I'll see. The swell of tears. The sting of her loss. A loss I know all too much about.

"I'm sorry," I offer, my voice cracking on the apology. The words are bile in my throat, weak and hopeless, like I feel in the moment. They aren't enough. Nothing will be enough.

"It's why I've been so hesitant with you." She shrugs and twists her lips as she looks back at me and the heartbreak in her eyes tears me up. "At twenty-one, I internalized the guilt they placed on me. I'd gone against God, my upbringing, and my parents and gave in to the greatest temptation of my life." She doesn't have to clarify. I was that temptation. The snake in the grass.

"I couldn't forgive myself and their blame hammered in the burden. Jebediah's death was because of me. I called him for a ride. He shouldn't have been on that road, at that time of night. His death was a reaction to an action I set forth. Of course, I didn't think like that at first. I only thought of myself as bad. *Very bad.* I lasted a week at home before I took off for Beverly's farm. I didn't have a plan. I didn't know where else to go. Then she told me about an opening at the library, and I just sort of stuck in Green Valley." She swipes at a solitary tear and her shoulders fall. She takes a deep breath. "That was probably more information than you wanted."

"No. I appreciate you telling me. I mean"—I blow out a breath —"that was a lot, and it sounds rough. I'm so sorry." What more can I offer her? She's going to hate me. I have so much to tell her and yet the words cling to my throat, refusing to leave. I don't know where to start because I know this will be the end of us.

The Tail of the Dragon. The road runs from the Fugitive to Cedar Gap. The reason I remember Naomi—it wasn't just because she was the girl who caused me to be late for the Iron Wraiths. It was the same night *I* caused an accident.

Two high-speed bikes coming at one another, both on a mission, in the blinding darkness. On that road, you can hear the screech of another biker, but you can't see him approaching. It's difficult to judge the distance between opposing drivers. With three-hundred plus swerves and dips, the road intermittently caught headlights and then they'd disappear behind rock formations jutting forward, hiding the next pass. *What surprise awaits ahead.* It's part of the thrill and the treachery.

I was running late.

He was coming toward me.

I had somewhere to be.

He veered into my lane.

Startling us both.

The skid of tires ripped through my ears. The sound of metal colliding against rock reminded me of breaking bones. The drone of a dying engine like a fading scream. The thump of a body against the blacktop like a final pulse.

I hardly kept my own bike upright, wobbling side to side. With a fear of losing control, I narrowed my focus.

And once righted, I didn't turn back.

Cedar Gap was in sight before my throbbing lungs finally refused to draw in any more air. I pulled off the Dragon into a little diner's parking lot just outside the small town. Shaky hands dug through my jacket to find my cell phone. Then I remembered—I'd left it on the bed, in a motel room, with a girl. My legs carried me without my knowledge to the counter inside the restaurant. I don't remember the waitress. I don't remember any other patrons, but I turned my back regardless as I dialed Catfish on a payphone in the corner. It was a miracle I recalled his number.

"You're late," Catfish snapped. I don't know how much time had passed since he called me. I was a prospect for the Iron Wraiths and that meant I was a slave to the whims of the club. Catfish wanted a drink, and although I'm certain he could have reached for a bottle not more than an arm's length away, it was up to me to jump when he said jump and pour when he said fill. Hanging out at the Fugitive had already made me more than an hour late. And then there was the girl. And the biker.

"I think I killed someone," I shakily whispered into the phone. I sounded like I'd run a marathon and my heart raced like I had as well. The phone shook against my chin and I patted my jacket for a cigarette. I didn't smoke

them, but I carried them just in case. Like I said, prospect meant bitch to the others for ninety days. I'd smoke the whole damn pack if it calmed my nerves.

"What happened?" Catfish barked. This would look bad on him if I didn't show in front of the others.

"I was on the Dragon." I took a shuddering breath. "Another bike."

"It happens all the time. That road is no shit. He'll need to hang his remains on the Tree of Shame." He laughed. I didn't. By remains, he meant the morbid parts of a broken motorcycle, collected and hung on a metallic structure, symbolizing a biker's shame for crashing along the road.

It was more than a broken bike, though.

"I think he's dead."

"How do you know?"

I didn't. I didn't check. I didn't turn back. I left him.

Oh God, I left him there on the dark, dangerous road.

"I have to go back," I muttered.

"Wolf, calm down," Catfish said, his voice lowering as if whispering to me. His tone turned soothing, reminding me he wasn't just my superior, he was my friend. He wanted to patch me in. Brothers for life. *I prospected because of him.*

"I need to call the sheriff," I added, my voice growing louder, cracking.

"No," Catfish snapped. "Absolutely not."

"I've got to go back," I repeated more firmly the second time. "I think I killed him."

It became a mantra. A bad one.

I killed him. I killed him.

"Stay there. We'll come to you."

"I'm going back," I said one more time.

"We'll get a cleaner. Don't do anything ra—"

Shaky fingers returned the phone to the cradle, cutting off his words.

I walked back to my bike, started the engine and turned back in the direction of the Fugitive. I took the curves and swerves at a slower speed, worried that I'd crash myself as my trembling arms struggled to keep the bike upright. My balance was lacking. My body too tense to move with the weight of metal under me.

I'd like to make excuses for what happened. The most dangerous curve at high speed. *The possibility of plummeting to death. A blind spot. But those were dangers that existed every inch of the road and the number one rule is stay in your lane.*

He hadn't.

Then I saw him.

His body angled in a way it shouldn't be.

"You stupid, fucking idiot," *I shouted, as if he could hear me.*

What were you thinking?

Stay in your lane.

I could only surmise I'd startled him as much as he'd startled me. In order to prevent a dip down the steep mountain drop, he collided with the rocks supporting the mountain instead.

"Don't be dead," *I whispered, although only the darkness could hear me. The road was eerily silent with only the trees and the rocks and the sharp drop to the valley below.*

I spun and vomited across the black street.

As the roll of my gut settled, the roar of engines filled my head. I didn't have time to think before I straightened and was blinded by two singular headlights. A truck pulled up behind them.

A cleaner. Dear God.

"Wolf," *Catfish called my name so sharply, as if to awaken me from a deep sleep. I wished I was dreaming. Someone tell me this is a nightmare. I stared into my friend's face, not really seeing him.*

"I killed him," *I said, my voice shaky and weak like a child who had broken a vase. Only I'd broken a man.*

"We've come to take care of things." *Another voice drifted to me, but I couldn't make out who it was. Repo? Darrell Winston? Dirty Dave?*

Would they kill me? The horrifying thought crossed my mind as another man walked past me for the body.

"Did you touch him?" *the disembodied voice spoke. I must have shaken my head.* "Good. We'll leave him then." *The comment spurred me to action. I stepped into Catfish's space.*

"I gotta call the sheriff," *I yelled, trying to focus on his face, forcing him to hear me.*

"You don't gotta do anything, Wolf. We leave him be. Get on your bike."

I turned back to the man sprawled on the street. He looked my age. Early twenties, no older.

What was he doing here so late?

Why was he racing in the dark?

What did he hope to prove being on this road alone?

Another thought slammed into me. What if he had a family? An older brother, like Toad, who would wonder what happened to him. Or a mother who worried too obsessively, but only because she loved him. What if he had a girl, a wife, a kid ...

"Wolf. Bike. Now."

"I'm not leaving him."

I imagined the faint sound of sirens in the distance.

"I need to call the sheriff. What if—"

There were no what-ifs.

The world went black.

CHAPTER TWENTY-ONE

DEWEY DECIMAL CLASSIFICATION: 155.93
INFLUENCES OF TRAUMATIC
EXPERIENCES AND BEREAVEMENT

[Naomi]

Nathan's reaction to the story of my brother is not what I expected.

"Are you finished?" The disembodied tone startles me. His voice is hollow as are his eyes. I don't know if he means the history of my brother or my lunch, but when I nod, he absentmindedly folds up our wrappings. Crumbling them is more like it. He slowly stands, his movements deliberate, as if it hurts to lift each part of his body. Then he takes a step away from me, cups his hands behind his head, and paces a second before turning back as if he forgot something on the ground.

"Are you okay?" My voice cracks, weak and concerned. He doesn't answer me. His eyes don't meet mine, but his hand reaches out to help me stand up. He immediately releases me, bends for the blanket, and flings it over his shoulder. Hastily, he grabs the sack with our unfinished lunches and stalks forward.

All I can think is the story confirms my guilt, and Nathan wants nothing to do with me.

We walk back to his truck in silence. Ride to my house in silence. He drops me off in silence.

"I'll call you," he mutters just before I close the door to his truck, and I hear the falseness in his tone.

Don't look back, I tell myself. Although I don't believe in a woman turning into a pillar of salt, I fear I'll matriculate into the fine grains and blow away in the wind if I turn around. His ticking jaw and hard-edged cheeks told me he was deep in thought while we rode to my house. The kicker was his lack of physical contact. I'd just bared my soul of sin and guilt, and Nathan did nothing to comfort me. He didn't hold my hand. He didn't embrace me. He said … nothing.

I guess that settles things. I'd found the breaking point. My thoughtless actions resulted in my brother's death and Nathan's reaction is he doesn't want anything to do with me again.

The universe had spoken.

I hadn't even reached my front door before the crunch of tires on gravel signals his exit from my driveway. The screeching squeal of rubber on blacktop shortly follows as he speeds down the road. Once inside, I release a heavy breath and I collapse onto my couch, tears stinging my eyes. I'm heartsick at the possibility of not seeing him again, especially after fighting my feelings and denying my desire. I don't need a man to complete me, but I admit Nathan fit me like a missing puzzle piece. He is patient and kind, and doesn't make me feel awkward even when I am. He's been a comfort in the storm of the library closure, and I welcomed the safe harbor I found in him. He has allowed me to blossom and he rekindled my sexuality.

The inner goddess is unleashed.

I still want him as much as I did the first time we met, and once again, he's ridden off, and I worry I'll never hear from him again.

A fragile sensation returns on Sunday afternoon, when I feel sluggish, solemn, and so alone at the Save Our Library community meeting in the library, doomily nicknamed S.O.L. —*shit out of luck*—which should really read S.O.O.L but you get the point. The campaign efforts swirl around me like a mist and I feel discombobulated and separate from the crowd. My thoughts remain on Nathan's disappearance.

He hasn't called.

Unfortunately, Julianne isn't a good public speaker and the audience is lacking. We learn Billy Winston is no longer our hometown congressman. He resigned. The absence of several of the Winstons leaves us with an ominous feeling. Their mother had been the needle to knit our thriving library together. She originated so many of our special events and programs. Her children practically grew up within these walls and their absence doesn't go unnoticed. At one point, I see Cletus in the back along with his sister, Ashley Winston-Runous, but it isn't the same without the twins or even little Roscoe, who is now a man.

The heavy sense of loss isn't only from the missing Winstons. Diane Donner-Sylvester, who had been a strong champion to the library, especially our Thursday night poetry readings, has been missing from the area for years. I still feel her absence. She would have been a vocal supporter of our cause, and with her social media experience, a proponent of the S.O.L. campaign.

Then there is the fact Nathan isn't present. I shouldn't have expected he'd be there. Hoped rather. He can't do anything directly to aid our situation, but it would have been nice to see him in the room as the library has done so much for children like Clementine. I understand, though. This is about me. It's not like he hasn't disappeared from my life before. I want to blame my brother's tale, but I accept Nathan's absence as my fault. My irresponsibility. My thoughtless action. My brother would never have crashed if I hadn't called him in the first place, he wouldn't have been on that road. If I hadn't had sex with a man I didn't know. If I hadn't been in a bar celebrating my birthday. If I hadn't been left behind.

If, if, if ...

Our library meeting ends without a rally for reform. It's hard to evocate passion when the three people representing the spirit of the library include a stern old-school librarian, a debilitatingly shy one, and another most people saw as a witch.

With Nathan missing, I feel even more like an outlier.

Defeat is in the air, the aura around us negative and oppressive. No amount of black tourmaline can soothe my anxiety although I've been holding the crystal between my breasts for over an hour. When those gathered disperse, Julianne and I settle at a table near the lobby.

We placed a suggestion box on the counter with another sign from Julianne.

Offer us your ideas and then give us your prayers.

I'm not the praying type by traditional standards but I've been burning candles and calling on all the good juju Nature can offer us. I'm planning a protective ritual around the building for later this evening with crystals and prayers of my own, asking the Goddess for assistance.

After the lackluster meeting, we read the suggestions.

Hire a famous author to speak.

Taco Tuesday.

Bake sale.

Feeling hopeless, I make my own suggestion to Julianne. "Maybe we could expand to provide more variety."

"How could we expand if we don't even have the funding to keep the doors open?" Julianne has a point, despite her snippy tone.

"Maybe we need to add some unique features. Something that makes us stand out from other libraries," I add.

Julianne looks at me quizzically before replying. "What do we need variety for? We have thousands of books."

I love our lead librarian, but she doesn't see the bigger picture some days. The world outside Green Valley is changing—rapidly— and while I don't want books to be a thing of the past any more than she does, we need to make concessions to the modern age. A 3D printer is one of the changes we need. Author nights might be another, but we need something even grander.

"What about a fundraiser?"

"Like a bake sale?" Julianne wrinkles her face, holding up the slip of paper with the suggestion, knowing full well brownies and muffins sold for fifty cents apiece will not garner the funds we need.

"I don't know." I sigh in frustration as I comb my fingers through my hair. "Where is the ALA in all this?" The American Library Association should be our biggest advocate for remaining open. Julianne dismisses me with a weak wave.

"What about private investors?" I suggest next.

"Privatizing the library!" Mrs. MacIntyre interjects and adamantly objects. She's kept up to date on companies trying to take over the once-public institution and outsource them to private entities. This destroys union control and allows the individual organization to decide what books are shelved and what programs are offered. *We won't be burning books*, she once admonished. Her fear is censorship, although she's had her day of banning books and refusing programs.

"Not privatized ownership, but an individual investment. Like a GoFundMe or something." Julianne stares at me like I've suggested we swallow nails and drink castor oil. Dismissing my own suggestion, I shrug and shake my head. "Never mind."

But I do mind, and I believe there must be a way to save our library.

Every Tuesday is Teen Night at the library, although most of the kids who attend are of middle school age. It doesn't matter to me. Teenagers are mean, while pre-teens can still be curious and kind. Clementine Ryder is one of our regulars. Tonight's activity includes a book discussion of *The Halloween Tree* by Ray Bradbury followed by the production of homemade Halloween costumes. Kids are encouraged to bring materials or use some of the things we've collected over the year through a recycling bin we leave in the community center. Old newspaper. Scraps of yarn. Used but clean T-shirts. I like to say we are repurposing.

Clem arrives without a trace of her father. I know because I peeked through the windows in hopes of seeing him. I quickly ignore the sting in my heart when I don't see him. Instead, I consider how he wasn't present on Sunday at the town hall meeting and wonder once again, how do I think I can save a library, when I can't even seem to save myself. I've fallen hard for him and he's left me dangling once again.

I lead Clem to a table where we play a guessing game of who she wants to be for Halloween until she runs out of hints.

"Professor Trelawney," she announces. "She reminds me of you."

I shake my head, a little stunned. I hope I don't look as scattered as the character portrayed by my idol, Emma Thompson, in the *Harry Potter* films. However, Clem has read the books and I'm honored she envisions me as a fictional character I adore. I suppose I do seem rather eccentric like the Divination professor, and I know Clem means the comparison with respect.

"If only I were a Seer," I mumble. Then I could have predicted the future and anticipated the broken heart I feel once again from Nathan Ryder. Mustering some enthusiasm, I say, "Let's make you a Seer instead."

I give Clem an old scarf of mine to tie around her head to hold her wild fuzzy hair back from her face. I've worn something similar, wrapped high on my forehead to tame my reckless waves. "This is perfect for you."

Securing it in place and straightening her glasses, she instantly looks like a younger version of the professor she wishes to imitate.

"You'll need some kind of blouse, loose and full, and a skirt, too. Do you have something like that?"

"I'll check my closet."

I'd offer to make her something, repurposing some of my old things, but I don't want to overstep my boundaries. Making a costume seems like something a mother should do.

"Now, you need a prophecy ball."

Clem's eyes widen as I pull out a clear glass globe left over from last winter's ornament making class.

"I have blue, red, or yellow paint. We'll paint the inside of the ball and add some glitter for effect. We can use a piece of wood for a base, and then hot glue the globe to the wood. After that, all you'll need is a prophecy," I cheerfully suggest.

"A prediction, right?"

"Yes." I nod finding myself growing in excitement as her cheeks glow with the emotion. "For good purposes, though. Not evil," I warn. I'm very particular that any wishes into the world should be positive or helpful, and not negative or for harm. Clem has told me about kids bullying her at school. She's teased for her magnified glasses, her wild hair, and her overall knowledge. She makes a pouty face but begins to work while I circle the table aiding others.

Two hours later I've helped design a yarn-hair wig for a Rainbow Bright costume and an aluminum-foil sword for a knight. When the others leave, Clem continues to stare at her prophecy ball. Her concentration remains intense as her arms cross on the table and her chin rests on her hands.

"Whatcha thinking, Clem?"

"Miss Naomi, why aren't you married?"

Oh my. "Well, Professor Snape could never get over Lily." Some of the kids like to believe I went to a school for witchcraft and wizardry. I don't mind playing along. I'll admit to having a crush on the professor of Defense Against the Dark Arts, and always felt he's a little misunderstood and a lot sad from his broken heart. *Sounds familiar.*

She giggles and rolls her eyes. "I'm serious."

"You know, it's not really polite to ask such a thing," I gently admonish, raising a brow, and hoping to avoid answering.

"I'm sorry," she mutters, lowering her voice and her eyes, and my chest pinches. It won't hurt to answer her honestly with a small dash of mistruth.

"I just never fell in love and no one fell in love with me." It sounds pathetic, although a little romantic, even if it isn't all true. I'm in love with Nathan which totally baffles me. I can't seem to get him out of my system.

I'm stuck on you.

"What if someone fell in love with you *now* or you fell in love with him?"

I smile weakly. "I don't know, Clem." And I don't. If I'm in love with Nathan, and he doesn't reciprocate, it leaves me right where I am. Alone.

"But you'd say yes to it, right? If someone wanted to marry you?" Clem's eyes sparkle behind her glasses as she presses up on her hands.

Oh, to be young and dreamy about all things happily ever after.

There's a pinch in my chest, and I absentmindedly rub at it. How do I explain to a child that love is complicated? "I suppose I might," I reply although I don't believe marriage and I are meant to be bedfellows. I'm almost forty and there really isn't a prospect in sight. There was Nathan, but … "But I don't believe marriage defines a woman." I think of my sisters, both with broken marriages and hearts. "A woman can be her own best person."

"But you'd say yes?" Clem questions, not appreciating my deeper emphasis on independent women and the institution of marriage. Girl power. Silent fist pump in the air. Cue dying party horns. I sigh.

"Definitely," I say, because I can't deny I'd answer favorably if I was ever asked.

Clem nods, satisfied with my answer, and lowers her head, returning her concentration to the prophecy ball.

"You're staring awfully hard at that thing," I tease, hoping to redirect our conversation. Who's coming to pick her up? It's getting late and the library closes soon. My heart skips a fruitless beat with hope her father will be the one.

"I want to pick a good prophecy. Something I know will come true." If only it were that easy to make a prediction. *I predict Nathan will walk in that door and tell me what happened*, a deep masculine voice rumbles through my head. Then I scoff at myself.

"Well, whatever you decide, don't share it. It's like a birthday wish. You can't spill the secret, or it won't happen."

"No, a prophecy can be shared, like a warning or encouragement," Clementine corrects me in a voice as if she's all-knowing.

"Like fortune telling?" A female voice mocks from behind me, and I spin in my seat to see a beautiful teenager with dirty blonde hair, streaked with highlights. She's wearing a bit too much make-up for a Tuesday evening, but I recognize her instantly.

"Dahlia." I exhale after her name, and peer around her in hopes of seeing her father.

Wishful thinking be damned. It's been three days.

The booklover bug hasn't bitten Dahlia like it did Clementine. She isn't a fan of the library as much as her younger sister. She uses the library as more of a social gathering place than a study center and Mrs. MacIntyre has asked her to remain quiet or leave on more than one occasion.

"You're filling her head with nonsense." Dahlia snaps at me while she reaches for her sister's backpack hooked over a chair. "Let's go. You were so supposed to be waiting outside for me."

"It's cold and dark out there," Clem whines and I don't care for Dahlia's rough tone. I turn once more to the front windows to notice the night is black and the trees dance in a swift breeze. Winter is coming.

"Darkness doesn't hurt anybody, right, Miss Naomi?" Mockery fills her voice as she sing-songs my name. The hint of my witchery doesn't go unnoted by me, but I falsely grin in response.

"I was formulating a prophecy," Clem tells her sister, cutting the tension between her teenage sister and myself. Lifting her homemade prophecy ball with reverence, she holds it by the base with both hands to show her sister. "It's important to get it right."

"Whatever," Dahlia mutters, hitching her sister's backpack over her shoulder and ignoring the ball. "We need to get going. Dad's at home waiting on us. I think he's going out tonight."

My heart skips a beat as Dahlia's eyes meet mine. Is he coming to see me? Foolishly, my mind races through scenarios of him coming to explain himself. Explain why he hasn't called me.

Dahlia's eyes lower to take in my attire. My denim skirt is a shorter one. My tights are black to match my turtleneck. I've found myself shifting my clothing selection, feeling more confident wearing something outside of my loose-fitting, body-hiding attire.

"I think he has a date." She pauses a beat. Thoughts about my clothing crash within me. "You know he might have been more attracted to you if you dressed differently."

Out of the mouths of babes, or malicious teenagers without a filter.

"Dahlia," Clem shrieks, but too late. There's spite in Dahlia's gaze, and I read the meaning in her insult. She knows I went out with her father and she didn't like it.

Does she also know he hasn't called me in days?

"It's okay." I wave at Clem, offering her a forced smile. "Remember, only words," I remind her, as I've told her on several occasions how to handle what others say about her appearance or her books. *Only words*. People say mean things when they don't understand someone different from themselves, or they are afraid of that difference. If they feel threatened by it, or uncomfortable with their own reaction, they lash out. They scorn the unexplained, and some kids don't understand Clem's advanced vocabulary or her love of fantasy. Heck, some adults don't understand me, and do the same thing.

"Maybe one day you can give me tips." I don't know why I suggest it or even why I address the pettiness of a seventeen-year-old. Perhaps it's who she is, or who she belongs to, or maybe a teeny-tiny-part of me wonders if she's right. Nathan and I don't match.

Then again, if Nathan Ryder doesn't like me because of what I wear, that's too bad for him.

Maybe he should see you naked again, my thoughts whisper, but there's no chance of that ever happening again.

"We should go shopping. A girl's day," Clem says, her excitement pinkens her cheeks as her hands press into the table to help her stand.

"Don't count on it," Dahlia mutters holding out Clem's jacket to her. I take it from Dahlia and help Clem into her coat as she doesn't appear willing to set down the prophecy ball.

"I predict you'll take us shopping," she says to the false crystal in her hand but mocking her sister.

"I predict, I'll kick your butt if you don't get walking to the car."

"Excuse me," I say, addressing Dahlia and her tone. "There's no need for that kind of talk."

Clem looks from me to her sister and back again. I remind her: "Just stop, right, Clementine?"

She nods and looks up at her sister as she speaks. "You don't have to be so mean."

Dahlia's eyes narrow on me. "Don't be putting a spell on her like you did my dad."

What?

"I already made her and Daddy my prophecy," Clem interjects, holding up the false crystal ball.

Oh no.

"Clem, it doesn't work—"

"You'll be at the Halloween party, right?" she reminds me I promised to attend.

"Oh, I don't—"

"You have to come. I want you to see my costume, and my dad will be there."

"Clem, I don't think—"

"Please."

Sweet Goddess, how does Nathan resist her? I glance up at Dahlia who smirks at me. She senses the superpower of her little sister—a pout and excessive blinking behind those magnified glasses—and I'm putty.

"I'll think about it."

"I predict you'll be there," she says, holding the prophecy ball before her as she walks around her sister, heading for the front doors of the library.

"I predict, you won't," Dahlia sneers under her breath, as if suddenly she's the seer.

"What's wrong with you?" Beverly asks as I stare out the window of Daisy's Nut House the next morning.

"It's nothing," I lie, dismissively waving a hand and drawing my eyes back from the parking spot where Nathan first kissed me, and I didn't kiss him back.

I think he has a date. Dahlia's words ring through my head for the millionth time in twelve hours. I guess that could explain why he hasn't called, but I don't like that answer. Either way, I deserve an explanation for his silence.

I'll call you. His hollowed voice ripples through my thoughts.

"Here you go," Daisy says setting down two mugs, a small chrome kettle of hot water and packets of tea in a dish along with a vanilla Long John for Beverly and a cake doughnut with Halloween sprinkles on it for me. "Haven't seen you in here lately with Nathan," Daisy comments. Beverly raises a brow at me.

"Oh, yeah, that was just … one night." I don't know why I stutter, but I choke on the final words. *One-night.* That's what we'd been at first. Maybe that's all it was ever meant to be.

"Well, that must have been some night," Daisy teases, winking down at me. "He had quite the smile for you that evening." My face heats although Daisy has no idea what that one night was like, all those years ago.

I nod, unsure how to respond.

"Enjoy your tea and doughnuts, ladies." She pats my shoulder and returns to the counter when Jethro Winston and his small crew of children walk in.

"Hmm … is this Nathan the reason your mind has been a million miles away today?" She lifts her mug to her lips and blows on the steamy tea before sipping.

"Bev, do you think you'll ever love again?" My sister sputters. A brown spray of liquid showers the table. She continues to cough, choking on my question.

"Would I *what?*" She doesn't look at me as she swipes a paper napkin over her white blouse with a Peter Pan collar. Once again, I notice her clothing and wonder where she gets such items. Pulling a handful of napkins from the dispenser on the table, I dab at the mess on the surface, as she admonishes me. "You made me ruin my shirt."

"That shirt needs to be ruined," I bite. The style makes my sister look like a hundred-year-old bitty instead of forty-five. Not to mention, it looks like something she might have worn when she was thirteen. She could also use a haircut and maybe a little color to either darken the grays or give into the lightning streaks in her hair. I don't know why I think of these things, but my sister needs a makeover in both her appearance and attitude. Strangely, I feel like I do, too.

"What makes you say such a thing?"

"That blouse isn't flattering on you."

Beverly's dark eyes open wide as she stares back at me. "I meant, why would you ask me about love?"

I shrug and look out the window once again. After a moment of silence, I glance back at my sister who scrutinizes me like Nathan did the first night we sat here.

"Did something happen? Did you meet someone?" My sister's brows rise, forcing her forehead to wrinkle. Her surprised voice softens when she asks a second question. "Who is he?"

Meet someone? Not exactly. "Remember, the night Jebediah died." My voice lowers as I sit up straighter and my hands clasp together on the table. My sister's eyes narrow on me. She hates how I've beat myself up over the years. She understands the mind games my parents played and she's the first to remind me it wasn't my fault.

It was an accident, Nae-Nae. Jebediah shouldn't have been riding in the first place.

Beverly's gaze remains on me, waiting.

"Do you remember Nathan Ryder?" I don't think I need to remind my sister who he is. Back then, I told her in one sentence—*I slept with a stranger at a bar.* "I've recently seen him."

"What?" Beverly chokes again, this time minus hot tea on her tongue. I go on to tell my sister everything. How I saw him at the Piggly Wiggly. How he checked out books. How we kissed and the arrangement for three dates.

"Then I told him about Jebediah and how he died after we were together."

Beverly doesn't need me to spell out my shame. She knows I've lived with it for years and she sighs with exasperation. "You know it wasn't your fault. You've given too much power to Mother and Daddy's words. What they said wasn't true. It wasn't you and you aren't going to hell." Her words remind me of what I tell Clem about the bullies in her life. *Only words.*

My sister's right. At my core, I know I'm not to blame for Jebediah's crash, any more than it was my fault he drank too much that evening, but it's been difficult to accept all these years, living with the guilt placed on me. Even with a new religion and acceptance of my womanliness, I haven't released the shame I felt, at least not in its entirety.

I called my brother for help and he died trying to get to me.

"Did you sleep with him again?" Beverly's voice waffles between judgment and jealousy. Sex wasn't an open conversation between us as teenagers, but as we've grown older, the fence around off-limit subjects has crumbled. She has admitted to missing her estranged husband despite his stepping out on her. Not because he was a great man, but because she'd given herself to him, and only him, in her lifetime. She missed the intimacy, she once told me. Unfortunately, he was sharing *his intimacy* with several others, so I don't know how precious the moments as man and wife could have been.

"No," I whisper, as if ashamed that I hadn't, or am I ashamed because I wish I had? Beverly waits for more details. "I just ... I like him, but then I told him about Jebediah—"

"Stop blaming Jebediah for everything that happened to you. You didn't hold the bottle before he drove," her voice falters knowing something similar happened to her: she did drink and drive.

"I called Jebediah." I point at myself emphasizing the blame, but Beverly rolls her eyes, disgusted with my return to an old argument.

"He made his own choices. Besides, Nathan's the one who walked out on you so quickly. Did he ever explain why he didn't call?" Leave it to Beverly to blame the man who walked away, so similar to her own circumstances. I quickly fill her in on what I know of Nathan's history. His moves. His girls. Beverly's head tilts and her brows severely pinch. A crease furrows between her eyebrows.

"That's not an explanation. He could have still called you."

"He left his phone behind. He also said he had his reasons, and that it wasn't because of me," I protest, uncertain why I'm defending him.

"That's a copout. You deserve to know the reason. In fact, you deserve it right now." My sister's growing agitation is contagious, and she bangs on the tabletop for emphasis. Once again, I think her passion comes from her own experience. Howard left without giving her an explanation.

"You're the one who's all girl power and go Goddess. You need to make better choices for you. You're still choosing to blame yourself and you need to stop." *Just stop.* "Quit faulting yourself for everything related to that night." She exhales after her rant. "Maybe you should have slept with him again."

"Beverly!" I'm utterly shocked my sister makes such a suggestion.

"Well, it's one way to get over a man." It's my turn to choke on comments.

But what if I don't want to get over him?

I'm stuck on you.

Apparently, Nathan has become unstuck and a heaviness settles in my chest.

"Or you could have slept with him to keep him, but then again, what do I know. All the sex in the world didn't keep Howard home with me." Beverly's admission startles me, and I feel sorry for her. Howard was an awful man and Beverly wasn't always so bitter. "Then again, Nathan is older, and maybe he has that erectile dysfunction thing you so often see advertised on television, and his penis doesn't work like it sh—"

"It works just fine," I interject, holding up a hand, flushing deep red at my sister's verbal vomit.

"How would you know if you haven't slept with him?" My sister's lips slowly curl into a mischievous grin, a novelty on her face, and my heart pinches with hope that I'll see a full smile one day from her. Then, a puzzled expression crosses her face.

"So he hasn't called in three days?"

Four now, but who's counting? I nod.

"And you think he's ghosting you again?"

I shrug. That's a pretty modern word for being ditched.

"You need to go after him instead."

I startle at the suggestion, as this is what my sister did, and it didn't turn out favorably for her. Then again, if I went to Nathan, I'd go with a sober head.

"You need closure, Naomi. You need to confront him, and get your answers, so you can let him go. So you don't spiral again into believing something about yourself that isn't true. If he walks away, let it rest on him, not you, but at least you'll have said your peace. You can't allow him a free pass." For a brief moment, I wonder once more if Beverly is speaking about herself. She never had closure with Howard. She still has no idea where he is.

"I'm not allowing Nathan a pass," I say, but my voice sounds weak even to me. He said he'd call all those years ago, and when he didn't, well … I didn't have a way to question what happened. Nor could I concentrate on his disappearance at first. I rolled the absentee-Nathan into the death of Jebediah, and assumed his missing was part of my punishment.

My hand smacks the table. "You're right."

"I usually am," Beverly mutters sarcastically, not startled in the least by my determined voice.

"I can't let him get away with this again."

Nathan Ryder will not ignore me. If he doesn't want to see me because of Jebediah, so be it, but he needs to man up and tell me to my face. And if he's dating someone else, like Dahlia hinted, he can tell me that as well. Sweet Goddess, if he simply changed his mind, he's allowed that decision, too. But I deserve answers.

Make better choices for yourself, Beverly says.

I need to free my heart from him.

Although, those words are easier said than done.

CHAPTER TWENTY-TWO

DEWEY DECIMAL CLASSIFICATION: 126
THE SELF

[Nathan]

When I awoke, Catfish stood over me. I'd been unceremoniously dumped on the floor of a dark room.

"What the fuck happened?" I asked groggily as I took in my surroundings. An Oriental rug lay under me. Dark wood paneling covered the walls. I was in some kind of holding room in the Wraith's clubhouse.

"You passed out," Catfish stated, his voice rough, laced with disappointment.

"I fainted?" I asked, incredulous at the thought. I'd never fainted in my life. Sure, I threw up at the sight on the concrete but—

"Not willingly," Catfish smirked. I pressed up from the floor and felt a throbbing at the base of my skull. Wincing, I rubbed the back of my head.

Not willingly? They knocked me out.

"What happened to the other guy?" Catfish smirked at my question, as if I was being a smart-ass, as if I'd been in a fight instead of an accident. It was an accident, right? I clarified, "The guy on the bike."

The second the words left my lips, Catfish's expression dropped. "Why do you care?"

It was a strange response considering we both saw his body. Twisted. Mangled. Bloodied.

"Your little fucking freak-out was unnecessary."

I slowly stood, my head ringing. "What happened to him?"

"He was dead."

I swallow a lump in my throat. "What did you do with the body?"

"As you were smart enough to not touch him, we did nothing. We left him there."

Without thought, I reached for Catfish's cut, tugging him to me. Our chests collided, hard muscle against muscle. My heart raced so fast I was certain he could feel it ready to explode through my ribs.

"You left him there?" I couldn't believe it. He had been some innocent guy speeding down a dangerous road, just like me. It could have been me. The thought hit me hard and I pushed Catfish away from me. What if it had been me? Did Catfish care so little for another life? Had my oldest friend, Curtis, become so hardened because of his history that he no longer cared about people in general? He was only twenty-one.

"He was already dead."

"So, you left him," I repeated. "What if he was still alive?"

"He wasn't." But could he have been saved? Could he have been fixed? My thoughts collided like the bike against the rocky side of the road.

"I can't do this, man," I muttered, my fingers digging into my hair. "I can't be this." I couldn't be this cold-hearted. I couldn't leave a man behind. I couldn't watch a man die. Not an innocent man.

"It was an accident," I stated, eyes latching on to Catfish, searching for my old friend.

"And it's over."

"Who was he?"

"I don't care." The comment socked me in the gut.

"What happened to you?" I mumbled, staring at him.

"Don't be a fucking pussy. It's only death."

My mouth fell open. "I can't be one of you." The idea sucker punched me.

"What are you saying?"

"I can't do this," I repeated, my meaning clear.

"You've got to be fucking kidding." Catfish laughed, low and rough and

edged with evil. Then he sputtered to a halt when he noticed I wasn't joking. "You can't just leave." He stepped up to me, our chests nearly touching once again. His fingers curled into fists and I waited for a blow.

"I want out," I stated, willing my eyes not to close as I anticipated the beating he would give me.

"I did everything I could to bring you in, Wolf. I put my name on the line. I'd just made it in the club myself and then I hooked you up, man." He glared at me as he stated the facts. I hadn't seen myself going anywhere when I had asked him to put a word in for me. But I'd changed my mind now.

"I appreciate it, but I want out." Something in my tone must have gotten to him and the fist I expected connected with my stomach. I doubled over, waiting for more, but the door opened.

"What's going on in here?" The rough voice of Darrell Winston scraped over my skin.

"Just an issue with a prospect. I've got it covered." The tone of Catfish's voice brooked no argument. I should have known then the authoritative role Catfish would one day play in the club. He spoke like the leader he hoped to be.

"Damn straight." Darrell chuckled, and then stepped back out of the room at the sound of feminine giggles in the hallway. Once the door clicked shut, I stood toe-to-toe with Catfish again.

"You're my responsibility," he stated back to me as years of friendship sealed off in his eyes. "You want out. Fine, fucking go. We don't need cowards. But you'll leave town and never come back. You'll be a lone wolf now, my friend." The sneer to his voice spoke volumes. I was on my own. We were no longer friends and the club would always be watching me.

I stared at him, waiting for a punchline. He didn't flinch other than a tick in his jaw. If Catfish cut me loose, he'd have to bear the burden of the decision. If I fucked up in any way, he'd be killed. Then, they'd kill me.

"Never come back," he muttered. "Or you'll belong to me again."

"You have my word," I said.

"It means shit to me now." Then he punched me in the face.

"Hello." A sweet feminine voice interrupts my memories, the one that has haunted me since Saturday. I'm on the third floor of the Bickerton build, picking up my tools, and I pause with a drill in my hand, thinking I imagined the familiar sound of her voice for a second. The framing was nearing its end and the drywallers would soon begin, as long as the Bickertons didn't change their mind again. I'm hopeful this next step would put an end to whoever has been hanging out here at night and stop me from thinking so much about the woman next door. "Nathan?"

I take a deep breath and head for the stairs, taking them slowly, feeling as if I'm descending into hell. Naomi stands just inside the front door of the lower level. It's been four days since I've seen her. A halogen shop light illuminates the foyer, and as she spins in the direction of the staircase, my breath hitches. Her silvery hair. Those wild waves. Her deep-set chrome eyes. She's so beautiful with an other-worldly appearance despite the harsh glow of the work lamp. An aura of determination filters around her.

For a second, a smile graces her face and she steps toward me as I finish my descent down the stairs. Then she stops just short of me, too far away, and I hold my breath.

"Nathan Ryder, you will not disappoint me again."

The words startle me, like a fresh slap to the face. One I rightly deserve. I lick my lips as I look away from her. I can't face her, and my palms sweat.

I'm a coward.

"I'm sorry I didn't call." The words taste acidic on my tongue, as I scratch my knuckles under my chin. Her eyes follow the motion and my heart pinches at the absence of her lick-me looks. A simple phone call is the one thing she wanted from me.

I've been waiting for him.

Me.

"You need to do better than that," she snaps, and I turn back to her as her fingers curl into fists at her side. Her long coat covers her entirely, but it's open in the front and I see a hint of a deep red dress inside.

She's a present you'll never unwrap again.

"You can't just apologize. I need a reason." Her voice trembles. "You ... you owe me."

Her arms cross over her ample chest and I swallow. I want to pull her to me and crush her against me. I want to hold her tight and bury my apology into her hair. I want to tell her how I feel about her before I confess ...

"If you're seeing someone else, I need to know the truth. From you."

"I killed your brother."

The confession cracks through the stud-framed room like the smack of a hammer on a nail. The words reverberate like a hollow echo. The silence afterward is thicker than a two-by-four.

And the look on Naomi's face is indescribable. The question. The puzzlement. The pain.

"You ... but ..." Her mouth opens but she can't find the words. Her lips snap shut. Her eyes blink in confusion.

"I got a call. The Wraiths. I told you I was a prospect for them, and when they call, you jump."

Her chrome eyes turn to tarnished silver as they narrow, and she processes what I'm trying to explain.

"I was late. There was a girl ..." My voice fades again, and I weakly grin. There was a girl with raven hair, wild and spread on my pillow. *One more kiss.*

Naomi steps back, but it's more like she tilts, and I step forward, afraid she'll faint in the foyer. Reaching out for her, she quickly rights herself before I can touch her. Her arm flinches away from my grasp and I retract my hand.

"Don't ... don't touch me." Her voice is devoid of warmth and she glares at me, demanding I continue.

"The Dragon is dangerous. It's so hard to judge the distance between drivers. At some point, you hear the buzz of another bike, but you question where it's at. Is it behind me? Is it in front of me? You don't often see it until it's upon you, and in the dark ... and with the curves ... and the rocks ..." I don't need to give her all the details. "He swerved into my lane. We both panicked, afraid we'd collide into one another. He didn't regain control of his bike and he—"

A raised hand stops my speech.

"He'd been drinking."

The words linger between us as if that explains everything, but it's not stated as if it absolves me. The words just float between us and flutter to the floor like someone ripped up a piece of paper and tossed it into the air, watching the shreds coast to the ground.

"I should have gone back."

Naomi's head pops up and she stares at me. Her lower lip trembles. "What do you mean?"

I lick my lips again. My mouth is so dry, yet my palms drip with moisture. "I didn't turn back."

"You hit and run?" The question in her tone punches me in the gut. Shaky fingers raise to cover her quivering lips.

"Technically, we didn't collide." It's the wrong thing to say as her eyes widen. She doesn't even blink. The accusation in her wide-eyed glare travels to my soul. She isn't incorrect. I should have turned around for him. I have no excuse.

"Was he ...?" Naomi closes her eyes and I guess what she's trying to ask.

"I think it was instant." He died on impact.

"But you don't know? Because you left him there." Her frame visibly vibrates, and I step toward her again, hands lifting to steady her tremors, but she steps back once more, demanding I keep my distance. She bumps against the wall behind her.

"Please let me explain." Although, I can't think what else to tell her.

"There can't possibly be more," she snaps, and she isn't wrong again. There isn't much else to say. Then her head tilts and her voice simmers with disgust when she asks, "How long have you known?"

"What do you mean?"

"How long have you known it was my brother ... and me?"

My eyes open in shock. "Only when you told me on Saturday did I put it all together."

She shakes her head back and forth. Her expression reads unacceptable. "Why didn't you say something on Saturday?" Her voice cracks in disbelief.

"I didn't know how to tell you it was me." I hang my head and hear the roar of motorcycles echoing in the background. The volume jacks higher until the sound is nearly upon us and I realize they've pulled into the gravel drive.

"Shit," I mutter, stepping toward the slim window pane edging the front door. Instantly, I turn toward Naomi.

"Go upstairs. Don't say anything," I whisper as if the men are already upon us. Surprisingly, she doesn't flinch as my hands grasp her shoulders and I nudge her toward the staircase. She notes the concern in my eyes and takes a step to the stairs. I watch her climb before I hear the doorknob twist.

"Wolf," Catfish greets me, not in the least surprised to find me present. It's late and I'm still on the job to finalize an interior inspection. I hold my breath wondering how he could have known I was here, and then I remember my truck out front.

"Catfish." Our eyes meet. In his leather cut, near the bright work lamp, he's half illuminated by light, half in darkness, and I ponder the juxtaposition of him for a moment. My old friend is falling further into the dark side.

"Where's Henderson?" Dirty Dave asks. Catfish turns his head to the older man as he enters.

"I don't know anything about Dwight," I admit. This draws Catfish's attention back to me. His eyes narrow.

"He told us to meet him here. Has a special delivery," Dirty Dave explains.

"It ain't me," I clarify, although now I'm concerned. Did Dwight promise them me? Is he using the house as a meeting point? His son has already been here. Just what are those Hendersons up to?

"Too bad. Thought you'd come to your senses," Catfish responds, crossing his arms and eyeing me as I hold my ground. I need to get them out of here before Dwight shows up and I need to finish talking with Naomi. We can't be done yet.

A creak from the upper floors echoes down to us and Dirty Dave's head turns toward the staircase. Catfish looks past my shoulders. "Someone up there?" he asks.

"Just me, fixing a mess from your weasel."

Dirty Dave chuckles at the name. Catfish glares. "Who you hiding?"

"No one," I answer, holding my breath. I don't want them to discover Naomi.

"Still seeing that strange bird?" Catfish inquires, tipping his head once in the direction of Naomi's home. How does he know where she lives?

"We broke up." I'm not wrong. She's not going to want to see me again. I killed her brother. While we didn't hit head-on, I'm still indirectly responsible. And man, how I wish the circumstances were different.

Dirty Dave snorts, and the tone itself suggests something. He wants her next.

"You leave her out of it," I rush. My fists clench and I fight the force pulling me to step into Dirty Dave's face. The venom in my warning gives away my still yearning for her.

"That's what I thought," Catfish drawls, with a knowing gleam to his eye. "She the one holding you back? Do we need to let her know you owe me?"

"Don't you go—"

"Easy, Wolf," Catfish warns as I step up to him and we stand toe-to-toe.

"We could take care of her. Chirp-chirp, little birdie." Dirty Dave snickers and my hackles raise. My fingers unfurl and then return to fists. "Or should I be calling her a witchy woman?"

An old song from the Eagles comes to mind, but I shiver at Dirty Dave's hint at the gossip around Naomi.

"Are you threatening me?" I glare at Catfish, ignoring the older man. My eyes burn with my own ultimatum: come near her and I'll toast him.

"Ahhh." Catfish lets out with a devious grin but doesn't elaborate. We stare at one another a long moment before he speaks. "You tell

Henderson we don't have time to wait for his nonsense, and as for you, I hope you come to your senses soon, Wolf."

"Never," I hiss under my breath.

"You will," Catfish states. "Sooner than you think."

My body hums and I hold my breath as the two men turn for the temporary front door and exit. Once I hear the roar of motorcycles, I turn to race up the stairs and nearly collide with Naomi tucked into a dark corner. I grip her upper arms and tug her against me, displaying my inner caveman and a bit of fear. I don't want them coming after her to get to me.

"What was that all about?" she asks, pressing her face into my flannel and gripping handfuls of the fabric.

"Nothing," I lie.

"You didn't explain to them who I am?" There's a question in her eyes, wanting an explanation and maybe a definition of what she means to me, but I can't make declarations with the anxious energy rumbling through me.

"I don't want them to come near you." I pause as I grip her shoulders and push her back from me. "This is between him and me."

"You told them we broke up." Her voice falls soft and uncertain. Is she questioning us?

Didn't we?

"Can we get past this?" Her brother. Me.

Tears fill her eyes as her lips twist. Her head shakes side to side. "I don't think so."

She shrugs out from under my hands, and this time, I'm the one left standing alone, while she walks away.

CHAPTER TWENTY-THREE

DEWEY DECIMAL CLASSIFICATION: 168
ARGUMENT AND PERSUASION

[Naomi]

He follows me at a distance which both startles me and settles me. I want to walk away all brave and determined to be free, and yet I want his comfort and reassurance. The emotions conflict inside me.

I killed your brother.

Not in a million stars did I think that would be his reason for not calling me.

Another woman.

A change of mind.

But this …

He isn't trying to hide the fact he follows me. The snap of a twig. The crackle of brush pushed aside. Loud sounds echo in the forest on this quiet night meant to reassure me he's there for protection and because he's a gentleman. I don't know what those men wanted with him and it's yet another mystery surrounding Nathan Ryder.

Who is this man?

I break free of the thick bush between the properties and continue to my door. At the edge of my land, I expect him to turn and retreat.

I've made it safely home. He can disappear once again. So the sound of his voice directly behind me startles me.

"Do you hate me?"

"Hate is a strong emotion," I say spinning to face him. "And I don't feel that—"

"I know." His voice drops as he holds up a thick hand to stop me. "You don't feel that strongly about me."

"No, you don't understand. I do feel strongly about you … in the opposite direction." I blow out an exasperated breath. He couldn't possibly be this dense. He couldn't possibly not know how I feel about him.

"What do you mean?"

"Nathan." I sigh. "I've fallen for you. Again." My arms flap and then my hands slap at my sides, frustrated with him, with myself, with these feelings that I shouldn't have in our situation. I visibly shudder.

His breath catches but his eyes remain uncertain. "Maybe we should step inside to talk. It's cold out here."

Is it? I don't feel the cold. I only feel the heat rushing through me from his revelation.

I killed your brother.

"I don't think that's a good idea," I say, slipping my hands into my coat pockets. I inhale in hopes of drawing myself taller, to ward off the pull to hug him or hit him. I don't trust myself to bring him in my house. Besides, he hasn't responded to what I said. I've fallen for him.

"We need to talk," he says.

"Isn't that what we are doing?" I admonish and then my head lowers. "I don't know what's left to say."

Nathan wraps both his hands behind his head, turns in a circle, and then faces me again. He's wearing only a flannel, rolled to the sleeves and exposing his strong forearms. My eyes leap to his wrist, noticing the gratitude bracelet I gave him.

Am I still thankful for him?

What's his purpose in my life?

Right now, I can't think straight.

Nathan lowers his arms, slipping his hands into his pants pockets. He blows out another breath.

"Look, I just want to explain. I didn't mean for it to happen. I didn't see him. He probably didn't see me. You mentioned he was drinking."

Tears fill my eyes and I shake my head, willing them away. Willing away the memories of my brother, a fun guy who took things too far, too fast, too often.

"Did he do that often?" Nathan's voice softens. I swallow past the lump in my throat and nod. A thick finger comes to my chin and presses upward. I lift my face to meet his. "I'm sorry he did that."

He's not blaming Jebediah. Mother Earth knows, Jebediah didn't have it any easier than the rest of us under our parents. As the precious, only boy, the pressure to conform was tripled, which was something he simply could not do.

"I'm sorry I didn't stop immediately, Nae." The nickname turns my stomach. I'm going to be sick. "I was young and stupid and in a hurry and ..." He licks his lips and I close my eyes. "I don't have a good reason."

I nod. He doesn't. There isn't any reason in the world I can accept for not turning back to help another human being.

"When I went back, I didn't touch him, but I knew ..."

"You went back." I'm not absolving him, but I'm curious. "Why?"

"I felt guilty." He lowers his finger from my chin. "It took me a minute, but it hit me hard. My mind raced. Did we touch? Did we somehow clip bikes? I knew I'd lost control, but I righted myself. He obviously didn't. I called Catfish. He warned me not to go back but I did anyway. I had to be certain. If there was a way to make it right, I was willing to try ... but I just knew."

His head falls forward and two thick fingers pinch at his eyes, pressing at the lids. He swipes to the center and draws down his nose after a second.

"Why did you call Catfish?" Another thought occurs. "*How* did you call him?"

Nathan had left his phone on the bed by me. I always assumed he returned to the motel, retrieved the phone, and decided not to call me again. He'd got what he wanted and left, that kind of thing. I never imagined this. Never.

"I stopped at a diner in Cedar Gap."

My breath hitches. The Water Pump. A greasy spoon on the edge of the highway just off the pass where drivers decide: do I take the Dragon or the safer yet longer route around the lake?

"I used a payphone." The comment interrupts flashbacks of visiting the Water Pump, drinking contraband soda pop and hanging out with boys I shouldn't have been with at thirteen. I'd giggle at the thought of a payphone if the moment wasn't so serious between us.

"Catfish was my brother."

My brows instantly pinch. "I thought Todd was."

"Catfish was going to be my biker brother. He's the reason I was patching into the Wraiths."

Ah, yes. The Iron Wraiths. The reason Nathan left that night.

"And the reason Catfish was next door tonight?" I question.

"He wants me to patch back in." My insides tumble and the nauseous sensation returns.

"What did he mean, you owe him? Is this why he wants you to patch in again?" I pause a moment while Nathan looks off to the construction site. He scoffs bitterly and scratches his knuckles under his chin, making raspy noises from the contact of skin on scruff. "He wants me to patch in because the Wraiths are a hot mess. They need to rebuild. Restructure."

"And," I ask, not satisfied with this curt answer.

"And I owe him because he let me go the first time."

My forehead furrows. "I don't understand." I'm not versed in biker culture.

"I couldn't handle what happened." Nathan's dagger-silver eyes hold mine without flinching. "I couldn't take a life … whether by accident or on purpose … and that's what I'd need to do to become a Wraith. It hit me that night. The near miss on my end. I couldn't be responsible for taking away someone's life. I told Catfish I wanted out."

His brows soften. "He did it." Nathan shakes his head, shifting his eyes from mine. "He let me leave."

I continue to stare at him, not understanding. Nathan exhales with a shudder, and for a moment, I picture the brown-haired young man with his brilliant eyes, carefree and careless, but not without a conscious.

"I wasn't supposed to come back here. I wasn't supposed to ever return. I took their secrets with me and Catfish knew mine. I was a coward."

"Nathan," I admonish. His refusal to purposefully take a life doesn't make him less of a man. It makes him honest with himself and the fact he didn't patch into a notorious MC makes him a better person.

"Catfish had to take responsibility for my desertion. I can only imagine what he went through when he told them he let me go." His body trembles again.

"So you didn't patch in because of what happened with Jebediah?" The question rings in my quiet voice.

He nods. "It's also why I didn't call. When Catfish told me to leave, I left. I hid in Nashville for a bit before defecting down to Florida. I never returned for that phone with your number." He sighs. "And what could I say? I want to see you again, but I think I killed a man and now I'm running away."

The defeat in Nathan's voice slays me. For such a big man, the slouch of his shoulders and the hang of his head speaks volumes to a trying time in his life. That was eighteen years ago. The silver in his hair and edging his sharp jaw hints at the passage of so much time, and I know all too well how guilt and blame can ripple like a current from the decisions you make.

"Why did you come back then?"

"Ma missed the girls, and after Margie went off with another man … Dahlia was in trouble at school … and I just wasn't happy. Something was missing from my life."

An unsolved puzzle with a missing piece.

Me?

I shake my head. "Your mystery is solved." My voice teases without humor.

"What if it was the universe speaking to me?" He steps forward and my back hits the front of my house. Nathan fills my space and I breathe him in. Sawdust and cinnamon. "What if the universe drew me back here to find you? For us to be together?"

"We can't be together," I whisper. This revelation confirms it for me. Jebediah has been my cross to bear in life, and now I hold Nathan's as well. He's the last man I should be with. "Your story confirms what I've always known. You plus me equals catastrophe."

"Don't say that." Nathan's hand cups my cheek and while I should reject his warm touch, I lean into it. For the first time, in a long time, I want the comfort of another person.

"There's no other explanation. There are a million what-ifs in this scenario, but the result remains the same. You left me. I called my brother. He's dead."

Nathan's eyes narrow. "You don't really believe it's that black and white. I know you. You don't see with such tunnel vision."

"You don't know me at all," I state, confident in his lack of knowledge. "You've been searching for the girl in your head, in your memory, but she doesn't exist. She's dead, too. And I ... I don't think I know you either."

Nathan's breath hitches, his chest expanding in disbelief. "Don't say that. She's right in front of me. I'm right in front of you." The pain in his tone almost breaks me.

"She's not," I say louder. I'm not her anymore. I'm not the girl dancing around the room with a drink in her hand flirting with all the boys. I surround myself with safe places. The library and books and my home with all the lights on.

It's like someone is waiting for me.

I take a deep inhale, my lips trembling. Tears sting my eyes and my nose burns again.

"I don't know who you are," I whisper.

"Nae," Nathan softly hisses.

"Don't call me that." I pull back from his touch, no longer allowing myself to melt under the warmth of him, or the ashen tone of his voice, or the look in those silver eyes. He's a full body seduction that I won't allow to take me again. I refuse to fold under his spell.

"The universe did speak once before, Nathan. It told you to leave me behind and it told me to accept that you didn't call. It took my brother and that's the end of us." With tears leaking, I spin away from him and press open my door. I don't look back as I close it, and once shut, I slump to the floor with my back against the wood.

There will be no phone call tonight. He won't remain in my yard. All our dates are done, proving what I've known all along. Nathan Ryder and me were never meant to be.

CHAPTER TWENTY-FOUR

DEWEY DECIMAL CLASSIFICATION: 309
CUSTOMS, ETIQUETTE, FOLKLORE

[Nathan]

I'm stuck on you.

I don't want to let her go, but with the door closed in my face, I've lost her once again. Only this time, the only excuse I have is myself. My hands rest on either side of the casing while I press my forehead to the wood. I should bang on it, demand she let me it. Be the wolf that I am.

But I can hear her response. *Not by the hair of my chinny-chin-chin.*

She says she doesn't hate me, but she'll never love me after this. I don't know how to get *us* back. I didn't want it to end.

On Saturday, I took her to the woods with the full intention of discussing what was next for us. *Us.* I wanted her to meet Dahlia and Clem outside the library. I wanted to introduce her to Todd and Big Poppy. I wanted Ma to see I found a good woman. Only here I am again. Alone.

I press back from the door and stalk through the thick twigs and rough stems of foliage-free fauna. I turn back only once, watching as lights slowly go out in her house.

She's no longer waiting for someone.

I've been found and lost once again.

After a restless nights' sleep, I wake with a heavy heart. I'd spent the night thinking about Naomi Winters. Her independence and yet her innocence. Her pride and yet her personal punishment. Her guilt compared to mine, or should I say the guilt we share which is one and the same—*her brother*. And I decide I won't walk away so easily this time. I need to fight for her. I need to show her I'll come back for her. I'll make that call I didn't place. But first, I need her forgiveness.

Arriving early to work, I cross next door to leave a collection of fall flowers and a pumpkin carved with the image of a jar releasing lightning bugs. I haven't carved in years and typically wood is my medium, but we had the pumpkins and I needed to work my fingers. The image feels symbolic to me. Naomi and I each need to let our shame go, instead of containing it inside. In fact, maybe we need to release the blame by working through it together.

The lightning bugs remind me of Naomi. She was a light in one of the darkest parts of my life. A spark when I was ready to commit myself to a club that would have led me down the wrong path. Maybe, just maybe, the universe intended her to be a flame of hope for me. It blew out too quickly. This time, I don't want her to burn once and be out. I want her again and again.

I leave my offering on her doorstep, smiling to myself with hope she'll see it and it will lessen the pain I know she must feel after learning my role in her brother's death. I don't know what will make me feel better, but I believe her forgiveness will be enough. I also want her to have a sense of peace. She knows what happened to her brother. She knows what happened to me. Maybe this will give her what she needs to move on.

Throughout the next week, I leave her little things. An extra-large, fallen leaf with a heart cut in the middle. Another poem with my feelings. A 'thinking of you' note on her windshield. A miniature doghouse I made which was intended for her hedgehog, Dewey. And through it all, she doesn't call me, and I don't call her. I give her space.

But the day of Halloween, I'm coming out of my skin. It's been nine days since we spoke, and I promised Clem I'd attend the Halloween party at the community center. Secretly, I'm attending because my Dandelion told me Naomi would be present. I'm hoping seeing her in a public setting will at least get her to speak to me, even if I feel like a heel using my child as the bait.

I'm such a bad father.

I'm turning into a desperate man.

I've missed our nightly phone chats, but more so I've missed her touch, her kisses, her laughter. She's easy to be around despite the fact she thinks she's awkward. I love to learn about her, hear her philosophies. She grounds me, and I need grounding.

By Friday afternoon, I'm already on edge for the evening which is creeping closer by the minute when Deputy Sheriff James arrives to investigate an issue at the project site. Someone's been in the framed house again, although we have a security door and Tyvek sheeting over the window cutouts, not to mention a privacy fence around the project. It's obvious someone had a little soirée at the construction site and dislodged some supports. Whoever it was, they were lucky the place didn't collapse on them. As the builders, however, we were equally fortunate the place didn't ignite as the floor was littered with used matches. The scent of pot permeated the enclosed space. It must have been some party.

"I bet it's that witch next door," Dwight mutters to me as he stands next to me, knowing I won't touch him with our foreman Garrett Monroe present. Bill is also here today.

"Nathan," Jackson addresses me, walking to Garrett for the particulars. Beer bottles and a lighter were collected for evidence. Jackson speaks with Garrett and Bill a few minutes while Dwight remains next to me.

"It had to be her practicing some ritual or voodoo or who knows what," he mocks.

"Shut up, Dwight," I mutter, keeping my arms crossed so I don't strangle him. "You don't know what you're talking about."

"Ah, see she's got you under her spell, too," he teases without humor.

"Unrequited love isn't a good look on you," I snark and Dwight's head spins to me.

"I don't know what you mean," Dwight sings, tipping his chin upward.

"You're a little old to still be hanging on to a schoolboy crush," I say.

"You're crazy," he snaps. "Just like her." Dwight stalks away from me, and I have a mind to follow him and knock some sense into him, but then again, you can't hammer into rotted wood.

"Nathan." The sharp tone of Bill's voice brings me to Jackson and Garrett. "Nathan, I've just learned some disturbing news about next door and in light of this party—"

"What happened?" I growl, turning on Jackson.

"Now, Nathan—"

"Don't you 'now, Nathan' me." I tolerated Jackson's flirtatious innuendo with Naomi at Genie's but I'm not playing around with him.

"We understand there was an issue next door. Jackson just wants to know if you know anything, seeing as you're dating Naomi Winters." Bill's calm tone draws my attention. I'm not about to correct him on my relationship status. I want to know what happened.

"We also understand there have been sightings of a few motorcycles stopping here at night. Know anything about that?" Jackson's tone drops, but it drips with suggestion.

"Are you insinuating I've had something to do with this?"

"Just heard they're looking for new recruits. Thought you might be one of them." Jackson nods his head, acting like he has any authority, when he's more like a glorified traffic cop.

"Not everyone who rides belongs to a club," I bite, and then decide arguing with Jackson isn't worth my time. "Tell me about Naomi."

"Seems someone removed all the signs along the property ..." Bill begins. I noticed they were gone this morning, and thought it was a statement from Naomi. Like she'd given up on her cause. Given up on us. I swallow back the lump in my throat as my body vibrates, and I cross my arms to hold myself steady.

"And," I prompt Bill to continue.

"Someone set them on fire in her yard, leaving a sign of their own to her," Jackson adds.

"What?" I screech. My arms fall to my side, fisting in anger, frustration, and fear. "Is she okay? Did something happen to her? Her house?"

Shit, her house means so much to her. It's more than a building but a precious gift.

"She's shaken but fine. Seems this is the second fire in two weeks. Damn kids, I think." Jackson is an idiot. It isn't kids.

"What did the sign say?" I growl, glaring at Jackson who is almost gloating under my growing agitation.

"Capture the witch."

Son of a bitch.

"Naomi Winters doesn't need any trouble from us, like I don't want trouble with her. Arson this close to a project could be disastrous," Bill adds.

Forget the damn building. I want to know if she's okay.

"And you're certain nothing happened to her?" I ask, my voice vibrating with tension.

"She's fine," Bill dismisses. "I went to see her this morning at the library, ask her if she needed anything."

"And what did she say?" *Does she need me?*

"She blamed it on some kids, but I'm not convinced," Bill says, shaking his head.

"I'm not convinced either," I harshly offer.

"Oh really, and what do you know?" Jackson asks me. Here's where the crossroads begin for me. I can't rat out Junior as I have no evidence and I don't want to turn into a tattletale like Dwight. And whether I want to admit allegiance to the Wraiths or not, I'll always owe Catfish, so mentioning his name is a death sentence for me.

"I've got nothing but a hunch," I say to Jackson and Bill snorts.

"Well, we can't go with our gut," Bill adds.

Still. Sometimes we need to let our heart lead, and that's my decision. First, I need to get Naomi to talk to me. I'm not making light of her predicament, but I have my own capturing to do this evening.

I need to get to the community center and speak with Naomi, tell her how I feel, beg her to give us a chance. We can work through this, I'm convinced. I practically vibrate as I finalize securing the construction site from additional trespassing. With tonight being the Halloween party, who knows what trouble hooligans will want to cause in a vacant building. Or teenagers. Or MC prospects.

As I'm heading to my truck, I notice I've missed three calls. The first is from my mother who is most likely calling to tell me I'm late, as if I don't already know. The second two are from my brother who would rather text me than call.

"Toad," I gruffly address him as I hop in my truck. "What's up?"

"You'll never guess who's at the Fugitive."

If he's about to tell me Charlese, it won't surprise me. Charlese would move on to someone else if we didn't last, which we obviously didn't. We had a good thing going. No complications. Which is certainly not what I have with Naomi, but I'm rethinking my thoughts on that. Maybe it's not such a bad thing. I still have to prove myself to her, but I don't want her giving up on us.

"Who ya got?" I chuckle, waiting for her name. Maybe it's someone special for him.

"Dahlia."

"What?" I slam on the brakes as I'm reversing out of the Bickerton drive.

"Walked in with two friends, looking like her own kind of Halloween nightmare."

"What's that mean?" My stomach pitches.

"She doesn't look seventeen."

Shit. "Don't let her leave."

"Didn't plan to. In fact, she's lucky I don't haul her ass to my room and lock her up."

Shit. Shit. *Shit.* Why does she need to try my patience? And why tonight of all nights? Clem's waiting for me at the community center. So is Naomi without knowing it. Then it hits me. Dahlia is counting on me going there.

"Has she seen you?" I ask, reversing with tires squealing, kicking up gravel as I rush down Green Valley Road. Taking the Dragon in my truck, in the dark, is the last thing I want to do right now. It will take me an hour to get to her and an hour to get back. I need to get to Naomi, but Dahlia is my priority.

"I'm sure if she did, she'd turn tail and bolt."

I can't have Dahlia seeing her uncle and getting skittish. Who knows where she'll go next?

"Keep an eye on her. I'll be there." I call Ma next, leaving a voice message she won't know how to retrieve. My mother's worse than Naomi in refusing to use modern technology.

"What's I need a cellphone for?" Her accent thick in disgust.

"To call me."

"If I holler your name, you hear me."

"No, Ma. For emergencies. When I'm not here and you're out with the girls."

"What emergencies? I always have everything under control."

I can't even list all the times she hasn't. Apparently, I don't either.

I take the steep ascent up the mountain road, palms sweating as I maneuver my truck slowly through the curves. If I were on my bike, I might risk some speed, but my pickup is too big. I could use this time to strategize—figure out how I'll win Naomi back—but instead, I'm cursing my seventeen-year-old for being a rebel and a pain in my ass.

As I hit the true Tail of the Dragon, my thoughts travel back to *that* night, and I sober thinking of the loss of life. All of our losses. Naomi's brother is dead, but that night also changed the course of history for her and me. We could have been together all those years ago. Guess the universe had other plans in between that time and now. I definitely wouldn't have Clem or Dahlia if I changed my past, and for those two reasons alone, I can't wish it all away.

I navigate the road, old ghosts at every twist and turn.

"You need to ride again," my brother told me. "Prove to yourself you can do it."

I have. When I eventually returned to Green Valley, I took the slithering curves at high speed. Part death wish. Part proof of life. I needed to prove to myself I could handle the road and the memories.

A frustrating hour later, I enter the Fugitive hellbent on hitching my daughter over my shoulder and carrying her ass out of the club, but not before I make it known she's my daughter and I'll murder anyone who touches her. Fortunately, I don't need to do any Daddy-caveman routine as I don't find her in the bar.

"In Todd's room," Big Poppy tells me. I head through the pool room and out an emergency door to the attached motel where Todd lives. Owned by Big Poppy, the bar and motel are a mecca for riders to stop and hang out, putting aside club differences for the risk of riding down the Tail.

I don't knock when I get to the room but turn the handle and find my daughter sitting on the edge of Todd's bed. My brother sits casually in a chair with his booted feet kicked up on the mattress.

"You called my dad?" she snaps as she turns to Todd, glaring daggers at him.

"Whatcha think I'd do? Thought I brought you here to watch television?" Toad asks. He was the one watching out for my baby girl those years I was gone, and Dahlia and I were separated. She has a closeness with him that I lack as her father. It stings sometimes.

"What are you doing here?" I interject, drawing her attention back to me.

"You wouldn't let me go to Knoxville for Halloween." The university boy in Knoxville hasn't called her as often when I didn't allow the quote, unquote "college visit." *Surprise, surprise.*

"You never let me do anything," she pouts, crossing her arms at her waist. I finally take in my seventeen-year-old's appearance. A racy red bra fully exposed under an open black shirt. Her midriff on display. A short leather mini-skirt, fishnet stockings, and a giant red bow in her hair. With bright blue eyeliner and deep pink cheeks, it looks like the 80s vomited her.

"I'm trying to protect you from a broken heart."

"You're trying to keep me from living my life." *Ouch.*

"That's not true."

"You're always asking me to do stuff for Clem. I have my own life."

"Dahlia," I sigh. She's right. I need her help. But then I look at her and despite the woman she's becoming I realize she's still a child. She isn't my wife or my partner, she's my kid. "I'm sorry. I haven't been able to do it all alone. We're a team." *It takes a village,* Ma always says. Or in my case, a valley.

"I don't want to play." She swipes at tears leaking from her eyes and my chest constricts. It's rare to see Dahlia cry. She's grown more confident and stubborn since the move here. I might know someone like her.

"And now you have another girlfriend." Dahlia's voice takes on the sarcastic sassy tone that makes my skin crawl. "And Clem's all like, Daddy's in love," she mocks.

My breath hitches. *What?*

"She'll just leave you like the rest of them."

Man, can my kid throw a sucker punch.

"Dahlia," my brother warns, and I'm reminded we have a witness to her meltdown.

"It hurts to be left behind, doesn't it?"

It does hurt, but I don't know what she's getting at. Becca was a mistake. Margie wanted more than who I was. Both left me. My brows pinch.

"When did I leave you?"

"When I was little. You left me with Gramm until you fell in love with Margie. Ha." She drags out the words before her big finish. Dahlia didn't like Margie who didn't even try to get to know Dahlia. With Clementine as Margie's focus, Dahlia felt rejected by someone I thought would be my wife. Fuck Margie.

"Dahlia, I've explained this. I had to work. Green Valley didn't offer much. I sent home everything I had."

"Except you. Then you got another baby."

"What are you saying? Do you resent Clem?" I've never, ever heard Dahlia speak negatively about her sister. I mean, sure they fight as sisters do. Todd and I still fight, but in general, Dahlia's been an amazing big sister minus the menstruation books.

"No, I love her. I just ..." She's crying uncontrollably now, and I don't understand what she's trying to tell me. I don't understand seventeen-year-olds! "I want you to let me be my own person."

"And what? Visit some random guy at a college or hook up with a biker in a bar?"

Her head snaps up and just when I think she can't rachet up the death glare, she does.

"You don't understand anything. I hate you," she says.

I've heard enough. "Well too bad, because I love you, and now we're going home." I don't reach for my own child. I'm too upset. I nod at Todd who stands from his chair and steps forward, scooping her into his arms. I'd do it myself but I'm shaking so badly I wobble as I walk. While I want to hug her and tell her she's wrong, I'm afraid to touch her. Either way, we're getting out of here.

When we settle in the truck and I'm preparing to give Dahlia a lecture of a lifetime, I receive another call from Ma.

Goddammit. I answer instantly.

"Ma?"

"Daddy," Clementine's voice chokes and my heart aches. I hate that I'm disappointing her for Dahlia's behavior.

"Hey baby, I'm sorry I'm—"

"Daddy," she interjects, her little voice choked up. "They took Naomi."

CHAPTER TWENTY-FIVE

DEWEY DECIMAL CLASSIFICATION: 391
COSTUME AND PERSONAL APPEARANCE

[Naomi]

The annual Halloween party occurs before the weekly Friday night jam session at the community center, an old school converted for valley gatherings. The party will go in waves as couples with young children will leave first for trick-or-treating. Then, the older members will return to their homes, and finally, the younger crowd will head to bonfire parties throughout the valley. I tell myself the party won't be so bad, and mustering courage I hardly feel, I pull into the center's lot because I promised Clementine I'd attend.

"Get in. Get out. How hard can it be?" The difficulty lies mostly in seeing Nathan. I don't know what to do about him. Would it be wrong to forgive him? Is there anything to forgive? I've been so confused, muddling through my emotions this past week. Am I angry that he was involved in my brother's accident or am I angry he didn't tell me? Am I worried that he knew all along and played me out of his own sense of guilt? Or is he really attracted to me? We haven't spoken since his confession, but he's been leaving me little treats. Flowers. A pumpkin. More poems.

I've been constantly thinking about him, and my determination to stay away has turned into desperation to see him again. In my heart, he's forgiven. It wasn't his fault. It wasn't mine either, and I need to forgive myself, like Beverly often admonishes me. I just needed a little time to come to terms with everything. Now I'm back to putting my fate in the hands of the universe. If Nathan shows at the party, and doesn't run from me, then I'm taking it as a sign our connection might be destiny.

Does he love me? Does he love me not?

I'm scared either way. I wring my hands before I pull open the door of the former school building and find it bustling with people. Julianne will be here somewhere with her grandchildren, who are visiting from Knoxville. Sabrina will hopefully be here with Harry, and possibly Wyatt Monroe. Familiar faces stare at me, questioning who I am as I wander through the crowd. My costume is quite different from what I normally wear, but then again, it is Halloween, a ritual I don't celebrate but I will participate in for the sake of Clementine.

Jackson James is the first person who speaks directly to me.

"Miss Naomi?" His eyes roam my costume and I'm not certain if his surprise is my presence at the festivities or my appearance. I'm wearing something more revealing than I've ever worn before. On that note, so is Jackson.

"Deputy James," I drawl. "Why, who might you be?"

Jackson juts his hips side to side, like he's impersonating Elvis Presley, but with his uniform unbuttoned to almost his waistline, he looks more like someone from the Village People.

"I'm a hot cop. You see them all the time on social media."

I have no idea what he's talking about and I'm not good at hiding my surprise, so my brows rise high and my forehead wrinkles. I'm not certain hot cop is the category I'd place Jackson in presently, and I feel the urge to remind him he's not a police officer but a sheriff's deputy, but instead, I keep my comments to myself.

"Indeed," I say, not certain why I break into a British accent, but I don't know how else to respond to him. "You just need a cowboy, a

Native American, a military man, a motorcycle guy, and a construction worker and your band will be complete."

Jackson stares at me, not understanding the reference.

"Speaking of construction workers, Nathan Ryder was sure riled up earlier when he heard about the fire in your yard."

My back stiffens. I didn't want anyone to know what happened, least of all Nathan. I don't want him to overreact like he did at Genie's. Although the fire did concern me. The blaze roared to life in my driveway and I had to call the fire department immediately this time. A kitchen extinguisher wouldn't have been enough, especially as I haven't even replaced the last one yet.

"I assured him we'll continue driving by to make sure you're protected. One can never be too cautious. Protection is important." Jackson winks at me and for a moment, I hear innuendo in his little speech. *Oh my.* Simmer down, hot cop wannabe. I nod and excuse myself when I see Beau Winston following Julianne MacIntyre to the cafeteria. Her coleslaw is her signature contribution to events.

When I reach the food, I sidle up next to her.

"Is that your coleslaw?" I ask, knowing full well it is.

"My specialty," she states, her eyes widening when she finally turns to look at me, roaming over my costume. "My, you are a sight." Then she glances down to my empty hands. "What did you bring?"

I stare back at her realizing I haven't brought anything. I'd been so concerned about getting myself here in one piece I must have left the brownies I made on the counter at home.

"Mrs. MacIntyre." Beau Winston nearly accosts Julianne for a scoop of her salad and then turns to me. "Miss Naomi?" I'm sensing a theme, as people stare at my outfit. Beau digs into the coleslaw and then quickly walks away, carrying a plate full of Julianne's best.

"If I didn't know he was Beau, I'd swear he was Duane. Duane's the one who loved my coleslaw so much." Julianne and I both follow the retreat of the red-bearded twin, noting the curve of his backside in his signature mechanics costume, before looking at one another and giggling like school girls.

"I may be old, but my eyes still work just fine," she purrs, and I nearly stumble over at the suggestive tone. "Bethany sure knew how to produce 'em even if she didn't pick a good one to do it with."

My mouth falls open and then my gaze travels back to Beau. Julianne isn't wrong even if I do feel like a cougar watching him. I notice Hazel and Mabel, who are roughly my age, across the cafeteria watching with equal rapture as the Winstons gather at a table. The twins' pink cheeks hint at thoughts similar to myself and Julianne, and I feel all kinds of wrong admiring the rightness of the men in that family. Jethro is the hottest in my opinion and watching him with his children only adds to his appeal.

I quickly turn away as I hear Julianne's grandchildren call out to her. Her granddaughter has gotten so big in the last five years and has finally outgrown the Tinkerbell costume. Julianne didn't think she'd ever want to be another character. It looks like she's simply traded up to ballerina which is practically the same costume, minus wings and a wand. Her little brother is in tow dressed like Batman, cape and all. Julianne scoops up her grandbaby much to his dismay and excuses herself.

Not moving from the food table, I watch as Cletus Winston enters the room with his wife, Jennifer Sylvester-Winston holding his fingers. They're dressed like Sherlock Holmes and Watson, complete with top hat for Jenn as Watson and a vest for Cletus slash Sherlock. Vest-porn. Is that a thing? Because Cletus wears one well. Jen says something to her husband and then walks over to the dessert table, inspecting the supply of her famous banana cake cupcakes.

"Miss Naomi," she greets me, giving me a nod. Her smile reminds me of her mother. I liked her mother even if she was too tough on her daughter. Diane took me under her wing for a year when she discovered Vilma's Videos, and an unlikely relationship developed between us despite her friendship with my older sister Scotia. My chest pinches at the loss of another person important to me. It reinforces my desire to see Nathan. We have a lot to work out, but just maybe ...

"Miss Naomi," Clementine sings and I turn in her direction as she enters the cafeteria. Emma Rae follows her and shrinks back, startled by my appearance, but Clementine gives me a slow smile, similar to her father, and I realize I have nothing to worry about tonight.

"Jack Skellington," Clem says with a knowing smirk. I'm dressed in a pair of black leggings, feeling rather exposed without my full skirts. Thankfully, the long-tailed jacket I made covers my backside, although it's equally fitted, outlining my shape. A white shirt under the jacket and giant bow tie fashioned like Jack's completes the outfit. It's my face and hair that shock people. I've painted my face white to mirror *The Nightmare Before Christmas* character, and additionally given myself the appearance of hollow black eyes and stitched lips. Piling my hair on my head, I powdered it to blend with my face.

"Oh my," Emma Rae says, holding a hand to her chest. "You do look like him."

I smile and Nathan's mother flinches. I redirect my attention to Clem.

"So, Professor Trelawney, how goes the fortune telling this evening?"

Clem giggles. "I've predicted big things," she says. "As soon as my dad gets here."

I'm haunted by the fact she made a prophecy about her father and me. For her sake, I worry she'll be disappointed.

"Your father's coming?" I'm a little surprised. I mean, I am hopeful, but not certain what that means. He doesn't seem like the type to hang out at a community Halloween party. Most days, Emma Rae is the one bringing Clem to the library. I assume she is more involved with the girls day to day while Nathan works.

"Yep, he promised he'd come this year." Clem's hesitant smile tells me she's equally concerned he might not keep his promise.

Time passes with games for children. Food for all. Enough candy to cause sugar shock. As the evening draws on, Clem becomes more and more quiet. Her father hasn't shown. It's one thing to make unfulfilled promises between adults, but from a parent to a child, it's hard to watch the disenchantment.

Clem hasn't set down her prophecy ball the entire evening, and when I find her sitting in a folding chair, her concentration firmly on the mystical object in her hands, my heart pinches.

"Clementine," I softly address her as I squat before her. "Whatcha doing?" She should be running around with the other children but she's not. Sitting here, she looks like a wallflower. A child on the edge of the fun instead of enjoying the middle of it.

"He promised he'd be here."

My hands cover her knees. She did a good job finding a gypsy-looking skirt and a white blouse to complete her costume. She really does look like a young version of the Divination professor.

"Maybe something came up?"

"Something always comes up," she mutters. "Dahlia warned me. *He won't show,* she said. He's typically there for me, though. He knew tonight was special."

I swallow a lump in my throat. "Why was tonight special, honey?"

"Because of the prophecy." She shakes the ball in her hands. With trembling fingers, I brush back some of her hair as her head hangs low.

"What prophecy?" I keep my voice steady, although a chill raises the hairs on my skin.

"You and Dad. You went on a date with him and he was happy. Then I don't know what happened, but he's all grumpy again. I wanted him to come tonight, so he could see you. He'd smile again. Then he'd kiss you and you'd fall in love. I don't care if you're a witch and become my stepmother."

Whoa. There's a lot in her declaration. How do I explain to a child that dating doesn't work the way she thinks—Nathan can't just kiss me and then I'd fall in love with him. That's a fairy tale. But when I think about it, it's exactly what did happen. He kissed me all those years ago and I've been foolishly waiting for him ever since. Let's just gloss over the fact she thinks a kiss will lead to my becoming her step-mother. We're fifty steps away from something like that, but I need to address the disappointment Clem feels.

"Sometimes we only have wishes, Clem. Not predictions. Not prophecies."

I wish my brother hadn't died. I wish he hadn't drunk before driving. I wish Nathan had called me all those years ago.

Her head pops up. "Then what good is the ball?"

How do I tell her wishes are only wants and we don't always get what we want? How do I remind her the object in her hand is only make-believe?

"Clem, there's nothing wrong with wishes and dreams, but sometimes they don't happen like we want." I wanted to dance. I wanted to drink. I wanted to cavort, until my brother's death and the guilt froze me.

Clem stares at the ball. Then clasping it in her hands, she lifts it above her head and throws it at the tile floor. It instantly shatters.

"Clementine," I gasp. She quickly stands up, forcing me back and my hand lands on a jagged piece among the scattered shards. She races for the exit, and I stand to follow her, calling out her name. She pushes out the front door. When I make my way through the same door, I see her round the building. I call her name one more time before I curve around the side of the community center and stop short.

"Broom, broom, broom, look who's under the moon?" A male voice slithers down my spine.

It will never happen again, I tell myself, but my heart knows better.

"Itchy witchy gotcha, bitchy."

CHAPTER TWENTY-SIX

DEWEY DECIMAL CLASSIFICATION:
649.125 TEENAGERS

[Nathan]

We ride in silence at first. Dahlia cries softly and I reach out a hand for hers, but she ignores mine and I retract it to my lap. I'm white knuckling the steering wheel caught between the need for speed and the will for safety. My mind is completely focused on getting to Naomi. All Clem could tell me was that three boys captured her on the side of the community center. I didn't think to ask who did it. I asked for my mother. Ma assured me everyone was okay. Clem was shaken. But Naomi ... she's missing. Kidnapped.

"Didn't you, like, have, like, a fight with, like, the witch or something?" Dahlia says to me halfway through the drive. "Why are you, like, so anxious to get to her?"

My eyes close. *Give me strength. Someone, anyone. God. Goddess. Any supreme being who will listen.*

"No, we did not have a fight. We ... we're unfinished business. And don't call her a witch," I say. I don't know how to explain to my daughter the second chance I want with this woman, or rather the third. The power of three.

"Do you know something about this capture the witch stuff?"

"Capture the witch," Dahlia says, twisting in her seat to stare at me.

"Dahlia," I growl, my heart racing in my chest. "What do you know of it?"

"Like, I thought it was, like, all a joke."

"Out with it," I bark. Dahlia tugs at her too short skirt, sensing the severity of my tone. *My God, that scrap of material hardly covers her.* "Tell me more."

"Kids talk. Iron Wraiths. Said they were, like, planning to, like, rekindle the old game, like, only this time, like, they'd, like, do more than, like, rekindle it."

"What's that mean?"

"Rekindle means, like, relight a fire, Dad." *Her sass, so help me.*

"I know what the hell the word means, Dahlia. What do you think it means to the boys?"

Her eyes widen, and a hand covers her lips. "They wouldn't, like, set her, like, on fire, would they? Like an old-fashioned witch burning?" But there's no doubt between either of us, they very well could intend to burn Naomi at the stake. I'm ready to vomit.

"Which kids?" I snap.

"Wraith wannabes. Junior Henderson and Toby Bryant."

My hand smacks the steering wheel and Dahlia flinches.

"Why didn't you say anything to me?" My voice rises.

"I didn't think, like, they were, like, serious. They're always, like, joking about things, like, saying stuff they, like, do, like, plan to, like, do. No one, like, believes them." Dahlia's head dips and I shake mine. I remind myself Dahlia is still a child, a teenager no less, and they just don't always use their head. Case in point, this evening. I can't drive any faster down this damn road and my nerves are almost shot with the lack of speed, the questions in my mind, and the fear racing through my blood.

I fumble for my phone, wanting to call the sheriff's department, only to find I have no reception.

You've got to be kidding me. How did we survive without cellphones?

"Why, like, can't it work out with you two? Is it, like, because she's a witch?"

"Damn it, Dahlia, no. I don't care if she's a witch or the freaking Wizard of Oz. I like her, okay?" I smack the steering wheel once again and shift my eyes to my daughter.

"Look," I sigh. "Naomi is not a witch, okay? And even if she is, she's important to me. I heard what you said back there, and I appreciate your concerns about girlfriends and getting left behind." I stop short, no longer knowing which direction I'm going with my thoughts or what I want to say about Naomi and me. I think I love her, and I want to be with her.

"Too bad about it not, like, working out then," she mutters, a touch of sincerity in her voice. Here's the other thing about seventeen-year-olds, they can totally surprise you sometimes.

"Why?" I feel like I'm falling into a trap asking this question but I'm too curious to ignore Dahlia's comment.

"You were smiling more lately. It's been kind of nice." *See?* Surprise. My eyes shift to my daughter who refuses to look at me, keeping her eyes focused forward.

"I was smiling?" I question, a grin joining my inquiry.

"Yeah, you weren't, like, grumpy like you've been, like, the past week. You were actually … pleasant."

Big word there, I want to tease, but then my chest clenches.

Was I smiling? I was happy. I miss talking to Naomi each night on the phone. It is a bit adolescent, but I looked forward to that time. I also liked popping in to see her on my lunch hour. She always seemed so surprised at the spontaneity and I loved the look on her face. Like she was equally happy to see me. I think of poetry night, how she was tickled by my weak attempt at a poem, and how she said it was a gift. In less than a month, this woman has turned me upside down and inside out.

"I don't know if it's going to work out or not, but I want it to. I want to try to make it right," I tell my daughter.

"Clementine thinks you, like, love her," Dahlia softly teases.

I'm stuck on you.

Maybe I do.

"I'm sorry she's missing," she adds even quieter. "I hope she's okay."

Me too, I think. She better be okay or heads are going to roll and I know right where to start.

"I like you better when you smile," Dahlia whispers and my head briefly turns to her. I can't take my eyes off the road for more than a second.

"Yeah? Look, I'm sorry, okay? I've had a lot going on lately," I say, not needing to explain the pressure from the Wraiths or the fear of Dwight's retaliation on Naomi. "You and Clem make me smile, I just want to have Naomi smiles, too. Okay? I like me better when I have those smiles as well."

But right now, I'm afraid I'll never have one of those smiles again.

Finally, I pull up to the community center, and Dahlia turns on me again.

"What are we doing here?"

"I need five minutes with Clem and the sheriff. You can stay in the truck or come inside."

"I can't go in there," Dahlia scoffs, pulling down the visor for the illuminated mirror. Her face is streaked with tear-stained makeup. She snaps the mirror shut and hastily returns the visor to its place. Crossing her arms over her midriff, which I noticed is newly pierced at the belly button, she says, "I'll wait here."

As I exit the truck, an ominous feeling ripples up my spine when I see the blinking lights of the sheriff's car.

"Jackson," I address him as I pause by the front door of the community center. "Where's Clementine? How is she?"

"She's fine. A little shaken up but okay. She's inside with your mother."

I step up to him, our heights nearly equal. "What happened?"

"Seems your daughter witnessed some men take Naomi Winters from the side of the building."

I already know this. "Why were they outside?" I ask. The front door to the community center opens and Clem races toward me.

"Daddy." I bend as she tackles my waist, and I cup her head against me. Holding her, I try to process what the deputy said. Clem coughs.

"You're squeezing too tight."

I release her and skim my hands down her arms, examining her face. "What happened, Dandelion?"

"Miss Naomi and I were outside, and some men took her. They pushed me down and then grabbed Miss Naomi. She put up a fight, kicking and screaming like you told me to do if anyone ever tried to take me, and she told me to run inside."

Sweet Jesus. Why didn't Naomi run, too?

"Did you see who it was? Did you recognize any of them?"

Clementine grows quiet, her lips sucked into her mouth.

"She hasn't opened up to us. We want to help but we need a name," Jackson interrupts.

"Clem," I say, shaking her wrists in my hands. "Please, baby. This is important."

"Junior Henderson is the only one I recognized." Her voice is shaky as she speaks.

"How the hell do you know him?" I shouldn't swear at my child, but I'm equally shaken. Clem's eyes fill with tears as she shrugs and I'm sensing there's more she isn't saying, but it's a name and a start.

I'm gonna kill that boy. Then his father who I'm certain is behind this. This was his sick game to begin with.

"Okay, we'll send an APB out on the boy, see if we can figure out who he's with tonight or where he went."

"Where's Gramm?" But I look up to see my mother inside the front door, holding the handle, watching Clem and me.

"Go back inside, sweetheart. I have Dahlia in the truck. I'm gonna send her in too, okay? All my girls go home, and I'll be there soon."

"Dahlia's here?" Surprise and excitement fill Clem's voice, but I don't have time to consider the sisterhood of my daughters. I need to find Naomi.

"Daddy," she says, still holding my hand as I stand. "I'm sorry about the prophecy."

"What prophecy?" I ask.

"The one I made for you and Miss Naomi. I got mad that it didn't come true and I smashed the ball. It's the reason we were outside in the first place. Miss Naomi followed me."

What the fuck? "Dandelion, you can explain everything to me later, okay? But I need to go look for Miss Naomi and you need to go home with Gramm."

I press a kiss to Clem's fuzzy head and note the scent of honey and almonds coming from the scarf around her hair. *Naomi.*

"Now, Nathan, let the sheriff's department handle this," Jackson says, hitching a thumb in his belt. Ignoring him, I nudge Clem toward the front door and turn to my truck.

Yanking open the passenger door, I say to Dahlia, "You need to go home with Gramm and Clem."

"I am not going in the community center like this," Dahlia replies, drawing a hand down her costume, horrified.

"You should've thought of that before you selected your outfit. Naomi has been kidnapped, Dahlia, and I need to go after her. Out."

As Dahlia steps out of the truck and heads toward the community center, she calls back to me. "Dad, I'm sorry for what I said before." Her voice lowers as I open the driver door. I step up on the sideboard and peer back at her. "I don't hate you."

"I know, baby. We'll talk later, okay?"

She nods as I slip into the cab and start the engine.

I feel like all I've done this night is chase my own tail—racing after Dahlia, running to Clem, and now searching for Naomi. Suddenly, the Tail of the Dragon doesn't seem like the hardest journey of my life. My ride to find Naomi does, and I just hope I'm not too late.

CHAPTER TWENTY-SEVEN

DEWEY DECIMAL CLASSIFICATION: 364
CRIMINOLOGY

[Nathan]

"Where the fuck is she?" I snap, barging into the Dragon Biker Bar. I'm asking for trouble, going all lone wolf into the Wraiths' lair, but I need to know where my girl is, and this is the first stop. I have no doubt Dwight is part of Naomi's kidnapping with Catfish behind it all to get me to join the Iron Wraiths.

I glare at Catfish as he slowly stands from a stool. "Now, Wolf, what makes you think you can barge into my bar and make demands?"

"When did you become the prez?" The chatter and music around us lowers as it appears the others near us await an answer. The Iron Wraiths had a president—Razor Dennings, who's incarcerated. Second in command was Darrell Winston, hospitalized, and another lieutenant in arms, Repo, has been missing for years. Even Razor's old lady has disappeared. The club should be renamed Chaos because that's what they are in the middle of, and because I know all these facts, I'm not concerned about speaking up to Catfish. I haven't heard he officially holds any title yet.

"I don't want any trouble. Just tell me where the girl is."

"What girl is that?" Dirty Dave steps forward, licking his lips like he might have eaten said girl. I swear he makes chirping sounds under his breath.

"My woman. Naomi." I'm making a bold statement, a true one. Naomi Winters belongs to me. I want her safely returned first and then I'll worry about why they took her.

"We have no business with the birdie librarian," Catfish says, raising his hands in surrender.

"The fuck you don't. She's been harassed ever since I saw you at the Canyon. A fire in her yard. Broken taillights." I pause. The broken car lights were before we went to the Canyon. "Where is that weasel, Dwight?"

Dirty Dave laughs. "Weasel. Huh, good name for him."

"We haven't seen him tonight," Catfish says, sitting back on the barstool.

"Where might he be, then?" My anger is reaching a new level. Any second, I'll make a mistake in judgment and reach out for Catfish like I'm going to do the moment I find that jackass Dwight.

Catfish shrugs. I step forward.

"If it were Daniella, you'd be turning this valley upside down."

Catfish's eyes pinch to slits. "I don't know what you're talking about."

"The fuck you don't." It's no secret that Daniella Payton's family would not approve of Catfish and Daniella renewing their relationship from when they were kids, and yet, it's also not a secret they've been seen—*kissing*—while she was engaged to another man. A Winston of all men.

Catfish stands up fully, but I still have size on him. "You're mistaken."

"I'm not, and you know it. If she were missing, you'd see red." I don't have to tell him how I know about their affair. All Catfish needs to know is I'm willing to speak to her parents. Her father is a judge, and I'd start a personal war with Catfish, because love makes us do crazy shit.

"You have my word, Wolf. I don't know where he is. Or her." His word means nothing to me, and we continue to glare at each other—two pit bulls waiting to be unleashed. But there's something in his expression which makes me believe him. Maybe it's the slight softening of his hard-edged jaw when he sees I'm not backing down until I have my girl. My shoulders fall, the weight of unanswered questions pressing on me.

Where could she be?

"How are things going up at the mansion in the mountains?" Dirty Dave interrupts, a twisted gleam in his eyes. "Looks like a beauty of a place."

I'm about to tell him to shut the fuck up until something clicks.

A party at the construction site.

I turn for the door.

"Hey, I'm not done talking to ya," Dirty Dave hollers after me.

"You are now," I say, flipping him off and exiting the bar.

I make it to the Bickerton's in record time, although each minute it takes me to get there means one more minute Naomi might be in danger. I refuse to believe I'll be too late. I also refuse to consider the extreme.

Would they truly burn her?

I shiver at the thought.

I cut the engine the second I arrive. A light flickers and then dies inside the construction site.

Please don't let it be a fire.

I'm not surprised when I hear the purr of motorcycles behind me, but I don't look back. This is my business. I'll deal with the Iron Wraiths afterward. I don't go for the front door but sneak around the back where, I'm assuming, they cut into the Tyvek. However, I don't find an opening anywhere as I circle the house and find myself returning to the front. Catfish and Dirty Dave help themselves to the door. It opens without a catch.

Mother— I follow them. Inside, I'm surprised to find four people in addition to Catfish and Dirty Dave.

Three teenagers and one Dwight.

"Son of a bitch," I say the second I see Naomi tied to a chair, tape over her mouth. I do a double take as her face is streaked in black. Her hair is a tangled mess, looking extra white. A bigger shock is she's wearing pants and a giant tie at her neck. It takes a second to register she is dressed in a costume.

"Well, well, well, look what the cat dragged in," Dwight sneers and I turn on Catfish.

"Didn't know where she was, huh?" My fingers curl to fists as I stare down the wannabe president.

"Wolf, I just gave you my word. We followed you." Catfish turns his eye to Dwight. "What's going on?"

"Capture the witch," Dwight gleefully gloats, sweeping a hand toward Naomi. Tears pour from her wide eyes. I want to go to her, but I need to get the situation under control. There's five of them.

"Explain," Catfish demands, his booming voice cutting down some of Dwight's fun. Junior steps forward and speaks.

"We captured the witch," he states, like this is something out of a play, only there's nothing heroic going on here. "Ding, dong, the witch is *gonna die,*" he mocks, and I lunge forward. Dirty Dave catches me, and Catfish steps up to Junior.

"Why'd you take her?" he addresses the messy-haired teen.

"Wanted to show we could." His expression is almost the same as his father. "Wanted to prove we could deliver any package."

Dirty Dave snorts. The boy turns to his father, a menacing glare in his eyes, but there's something more. Something I remember from the night I witnessed Junior and his friend swapping something with Catfish. Junior is seeking recognition from his father. Acceptance. And it's pathetic he's gone to such lengths.

"What did you plan to do?" I demand over Dave's shoulder, although I'm already predicting the answer and my stomach twists with the thought.

"We have unfinished business," Dwight answers, turning to face

Naomi. "The boys were helping me. Although now that you're here, my intention might be different."

What did he originally intend to do? The unimaginable crosses my mind. Naomi whimpers behind me.

Catfish turns to Dwight. "What do you mean?"

Dwight's lost in thought as he glares at my girl. His voice lowers to an angry hiss as he says, "Itchy witchy, little bi—"

Catfish grabs him, cutting off the insult.

"It's just a little joke." Dwight's eyes flick over to me, glassy and dazed. Is he high?

"What's the joke, punk?" Dirty Dave asks of Dwight's son.

"Burn her." Junior's words turn my insides to ice.

Naomi's feet begin to kick and the chair she's secured to tips. I shrug out of Dave's grasp, and reach for the tilting chair. Kneeling next to her, I place a hand on the nape of her neck, in hopes of settling her. Her skin is cool but sweaty and I can only imagine the fear running through her. Her eyes widen as she looks at me, confusion and pain mixed together. *Does she think I'm part of this?*

As a construction worker, I always have a pocket knife with me, and I pull it from my jacket. The snap of the switch causes a chain reaction. Dirty Dave pulls a gun and Catfish turns his back on Dwight Henderson.

"Maybe we can offer a trade," Dwight suggests.

"I'm setting her free. She's not a part of this," I announce. "This is between us. This other ..." I point at Naomi. "... is some stupid kids' shit that went too far. Again." My eyes flick to Catfish as I begin to cut Naomi loose. Slipping behind her, I work at the ties on her wrists while shifting my eyes to Dirty Dave. "Catfish, how about you get the hound to lower the gun?"

"Put that away before you hurt yourself," Catfish snaps.

"Him for her," Dwight demands, although he's in no position for demands. Then it hits me. Did Dwight take Naomi in hopes I'd patch in? Me for her? It doesn't make any sense. He hates me.

Catfish doesn't move while I saw at the ropes on Naomi's wrists.

With Junior's attention on his father, the other two teens hover in silent stupor behind him. No one makes a move to stop me.

"You're not going to let him get away with this, are you?" Dwight demands of Catfish, stepping toward him. *Big mistake, prospect.* You don't question the authority of the club.

Catfish turns on Dwight. "What did you hope to accomplish with this?"

"You're the one who wants him back. Here he is. Take him." Dwight waves a hand out to me as if I'm the prize.

"You don't know shit," Catfish snaps, and I'm a little relieved as I can't imagine him sharing our history with someone like Dwight.

Dwight's face falls, panic setting in. "It's their fault. They just called me in after they got her." He points at his son and friends, and I'm shocked. Dwight Henderson is ready to sell out his kid to save his skin. Then again, I shouldn't be surprised. He's never to blame for anything, according to him.

"You asked us to do it," Junior snaps, and Dwight raises a hand to smack his son. Instead, Catfish slaps Junior. The crack of skin on skin resounds in the emptiness of the framed first floor. One of the boys behind Junior flinches at the action.

"Don't you lay a hand on my son," Dwight snaps although seconds before he was ready to do it himself. Catfish grabs Dwight by the throat.

"Your son? If you were a Wraith, he'd be my son. Son of the club. I'll treat him any way I want for this ignorance."

The club is your family. All members belong to each other, even children. Catfish isn't wrong. If Dwight were to patch in, Junior would be handled how the Wraiths saw fit. Catfish smacks Junior again, waiting on Dwight to respond. When Dwight doesn't, I'm sick, and I'm also done. This is another reason I can't join the Wraiths. I'd never manhandle a child.

"This is gonna hurt like hell," I mutter as I reach for the corner of the duct tape over Naomi's mouth. Her eyes widen in understanding, but she nods once. She lets out a horrific scream as the tape rips at the delicate skin around her lips. It's swollen and red, and I imagine it stings, but I have no time to comfort her. I need her out of here.

With hands on her upper arms, I slide Naomi from the chair and shift her behind me. She grips the back of my construction jacket. We don't have a moment for the reunion I want which involves me never letting her out of my sight again. Instead, I walk us inch by inch closer to the open door.

"No matter what you hear next, you run like hell to your house and lock your door. Then call the sheriff," I mutter over my shoulder to her. My tone remains steady, although it's opposite of the vibration hovering over my body.

"What about you?" she whispers and my chest clenches with hope. Is she worried about me? Does she still care?

"Go," I press, keeping my body before hers, blocking the door so she can escape.

"What the fuck?" Dwight says, making eye contact with me as the door cracks open and Naomi slips out. He rushes me but not before Catfish has him again by the shoulders. Dwight yells at me around Catfish. "You son of a bitch! She's gonna squeal!"

"And you'd recognize a squeal, you fucking pig," I bark, stepping forward, ready for a fight.

"Ha, Piglet. That'd be another good name for you," Dirty Dave says as if figuring out a gang name was the most important item at hand.

"I'll kill you for this, Nathan," Dwight threatens.

"Actually, there's no killing under our protection." Catfish twists to eye me, willing me to accept the position. He's here offering me asylum against Dwight if I'll only say yes. Whether his intention or not, Catfish fell into Dwight's trap. Me for her. An Iron Wraith prospect again.

I'll find another way.

I can't be one of them.

Suddenly, Junior Henderson has Dave's gun and the click of the trigger grabs all our attention. He's pointing it at Catfish.

"You hit me," Junior bites, a single tear slipping down his swollen cheek, but the edge of his jaw gives away a more murderous expression.

"Don't cry, you big baby. You want to be a man, act like it," Dwight commands. The disgust in his tone unsettles me. And that's the thing. He's not a man. I bet, he's not even seventeen. What has this boy suffered under this man?

"Now, son," Catfish begins, keeping his voice calm as he slowly raises his hands. "That's not a toy."

"Shut up," Junior replies with a shaky grasp on the trigger.

Oh boy. Catfish looks like he's going to eat this kid for breakfast.

"Steady boy," Dirty Dave says before lunging for the kid and a shot explodes. Without thinking, I tackle Catfish before I hear the thud of another body behind me. The gun clatters to the floor. Still covering Catfish, I search his body, looking for a puncture to his skin or blood. Wide eyes meet mine as I find him clear of injury. I look over my shoulder to see Dwight slumped against bracing two-by-fours, his hand covered in blood.

"You fucking shot me," Dwight mutters, his hand at his thigh which is seeping. For a split second, I think I'd like to watch him bleed to death for being a prick, but that's not the kind of man I want to be.

"You saved my life," Catfish mutters under me and the comment spurs me to action. I crawl over to Dwight and remove my jacket, pressing the thick material to the wound on his upper leg.

"You shot me," Dwight says, his voice shaky and confused as he watches the blood oozing from his leg. His eyes remain focused on his thigh although the words are intended for his son. Dirty Dave has his arms wrapped around the boy, holding him to the ground.

"You let him hit me," Junior states, his tone weak and uncertain, as if he's startled himself. Perhaps he fired the shot unknowingly. The adrenaline coursing through him could have made him shoot. The high takes over and you pull the trigger without thought.

"I'm tired of people thinking they can hit me," Junior states, trying to straighten under Dirty Dave's grasp while his lower lip quivers and he glares at his father.

He's only a kid, I remind myself.

Catfish stands and Dave pulls Junior up before him. The two other boys remain shocked and startled until the low sound of sirens filter through the sliver of the open door.

"Get out of here," Catfish tells them. "You didn't see anything." The two youths scramble toward the back of the house and disappear. Catfish looks at me and I tip my head. He nods in return. Dave releases Junior and the Iron Wraiths step out. I'm not certain how the remaining three of us are going to explain this—my word against the Hendersons—but I'll tackle that in a minute. It seems hardly any time passes before the sound of sirens echoes louder down the road, and then red and blue lights flash through the open front door.

Thank you, goddess next door.

CHAPTER TWENTY-EIGHT

DEWEY DECIMAL CLASSIFICATION: 306.87
PARENTING

[Nathan]

W *hat a fucking night and it isn't over yet.*
I'm totally beat when I reach my house after a statement to the sheriff. I don't know what exactly will happen next for the Hendersons. Junior admitted what he'd done to his father. Both kept quiet on what they did to Naomi, though, and I had no problem bringing that part of the evening to Sheriff James' attention. He's a good man and I know he'll look into the matter. For now, Dwight will be in the hospital for surgery and recovery, along with an arrest as an accomplice in the kidnapping of Naomi Winters. Junior's headed for juvenile detention and hopefully some mental care. His guilt could eat him alive. I know all about that.

I'm torn between heading next door and going home to my girls, but the blood on my hands needs to be washed away and the ruined jacket needs to be replaced. I need to clean myself up before I go to Naomi. Despite Sheriff James's assurance that she is safely in her home being interviewed by his son, Jackson, I need to see Naomi for myself.

It is more than that.

I need to touch her. Her hair. Her face. Her lips. I need personal confirmation she is whole because this evening, I'm broken.

I could have lost Dahlia.

I could have lost Clem.

I could have lost Naomi.

The final thought hits me hard in the chest. It isn't that Naomi ranks higher than my children, but she rates among the most important people in my life—the people I never want to lose—and the people I love most.

After I toss my construction jacket in the trash and take a quick shower, I stand outside Clementine's door, watching her sleep. My heart expands with love and fear. What if those boys had taken her? What if they had touched her? Emotions swirl within me. In her pink room with a nightlight projecting stars on the wall, I want Clem to remain as innocent of this world as she is in this moment. Yet, the reality is, she'll grow up. She is becoming a woman in her own right: intellectually as well as physically. I think back to the books I checked out at the library. The ones which re-introduced me to Naomi, rekindled my attraction to her, thus beginning this wild ride. My sweet Clem was part of the universe reconnecting Naomi and me, all because I needed books to help her understand her changing body. There needs to be an adult book titled *I Have a Heart*. The subtitle could be how to understand the constantly evolving emotions within it.

Speaking of a child growing into a woman, I sense Dahlia behind me in the narrow hallway. Not quite a woman. More than a child. Who knows what could have happened to her this evening at the Fugitive if my brother hadn't been there? She might have given her virginity to a boy, who was lost, who got called away, who followed his head instead of his heart.

"Is she okay?" The small sound of my daughter's voice turns my head. She looks young again with her hair freshly washed, long and straight around her face. She wears baggy pajama pants with giant smiley faces and a faded pink T-shirt. *Why can't she stay like this?*

"Clem will be okay. She's pretty resilient." When I moved Clem away from her mother, I worried about the repercussions of her not seeing Margie as often. A young girl needs her mother. Clem has never once hinted she misses her mom or wants Margie more than me. "She isn't hurt physically. I just hope she doesn't have a nightmare."

"I didn't mean Dandelion, but if she wakes up, I can get her. She'll probably come to me anyway." I search for sarcasm in my daughter's voice. She's hinted often enough lately that she feels responsible for Clem in a way she doesn't appreciate. On the other hand, if Clem does have a bad dream, I usually return her to her own bed as I feel she's too old to crawl in with me. Since our return to Green Valley, I have found Clem in Dahlia's room if she's had a nightmare. Dahlia's head lowers, as she swipes hair behind her ear. Sheepishly, she adds, "I meant Miss Naomi."

I take a deep breath, shuddering when I consider that my daughter knew how this night might play out, and she didn't tell me. I pause with my hand on the doorjamb, taking a deep breath to steady myself before I face her.

"She's shaken up and frightened, which I'm sure was their intention." The boys didn't appear to know what to do next with Naomi, despite what they said about burning, and who knows what Dwight was thinking. After the initial capture, there wasn't a physical plan. Junior Henderson was too wound up to confess anything other than the *idea* of capturing the witch, reviving an old legend and proving themselves to a bunch of men—the Iron Wraiths—who could have cared less about the child's play of kidnapping an innocent woman. If I told Dahlia the names of the offenders, I have no doubt she would recognize them. She already told me who was talking in her school. My only hope is she isn't mixed up with either of them.

"I'm sorry something happened to her." The quiet tone is disconcerting. Dahlia isn't often contrite or sincere, especially since we moved to Green Valley. Uprooting her to this small town has spurred her sarcasm levels off the chart.

"I'm going to check on her," I say hesitantly, although I don't need my daughter's approval. She nods slowly.

"I didn't mean what I said," Dahlia states, lifting her head and swiping loose hair behind her ear again.

"Which time?" It appears my sarcasm has resurfaced, but I'm not in the mood to argue with my child.

"That I hated you." A single tear slides down her cheek, but she quickly wipes it away. My shoulders fall, and I step toward my girl. I have already forgotten those words from this evening. I wrap her in my arms, tugging her to my chest.

"I know, baby," I tell her, because while she might say she hates me, her words are only words, lashing out for attention. Her slim arms wrap around my middle in a surprising reciprocation of my embrace and she hugs me tighter. My hand cups the back of her head and I kiss her hair. *Why can't she always be like this?* Instead, I tell her how I feel, with words I do mean. "I love you, sweetheart."

A sharp inhale escapes her. The phrase isn't something I say often enough to my children, and I need to do better.

"I love you, too, Daddy. And I meant the other thing I said."

I pull back to look down at her. Liquid eyes the color of fresh-tilled earth stare up at me. With her face clear of makeup, her youthful beauty makes my heart ache. "Naomi did make you smile more. Do you think you can win her back?"

My thumbs swipe at my daughter's cheeks. "I'm hoping I can get her to make me smile again."

Dahlia's lips twist in a knowing smirk. She nods once before whispering, "Go get her, Dad."

Another quick hug and I'm down the hall and out the back door but not safely in my truck yet. A large body looms against the side of my garage. I'd prepare to fight if I didn't recognize the outline and have expected him to show up sometime.

"Curtis." The use of his given name reminds us both of a time long gone. Nights when he stole to my home needing refuge from his uncle.

"Wolf." The use of my biker name reminds us both I'm still obligated to him outside of our past friendship. We stare in the dark at one another, both nothing more than an outlined shadow. If he's going to kill me, I wish he'd get it over with as I have somewhere important to be other than my own funeral.

"You saved my life."

I'm stunned a moment, remaining silent as I repeat the statement in my mind. *I saved his life.* Honestly, we have no way of knowing if Junior Henderson intended to kill Catfish, or merely shoot him. Either way, a bullet could have been fatal. Or not. My head lowers, shaking side to side. I don't know what made me jump over him, taking him to the floor. Maybe it was our long-gone friendship, a relationship once valued by both of us. Maybe it was some sick obligation to him for setting me free.

I shrug.

"Not many would do that for someone they owe."

Oh man, here it comes.

"So I'd like to consider us even. A life for a life."

My head shoots up and I glare into the darkness at his imposing form. I clear my throat before I speak, not wanting to betray my surprise. One was taken too soon. One was saved tonight. "I don't know what to say."

"I'll still be watching out for you, but I think you've proven you aren't going to take us down." The collective *us* really means him. He's a Wraith now, in more ways than one.

It's the closest I'm going to get to any gratitude from him. Not that I expect any. I did what I had to do, just like I tried to save Dwight the dweeb. Just like I wanted to save a dying man on a dangerous road. It's all more of a reminder I'd never fit in with a club, not one like the Wraiths.

"I hope the chick's okay." He references Naomi and I'm hopeful he understands. Maybe he has a conscious after all. His heart certainly belongs to Daniella Payton.

I tip my chin. "I'll see ya around."

"Let's hope not," he responds, stepping back into the dark shadows at the side of my garage. I hear him walk away and hold my breath until the gentle hum of a motorcycle breaks into the late night somewhere off in the distance.

Finally, I turn for my truck.

No more waiting, Naomi. I'm on my way.

CHAPTER TWENTY-NINE

DEWEY DECIMAL CLASSIFICATION: 269
SPIRITUAL RENEWAL

[Naomi]

I sit outside by the firepit, holding a glass of wine in my hands. I can't seem to get warm although I stood in the shower for the longest time. I scrubbed at my hair and my face, removing the makeup and powder as best I could. It's the rest of my body that trembles with the grime of them touching me. Nothing sexual, *thank you, Mother Earth*, but enough manhandling to make me feel dirty.

I reflect on the night. Sheriff Deputy Jackson James arrived at my house shortly after I got out of the shower. He wanted details of my night and it was hard to recall them all. I'm not a good witness under the stress, but I explained to him how I followed Clem, and found her in the middle of three teens outside the community center.

"Not men, but definitely young adults. I recognized two of them, but I don't know their names," I told him. One was Dwight Henderson's son, whom Jackson said has been taken to the station for shooting his father.

"He shot his dad?" My heart breaks a little. What would make a young man pull the trigger on his father?

"It's a little messed up but we'll get to the bottom of it. He clearly needs some help."

I nodded. The younger Henderson does need support and guidance. "Will he go to jail?"

"Juvie."

Wow. "What about Dwight?" I don't want to care about him, but my religion centers on concern for all humans equally.

"Shot in the leg. He'll need surgery, recovery, and some jail time himself for what he did to you."

Dwight Henderson was being charged as an accomplice in my kidnapping even though he wasn't present for the actual capturing. I don't know how this will play out and I'm exhausted just thinking about testifying in court if I need to.

"What about the other boys?" I asked but Jackson just stared at me.

"What other boys?" He pauses a beat. "Why don't you start at the beginning again?"

I exhale with frustration and recall the evening's events one more time.

It will never happen again, I told myself, but my heart did not believe me.

"We don't want any trouble," I recall saying in defense of Clementine and myself, trying to keep my voice calm. My hand throbbed and I cupped my left with my right. Blood dripped from the stinging wound. Clem looked at me over her shoulder and took one giant step in my direction. Thankfully, all eyes seemed trained on me.

"Broom, broom, broom, look who's under the moon?" Dwight's son said.

"Seems the witch has transformed to a skeleton tonight." The blond from the Stop-and-Pump spoke.

"I'd like to check out her bones." Another boy sneered.

"I'd like to bone her," the blond added. I shuddered with the thought.

"Ewww ... she's old," Dwight's clone replied. They're children in the form of men which made them no less ruthless or strong, I reminded myself.

"Clem," I muttered. "Go back inside."

"Before she casts a spell on you, my pretty," Dwight's son mocked in an

evil witch imitation. He looked exactly like his father once did. On the verge of muscles. Spiky dark hair. Questionable eyes.

My heart pulsed in my ears and my hand throbbed. My only concern was Clem.

"Let her go. She has nothing you want," I warned.

"Except her older sister." One of the other boys chuckled, and my stomach rolled. Dahlia.

I stepped forward, hoping to place myself between Clem and the boys. In doing so, I entered their circle.

"Clem," I hissed. "Run." I turned as she did, watching one of the teens bump into her and knock her to the ground. I screamed her name as one grabbed my waist. Lifting me off the ground, I kicked back at my captor while my hands pulled at the arms around my belly.

"We've got ourselves a fighter here," the boy at my back said, his voice slithering around my neck. "Grab her damn legs."

Another boy stepped forward to clutch each of my ankles. I twisted my hips hoping to loosen the hold they had on me. I remembered dropping, and gasping, but I was caught before I hit the ground. My hand shot up and I weakly connected with the chin of the teenager holding me.

"Bind her hands." Someone stepped forward and cuffed my wrists at my waist. I saw Clem smacking at the back of the boy at my ankles.

"Clem, run," I said. "Tell someone." It's part of the advice I've given her on being bullied. Tell a teacher, the school social worker, or a friend. Tell someone until they listen. She'd been afraid to tell her dad and I didn't understand why.

"Get her," one of the three demanded, but Clem made it around the building before someone could snatch her.

Sweet Goddess, don't let anything happen to the child, I prayed.

I screamed "Run!" until a hand covered my mouth. A bag went over my head.

"There were two other boys. One blond. One with pink streaks in his hair," I told Jackson.

"They weren't at the crime scene, but we'll investigate further," he assured me.

"I can't believe it happened again," I muttered, not realizing I said it aloud.

"It won't ever happen again," Jackson stated, although how he can be certain is beyond me. There will always be someone who doesn't understand a religion or political view or sexual orientation. And there will always be discomfort and disconnect from prejudice. Someone will always have a differing perspective, and either act or react based on it. And yet, I don't get the sense any of what happened tonight revolved around my religious practices.

What a cluster ...

I nodded as Jackson closed his tablet and stood to leave.

"What about the Iron Wraiths and Nathan Ryder?" Did something happen to him? He defended me, but we certainly didn't have time to chat about what was happening. From the moment Nathan had entered the house, my heart raced. Was he hero or foe? I hated that I doubted him. It was all so confusing.

"Nathan Ryder gave a statement. He was holding his jacket to Dwight's wound when we arrived, trying to staunch the blood flow. There weren't any other men present. Just the boy. The other kids must have run off, but we'll find them. Some of the Wraiths were present, you say?"

I pause a second, considering how I should react.

"I must have been mistaken. They were all wearing leather and such," I lied, waving off my absentminded assessment and hoping Jackson falls for it. *See, terrible witness.*

"Will you be okay alone tonight, Miss Winters? Want me to call someone? Your sister maybe?" There's nothing Beverly could do for me and Scotia would never come. For a moment, Jackson lingered, and I worried he was about to suggest himself for comfort.

"I'm fine," I lied, still shaky and spent, but I had something I needed to accomplish this night.

"We'll be patrolling the area again later tonight. Lock your doors, but you're safe now," he said, confident in his protection.

When Jackson left, I dressed in a simple shift nightgown. It's gauzy and light and slightly opaque, but it brought me comfort to be dressed in the vintage linen. I had an obligation to myself this evening and it involved a celebration of life and gratitude despite my recent scare.

Currently, a small pyre is assembled in my backyard, contained within an iron fire-safety ring. A traditional bonfire isn't permissible so close to the trees surrounding my property, and as I'll be a singular dancer for this celebration, there's no need for a raging flame. Tonight is Samhain, and I intend to honor my obligation to remember the dead. It feels especially appropriate this year as recent events have brought so many reminders of my brother's passing. I'm hopeful the ritual of bread for the deceased, a fire for life, and the spiritual dance will finally put my brother to rest in my heart. I'm ready to release my guilt.

I take a sip of the celebratory wine. This is the rare occasion I drink, and tonight, I need it.

With the fire started, and my bare feet slowly warming to the cool earth under my toes, I sit with my knees bent and my shift tucked around my legs. The late October mountain air ripples through the light material but I patiently wait for the fire to heat me. The wine warms my insides and I take another sip of the crisp berry, fall harvest red as I stare at the flames, forming their own dance in the nighttime breeze.

Samhain dances differ from Beltane as it's a private affair. Open to my interpretation, tonight I dance to remember my brother, offer gratitude for the past year, and open my mind and heart to a new year. Traditionally, I'd call forth my brother. Not that he'll appear to me, but I'd reach out to him in mind and spirit. Tonight, I hope to let him rest. I hope he accepts my apology for the eighteenth year and one-hundredth time, and then set us both free.

I stand and pace around the firepit. I'm no longer a dancer, but I follow a simple set of steps, relaxing my body and attempting to free my mind. I also need to forgive. Forgive myself. Forgive my brother. He drank. He drove. Those were his decisions. Finally, I need to forgive Nathan for his part. I want to blame him for not reacting instantly to my brother's crash, but I'm doing what I strive not to do—project action. I have no idea how I would have reacted in a situation similar to Nathan's, and it isn't fair to judge him for his response. It isn't fair to hold against him decisions made so long ago.

From my sister Beverly I've learned bitterness hurts and takes so much energy to maintain. So much negativity. It's easier to let it go. It's harder to allow the hatred or guilt or shame to fester. And I'm tired. I've strived to be the person I want to be, but something has always held me back from fully embracing myself.

As I increase my pace, twisting and turning sensually with arms lifting and lowering, I release myself to the night. *Let the inner goddess remain.* The independent woman who knows her mind and body and spirit. Let the things which clog the growth of those counterparts disperse. Within minutes, I feel lighter. I feel braver to go after what I want. It hits me hard that the first thing that comes to mind is Nathan Ryder. He's what I want.

I smile as I slow my steps. Taking one and two and three, and then stop. I almost feel giddy with decision, making new choices for myself, and I bow to the fire, which isn't necessary.

I reach for a bottle of bubbles near the bottle of wine, swirl the wand in the sudsy liquid, and raise the plastic stick to my lips. Blowing gently, I watch the soapy bubbles drift above the fire and abruptly pop. Bubble-blowing is a practice I adopted at Bethany Winston's funeral years ago, and I continue it each year as I remember those who have gone before me. I'm sending a message to the dead, willing their spirit to flow back to the heavens on this night when the portal of life and death is open.

One bubble. *Bethany Winston, your friendship meant everything to me.*

A second one. *Jebediah Winters, your love and acceptance set me free.*

A double bubble for my deceased parents. *Mother and Father.* I pause and take a large breath. *I forgive you for what you said to me.*

I'm hopeful spirit fairies will find them all settled in the afterlife. I follow the drift of the double bubble until a floating spark from the fire nears the edge of the suds and pops the conjoined circles. I smile as a tear falls and then I turn back for my seat. I lower to the ground, pulling the bottle of wine to me and pouring a second glass. Looking up through the haze of smoke flowing around the flames, an image forms and for a moment I believe I'm hallucinating. The outline of a man becomes clearer, approaching from the opposite side of the small fire. Our eyes find each other. Silvery orbs stand out against the backdrop of the dark trees. In a leather jacket, deep blue dress shirt, and dark jeans, he stands tall and imposing and delicious looking.

"Nathan."

CHAPTER THIRTY

DEWEY DECIMAL CLASSIFICATION: 129
ORIGIN AND DESTINY OF INDIVIDUAL
SOULS

[Nathan]

"Nathan."

My name whispers over the flames dancing in the small fire contained with a metal ring. The flame illuminates the darkness around us, and a strange sense of calm settles over me as I observe her. Her eyes glow like silver jewelry and remain fixated on mine as I slowly circle the firepit to stand before her.

"You're drinking," I say which isn't really the first thing I want to tell her. I want to tell her she's beautiful, and I'm so relieved she's physically okay.

"It's the one night I let loose," she replies, charcoal eyes looking up at me. "It's Samhain."

"Sam who?"

"Samhain. It's like Halloween. The *original* Halloween celebrated by the Celts. It's the night when the realm between the living and the dead opens and souls run free."

"And you're blowing bubbles because?" I knocked on the front door but didn't receive an answer. Then I smelled the faint scent of a campfire and worried another fire had been set somewhere on her property. Nothing could have prepared me for rounding her house to find her dancing around a flame, blowing bubbles in the air.

"The bubbles are like fairies, carrying the restless spirits back to their resting place."

I stare down at her, my hands slipping into the pockets of my jeans. I'd like to think she hit her head, but I know she believes in what she's telling me. I'm trying to understand her, and I know some of what she explains is similar to the original meaning of Halloween, not the trick-or-treat stuff we celebrate in the United States, but more a traditional festivity.

"Tonight's a night to give gratitude for a hearty harvest and honor the dead. And celebrate a new year beginning. It's my New Year's Eve."

My knees crack as I squat next to her, and absentmindedly rub at the gratitude bracelet she gave me. I need to give gratitude tonight as well. I'm so thankful she's alive and unharmed.

"So, blowing bubbles and drinking wine is how you honor your brother and ring in a new year? Does he visit you on Sam-ham?"

"It's pronounced Sam-*ween*, and now you're just laughing at me," she teases, her voice dreamy and rich. *Is she drunk?* "I'm not talking to the dead, Nathan."

At her sharp tone, I lift a hand and rub my knuckles over the scruff under my chin. It's a nervous habit when I don't know what to say.

"You feeling okay?" I ask. My eyes drift to the wine. She lifts the glass and takes another sip. "You mind?" Without waiting for her response, I remove the glass from her hand and drink. It's sweet and fruity, not my thing.

"I've been better." She pauses and tilts her head. "Actually, I think I might be at my best."

"Whatcha mean, sweetheart?" I ask, lowering myself to sit next to her. The flames at my back are making me too warm in my leather jacket and I remove it to place under me. I notice she's only wearing some thin dress, draped over her raised knees. Are her feet bare? Where are her shoes? It isn't that warm out here.

"I feel like I've been holding something inside me for a long time. Keeping it contained in a jar, but like the pumpkin you gave me, I've set the lightning bugs free." Okay, I definitely think she's tipsy, but I like what I'm hearing.

"So you liked the pumpkin."

"It was very sweet."

"I carved it myself."

"You did?" She turns to look at me, her eyes glittering from the firelight. "All your gifts were very sweet." She slowly grins at me, and although it doesn't reach her eyes, it's a start. "What are you doing here?" She looks around as if she's suddenly realizing it's dark and late and we are in her yard.

"I came to see if you were okay. It's been a frightening night." I bend my knees to sit like she is and wrap my arms around them as best I can. My gaze drifts to the flames. "I was frightened."

"You were," she states in surprise. I feel her looking at me, so I turn back to catch her eyes.

"I don't know what they planned to do to you, but anything was too much. I don't like to think of them manhandling you or tossing you about." My eyes roam her bent body. "Did they hurt you?" I gaze at her mouth which was raw and red when I removed the duct tape. She lifts a wrist and shows me the pink, raised lines cut into her skin. Reaching for one wrist, I tug her arm toward me by her forearm and kiss the delicate skin, taking a liberty I'm not certain I deserve yet but wanting to offer comfort anyway. "I was afraid I'd lost you forever this time."

She tips her body to lean against mine and I wrap an arm around her, noting once again how thin the fabric of her dress is. Heat emits from her skin through the material.

"I'm not going anywhere, Nathan."

I lean over and kiss her temple, lingering at her hairline. She smells like I remember: honey and almond and delicious.

"You sure you're okay tonight? I mean ... more than what happened next door. This ..." I nod off at the fire. "It looked like you were dancing when I walked up."

"You saw that?" she quietly shrieks, lifting her head from my chest and turning to look up at me. "It's tradition to dance around the flames. Once upon a time, Celtic communities gathered to celebrate with feasts and drinking."

"Sounds like foreplay to an orgy."

She chuckles and I notice her feet shifting under her dress. "Drinking and cavorting." Her eyes return to me. Are those ... have her eyes returned to ... lick-me eyes?

"Is this like an *Outlander* thing?" My ma watches the show and I've seen glimpses of it.

"What?" She laughs again and I swear it's the sweetest sound.

"You know, those dudes in skirts in Scotland," I say.

"Kilts. And I guess you could compare it to that, sort of." Her voice remains playful, so she isn't mad at me for asking and she sees I'm not teasing her. I'm trying to understand.

"So dancing around the fire ..." My eyes drift back to the flames and I reach for the bottle near her toes. I take a swig right from it and then lean back to tug my shirt from my pants. I'm wearing a deep blue button-down and dark jeans, trying to clean myself up before I came over here to beg her forgiveness once I saw she was unscathed, or if she was scathed, ask her if I could hold her so she felt safe. Now I have another idea.

I stand up enjoying her eyes on me as I slowly unbutton a few buttons and then tug my shirt, T-shirt and all, over my head to remove it. I tie the arms around my waist and lower a hand for her.

"Pretend it's a kilt. It's the best I can do on short notice." I wiggle my fingers at her.

"Nathan?" she questions, her deep eyes flaming from the fire.

"Dance with me, Naomi." She doesn't take my hand at first and I hold my breath as I stare down at her. "Let's celebrate your brother together."

Slowly her hand comes to mine and I tug her upward, watching her gracefully rise. Her hair is intricately braided like the night of our date at Genie's and I want to wrap it around my fist and draw her to me. Then my eyes travel down her attire.

"Sweet Goddess," I hiss. *What in the name of all things holy is she wearing?* The material is opaque, and I can see every detail of her through the thin fabric. She's not wearing a bra and she's not wearing ... *Mother Earth*, as she says. I swallow hard at the sight of her. Dark nipples peak at the fabric. Her curves are on display as the dress hugs her hips and outlines her breasts. My mind instantly envisions her completely naked and my body wants to lay her under the stars and celebrate her, but I don't want to cross a line I don't think I'm allowed to pass. The racing of my heart behind my ribs is almost visible. I want this woman with every part of my being.

She slowly smiles up at me when my eyes finally return to her face. She knows what I'm thinking. She has to know.

"You're so beautiful." It almost hurts to look at her in this flimsy dress with the firelight dancing on her. Hurts, in the best way.

"Thank you," she whispers as the color of her cheeks deepens. I hold up our collective hands and wrap the other around her lower back, drawing her against my bare chest. Her nipples crush against me, hardly contained with the thin material between us. Her breasts rise and fall against me, dragging slowly over my skin. Her hand tentatively comes to my shoulder, wrapping over the muscle, and the heat from her touch singes me. I'm so turned on I forget for a moment what our purpose is in standing here.

"Shall we?" she suggests, and I slowly lead us around the circle. It's not the dance I witnessed earlier, twisting side to side, arms elegantly raised in some kind of praise, like she was reaching out for something, or someone. No, we have a more traditional dance happening, taking our time to move around the flames in a lazy sway. The crackle of the fire and the lofty mountain breeze is our music, and I concentrate on her lips as my thumb at her back forms soothing circles, absorbing the heat of her against me.

"Is there something I should say? Something I should be thinking?" Because all I'm thinking as we circle the flames is that I want her.

"We should be thinking of my brother."

"I'm sorry about your brother." My voice is quiet and the air around us suddenly feels cooler.

"I know you are, Nathan."

"I want you to forgive me." I won't say I caused the accident, but I do harbor guilt over it happening, over witnessing it. Her hand slips from my shoulder, palm flat against my left pec. She must feel my heart racing underneath it.

"I've lived with regret for so long, Nathan. My sins from that night. Calling my brother, making him feel he had to come get me when he was clearly in no condition to do it. I don't know if I can ever forgive myself."

Which means she may never forgive me, either. My shoulders fall, but I pull her a little closer. My lips come to her forehead.

"Why are you here, Nathan?"

"I told you, I wanted to check on you and see that—"

"No." She stops moving. Her hand hasn't left my heart. "What are you doing here? You could have called me. It could have waited until tomorrow." Her deep chrome eyes look up at me, all shiny and silvery and questioning in the firelight.

"I don't want you to wait anymore for me. I want to be here. Now, in this time, in the present." I pause a moment, something she said a second ago still bothering me. "I don't want to forget the past. I'll never be able to let it go either, but I need to move on. I want you to move on, too. You mentioned sins from that night and regret. Do you regret being with me? Can we not think of your brother for a moment and only think of us?"

Her forehead furrows and her eyes drift down to her hand on my chest. Her fingers splay open across my skin.

"I don't regret you. Then or now." I tug her a little tighter in my relief, but then she adds, "But if I hadn't been with you …"

My arms drop and I step back a little. *If she hadn't been with me …* I look over at the fire, my hands slipping back into my jeans, so I don't drag her to me.

"You know, Nae, we can't live with what-ifs. What if you hadn't ever shown up at the bar in the first place. What if I'd never met you. What if I hadn't returned to Green Valley. Those are questions we will never have answered. We can only live with what we do." I turn back to her. "Can you accept what happened between us? Between you and me and that night?"

Her breath hitches. She understands I'm talking about us and the physical chemistry we had. "I think about it all the time."

My hands instantly come to her cheeks and I lower for her lips, drawing her into me. Her hands hesitate as they return to my skin, spreading over my shoulders and around to my neck. She tugs me to her as the kiss deepens, and I release her cheek but not her lips. I slip an arm around her back, pressing her against me again.

"Do you feel this, Naomi?" I say, pulling back but holding my forehead against hers. "Do you feel something happening to us? Now. Here." She nods against me and my hand slips from her other cheek to the swell over her left breast. Her heart hammers like mine, rapid and wild.

"Here's a what if, Naomi. What if I fell in love with you? What if I never stopped thinking of you? What if I always wondered what happened to you?" Her breath hitches, and she pulls her forehead back from me. "I'm stuck on you, Naomi, and I think that means I've never let you go. I've been *waiting* as well. Waiting to find my way back to you."

"Nathan," she moans.

"Forgive me. Forgive yourself. Let's move on, Naomi. Together." This is my plea. A prayer. A spell.

Her lids lower and my shoulders fall with the hesitation. She's going to walk away and I'm going to let her go this time. I have to if she doesn't want us. My hand skims up her back, memorizing the curve of her under my touch. The hand on her heart stretches up to her shoulder until both of my hands meet on opposite sides of her, cupping her shoulders. My chest suddenly aches, and I feel like I'm going to be ripped in two. I prepare to step away and leave her to the night.

Then her lips press at my chest, just over my heart. She lingers and my breath hitches forcing my pec to flex under her tender lips. She smiles against me, pebbling my warm skin in an opposite reaction. Goosebumps.

Her eyes lift to mine, and I recognize the look. She tips up on her toes, and kisses me, reminding me of the time in the library when she caught me off guard. Everything she does surprises me, and a new thrill runs through me. The tip of her tongue comes forward, sweeping into my mouth, and I moan as pleasure shoots down my abs and settles below my belt. She giggles as she pulls back. She must have noticed the twitch in my jeans.

"*What if* ... you come inside with me?" she shyly asks, but she's not going to be shy with me if we cross her threshold. I'm going to show her how I feel and take away all her regrets and remind her how good we were. Together.

"There's no turning back if I do," I gently warn her. I'm going to want her again and again.

Her lips slowly curl up and her eyes sparkle.

"What about Samhain?" I want to be respectful of her night and her rituals. I won't rush us, if we need more time out here.

"I think it's time I let the spirits rest and awaken my heart."

Sweet Mother.

She steps back, dragging her hand down my arm until she lands on my wrist. Her fingers toy with the beads of the bracelet she gave me. Then her fingers circle my wrist, and she tugs me forward. I'm under her spell again, and I don't want her to ever let me go.

CHAPTER THIRTY-ONE

DEWEY DECIMAL CLASSIFICATION: 306.73
CULTURALLY TYPICAL PATTERNS OF
SEXUAL RELATIONSHIPS AND BEHAVIORS

[Naomi]

I am not a seductress, but the way Nathan's eyes follow the movement of my body, I feel empowered. Like I can be the sexual being I want to be *with him*. I can lead him into my home. I can take him to my bed. I can allow him into my heart.

The inner goddess wants these things.

And I do as well.

I'm ready to give in to everything that's been between us for the last month—unresolved desire—and a second chance.

We pause for only a moment to douse the dying flames of my celebration fire. Fire and water—two elements of nature—mixed together. While one smothers the other, the other sizzles under the connection. This strange metaphor fills my thoughts as I continue to lead Nathan into my home. I flip off the lights as we pass through my kitchen and living room. We climb the stairs in darkness, and my heart races with each step I take upward. Nathan clutches my hand as he follows me. We don't speak.

Once we enter my room, the soft click of the door sounds like a shot to begin the race and I leap for him. My mouth crashes against his in another unpretty kiss of eager lips and clashing teeth.

"Ow," I whimper, giggling as I pull away from him. Nerves kick in. "I might be bad at this."

"You're perfect," he states, lifting both his hands to cup my face and draw me back to his mouth. I conclude it's safer to let him lead and give in to the pressure of his lips over mine. He pulls me into him, sucking and sipping, taking his time to outline the lower curve and nip at the corner. My body softens against the firmness of his, leaning on him, allowing him to take control. He continues to meld our mouths together. Slow. Purposeful. He's not leaving a portion untouched.

The heat of his hands on my cheeks lowers to my neck, massaging before his lips follow. Open mouth kisses suck at my sensitive skin while his hands round my shoulders, forcing the neckline of my nightgown to spread over them and slip down my arms. He nips me near my clavicle, and I squeak as my knees buckle. I feel like I'm going to crumble to the floor, but Nathan's firm hands hold my upper arms, keeping the stretched-out nightdress in position. He speaks against my shoulder.

"We'll only go as far as you'd like, but I'd very much like to see what you're wearing under this thing."

"I'm not wearing anything," I whisper.

"And that's what I want to see." *Is he being cheeky while sexy at the same time?* I smile as his mouth continues a trail to my left shoulder, teeth tenderly closing the path before moving lower. My nightgown dips, catching on my rock-hard nipples briefly before allowing both breasts to spring free of the material. Nathan pauses his undressing and stares down at the heavy swells, ripe and ready for him.

"You are so fucking beautiful, Naomi." His eyes haven't left my achy globes, and a hand releases my nightdress and tenderly cups one, lifting the weight to meet the heat of his mouth. I cry out at the sensation, and Nathan smiles against my skin.

He continues to suck at my breast, drawing it deeper into the warm cavern of his mouth and then slowly releases me to circle the nipple with his tongue, forcing it into a tighter peak. I don't think the nub can take much more and then he moves to the other one, giving it equal treatment. My hands cup the back of his head, holding him against me. I don't want him to ever stop and my breath hitches when he nips at the second sharp peak before releasing me. I want to pull him back to me, but his mouth continues down the center of my belly as does my nightgown. Nathan drops to one knee.

"Nae," he whispers against my tummy, a question in his voice. The material of my shift circles my waist as do Nathan's hands, curling at my sides. He pauses, continuing to kiss me as my stomach quivers with anticipation of his mouth dipping even lower on my body.

"I want this," I say, almost a replica of the words I said to him the night we first slept together. My fingertips continue to stroke through his hair, hinting for his head to continue down my body. As if reading my command—my desperation—his hands drag the soft fabric over my hips and release it to fall the remainder of the way to the floor. Nathan rocks back on his heels and stares at the dark mound at the apex of my legs. His eyes drift upward until they meet mine.

"You're a goddess, and I plan to worship you." Before I can respond, his nose presses against the coarse hair and his tongue stretches forward. The tip meets my swollen, pulsing, sensitive nub, and I gasp. I reach for his shoulders, not certain if I'm pushing him away or pulling him closer.

As his tongue delves deeper, swirling and curling, my knees give out.

Closer, I realize. I want him so much closer to me.

Releasing me with a lavish lick, he holds my hips and guides me backward until the back of my knees hit the mattress. Nathan tugs me to the edge and returns between my thighs. I'm grateful for the seat as my legs continue to shake. He's tucked a hand under each knee and pushes upward. The movement forces me to fall back and spread wider while his mouth devours me.

Forget Vilma and her stupid videos. This is so much better.

"More." Without realizing it, I'm crying out for it.

Nathan chuckles against sensitive folds, drawing out a kiss down there before returning his tongue to its mission.

"Nathan," I squeak. I'm not certain if I'm asking a question, making a statement, or warning him, but I feel a building, a creeping, a climbing like I've never felt before. Not alone. Only with him.

His name becomes a strangled scream as the release is like nothing I've experienced. I flit. I float. I'm outside myself as tingles race from my feet to my core. My lower belly explodes with a rush of flutters. Pinpricks of light flash before my eyes. I'm clutching at Nathan's head, holding him between my thighs in the most compromising position I've ever been in, and I don't want to let him go.

Eventually, he pulls back with a final lap at my seam, and then sucks at my inner thigh. My hands fall away from his head, landing on the bed beside me. I can't move. I can't think.

"Nae?"

I groan in response, or at least, I think I do. I'm not even certain I'm me and he's really here.

Is this a dream?

Then he stands. His glorious bare chest with a sprinkle of hair forming a V near firm, smooth pecs. His silver, finger-swept hair. His gray gleaming eyes. He's real all right, and he's staring down at me with his hands on his belt buckle, hesitating. I blink. I blink again. Then I lift my head.

Nathan chuckles softly. "I asked, can we keep going?"

He's asking me for more and I'm so willing to give it to him. For a second, I don't think I'll recover from what we just did, but my eager body is already revving up for what will happen next. My cookie crumble reheats and I'm melting before he even touches me.

"Yes." I emphatically nod to assure him.

Nathan strips and the sight of him doing so nearly brings a second orgasm. I watch in wonder as he tugs off his boots, peels off his socks, and then, torturously slow, removes his jeans. He keeps on his boxer briefs but bends down for his jeans again and pulls something from the pocket. Tossing it up on the bed, I twist my head to find two foil packets.

Condoms. My stomach sinks with relief that we don't need to have this awkward discussion. Then I recall when I saw him a month ago at the Piggly Wiggly. My head turns back for him.

"I haven't been with anyone since that night," he answers as if reading my mind. I nod once. The euphoric emotions of the moment slowly slipping away from me. "Let me assure you I won't be with anyone else from this night forward." He crawls over my body, leveraging his lower half to spread my thighs. He balances on his elbows as his fingers reach for my hair and twist the braid around a fist.

"I don't want to be with anyone else, goddess. Do you get me?"

I nod my understanding.

"You're giving me something sacred," Nathan whispers before leaning forward and resting his forehead on mine. Something must tell him what we are about to do is catching up to me. I'm giving up my virginity. Again.

"I've already given it to you," I attempt to tease, and hope I've disguised the trembling in my voice. I'm nervous, and anxious, and beginning to overthink. He pulls back to look down at me. A shaky hand brushes over loose hair around my face.

"But this time, I'm hoping you'll give me more. I'm hoping you'll give me your heart."

My eyes sting and I blink a few times willing the tears to stay hidden. The anxiety in me retreats, almost as if marching away from the part he wants the most.

"I gave it to you before, as well." I reach up for his scruff covered cheek, holding my palm against the scratchy hair recently between my thighs. He turns his face into my palm, kissing the center of the pad and closes his eyes for a second.

"I'll definitely be bad at this," I whisper.

"It's going to be so good." Softly, he kisses my lips until my girlie parts tingle again and I begin to wiggle under him, seeking friction. There's no hiding his arousal as the firm length presses against me. His hips roll forward and we start a new dance. Fingers dip into my hair as our kisses heat. My legs open farther as we grind together.

Nathan's hand outlines my body, caressing a breast before wedging between us, prepping me for what's next.

"You ready for me, Nae?" His voice roughens as his fingers gently trace over sensitive folds. I buck against the delicate touch, my body reaching toward his for more. "You feel ready."

He's teasing as slickness coats his fingers. His mouth nibbles at my neck while he primes me with one finger and then a second. I hardly recognize the sounds within my room—the moaning, groaning, whimpering—which can only be coming from me. Nathan withdraws from my center and pushes at his boxers. His eyes stay on mine as he blindly reaches for the packet on the bed. Then he kneels back between my thighs. I watch as he bites the foil and then close my eyes. If I see him touch himself, I'll spontaneously combust before anything happens.

Leaning over me again, the tip of him touches my entrance. He's nudging but not pressing, like a knock at the door, waiting for an answer.

"I want this," I assure him.

"I don't want to hurt you." Whether he means physically or emotionally, I don't know. Either way, the intrusion into my body—and my heart—runs the risk of stinging.

And I want the sting. He presses forward and there is a slight burn. The stretching. The pulling. The filling.

He stills for me to catch my breath.

"You okay?"

"It just ... I don't know ..." He tips his head as he peers down at me and I lick my lips before I explain. "I'd say I've never felt anything like it before, but I have felt it. With you."

He smiles and leans forward to kiss my nose.

His hand slips down my arm to my fingers, entwining his with mine. Squeezing tightly, we make a collective fist and he thrusts forward. I'd like to say it was an overwhelming experience—that first thrust. All the romance novels make it sound romantic. I'd like to say it didn't hurt. The books also act like it doesn't. The truth is—both occurred at once. I lost my breath as he filled me in a way I hadn't remembered. I also felt a sharp sting and my eyes watered as he tapped deep inside me. I couldn't help it. A tear escapes.

"Shh, sweetheart." Nathan swipes a thumb at the corner of my eye, watching me with a wary expression as he stills. The weight of him over me is incredible. Heavy, pressing, fulfilling. "How do you feel?"

"Full." The word comes out breathless and quiet, and Nathan smiles again.

"I feel full, too." He kisses me, dragging my lower lip between his and then opening wide to take my mouth. Seconds pass as we lay connected. Mouth on mouth. Him in me. He pulls back with a teasing nip at my lower lip.

"I don't remember it being like this," I say. My memory is so vague in comparison to the current reality.

"Oh yeah? How do you remember it, goddess?" He's teasing me again, but not making fun of me. With his question, he draws back, threatening to leave me. I whimper.

"Tip your hips up," he softly commands but his voice shakes as if he's on the edge of losing control. I do as he says, and he plunges forward in response. "Move with me."

"Again." My breath hitches and my eyes roll back. He stills and I open to meet his gaze. My mouth opens but no sound comes out. *Again.*

We repeat the movement, my body following his lead until I begin to naturally react to his, and I chase the pace he sets, beat for beat until the climbing sensation skitters along my legs and the flutters drop in my belly once again.

"Nathan?" I question, although I know what's about to happen. The thrill climbs higher. His hips have begun a pummeling rhythm, as he taps deeply into me. A hand slips under my backside, slightly lifting me to meet him—thrust for thrust.

"That's it, goddess." He knows what's about to happen, too, and his driving increases. My fingers dig into the firm globes of his backside, holding him in me. I whimper each time he pulls back and relish the fill each time he propels forward. Finally, I can't take it any longer and I still, my body humming, spiraling, exploding all around him.

Near to bruising, fingers squeeze at my backside as Nathan curses and then I feel a pulsing, thumping, deep within my channel.

"Nathan?" I question again, as if I don't realize what he's doing.

Sweet Goddess! Nathan is gorgeous as he strains over me. A vein swells along his neck as he bites his lip and holds himself above me. My eyes lower between us, wanting to see us connected, as if feeling it isn't enough. The firm evidence of his manhood has disappeared within me and my peeking confirms what I already know—Nathan and I are one in this moment.

He collapses over me, the weight again a reassurance of sorts. I hold still not wanting to lose the sensation. Never wanting him to leave me again. The thought hits me hard.

He's going to leave.

He has his own home. His own life. He has a family. He has children. He ...

"Stop thinking so hard," he mutters against my shoulder.

"I'm not thinking," I defend, wondering how he knew.

"I can feel your thoughts." He presses up on an elbow and peers down at me. I'm overly aware of our continued connection as well as a stickiness. "I'll be right back."

He slips out of me rather quickly, leaving me with a strange sense of emptiness. I hear, rather than see, the snap of the condom being removed, and he enters my hallway, heading for the bathroom. I don't know what I'm supposed to do next.

All those years ago, Nathan received a phone call moments after we finished. He slipped from bed, instantly answering it. He muttered into the phone, hung up, and swiped a hand down his face. Then he tossed the phone to me.

"Put your digits in there." He nodded at the phone.

"I gotta go, babe, but I want to see you again. I'll call you." The words stung more than him taking something so precious as my virginity. His voice hid something that settled sourly in my stomach. He kissed me one more time —quick, firm, harsh. And then he left.

"Naomi?" My head rolls against my pillow and I look up to see Nathan peering down at me. His eyebrows pinch as he searches my face. My heart races with anxiety, anticipating what he'll say next. "You okay?"

"Why wouldn't I be?" Brittle words snap out of me after I've just experienced one of the best moments of my life. Why did I say that to him in such a tone? This time it isn't shame that steals my moment, but fear.

"You have a funny expression on your face. I just asked you if I could stay."

I quickly sit upright. There's no sheet to clutch over me as we did this on top of my bed, so my arm covers my breasts as if that hides me. I sit in all my nakedness, baring not only my body but my soul to him as my voice squeaks.

"You'd like to stay?"

Nathan reaches for the back of his neck and scratches. His eyes shift away from me. I notice he has put his boxers back on and dangles something in his hand.

"I mean ... well ... I'd like to stay if you want me to."

"Do you want to stay?" I question, my voice lowering another octave.

"I just told you I'd like to stay." He nervously chuckles and I remind myself, *I'm so bad at this.* I stare at him, waiting for the other shoe to drop, waiting for the universe to implode.

It doesn't.

"I'd very much like you to stay."

His lip curls in a crooked grin, the dimple slow to release. "I brought you this, if you want to clean up." He holds out a hand towel from my bathroom and I nearly choke on my relief. He reaches for the cover on my bed after I take the towel and pulls back the sheets.

"I'll just be a minute," I say, hopping off the mattress and quickly stepping toward the hall for the bathroom. Inside the small, enclosed space, I thump my forehead against the door, taking deep breaths.

I just had sex with Nathan Ryder!

The thought hits me as hard as the ache between my thighs.

I just had sex with Nathan Ryder.

The excitement lessens as I clean myself and toss the towel at my hamper. I lean toward the mirror over the sink. Do I look different? Will Green Valley residents know what I've done? I stare at my face—rosy and flushed. My lips are swollen. My eyes stare back at me, wide and bright.

I do look different.

I feel different.

I had sex with Nathan Ryder.

What I don't feel is guilty. This time it's something more. It's something deeper.

I peer up at myself one more time, releasing the bed-wrangled braid and fluffing up my hair.

I feel complete. And in love.

CHAPTER THIRTY-TWO

DEWEY DECIMAL CLASSIFICATION: 155.3
SEX PSYCHOLOGY AND PSYCHOLOGY OF
THE SEXES

[Nathan]

As I sit on the edge of Naomi's bed, my body still shakes with the aftereffects of being with her. I've never been so nervous with a woman in my life. This was a big move for her, and I wanted her to lead, but Goddess forgive me, once I entered her, I was on the verge of breaking. Like a horse let free of the confines, I wanted to plunge and plunder. I kept it together until I told her to move her hips. Then, the tip of her head. The roll of her eyes. The sweet sigh, and we were off to the races.

She felt amazing. The heat. The fit. The way she looked at me.

It was no longer lick-me eyes, but something more.

Love me.

She's taking a long time in the bathroom, and I'm beginning to worry she has second thoughts about what we did, or me staying overnight. I'm not ready to leave. I should go home and check on Clem, but the pull to stay with Naomi and hold her all night is greater.

She needs me.

I need her.

I need to know we are ready to move forward together.

I'm holding my phone in my hand after I noticed it fell out of my jeans' pocket. It's almost two in the morning but I send a quick text.

When I look up, I see Naomi standing in the open doorway. She's replaced her nightgown for something shorter, more revealing, although it's nothing more than a long T-shirt.

She has legs, my brain screams.

Amazing legs, I clarify as I recall them wrapped around my hips. I imagine them in other ways as well—around my face, on my shoulder, and bent under me. I'm getting semi-hard again, just thinking about all the things I want to do with her.

Damn, boy. I thought I was supposed to settle down after forty, but I want her. Again. I picture her mouth forming the silent word as she asked me to move within her, over her. I'm growing stiffer with every thought and I rub a hand down my face. I need to calm down. This was her first time in a long time. It's new and I need to be patient.

She looks hesitant as she stands too far away from me, leaning against the doorjamb.

"Got a call?" The words ring accusatory and disappointed, and I should be offended, but I remember our first time. I won't let that night ruin this one.

"I thought I'd send Dahlia a text. Explain I'm staying the night. I want her to check on Clem for me."

Naomi instantly presses off the door, straightening as her hands clasp before her. "Should you go home? Make sure she's okay? What happened must have been traumatizing." Her voice fades off and as much as Clem might need me, Naomi needs me more. She isn't a child, like my daughter, but she still deserves comfort. I want to be that comfort.

"Dahlia said she's sound asleep."

"That's a pretty open relationship you have with your daughter if you're telling her you're spending the night with a woman."

"I'm not spending the night with just any woman. I'm spending it with my girl."

Her lids lower but her mouth twists like she's fighting a smile. The hint of it confirms I'm doing the right thing. I need to stay tonight. We can work out all the other nights tomorrow. I stand and her eyes drag down my body. I like how she looks at me. Eyes wide. Lips bitten by her teeth. She appreciates what she sees, and I'm flattered by her lingering gaze.

"I didn't know what side you slept on," I say, swiping a hand toward the bed. Instead of answering me, she steps forward, walking right up close to me, and I encircle her with my arms. She inhales against my bare chest. I smell of sweat, campfire, and us. Maybe that's not such a bad combination. I smile as I kiss her hair.

Releasing me, she steps out of my embrace and crawls into the bed, moving over to allow me space. I fold in after her. She lays on her side, two hands tucked under her cheek and intently watches me as I gaze back.

"How are you feeling?" I don't just mean physically, although that's what I expect her to explain.

"Is it silly to say, I feel a little whole and a little empty?"

My heart races in my chest. I feel whole as well. Complete. Like we were meant to be. It takes a second to react to her second sensation. "Why empty?"

Her eyes drift to the sheet between us and her fingers pluck at the fabric.

"It's going to sound silly." Her quiet voice sets my nerves ricocheting all over. Why does this feel so complicated? *You wanted complicated, remember?*

"Try to explain it to me."

"I miss you already."

I chuckle lightly as I reach out for her. "Come here." Tugging her to my chest, I press a kiss to her forehead as my arm slips over her and holds her against me. "I'm not going anywhere, Naomi. Not this time."

"It's not just that ..." Her voice drifts and I tip up her chin, so she looks at me.

"I ..." She swallows and the hand pressed on my chest pulls back and points downward. She whispers. "Down there."

My brows rise. "You mean, inside you?" My voice cracks like a prepubescent teen. *Does she want me again, already?* She shrugs and I chuckle. I lean for her lips before a sour expression takes her face. When I laugh, sometimes I think she misinterprets my meaning. I don't find her funny as in ha-ha, but innocent and sweet.

"You can have my body whenever you want, sweetheart."

Her head shifts on the pillow, and she stares at me. "Now?" She isn't teasing. Her expression is one hundred percent serious, so I fight the playful laughter rumbling in my chest.

"The reality is I need a minute to recuperate. I'm old." Maybe fifteen minutes or so.

"You are not," she huffs before pressing a kiss to my chest. "You're seasoned, remember?"

"Are you teasing me?" I ask, tickling her side. She squirms against me, wiggling and giggling before one of her legs hooks over my hip.

"Old man humor." She laughs louder. God, I love her laugh. I love her smile. I love her.

It doesn't hit me hard as it's been there from the start. I'm in love with this woman.

I have a vagina, she said, and I fell instantly. I smile at the memory as I pull her over me. Her hair cascades around her face as her legs instinctively straddle my hips.

Maybe I'm not as old as I think. It appears I don't need those fifteen minutes after all.

"I'll give you man humor," I tease as I cup her cheeks and draw her mouth to mine.

Sex the second time last night was more frantic and frenzied. Naomi says she's bad, but she's a natural with me. Her body moves like it recognizes mine, like we've been together for years. She quickly picks up on what I like and allows me to help her figure out what she likes. She's curious, and I'm willing to let her discover whatever she wants from me.

I awake with the typical morning wood. I should get home to my girls, but Naomi curls up against me all warm and comforting. I don't

want to leave her yet. Last night was like no other. A night of explo-
ration and rediscovery and new adventures. Reconnecting with
Naomi Winters might be one of the best things to happen to me. My
hand cups the braid she remade before we fell asleep facing each
other. Her feet rest against mine as her head buries into my chest. I
can't remember the last time I slept through the night with a woman,
but a man could grow used to waking up to this.

Then my phone rings.

It's set to vibrate, and it rapidly ripples against the top of the nightstand behind me. I unwillingly roll over and reach for the phone.
Dahlia's name pops up on the screen.

"Hey," I answer. My voice is rough from lack of sleep as well as
trying to remain quiet. I slip upward to sit. My dick sticks straight up
in my boxers and I try to ignore it.

"Dad, when will you be home?"

I glance at the digital clock on Naomi's nightstand. 7:03 AM.

"Soon, baby. What's wrong?"

"Nothing, I just don't want you to get in trouble with Gramm." I
sigh and scratch under my chin. *Ma?*

"Why? What's going on?"

"You've never spent the night out. I just thought I'd check in with
you so I can cover for you with Gramm."

My shoulders fall and I softly chuckle. My seventeen-year-old
wants to cover for me? Like I'm going to get in trouble with my
mother for spending the night with a woman. At forty-one!

"Just let me handle Gramm, okay? How's Dandelion?" Guilt
knocks on my chest. I'm so divided and I don't like the separation. I
need all my girls in one place.

"She's fine. Slept through the night. I told her you went to see Miss
Naomi."

"Does Clem know I spent the night?" *What am I, a teenager?* Then
again, I am a dad, and spending the night isn't my typical behavior. In
fact, I've never done this before with a woman. I always go home to
my own bed. A small hand presses against my lower back and I shift
to look over my shoulder at Naomi, sleepy-eyed and concerned.

"She just thinks you're out early," Dahlia explains. "Maybe bring home some doughnuts," she teases and then asks, "How is Miss Naomi?"

"She's ..." Perfect. Wonderful. Everything I've been waiting for. "... all good. Tell Gramm the same thing you told Clem, and I'll be home soon."

"Okay, Dad. I didn't mean to disturb you. I just thought—"

"No, it's fine." I keep my eyes on Naomi as I speak to Dahlia. "See you soon."

We hang up and Naomi's watchful eyes speak volumes.

"You need to go," she whispers.

"I do, but I'm not going anywhere. Do you get me?"

She bites the corner of her lip and nods. I toss the phone on the nightstand and twist completely so I can cup her face as I lay down another minute. I pull her toward me, meeting her lips with mine. What's the harm in one more kiss? Then again, that is how I got in trouble the last time.

CHAPTER THIRTY-THREE

DEWEY DECIMAL CLASSIFICATION: 153.7
PERCEPTUAL PROCESSES

[Naomi]

"How we going to work it this time?" he asks after greeting me with a toe-curling kiss. I can't ignore what's jutting into my hip and my fingers twitch to lower.

"What do you mean?" I ask, his lips lingering on mine. His entire body has made an impression on me. One I don't want to forget.

"I'm not leaving this bed without a plan. I don't want any second-guesses about my intentions. Only second chances." He pauses as his eyes soften and a fingertip trails over my jaw. "Are you giving me a second chance, Nae?"

Didn't I do that last night? I gave us both a second chance at what we had all those years ago. But if I'm honest with myself, I think I know what he's asking. *Do I want it too?*

"You have all the chances," I say, my voice dipping low.

A smile instantly breaks on his face. "All the chances, huh? Does that mean I'm getting lucky again soon?" His hip tips forward, forcing his firm length against my lower belly. It feels like instinct to lift a leg and hitch it over his hip, repositioning myself so we line up.

"Sex humor?" I blush as I speak but he's being so flirty. "Is now too soon?"

He chuckles into my neck as he nips me. "I should probably get home. Check on the girls."

Instantly, I retract my leg and loosen my arm curled over his. "Oh, right. Definitely." He isn't wrong. His daughters should be his priority. Poor Clementine. She's going to need some therapy after what she witnessed last night. And Dahlia. I don't have the full story but Nathan did explain why he was late getting to the community center.

"Nae?" he questions tugging at my cheeks.

"No, no … go," I admonish. I mean it. He needs to be with them, but I can't help the sting of tears burning my eyes or the prickle in my nose.

"Dammit, Naomi." He rolls me to my back and pins a leg between both of mine. He lifts up and stares down at me. "Tell me what you're thinking."

I shake my head. It's too much. Too soon. I can't say what I feel or want or think of him. My heart races as my mind sprints to thoughts of never seeing him again, just like before.

His weight settles over me. His arms lowering to brace on his elbows.

"Nae, I'm not going anywhere this time. If I don't call, you can call me out like you did last week. But I swear I'm going to call you later today, and tomorrow, and the next day. And we're going on more dates. No limit this time."

I slowly nod as a traitorous tear escapes. His thumb brushes at it, but another seeps from the other eye.

"What's this, sweetheart?"

"I don't know," I choke as I whisper. I don't know what's happening to me.

"I'm stuck on you," he says, and a lump forms in my throat.

"I'm stuck on you, too," I whisper again, knowing the words mean so much more.

"Let's be stuck together," he quietly teases, rubbing his nose over mine. "Get my underwear off." He slips his other leg between my thighs and I tilt my head. My hands have been resting by my sides, but he guides one arm to move toward the waistband of his boxers and I wrestle them down a bit with him over me. He slips easily into me and we both moan with the connection.

"What about your girls?" I ask as he slowly moves as if he has all the time in the world.

"Not leaving until I convince you …" His voice fades as his rhythm picks up.

"Convince me of what?" I wonder as my knees spread farther open and my hands climb up his muscular back. Nathan thrusts forward and I gasp.

"You and me. Third time's a charm."

"Are you being cheeky? Because technically this is our fourth time."

Nathan chuckles and the motion vibrates inside me. We both startle at the vibration and his mouth comes to mine. I'm not a fan of morning breath but I'm quickly lost in his kiss. We move together as we have before, only this round is lazy and sweet. Too soon, Nathan warns me he can't last long and the pace quickens. He reaches between us, working at my sensitive spot, encouraging me to meet him, and I do, still together, feeling each other let loose.

I giggle as I drift down from the brisk high. "What was that?" I tease, knowing it was morning sex, although I've never experienced it before.

"That was me showing you how I feel." He kisses me one more time before withdrawing and slipping from the bed.

I lay still a minute, dragging the covers over me and watching Nathan dress.

"Everything okay at home?" I question. Nathan snorts.

"Dahlia's worried I'll get in trouble with Ma for spending the night." Nathan's already slipped up his boxers which didn't fully leave his legs and steps into his jeans. He finds a very wrinkled shirt on the floor and slips it over his head. He dropped his leather jacket downstairs, so I imagine he'll retrieve it on his way out. He sits on the edge of the bed to slip on his boots. He's such a handsome man. I could watch him dress every day.

The thought unsettles me a little and I roll to my back, looking up at the ceiling. He flips his body and leans over to place a hand on my belly.

"I know you believe in destiny, right? All things have a purpose and a reason."

My brows pinch, uncertain where he's going with this thinking.

"What if ..." He tweaks one brow. "Destiny meant us to be together all along." He leans forward and presses a kiss to my covered stomach. "What if I'm back and you're here because we were supposed to be together. It just took a little time."

"You're thinking too hard," I tease, reminiscent of what he said to me last night. His silver eyes sparkle as he looks at me. I reach out to cup my hand around the side of his face and he leans into my palm, kissing the center.

"I'm serious. What if the universe was speaking to me before but it got lost in translation?"

"I thought you said no what-ifs." The corner of his lip hitches and he shakes his head. He knows I'm right, and so was he. We can't live by what-ifs.

"I just feel like this is right. Now's our time." With those words, he leans down and kisses me too quickly. "I'll call you later."

I don't want to feel the words are ominous, so I take a deep breath, send out a little prayer and watch him walk away from my room. Then he steps back into my view.

"Where's your phone? Because I'll be calling you from the truck in a minute." He winks and with that, he's gone.

"I slept with Nathan Ryder. Again." *Actually, it was three times, but who's counting?*

Restless and feeling like I could crawl out of my own skin, I make an impromptu visit to my sister's Sunday morning. Bev didn't look pleased at the spontaneous visit, but she wasn't kicking me out either. Thankfully, she also didn't spray out her tea when she choked on the sip she took. We are sitting in her kitchen, hot mugs of steamy goodness between us.

"What?"

"I had sex with Nathan Ryder."

Beverly shakes her head. "I mean, I heard you the first time, but what?" Her voice rises on the last word. "I didn't even know you were dating."

"Three dates. That was the deal. We completed them and then he disappeared for a week. Then I was kidnapped and we—"

"Hold up," Beverly says, holding up a hand to pause me. "Kidnapped? What are you talking about?"

"Capture the witch," I mutter.

Did I mention I'd never told anyone about the first incident?

Bev gives me a questioning look and I decide the best place to start is at the beginning. I repeat some facts my sister already knew and how it leads up to the present predicament.

"Why didn't you ever tell me?" she scolds.

"Because you had your own things to worry about." While Beverly hadn't had her accident yet, she had started drinking heavily to dull the pain of her husband stepping out on her. "Anyway, it's all over now."

"But what about the boys who took you? And this Dwight Henderson? And the Iron Wraiths?"

"I don't know about the boys yet, but Junior Henderson will be going to juvenile detention and once Dwight recovers, it's jail time for him as well. I'm of no concern to the Wraiths. In fact, I'm not certain why they were there, and I probably shouldn't have mentioned that part of the story."

Between rounds of lovemaking the previous night, Nathan shared his history with Curtis and Dwight's plan to kidnap me. He also explained how he thought the Wraiths had something to do with my kidnapping, thinking it was a ploy to get him to patch in again. He accused Catfish of such, but quickly learned everything was on

Dwight. I can't say I understand what he'd want with me all these years later. Nathan thinks it was the unrequited crush from when Dwight was a teen. I think that's preposterous but then Nathan reminded me, he's been waiting on me all this time, too.

I just needed to give it my due time before I found you again.

"But you're safe?" Beverly questions, concern in her eyes that I haven't seen in years.

"I'm safe from the Wraiths, yes."

Bev tilts her head and falls back in her chair. Her arms cross over her chest. She looks different. A little brighter in the cheeks. Is she wearing makeup? Maybe just some mascara and a hint of color over her lips. Her mouth doesn't look so pursed, but loose, as if she's been practicing grinning more often. She still wears a sweatshirt that looks too big for her and some outdated jeans, though.

"What are you *not* safe from, then?"

"Nathan," I sigh.

"Why? Did he hurt you when you had sex?" I marvel a moment at the cavalier manner of this conversation. When I was young and twenty-one, my sister never would have discussed such things with me, but now ...

"No, he didn't hurt me." I grin unwittingly, recalling with pleasure all the things he did do to me. His lips. His tongue. His fingers.

"Knoxville called, they can see your blush from there," Bev teases and I cover my face with both hands.

"It cannot," I mumble into my hands, the weight on my shoulders lifting a little at my sister's unusually good mood.

"Bev, did something happen to you? You seem different today." The words tumble out of my mouth before I think what I'm asking, and I reach across the table as if I owe her an apology.

"What? No." she stammers while her face flushes. "My goodness, what would make you say such a thing. No." *Huh.* Her adamant huff adds to my suspicion, while her eyes avoid mine and she swipes back at hair severely contained in a bun. There's a hint of something behind her emphatic defense. "Let's stay focused here, Naomi. You. Nathan."

Her tone reminds me once again of our mother, but I smile in spite of myself.

Me. Nathan.

Suddenly, the kitchen door flies open and in walks Jedd making a beeline for my sister. She holds up two hands like she intends to stop him, turning her face from him as panicked eyes meet mine. Jedd stops short, his pace faltering before he sees me.

"I didn't realize you had company," he says, halting in his quest for Bev and glancing from her to me. "I apologize."

"No worries," I offer, my eyes digging a hole in the side of my sister's head, as she's refusing to look at me.

"Bev, I ..." he begins and then stops. His lips clamp shut. He pivots on his work boots and storms back toward the door. It slams behind him and all the oxygen seems to leave the room along with him.

"What was that?" I ask, trying to catch my breath at the tension flaring between my sister and this strange man living in her barn.

"Nothing," she mutters, her voice sad.

"That didn't feel like nothing to me," I say.

We remain silent as Bev's eyes reach for the back door. Jedd is definitely attractive, but his stern expression and angular face do nothing for me compared to Nathan's more jovial, scruffy cheeks.

"Are you sure you're okay?" I ask.

"No," she whispers, and I grow concerned.

"Bev, you can talk to me." She shakes her head.

"Let's just stick to Nathan." She eyes me a moment before her face falls. "You said he was involved in the accident with Jebediah?"

The guilt still stabs through me, just not as strongly as it did before. Nathan and I have talked about that night too much. We'll probably talk about it again, but we can't change it. And we can't live with *what-ifs*.

"Can you handle that?"

I nod, understanding her meaning. "I need to forgive myself. And Nathan."

"He didn't cause the accident, Nae Nae." We'll never know who was at fault. That's what an accident is.

"Are you thinking you're in love with him?"

"Yes. No. I don't know," I reply, but I'm not fooling anyone, least of all myself. My elbows come to the table and I cover my face again.

"It's okay, you know? If you do." I peek through my fingers at her. Her face softens and the old sister, the one I had as a kid, returns. How I've missed her.

"Doesn't it seem fast?"

"How long you been waiting on him, Naomi?" Eighteen years. Eighteen years for a second chance. Is it too late? Then I think of last night. The connection with him. The sweet way we danced. His apology. And mine.

Jebediah would want me to live and I haven't been living. I've been hiding inside myself. Alone for too long. Another sharp zap of guilt taps at me. He'd be so disappointed I wasn't living life to the fullest, which had been his motto, even if he did live a little too full.

"Too long," I mutter in response to Bev's question.

"He's here now, so it seems you've waited long enough." Her eyes trail back to the door leading to her yard. Her voice lowers as she says, "Let love in." And I wonder if she's talking about me or herself.

Much to my surprise, my sister suggests we go shopping for the afternoon. Retail therapy. She wanted some new clothes and I don't object. I'm not a woman of fashion. I don't get worked up about styles and trends. For a long time, my clothes have been a shield of deflection. Loose fitting, long covering, and I've been hidden inside them. I've even made many of my own clothes, but I've been feeling a change brewing inside for a while. Long before Nathan, I've felt as if I was ready for something different.

On Monday, I arrive to work in a new dress. It's a deep red, one of my favorite colors, but it's a little shorter than my usual style, hitting just above the knee and exposing just a hint of cleavage. It might be a bit much for the library, but after spending the day with his daughters, Nathan called me last night.

Date number we-are-no-longer-counting. Be ready after your shift.

He assured me Clementine was showing no signs of stress and even Dahlia remained home on a Sunday to spend time as a family. They played an old-fashioned board game until Clem earned the most money and Dahlia stormed out saying Nathan cheated on Clem's behalf.

I don't understand women, he had sighed. I assured him, I thought he did.

When I enter the librarian office, Julianne sits in her swivel chair, staring at the computer. Her face looks grave until she sees me.

"What's wrong?"

Uh-oh, here comes the falling sky. Then I shake my head. I will not think like this anymore.

"We received an email stating there's a hold on our closure. There aren't any more details other than that we should wait for additional instruction before removing the books. We have a conference call later this afternoon to discuss this further. Can you stay a little later?"

"Um … sure." Nathan will understand, but my heart sinks. I don't want to give up a date with him. Julianne takes in my dress and then her brows pinch, but she doesn't comment. Instead, I ask, "Were we planning on removing the books?"

"The liquidation procedure includes selling them off or donating them to other libraries, but we hadn't received a directive, so I hadn't scheduled us to move forward either way." I shiver at the thought of liquidation. It sounds so final. I peek out the office window to the silent shelves. It'd be like I was selling off a piece of my soul, one book at a time.

"Well, let's hope this is a sign of good things to come." I nod to Julianne who is staring at me, her head tilted.

Can she see what I've done? Logically, I know it isn't possible to physically notice I've had sex, but I feel as if I look different, and I know I do in this dress.

"You look different today," Julianne states as she eyes the rich red color before dropping to my knees under the hem. Under the probing eyes of my boss, maybe I'm more exposed than I considered. "Is that a new dress?"

"This?" I hedge, pretending I don't notice. "I did a little shopping this weekend."

"I'm assuming you're wearing it for a certain someone," Julianne asks, an eyebrow twitching upward.

"Well ... um ... actually, I do have a date after my shift." When Julianne's forehead wrinkles and her eyes widen in surprise, I step forward, waving my hands at her. "But I can stay if the library needs me. I mean, I can go to any meeting you need. Nathan will understand."

"Will he?" Julianne nods to the window and I turn to see him standing by the check-out counter with two to go cups in his hands. He's devastatingly good looking in his leather jacket. His silver hair a little mussed. His scruff a little thicker today. He smiles the second our eyes meet and I'm a puddle on the floor. I turn back for Julianne who waves a hand, dismissing me while she fights a smile. I excuse myself and enter the lobby.

"Hey," he says, eying my dress.

"Hey. What are you doing here?" His eyes don't move from my body, starting from my ankles and making their way up my bare legs to the edge of my skirt and climbing over my breasts to the skin above them. My neck turns the shade of my dress and I blink as he catches my eyes.

"Is that what you're wearing tonight?"

I pull at the skirt, fanning the material. "I guess so. Yes. But now I have to ..." My voice fades as Nathan sets the cups on the counter, grabs my hand, and leads me between the stacks. I'm almost tripping over my feet he's walking so fast. He stops and tips up his head as if he can see over the book shelves he's pulled me behind. He twists left to right like he's looking for someone to be watching us and then he cups my face, and before I can ask him what he's doing, he's kissing me.

In broad daylight.

In the library.

Between the shelves.

It's hard and fast and I'm dizzy when he pulls back. He keeps his hands on my face, and my fingers clutch at his biceps, afraid I'll fall over from the impact of his kiss.

"I'm going to have a hard time concentrating all day knowing you're waiting for me in this dress." His eyes skim downward again and then he looks around us, as if he's noticing for the first time we're surrounded by books.

"Hey, I have a book I'd like to recommend to you." His arm remains around my lower back as he scans the shelves a second and pulls out a selection. He hands it to me.

I Have a Penis.

"Sweet Goddess." I laugh, holding the book. "Library humor?"

"This is where it all started." His voice drops and I look up at him. "But it's not gonna end, sweetheart. Seeing you in this dress, there's been a change of plans for tonight. Up for some adventure?"

I fight a smile, feeling helpless under his gaze. "I'll take an adventure when you tell me what you are doing here so early?"

"What? I can't pop in and see my girl?"

The fight gives up and I smile big. "Of course, but—"

"I couldn't wait to see you again." There's something deeper in his words, something unsaid and understood.

My wait for him is over.

CHAPTER THIRTY-FOUR

DEWEY DECIMAL CLASSIFICATIONS: 152.4
EMOTIONS AND FEELINGS

[Nathan]

C hange of plans. Just like our first date, I change my mind about where to take Naomi tonight. Seeing her in that red dress gives me an idea and I hope she doesn't think it's corny. I happen to think it might be romantic, if a bit understated, and I recruit Todd for some help.

"Do me a solid," I say to my brother as I call him after leaving Naomi with another heart racing kiss. *Who knew the library could be so hot?*

I explain to my big brother what I need him to do.

"I'm not breaking any codes for you, and if this backfires in any way, it's at your expense."

"Yeah, yeah," I say, knowing I won't let anything happen. Not this time. Never again.

The day is long and the crew at work is a little somber. Word of what happened spread fast among the workers, not to mention a cleaning crew had to take care of the mess. There's still an obvious stain on the floor, but drywall and tile are coming in this week. I'll be happy to move on to another project.

I pick Naomi up at six instead of five because of her meeting at the library.

"So, what happened?" I hold her hand on my lap as I drive down the dark switchbacks. It's going to take us an hour to get where we're going but I'm in no rush.

"It appears we might have a donor for the library, but we aren't certain yet. Someone from a financial management firm contacted Julianne and wanted some basic information. Most of our financial information is public knowledge but the interview included needs of the library, like a wish list to improve it." Her fingers rub over my knuckles and I like the feel of her hand in mine. I like how she's stroking my skin to give herself comfort. Hell, I like everything about this woman.

We drive on, talking about Clem and Dahlia, and the conversations I had with both of them on Sunday. Clem told me about the bullies at her school, and I feel just sick that I hadn't known. Naomi sheepishly admits that she did.

"First of all, I didn't know you were her father, and secondly, she didn't want me to tell you. I didn't want to betray her trust." I understand where she's coming from but if Naomi agrees to become a part of our life, like I want her to, she and I need to come to an understanding. No secrets.

I mention how Dahlia said something about going shopping with Naomi. "That was a surprise," I admit. Naomi's lips twist in a knowing grin, and I wonder what other secrets this woman has with my girls.

"Tell her to call me. I accept." She winks, and my chest constricts. Her getting along with both my girls is what I want next for us.

As we follow the curve of the road, we quiet and I start to think taking Naomi back to where we met might be a mistake. I'm taking her to the Fugitive, but as we slow to curl the Dragon, I worry her thoughts are falling to her brother, which dampens my romantic plans.

"I'm sorry," I say as we pass the particular spot I don't think I need to point out to her. "Maybe this wasn't such a good idea after all."

"Is this what you planned to show me?" Her voice lowers, sadness filling it.

"No, sweetheart. No." My grip on her hand tightens. "I wanted to take you back to the real beginning for us. When we first met."

I can't take my eyes off the road, but I feel hers on me. "Why?"

"I want to get it right this time," I tell her honestly. I pull her hand to my lips and kiss her knuckles. She leans over and kisses my cheek.

"You're already doing it right," she whispers and then settles back, leaning her head against my shoulder. Thank goodness for pickup trucks with bench seats.

When we finally arrive at the Fugitive, I escort Naomi to the bar, but she asks for the bathroom before I take a seat. Todd nods his head at me as I sit on a stool.

"Got everything all set?" My body hums with excitement. I can't wait to see the surprise on Naomi's face. Todd shakes his head at me in mock disgust.

"You owe me," he states, and I will. He won't forget it. "Give me five minutes." We both look in the direction of Naomi as she crosses the crowded space, heading right for me. She stops at the stool I pull out for her, and Herbie, an old guy who spends too much time at the Fugitive, glances over at us. "You're not Charlese."

"Who's Charlese?" Naomi asks and the wind knocks out of my sails a little bit. Todd shakes his head again, adding a chuckle as he steps away, leaving me to explain myself.

"What?" I choke, pretending I didn't hear her. I don't want to talk about another woman tonight. This could get complicated.

"She asked you, who is Charlese?" Big Poppy offers as he comes up behind me and smacks me twice between the shoulder blades, presumably helping me recover from my throat spasm. Where did he come from?

"I heard her the first time," I mutter, regaining my voice and twisting to glare at my brother's best friend.

"Then why'd you ask what she said?" he mutters, crossing his thick arms as he looks between Naomi and me.

"I'm Big Poppy," he states, offering her a hand and appraising her dress. *Don't look at her like that*, I want to hiss, turning a little caveman. She looks smoking hot chewing her lip as she's waiting out my answer. I want to kiss the scowl off those red lips.

"Walk away," I snap under my breath to Big Poppy, keeping my eyes on Naomi who's still waiting.

"Just trying to help a pal." He chuckles as he pats me one more time, pitching me off my barstool and into Naomi. I catch her by the upper arms as I stumble into her. She collides against my chest. Suddenly, I'm thrown back in time.

A girl with raven colored hair, wide eyes, and lips made for kissing.

I bumped into her as I wasn't paying attention where I was walking. I caught her by the arms, and she caught me off guard. She was so beautiful she took my breath away.

"Naomi," I whisper, my head falling forward intending to land on her forehead.

I'm lost in the memory, forgetting the moment at hand until she repeats: "Who is Charlese?"

She tries to pull back from me, but she's ... stuck.

"My hair," she whispers. The wild tresses swirled as we stumbled, and a strand caught on the teeth of my leather jacket. I tug her closer to me.

"You're stuck on me," I tease, but her eyes narrow. I hang my head again. "She's someone I used to know."

"Is that how you referred to me?"

"Naomi," I groan. How do I explain I never felt that way about her? She wasn't someone I used to know but someone I wanted to know more about, someone I wanted to see again. I'm going to strangle Herbie if he just ruined my chances to show her how I feel tonight.

"She was someone I was seeing before you." I don't want to mention the night I first saw Naomi at the Piggly Wiggly. Is the universe trying to fuck with me right now? "We're over."

"Did you bring her here, too?"

316

Aw shit. If I say yes, it might dampen how special I want tonight to be, but I don't want secrets. "Just for drinks and hanging out."

I saw Charlese a few weeks ago at this very bar when I came to see Todd. She made it obvious she wanted to resume our relationship, but I knew I no longer wanted just anyone. I wanted *the one.*

"Naomi, you're my only one. You get me? My. Only. One." I say, holding her chin with her hair still twisted in my zipper.

"Just kiss her already," mutters a deep male voice behind me. Herbie. This bar is too nosy.

"Come here." I disentangle her hair, smoothing the locks down with the others near her breast. My fingers twitch to touch her there but not in front of an audience. Instead, I slip my arms around her, and then my mouth slides over hers. I'm not arguing with her over another woman. Not tonight, not ever, and I don't need her hint of jealousy, although it's a fucking turn-on. Still standing in the middle of the bar, our lips are fighting the fight. Tongue. Teeth. Tension out of this world. Her mouth doesn't fight fairly, though, as she takes control, commanding mine with hidden curses and mysterious spells, and I fall under all of them.

Does she have any idea what she does to me?

I need her, and I need her now. I break the kiss leaving us both breathless.

"Come with me."

She hesitates for only a second before her dark eyes alight with the same memory.

A sexy girl danced at the bar, celebrating life. She leaned up and kissed me on the corner of my lips.

"Come with me?" I questioned, and she didn't hesitate.

Leading her by the hand, I practically drag her behind me, guiding her around the pool room, and out the back door to the motel.

First floor. Corner room. As I open the door Todd left unlocked for me, I wave her forward, and she stops just inside as I close the door behind me.

"Here?" Her breath hitches with recognition of the space. The place has been updated a little, but the plywood paneling remains. A flat-screen television replaced the old box set. A newer dresser. A better bed. But my addition, with my big brother's help—an incredible display of candles in varying heights and shapes—flicker in the dim room.

"Here," I remind her. She spins around, facing me with her back to the bed. I'd give anything to push her down and tumble on top of her, but she still looks a little stunned.

"There are so many candles," she says, taking in the display over the dresser, on the nightstand, and the small circular table with a chair next to it.

"I wanted tonight to be special ... magical."

She looks up at me, her eyes softening.

She's a goddess.

"This dress." I exhale. Her lids lower and the lick-me eyes appear.

Oh my. The girl inside the woman returns. Tempting. Teasing. Delicious.

"What are we doing here?" Her eyes question mine. If I only kiss her, I'll be a happy man. I just want to recreate a moment.

"I want to get it right this time."

She takes a step to the edge of the bed, and then lowers herself to sit. Slowly, she rolls back to her elbows, keeping her eyes up to my face. I fall to my knees and press a kiss to each exposed kneecap before rubbing my hands up her thighs and under her dress. I don't reach the promised land just yet but drag my palms back to her kneecaps. On my return trip up her thighs, I take the dress with the backs of my knuckles until I can see what's under the red material.

A scrap of black catches my eye.

Mothertruckerchristonacracker.

Has she missed me all day like I've missed her? We have so much time to make up for and yet, we only get what comes next.

"I want to make love to you, Nae. Here. Now. I want a do-over." She chews her lip and nods. I'm over her in a heartbeat, kissing those perfect lips and pressing her back against the mattress. I'm in a rush but I'll also take my time to savor every delectable inch of her.

I pull back to remove her dress which slips up and over her head.

When she's free of the red fabric, all black greets me. Bra with lace straps along with matching cups and panties. My eyes land on the tourmaline crystal. With her black heels still on her feet, she's a mesmerizing temptress.

"Is this for me?" I ask, skimming my knuckles over the swell of her heaving breasts and then dipping a finger inside the lace, not quite reaching her nipple yet.

"It's for me. I'm not changing myself for you, but you do make me feel … sexy," she says, catching on the word. I chuckle.

"Oh, you're sexy alright," I tease, slipping my hand behind her back to remove the bra and unwrap the prize beneath. Pink. Peaked. Ready for me, I devour one breast, swirling my tongue around the tough nip and sucking until she gives a sharp squeak. Then I pull back and take the crystal in my fingers to draw a circle around each breast. I curl and loop, marking her with an invisible infinity sign. I round the ripe tip of each nipple and release the crystal, heading for her other breast. Her fingertips stroke through my short hair, scrubbing at the back of my skull while I linger. My fingers walk down her belly to the elegant lace covering her and slip under the delicate material.

"Been thinking of you all day," I tell her as I tweak her nipple with my lips.

"Me too," she sighs, as I slip a finger inside her. So tight. So warm. Her hips respond instantly, following the drag of my finger, not wanting me to release her. Catch and release—it's all part of the pleasure. Only there's no more letting her go.

I pull back from her breast and lower to her lace undies, dragging them over her hips to her feet.

"Keep the heels on," I suggest thinking about her digging those spikes against my backside. I'm six-ways-to-Sunday hard but I'm not moving forward without tasting her. Slipping to my knees again, I wedge between her thighs and lower for her center. As my tongue splits her slit, she lets out a squeak and her fingers cup my ears. Her knees rise up to the bed, her heels against the mattress. My tongue delves and dips, and when I look up to see her head thrown back, I'm ready to lose it myself. For a self-proclaimed repressed woman, she's awfully free of inhibitions at the moment.

She's only been with me.

Every bit of pleasure I take from her is for myself, and yet every bit of pleasure I give to her comes from the heart. The thought spurs me on until the telltale sign of her stiffening. Her thighs clench around my head and she says my name on repeat. *Nathan-NathanNathan.*

I give a final kiss to her inner thigh as she comes down from the high. I slide up her body and her legs spread, embracing me between them.

"Condom." I pause, pressing up to move for my jeans. Her legs clamp around me and something fills her eyes as she stares at me.

"Have you ever gone without one?" She blinks and her legs slowly release me. "That was silly. Of course, you have." She's referencing the other morning when I so easily slipped inside her. Of course, there's also the matter of Dahlia and Clem. Discussing my sexual history is going to dampen this moment, so I put it as delicately as I can. "Dahlia was the result of an error in judgment, although I've never regretted her. I was just young and stupid and messed up in the head. Clem, was operator error with a condom."

"And Charlese?"

"Sweetheart," I sigh. "Never." I grip her upper thigh and wrap her leg over my hip. I've lost a little momentum, but I rub myself against her soaked center and return to full steam.

"I'm clean," I tell her, hating the awkwardness of this conversation.

"You know I am," she chuckles.

She's only been with me.

The reality of what's about to happen makes a part of me overeager.

"You're giving me something sacred," she whispers, and I slide into her. We both moan at the connection. She's so ... everything, and I'm overwhelmed. I should proceed with caution, but I want to ride with abandon. I want to bask in the tight fit, the deep warmth, and the look she's giving me with those charcoal eyes.

I slip back and then rush forward. Her head tilts back, and then returns to face me when I still.

"What?" she whispers.

"Your eyes." I stare marveling at the color, the questions, the desire I see in them.

"You already licked me," she teases, her voice low.

"They say something else." I slide back and then push forward again, building a slow rhythm.

"What do they say?" She strains, her legs slipping over my back and her ankles locking to prevent me from going too far.

"Love me."

Her head tips forward, her eyes landing on mine.

"Love me," I repeat as I increase the pace I've set, drawing her to the edge and then filling her again. She focuses on me while her body responds to the movement, the rhythm, the dance we've set together.

"Love me," I whisper.

"I do," she says, so quiet her voice pops. The words set me off and we begin to move in earnest as my mouth crashes hers, swallowing the phrase. The increase in our passion separates our lips and when I move in a particular way, her breath hitches.

"Again," she mouths, her hands squeezing at my shoulder blades.

"Say it again," I mutter into her neck and she begins a chant. *IdoIdoIdo.*

The plea is soft, but the meaning definitive. I love this woman and she loves me, and together we'll get to where we need to be to make us so much more. I repeat the motion she likes until we become a dance of drawing back and plunging forward. Naomi sets the beat with a new prayer: *harderfasterdeeper*, and I don't plan to disappoint her. Ever again.

"Holy crap," I mutter. "That was intense."

I collapse over Naomi, pressing her into the bed. After all these years, I can't believe we are in this room again. It would seem a bit surreal if it also didn't feel like we had come full circle. Only this time, there are candles. So many candles, and it's romantic. Magical. I wanted a do-over, and I'm giving us one.

I pull out of her and stand, commanding her to remain still. I return to clean her up and then toss the cloth on the floor. I reach to pull back the sheets.

"Are we spending the night?" she asks, and I don't like the hesitancy in her voice. I don't want anything to ruin tonight.

"We can't stay all night, but let's hang out a bit." I don't want to rush away like I did the first time we were here. We climb between crisp sheets, laying on our backs next to one another and I watch the candles flicker on the dresser, casting a sweet glow in the reflection of the mirror.

"Nae, I've got something to tell you," I say, bracing myself.

"Okay."

"I'm stuck on you," I say, rolling my head on the pillow to look at her. *I love you.* My eyes try to tell her everything, and I shift to my side. "Do you get me?"

I draw down her nose with a fingertip. "I knew when I first saw you. Way back when, you were someone special. I don't know how to explain it, but I knew. *I knew* you would change everything for me. And I fucked it up."

I trace over her jaw. "I planned to see you again. The next day, but then life got in the way." I swallow as we both know *death* was the cause. "But I'm seeing you now, Nae, and nothing will get in my way this time. Nothing."

A slow grin curls her lips and my thumb rubs over the bottom curve. I lean forward for that seductive mouth and kiss her softly. This kiss is different. I'm not rushing. I'm not devouring. I'm savoring. I'm taking my time. I can't make up for what we missed, or race to catch up the years. I just want this—a new beginning. I draw back and look at her.

"I don't want anyone else, and while your jealous spat was heartwarming and gave me a hard-on, it's not necessary. You're the only one for me. That's what I mean when I say I'm stuck on you."

"You've been with a lot of women," she reminds me, insecurity mixing with the truth.

"The past, goddess, that's where we need to leave all that stuff. Behind us."

"So what's next?" She cringes as she asks and it's cute how her nose scrunches up. She seems embarrassed she asked and sits up. I watch her struggle to keep the sheet over her breasts and braid her hair into an intricate twist. I sit up myself and kiss her shoulder.

"I like that braid on you," I say, watching her reflection dancing in the mirror opposite us. She has that otherworldly look about her again and I'd like to watch her form this braid every day. I meet her eyes in the glass and smile. "It's sexy."

Braiding her hair is an avoidance tactic, but I'm not letting her get away from me. I suck at the juncture of her neck and shoulder. She tips her head back and watches me in the mirror make my way up her neck and under her jaw. I fist the braid, tugging her head back for more nibbles on her throat.

"I'm so fallen for you," she says, and I feel the vibration under my lips. My mouth seeks hers.

"I want you again," I mutter against her lips. "I'm not going to even question why I want you so much, but first I need to answer your question. I'd like you to officially meet Todd, and Ma, and the girls. I want you to come over, and I want us to go out. I want to spend as much time with you as I can."

"Dates?" she asks pursing her lips into a pout and tapping a fingertip over them as she reminds us both of the proposal I gave her weeks ago. I tilt my head and narrow my eyes wondering what she's thinking. We've already discussed this at her house the other night.

"All the dates," I grumble. I press her back to the bed and she giggles under me.

"Sex?" she blurts, although not as reluctant as I remember when she first questioned me about it, when I propositioned her.

"Definitely sex, although I'm not opposed to kissing and nights of just holding you close."

"Deal." She leans up and kisses me, and I love that she's reaching for me. Taking from me. She quickly pulls back. "And phone calls?"

I pop up to my elbows. "That reminds me, I have something for you." I roll from the bed and I cross the room to open the dresser drawer. Naomi watches me, candlelight flickering over my body. She's staring at my backside and I catch her in the mirror. When I turn to face her, she gasps.

"You should come with a warning." Her eyes roam my abs, my pecs, and my flaccid dick. Even so, she's nearly drooling. A man could get used to this.

I tuck myself under the sheet, sitting upright, and present her with a box. A bow sits on the top covering the signature emblem.

"You bought me a phone?" She looks up at me, and I smile wide, pleased with myself.

"Now, you can text me too. Don't be shy. Photos optional." She gasps as I tease. "Seriously, I want you to call me whenever you want, though." I nod. "In fact, I want all the phone calls," I flirt and then lean over for her lips. Pressing her back into the pillows, I set the phone aside. For now, I want all of her. *Again.*

CHAPTER THIRTY-FIVE

DEWEY DECIMAL CLASSIFICATION: 027.4
PUBLIC LIBRARIES

[Naomi]

Dahlia did call me and we settled on a date for a girls' day: Dahlia, Clementine, and me. I'm nervous. This is a big step and once again I worry Nathan and I are moving fast, but Dahlia seemed sincere when she invited me to join her and her sister. Clementine is always happy to see me, but Dahlia hesitates. It isn't so much she doesn't like me as she's leery of me. I don't think she's convinced I'll stick with her dad, but she doesn't understand. I've been waiting for him for a long time. I don't think I'll be going anywhere now that I have him back in my life, so I offer patience without judgment. I remember being seventeen.

Clementine isn't really a shopper, which sounds like me, but Dahlia tells us she could spend hours at the mall. I prefer we do something a little less intense than shopping for a first time alone together, so I suggest we head into Knoxville for pizza. Brick oven pizza has become a local specialty. Slice of Heaven is a place where you can make your own pizza, pile on a variety of toppings, and then watch it bake.

"I like your outfit," Dahlia says to me while we sit at the table and wait for our pizzas. I refuse to believe I've changed my attire for anyone but me. However, I've had a few questioning looks lately regarding my clothing. Who knew so many people would get all worked up over me changing a few things in my wardrobe? I haven't worn the red dress again to the library. That was a one-time thing, and I'm saving it for another special occasion with Nathan. Today, I wear skinny jeans. Diane Donner-Sylvester would have been so proud of me. She'd always worn skirt-suits or dresses until her daughter talked her into embracing herself. *Release the inner goddess.* Diane shifted to slim pants and skinny jeans on occasion. I also wear ankle boots and a long cardigan sweater which drapes to the knee of my new pants. It's a compromise of sorts—*I like it*—and my black tourmaline remains prominent against a white tee underneath.

Eventually, we're stuffed from pizza, but the girls talk me into coming to their house to make brownies with them. I have an excellent recipe to make them from scratch, but Dahlia pipes up.

"That's so much work. Adding an egg, oil, and water seems so much easier." She's right. It is. But easy isn't always the best path in life. Of course, I rein in the philosophizing. I'll save that for another day.

As we stand in their modest kitchen, I grow nervous. I've been out with Nathan and his girls in the last week, but I haven't been to his home. Not like this. It seems intimate and cozy, like we're a family, baking together, and I wonder what he'll think when he walks in.

"Smells good in here," he announces as he enters his front door and makes his way to the kitchen. His eyes instantly fall to Dahlia and Clem with textbooks open on the kitchen table. "What the heck is this? Dahlia, are you doing your homework? It's a miracle." He good-naturedly teases his oldest who blushes as he walks over to Clem, kissing her on the top of her head.

He turns toward the counter where I'm leaning.

Turns away.

Turns back.

"Nae," he chokes, his voice groggy. He takes in my hair, piled up on my head and roams down my body, drinking in my long sweater and hip-hugging jeans. "You look hot."

His shock is one of pleasure, but it's a look that has me all tingly inside. Not to mention he just complimented me in front of his children. With one quick step forward, he cages me in against the counter. Leaning toward me, I want him to kiss me, but his girls are right behind him, although they can no longer see me with his large body blocking their view.

"I don't think you should kiss me," I quietly say, trying to look over his shoulder. He scowls.

"Why not?" he whispers. I want the girls to accept me, not think I'm another woman who will leave their father or want to replace their mothers. It's going to take time. I'm in no rush.

I run a hand down his chest, shrugging in response to his question. He knows I won't talk about this with the girls so close, but I notice his heart racing inside his jacket. He leans closer.

"Ew, are you going to kiss?" Dahlia asks behind him in her best tone of teenage disgust. I briefly wonder if she's kissed a boy yet. If she wants to go out with someone.

Will she be wild and reckless and fall in love?

A kitchen chair scrapes across the tile floor as Dahlia announces, "I'm leaving."

"See," I breathe cocking an eyebrow. Dahlia is being polite and cautious with me, but she isn't ready to witness something more between Nathan and me.

"Kiss her already, Daddy," Clementine giggles, encouraging her father. *Little instigator.* I shake my head as I lower it into Nathan's chest. A laptop snaps shut, and I sense Clem leave the room too.

"See," Nathan teases, into my hair. I lift my head, and he closes the distance between us with a soft kiss. Nothing overly sexual. Nothing suggestive. But I want to be sexual and suggestive and just everything in between with him. He pulls back quickly, but my eyes remain closed a second longer.

"This is a nice surprise and you look amazing," he says. "But you know I'd take you wearing anything. Although I prefer you wearing nothing."

"Nathan!" I admonish, twisting my head, hoping the girls can't hear his voice down the hall. He catches my hand swatting at his chest and brings it to his lips.

"You always look beautiful, but you look especially lovely in my kitchen. I love having you here." He leans forward again and rests his forehead on mine.

"I love being here," I reply, my voice quiet but filled with honest pleasure.

"I love *you*, Naomi."

What? My breath hitches as he pulls back to see me better.

"What?" The word is a whisper while my fingers lift to cover my lips.

"I said, I love you. I love you being with me, with my girls, and I want it all the time because I want you. I love you."

My face breaks into the biggest smile, like, the biggest, like, I'm not certain I've ever smiled so big before. I sound like Dahlia with all my likes.

"I love you, too." I tip up on my toes and press into him, gripping the edge of his open jacket. He meets me halfway and kisses me again, holding nothing back with this kiss. His arms loop around me, tugging me into him with one hand on my head and another on my lower back. We can't get close enough, and yet I remind myself we're standing in his kitchen.

"You finally bring home nice girl," Emma Rae says with her lilting accent, and I rip my lips from Nathan. Blinking up at him in confusion, he winks, and I lower my head again into his chest, mortified at being caught by his mother. "Now you marry this one."

"Ma," Nathan drags out.

Could the floor just open and swallow me whole? Suddenly I'm overly warm in my sweater, although I'm certain I'm not having a hot flash. It's the heat of Nathan and the embarrassment of his mother's suggestion. Nathan hasn't released me, and I don't know whether to be thankful or further horrified.

"What?" she draws out. "You kiss the girl, you marry the girl. At least, she's a good one."

I chuckle as I roll my head against his pec.

"She is a good one, Ma," Nathan assures his mother as he cups my chin and forces me to look at him. "And I plan to marry her. Someday. Soon-ish."

It's on a Tuesday we get our first positive news about the library from a company named Ernst, Ernst, and Ernst.

Dear Green Valley Library staff,

I'm pleased to inform you that a donation in the amount of $500,000 has been made to the Green Valley Public Library. The intent of this donation is to aid the library in remaining open for an additional year. In the time provided, it is assured, that with the benefit of our services, which will be retained by the donor, additional endowments will be procured to support the library.

In order to accept these funds, the donor would like to remain anonymous, however, there is one request: a portion of the existing library, or a necessary addition to the library, be named in honor of Bethany Oliver-Winston, and said section or addition be given her name in memory of her devotion to the library and her love of books.

Julianne pauses in reading the letter to peer up at me. Our eyes hold one another's filled with tears, questions, and relief. So much relief. Who could have done this, we wonder while at the same time we both feel a similar sense of gratitude. Giving something Bethany's name will be *our* honor.

"The letter goes on to quantify the collection is at our discretion, but additional librarians may be obtained to support these specifications and improvements." Julianne stares at the letter like Moses handed her the Ten Commandment tablets. The letter is sacred and our savior.

"Do you know what this means?" I keep my voice low, as if I'll break the glorious spell upon us. All kinds of thoughts form in my head, but I'm stopped in my pondering when Julianne looks up at me with genuine tears in her eyes. In all the years I've known her, I've never seen her cry. Not even at Bethany's funeral where she joined me in blowing bubbles to guide Bethany's spirit to her eternal resting place did Julianne shed a tear. But today, liquid pools.

"It means, the library is saved. *Praise Bethany.*" Julianne raises a fist in triumphant female-power. "I knew she wouldn't let me down." Yes, our patron saint of the library. Thank you, sister booklover.

"What do we need to do?"

"I simply contact this number and they begin the acceptance of the donation. Then they become a partner in searching for further endowments to keep us open."

"And for improvements," I add, a touch of excitement mingling with the preservation of the library. Not only will it be saved but it will be *changed*, and I can't wait for some of the innovative items we might gain to keep the library doors open ... and our books on the shelves.

When Julianne's shoulders fall, I note she isn't agreeing. I'd like to think she sees the vision of the future. There will be differences, but it won't all be bad. However, change can be a struggle. I'm the first to admit this. The shake of Julianne's head tells me she doesn't want to accept the truth. This change will be more difficult for her. She'll roll with the evolution like she did when card catalogs were replaced with computers, but sometimes, she doesn't desire a different path. Briefly, I wonder if she's considering retirement.

Julianne squeezes at her eyes with weathered fingers and stands as she sets the letter on the desktop. "I think I'll call Seamus and tell him the good news."

"Of course," I say, and smile at the love Julianne and her husband share. Then I think of Nathan. I think I'll give him a call as well, from my new phone.

I call Nathan and tell him about the library. He wants to celebrate but I tell him the ladies of the library already have plans.

"Sounds like a wild time," he teases knowing none of us are drinkers. I promise him I'll come to his place for dinner the next night.

"I'll be waiting for you," he says, and a smile breaks out on my face. I love this man.

Julianne, Sabrina, and I plan to meet at Daisy's Nut House for a celebratory doughnut, but to our surprise, Cletus Winston arrives in the library.

"Salutations, fellow book lovers," he greets us rather suspiciously. A knowing grin breaks within his thick beard.

"Cletus Winston, what did you do?" I admonish, hearing his mother's sweet voice ring in my head. Cletus was the quirkiest of her children, but definitely the softest despite a standoffish edge. He values family more than anything. And knowledge. And truth, which is what I hope to seek from him. "Did you donate to the library?"

It's a rather large sum, and while the Winstons seem well-enough off, I can't imagine having that amount easily available. Perhaps it was Sienna, Jethro's movie star wife who has the cash for such a generous donation. Maybe the boys at the Winston Auto Body Shop pooled their funds, sharing the responsibility. Drew Runous was the executor of Bethany's estate. She sold him all her assets to keep it from her deadbeat husband. Perhaps Drew gave us her earnings.

"I don't know what you're insinuating, Miss Naomi," Cletus says, his expression giving away nothing, but a little gleam in his eyes tells me he knows something. He always does.

It's almost closing time and I notice Cletus pause a moment, taking in the shelves of knowledge and entertainment.

"Momma sure loved this place," he mutters, and Mrs. MacIntyre walks up behind him. She rubs a conciliatory hand over his shoulders just once.

"She was the best of women," she offers him.

Cletus nods, staring off at the arrangement of our current library. The children's section with its beanbags in brightly colored fabrics. Planets, Sabrina's nephew calls them. The rows of literature and informational texts. Our little check-out counter and the lobby area with our holiday themed windows. Soon, it's all going to be different. A change is coming, which isn't all bad.

EPILOGUE

DEWEY DECIMAL CLASSIFICATION: 646.87
ROMANTIC PARTNERSHIP/MARRIAGE

[Naomi]

I *'d very much like to marry you, he said.*
I'd very much like to say yes, I answered.

That's how we ended up here, a place I never in my wildest dreams imagined I'd be standing—opposite Nathan. We were legally bound to each other in the eyes of the law through our civil service in Knoxville earlier in the day, but this is our celebration of marriage. We couldn't have predicted the weather for a winter day in Tennessee, but the universe is cooperating so far, although it's chilly.

I don't feel the cold as Nathan's hands warm mine. We stand amidst the trees behind my home. A ceremonial circle has been made around us with holly springs, boxwood, and cedar boughs. A Wiccan wedding isn't written in formal stone, so we've incorporated a mix of things to make this ceremony our own.

The firepit was moved within our circle, providing some heat and comfort for our few guests. Julianne and Seamus. Sabrina and Wyatt. Nathan's girls, Emma Rae, and Todd. Bev. Jedd. Even Scotia stands at the edge of our gathering. I wanted the ceremony in my backyard in order to *feel* Jebediah. I prayed for his blessing and I'm certain he's offered it. Forgiveness is the greatest gift, and I accept that Jebediah has done his part to free both Nathan and me.

Presiding over the wedding is a minister knowledgeable in hand-fasting ceremonies. She asks us to state our intentions.

Nathan goes first.

"Naomi, you believe in the power of three, a symbolic number and so I'm going to connect it to us. Three tries to get us right. Three dates to get back the only woman in my life. I'm sorry you had to wait for me. Eighteen years. Divisible by three. Love for my three girls." He nods to Dahlia and Clem before looking back at me. "But know that you are my number one. One woman. One love. One lifetime."

I'd cry if I weren't so happy by his words.

"I love you," he whispers, while squeezing my wrist.

"Naomi," the minister prompts.

"Nathan, I give to you my body, my heart, and my soul. It's all I have to offer you, but each part is sacred to me. The power of three, you just said. My body for your pleasure. My heart for your love. My soul for intellect, emotion, and trust. I believe in you for me. And all of me wants to love you. I'm stuck on you."

He chuckles as he blows out a breath and swallows.

The minister then leads us through lines we recite to one another, promising to love and honor the other. Nathan asked for us to include a blessing on our rings and in the tradition of modern marriage, we added this to the celebration. We already wear them from our cere-mony at the courthouse, so the officiator simply places a prayer of faith over them before wrapping our hands with a strip of linen, binding Nathan and I to one another for the rest of our days. When the binding finishes, Nathan looks at me, firelight twinkling in his eyes.

"Now, we're stuck to each other," he says, a smile growing on his lips, dimple exposed.

"Stuck together," I add, and he leans forward to join our lips. The kiss slowly heats until a throat clearing reminds us we aren't alone.

The final part of our wedding ceremony is a little unconventional, but Nathan and I aren't conventional. Our hands are unbound, and we take a stick to the firepit. Dahlia and Clem are each provided one as well and the four of us join them to light a candle, symbolizing our unity as a family. Emma Rae cries behind us as the flame brightens with the wind for a second.

A final blessing is given, and Nathan holds both my hands as our small family congratulates us with applause. I step forward to kiss him and I'm not surprised when one hand wraps around my back. But when his other hand grips mine and slips between us, I pull back because Nathan turns us.

"What are you doing?" I ask with laughter and confusion.

"It's not complete, until we dance." I think he's teasing me until he spins us, and we begin to make our way around the flames at the center of our gathering. "Full circle," he mutters under my ear and I giggle when he kisses me.

We certainly have come full circle and for once, I feel complete. We spin and my leg brushes Nathan's.

This time, he wore an actual kilt and my inner goddess warms within.

THE END

ACKNOWLEDGMENTS

(L)ittle (B)lessings of Gratitude

This work would not exist were it not for the intuitive and creative brain of Penny Reid, who first developed the Winstons and all the secondary characters bringing Green Valley to life in our imaginations. I'm eternally grateful for this opportunity to work with an author dedicated to the promotion of others in the romance book industry, and equally thankful to work with her assistant, Fiona; the SRU support team; and the other authors of Smartypants Romance Universe.

To Nora and Piper, both authors in the first round GV, thank you for your patience and conversations, including talking me off the ledge a few times. Piper (and Tracy), Green Valley will always be more than an imaginary place after our visit to Tennessee, so thank you for including me in that adventure. To Katie, for meeting me in Blue Ridge for my own nefarious reasons, and to M.E. for reading the first round of the first chapter and assuring me it was story people might like to read.

To Nick A., maintenance extraordinaire and motorcycle enthusiast, your information into the workings of MC life were invaluable.

Also, thank you for an introduction to the Tale of the Dragon. (P.S. I've really driven down that road – in a Jeep, though. No motorcycles for me. I also got lost after driving it. *Where is Jethro Winston when you need him?*). Additional thank you to Leigh Ann P. for further information into the "female" roles within a club.

To Jann S. and Lisa C., thank you for your insight into the Wiccan religion. I hope I've done the religion justice, and if I didn't, it was never my intention to offend. I appreciate the Goddess more than you might know.

To Maura, who gave me a little spark in Loving L.B., and it turned into this story. I hope you like it. I tried to "do me" like you encouraged, and to all the ladies (and a few men) in Loving L.B., who keep me in laughter and hot images every day of the week. Thank you for loving the "seasoned" man as much as me.

To Mel, for taking the detour in my personal adventures to walk me through this story. I hope you know how much you mean to me.

A special note to librarians everywhere – you are superheroes. Thank you for your love of the written word, still available in hard cover or paperback. I'd like to add, all Dewey Decimal Classification reference numbers were taken from the University of Illinois at Urbana-Champaign University Library. More specific numbers were obtained from http://bpeck.com/references/DDC/ddc.htm. Any errors in numbers and categories are the fault of this author.

Finally, always last on my list but first in my heart, my own Dunbar clan. Mr. Dunbar, as the original silver fox in my world, and my four littles who are all grown up: MD, MK, JR, and A. While reading is an adventure in fantasy, you are the best part of my reality (even if only one out of four of you is a reader!).

ABOUT THE AUTHOR

L.B. Dunbar loves the sweeter things in life: cookies, Coca-Cola, and romance. Her reading journey began with a deep love of fairy tales, medieval knights, Regency debauchery, and alpha males. She loves a deep belly laugh and a strong hug. Occasionally, she has the energy of a Jack Russell terrier. Accused—yes, that's the correct word—of having an overactive imagination, to her benefit, such an imagination works well. Author of over two dozen novels, she's created sexy rom-coms for the over 40; intrigue on an island; MMA chaos; rock star mayhem, and sweet small-town romance. In addition, she earned a title as the "myth and legend lady" for her modernizations of mythology as elda lore. Her other duties in life include mother to four children and wife to the one and only.

Newsletter: https://www.lbdunbar.com/newsletter/
Website: www.lbdunbar.com
Facebook: https://www.facebook.com/lbdunbarauthor
Goodreads:
https://www.goodreads.com/author/show/8195738.L_B_Dunbar
Twitter: https://twitter.com/lbdunbarwrites
Instagram: @lbdunbarwrites

Find Smartypants Romance online:
Website: www.smartypantsromance.com
Facebook: www.facebook.com/smartypantsromance/
Goodreads: www.goodreads.com/smartypantsromance
Twitter: @smartypantsrom
Instagram: @smartypantsromance

ALSO BY LB DUNBAR

Sexy Silver Foxes/Former Rock Stars

When sexy silver foxes meet the women of their dreams.

After Care

Midlife Crisis

Restored Dreams

Second Chance

Wine&Dine

Collision novellas

A spin-off from After Care – the younger set/rock stars

Collide

Rom-com for the over 40

The Sex Education of M.E.

The Sensations Collection

Small town, sweet and sexy stories of family and love.

Sound Advice

Taste Test

Fragrance Free

Touch ScreenSight Words

Spin-off Standalone

The History in Us

The Legendary Rock Star Series

Rock star mayhem in the tradition of King Arthur.

A classic tale with a modern twist of romance and suspense

Made in the USA
Columbia, SC
21 December 2019